Into the Ruins

Issue 6

Summer 2017

Published August 2017 by Figuration Press
Portland, Oregon

Into the Ruins is a project and publication of Figuration Press,
a small publication house focused on alternate visions of the future
and alternate ways of understanding the world,
particularly in ecological contexts.

intotheruins.com

figurationpress.com

ISBN 13: 978-0-9978656-4-6
ISBN 10: 0-9978656-4-4

Editor's Note:
There is a real glory in summer. Long walks, sunshine, the occasional evening wind. Admittedly, it continues to feel like an assertion of climate change: our cold and wet spring quickly followed by 100 degree days in June. And yet, there's a joy in it, too—in the change, in the fluctuation, in the world showing you all the things it can be.

Comments and feedback always welcome at editor@intotheruins.com
Comments for authors will be forwarded.

Issue 6
Summer 2017

Table of Contents

PREAMBLE

STORIES

PREAMBLE

EDITOR'S INTRODUCTION

CONSIDERATIONS AT THE EDGE OF PANTHER CREEK

BY JOEL CARIS

FOR WHAT MUST BE CLOSE TO TWENTY-FIVE YEARS NOW, I have been camping at Panther Creek. The campground is in Washington State, in the Gifford Pinchot National Forest, not too far from the Columbia River Gorge. The Pacific Crest Trail cuts through it—skirts through the edge of the campground, really, after crossing over the creek via a small but sturdy steel bridge. It's not a particularly rugged campground, nor a particularly fancy one: it's car camping, but with pit toilets and hand-pumped water. However, the sites are spread farther apart than in some campgrounds, heavy with trees, and feature easy access to the creek and trails. I've loved it dearly since the day I first arrived. I still do.

I first started camping there as a child, with my father, and it's a place I've known for two thirds of my life now. I know the different campsites, the various trails to the creek and beyond, many of the trees that live there. I know downed logs that jut out over the creek's rushing water, large rocks hunkered at its edges, and wide gravel banks than frame slow-moving bends of water. I have lain on the Pacific Crest Trail's bridge over Panther Creek late at night, staring up at the stars and contemplating the immense depth of the surrounding forest and universe above. I have been both awed doing that and disquieted by my own insignificance. In those moments, the never-ending rush of the creek below me—a constant and yet endlessly varied and complex, non-repeating sound—somehow opened that universe wider. Nights like that helped me to believe in mystery; to know that I couldn't know everything, or even very much.

I wrote stories while camping there. I hiked from there—so many miles and so many millions of steps over the years. I climbed up the mountain rising from the creek and descended back down it over and over again. I walked the campground's loop and played frisbee with my father on that gravel road. I spied animals; heard crows and ravens; listened to small critters—rodents, presumably—scrabbling across the canvas of my tent. I started fires, played with fires, trailed burning sticks through the air, roasted marshmallows, and lost myself in the flames as the night pressed in around me. I read uncountable books, immersing myself in their worlds even as I had lost myself in Panther Creek's world. All the food I ate tasted better than it ever could at home, the outdoors never hesitating to imbue me with a deep appetite.

Panther Creek has been a friend, confidant, counselor, teacher. Once, many years ago, I camped there alone for well over a week, the campground nearly deserted due to rain, talking mostly to the camp host who would drive in once a day and seemed always surprised to see me there yet again. My tent leaked at the edges of its base but I just mopped up the water with towels. My fires became more sporadic—hardly worth the trouble at times—and I huddled in my chair under a tree, hunched over to try to keep the books I read from getting too wet. I alternated my time between being outside and being in the tent. And to this day, that wet week comprises one of my strongest memories of camping. I spent a great deal of time in silence there, evaluating my life and discovering all the ways I felt I was wasting it. When I came home, I relentlessly sold off media I had collected over the years: CDs and DVDs and video games, perhaps even some books. I wanted less distraction. It worked for a while.

I swung on vine maples. I hung my head over the edge of a steep cliff. I built rock dams in the creek. I threw sticks into the current and then attempted to bomb them with rocks as they passed, my father and I taking turns testing our aim. I learned to skip rocks and I learned to pay attention to water skippers, to track their darting movements in the creek's lazy eddies.

I relaxed every time I arrived there: *Home at last.*

After a stretch of years away, I have made my way back to that home the last two summers for short visits. It can be harder now to get away for camping, though Panther Creek still calls to me. I avoid the weekends and its crush of visitors in favor of midweek excursions when the campground is sparsely attended. (When my father and I first started camping there, the place seemed almost unknown, but newspaper articles eventually revealed it to the world.) I always try to take a particular site: the last one on the main loop, where I have spent the vast majority of my visits. It's a favorite and even more secluded than most of the other sites, with its own spur trail that connects up to the Pacific Crest Trail and takes travelers to the creek.

I stayed at Panther Creek this July. I did not get my favorite site and instead took the first one on the main loop. It worked almost as well thanks to the empty sites next to it. Unpacking, setting up, and taking stock, I again felt back at home. I pumped water and walked to the creek to give my regards. I set up my camp stove and cooked dinner, swatting at the occasional mosquito. I made a fire, read, and eventually fired up the propane lantern as darkness settled in. I sat, and thought, and breathed—happy to be there once again.

As usual, I walked the campground and evaluated my surroundings. Nothing much seemed different than it had the year before—or twenty years before, for that matter. The pit toilets were redone some years back, constructed bigger and roomier with concrete floors and better ventilation systems. They still are pit toilets, though. The water pumps are the same as always. Some of the picnic tables, fire pits, and tent platforms (which consist simply of packed earth squares marked off by logs half-embedded into the dirt, raised a few inches above the surrounding ground) have no doubt been replaced or reconstructed, but the actual infrastructure you get when you camp there is no different than it was twenty-five years before. The gravel loop road and camp sites are in the same place. The trails are minimally maintained and, so far as I've noticed, no new ones have appeared. No doubt some trees have fallen and some new ones have grown into their place, but the forest seems largely the same. Panther Creek is an exercise in familiarity.

This amazes me in some ways. Almost no part of my life feels untouched from twenty-five years ago. Obviously, I am a significantly different person: an adult pushing inexorably toward forty years old rather than an adolescent. The world around me has changed in dramatic ways, not just through the rise of the internet and connected gadgets that so often are touted around as the sign of change (and "progress," of course) but through the economy, our politics, the size of the towns and cities less than an hour away from the campground, and the strength and resiliency of the ecosystems in which I reside. The state of the world and the ways in which I understand and interact with it are shockingly different; it is almost impossible to think of America now as the same country it was when I first discovered Panther Creek.

And yet the place itself feels so incredibly familiar. I know there are ways in which the surrounding forest is very different. Some of the differences are obvious, like the numerous new clear-cuts that have appeared along the drive to the campground over the last few decades. Many of them would take a more trained eye than mine to see, being rooted in the health of the forest and its ecosystems, the life found within, and the lifespans taking place within it and embodied by so many varied creatures. To be honest, I wish I could see and understand it better. I wish I had that knowledge and level of connection. But then, part of me probably doesn't want to know. What if I discovered that this place that feels so like home is slowly dying? What if this was just one more story about a loved piece of land ripped away, destroyed by a culture that refuses to make anything living truly untouchable? I've read that story so many times through the years. I don't want it to be my story of Panther Creek—of this place I love so completely.

Perhaps I don't know a story of destruction of Panther Creek—or don't yet—but I do know one of change, despite the familiarity the place holds for me still. In the early days of 1996, this part of the Pacific Northwest flooded. Rivers across the region registered record peaks and the Willamette River had to be sandbagged to keep from spilling into downtown Portland. A unique series of weather patterns created the floods and, while it did not create a major impact on my life, I do remember watching from my bedroom window over the course of several days as the creek behind our apartment in Vancouver, Washington topped its banks and crept ever closer to the edge of our back patio, eventually pushing up against it but never entering our home. I remember the seemingly endless rain. I remember that being a melancholy winter for me, a melancholy enhanced by the rain and flooding, but not caused by it.

That summer, my father and I camped at Panther Creek as usual. But the campground we arrived at proved to be different than the one we had left behind the summer before. It was not obvious at first, but became clear once we went down to the creek. We had our usual campsite, and for years we had always taken our chairs down to a small gravel island at the edge of the creek, just off the path leading out of our site. Upon going to do the same, we discovered that the island was gone, lost to the creek's waters. We were going to have to find a new place by the water to sit and read.

Soon I also realized that the creek had altered its course in several places. Whereas before, its approach to the bridge carrying the Pacific Crest Trail across its waters came as a wide and straight shot, with just a small sliver of a tributary splitting off to one side to meander and then rejoin, now the creek had split itself into roughly equal halves, creating a new island in the middle that stretched perhaps as much as a hundred yards before ending a small way from the bridge.

As I explored, I found that other banks and islands had disappeared and new ones had formed in various spots. Trees along the creek's bank had been lost to what no doubt had been an expansive and raging water during the winter floods. I hadn't been there to see it, but the land spoke to the change and echoed out the flood's memory. Sections of the bank fortified by erosion controls (large outcroppings of rock held together by wire netting) had been dug away, the creek unable to take away the netted rocks and therefore change course, but happy to dig away at the bank up against the rocks, ultimately sweeping chunks of it away.

We discovered still another significant change on a trip up the road from the campground, heading north for a visit to Panther Creek Falls, about four miles away. As we drove the familiar road, a new section suddenly cut in the opposite direction as expected, the blacktop fresh and unmarked and its connection to the old road obvious. The new section of road turned away from the creek and as we diverted on it, it was clear why: the old section of road had been swept away, the creek now far closer than it used to be, trees and shrubs washed away and the water having carved a very new path through the land beside us.

That's the thing: there *have* been changes to Panther Creek and its surroundings over the years, despite how surprisingly unchanged it sometimes feels. The very first ones I remember noticing weren't in the campground itself, and weren't the result of the '96 floods—they were the new clear-cuts that cropped up on the road to the campground within the first year or two after we started visiting there. Shocked by these disappeared trees and the slashed and gutted landscape left in their wake, I learned to loathe clear-cuts. This initial experience of them and discovery of what they were left me hollow and saddened, questioning the decisions we make as humans, understanding little of the history and economics of logging and seeing only the cruel destruction passing by our car windows and laying out so blatantly in front of me our culture's too-often devastating interactions with the natural world. It was not just depressing, but unnerving.

In a similar way, the changes wrought by the floods unnerved me, too, even though their source was not as disturbing or as clear an indictment on humanity. They were natural, really, in the way that we think of that term, and so logic would suggest they should not unnerve me at all. Still, seeing drastic changes in this place that held court within me as some place sacred, some place critical, left me wary, as though no place was truly safe from change. As unnatural as it would be, I didn't want change. I wanted this place to be apart from the rest of the world and to hold itself as a refuge for me, as selfish as that is. I wanted it to always provide a familiar comfort. I wanted it to be safe; to promise me one place I could understand completely no matter what happened to the rest of the world.

But the world rarely obeys such desires.

The island that the floods helped create on the approach to the Panther Creek bridge has long since populated with small trees: dominated by red alder and vine maple, if my memory serves me well, with douglas fir surely mixed in. These trees, and the other shrubs and plant life emerging out of that rocky island, found a new home thanks to the changes instigated in 1996. For perhaps twenty years now, they have grown. At some point, in some future flood, they may very well be swept away themselves, victims of the same kind of change that once opened their lives.

But no, maybe something will take them sooner. On my visit to the campground last month I noticed that a number of the alders both on the island and nearby, along the creek's banks, had their tops snapped off, their trunks ending high in the air in jagged spikes. I recognized the look well. It was how so many alders along the higher sections of Highway 6 looked. The highway crosses over the coastal mountain range in Oregon, stretching from Portland to the northern Oregon coast, and those mountain passes were hit by numerous heavy snow storms this past winter. I know that well, as I was often taking the bus across those passes this winter for work, the sides of the road (and often the road itself) blanketed with snow and ice. All that weight proved too much for these young, thin trees. It snapped off their crowns.

The sight made me think of a book I read recently, *The Hidden Life of Trees.* The book warned of the dangers to trees that grow too easily in open areas. A slow growing tree making its way up under the canopy of an already-established forest, surrounded by mature trees, will take a very long time to add height and girth, but the height and girth it does add will be of a very sturdy nature, its wood tight and dense. A tree exposed to full sunlight, though, will often grow recklessly fast, gaining height at a sometimes astonishing speed but putting on the equivalent of empty calories: its wood soft and too full of air, susceptible to stresses and strains in ways that the tree growing slow and steady, its sunlight rationed, is not. The trees left to grow anew on a freshly-made island in the midst of Panther Creek probably grew too fast. And the alders at the nearby bank likely did, as well; they grew in a much more open area in the company of heavy underbrush and may very well have established themselves after the same '96 flood swept away larger and more established trees. Along Highway 6, the disruptions that created fast growth were likely more man-made: trees planted after a past clear-cut, lacking the shelter of mature trees, in full sunlight and protected from faster-growing species by herbicide sprays. They grew fast, they grew weak, and they eventually shattered under the weight of snow and ice, just like those trees at Panther Creek born out of a flood twenty years past.

This, then, is one of the changes that I did not see, that I did not know the forest at a great enough depth to notice until the evidence became obvious. What else don't I see? No doubt there is an immense amount of knowledge about Panther Creek and its surrounding forest I can never gain through quick, annual trips. I would have to live there, be present day in and day out, and even then make a careful effort to pay attention. And still, being the child of a culture that goes out of its way to not understand the natural world and its own place within it, I would be at a loss of complete understanding. I would be handicapped by the lack of so much knowledge that, at a different time, would have been indigenous.

Maybe this is a confirmation of the mystery of the world, too. Not only is it that the world, the universe, is too vast and nonhuman to be knowable by any person such as myself, but that I am on top of that unprepared to come to know those things even within my grasp. The world is so big, it must be a mystery; but even the fraction that does not have to be a mystery is made one by our culture's determination to be incurious about it.

Yet it's that shallow understanding of the world that keeps bringing me back to the recurring thought about how little Panther Creek has changed. It feels remarkable. As the human-made aspects of our world (both comprised of humans and our artifacts, but also of the changes rippling out from our actions across our planet) accelerate in their alterations of the world we know, this small oasis in the Gifford Pinchot seems apart from all that, waiting as a refuge. But it's not apart, of course—it's a part of the whole, just as we humans are, and just as our artifacts are. The 1996 flood's disruption of the land is really no more or less natural than the disruption of the land caused by human logging or immense fires driven by climate change. All of these are natural processes. Humans are a natural process. And in many ways, it's the work of humans that has kept Panther Creek so unchanged over the years.

Without the designation pinned upon the place by humans, how much more would it have changed? The looping road is maintained and re-graveled as needed. The campsites are kept adorned with picnic tables, fire pits, and tent sites. Over time, the forest attempts to submit them to the same process of decay and rebirth it would any other element within its borders, and it's only through the work of humans year in and year out that the tent sites aren't overgrown with vine maples and sword ferns, the picnic tables don't rot and split, the metal cages of the fire pits don't rust and break apart until nothing is left except streaks of red in the soil.

In 1996, the course of Panther Creek changed, but that too was influenced by humans. Remove the erosion controls along its banks, and the river would have changed in different ways. Perhaps the new island on the approach to the bridge would never have formed if not for those erosion controls. Perhaps the creek would have remained in more traditional courses, cutting a similar path of disruption and uprootings through the surrounding forest as it had in centuries past. We can't know. The creek was not given free reign.

But even those constraints are in no way unique to the workings of humans. No creek or river is ever given free reign. No river winds its way through a landscape unadorned. It is always flanked somewhere—by trees, by prairies, by rocks and outcroppings, by sturdy shrubs or wetland plants, by sandy banks. Some give way easier than others, but none vanish without fight when the water comes. They all try to hold their place, to varying degrees of success, and the interplay between them and the water—no, between them and the water and their surrounding community of plants and soil and roots and stems and trunks and rocks and rotting logs and everything else, the infinitude of lives and artifacts and objects that surround flowing bodies of water across this planet—determine in an infinitely complex dance where the water will ultimately go. It's magic and mystery on an endless number of small scales, a whole systems interplay that our most powerful computers will never be able to model with precision. If gods exist, they certainly do there, in these unknowable interplays, reminding us—even if we don't pay any mind—the vast degree of nothing that we truly know. At best, we are witnesses here. We can never actually understand this world.

I suspect that lack of understanding is the only way I can arrive at Panther Creek, look around me, and marvel at how little it's changed. No doubt every time I arrive, it has changed tremendously from the last time I was there. I just don't see it. And when I do, it's because the change is crass and outsized, waving its crimson red flag and shouting to be noticed. Only then do I deign to. I imagine it's the same for most of the other human visitors. We just miss so much.

Here I am, attempting to understand the place of humans and our creations within the natural world—to see plainly the false lines that need to be erased so that we might better understand how we are all a part of the natural world, not apart of it—through the application of words and the flow of some kind of logic. Maybe that's an irony, since it seems we use logic delineated through words as a primary way of obscuring our place within the world. We attempt to step outside the planet and its ecosystems and then to view our impacts with a supposed dispassionate eye. We label ourselves something and non-humans something else, then discuss us and them as though each belongs to separate categories, when we all clearly do not (at least, not in the way we commonly imagine). I've done it myself throughout this introduction. It's hard not to.

Creating some theoretical structure of our place within and impact upon this planet, though, separates us from the direct experience of and communion with the broader world that illuminates our quite common place within it. We are animals living within ecosystems, interacting in complex ways with all the other creatures and energy flows within those same ecosystems, living and dying and changing the world around us even as the world changes us, a part of the same infinitely complex dance that determines the course of a creek—and unable to control that dance, no matter how powerful we delude ourselves into thinking we are. We take each step thinking we understand how it will impact the dance, but we don't understand at all. We take each step hoping to influence the dance in certain ways, and more often than not we fail in those aims. The dance is much bigger than us, and it doesn't particularly care where we would like it to go next.

Perhaps it isn't true for others, but I find that the best way to remember that I am part of that dance—and that, despite my fantasies and desires, I hold almost no control over it—is to give myself over to and remember the *experience* of the dance. It isn't to try to understand it, to predict it, to explain it, or to manipulate it to my own ends; it's simply to dance, and to feel and notice all the ways in which all the other participants react to me, ignore me, swirl around me, and determine their own steps. In that moment, I better see and feel my own small place in the larger movement, even if the vast majority of that movement is outside my sight. I know that it buzzes throughout an impossibly large radius, far bigger than I could ever grasp and cloaked in a mystery born of my own limited vision and understanding. I know that the beauty I can see circling around me, no matter how intricate, is only the most limited representation of all that is happening throughout: far too small and parochial to provide me any true understanding of the sheer breadth and singularity of movements taking place throughout the whole. And yet, even if I can never know it, I can sense it. I can feel its infinity. I can feel the impossibility of understanding.

That, I believe, is what Panther Creek has provided me throughout so much of my life. It is a place in which I can place roots into those direct experiences, shedding so many pieces of the human-made world that obscure complexity in favor of straight lines, right angles, human logic and understanding. Those are not bad, of course, nor are they unnatural. They can't be. But they do obscure; they do for me, anyway. They seed the ground with separations. They pull me from direct experience and place me back within the confines of my very limited human mind and our very limited human institutions and constructions. Again, they aren't bad or unnatural, but they provide only narrow views of the dance, and while we can never see it all, we can see far more than these limited vantage points allow.

But those broader sight lines come through direct experience of the world around us and the emotions, sensations, and perceptions it engenders. It comes through the sort of experiences I wrote about at the beginning of this essay. Experiences that, even as I wrote them, I wondered if they would resonate to any degree with the people who would read this. For me, those paragraphs are a joy. Not because they are particularly well-written or because they embody any brilliant use of language, but because they bring to my mind the echoes of the sensations, emotions, and pure joy and wonder that so many of those activities in and around Panther Creek brought to me as an adolescent, a young adult, and an adult. They remind me of the *experience* of those activities and the way they created small, passing communions with the natural world in which I played—and the way that those communions, those *revelations*, didn't just buoy me in the moments they took place, but carried me through future days and weeks and months, reverberating throughout my life, even years later. The memories are proof of my place in nature and its subsummation of me; are proof of my belonging here on this planet; are proof that my continual sense of coming home on my returns to Panther Creek are accurate and honest; are proof that the perceived separation of human and non-human so commonly trafficked in modern industrial society is a straight lie, whether or not it's recognized as so. All of that knowledge and feeling is embodied in my memories of Panther Creek, and it's that knowledge and feeling that I am evoking when I write about my experiences at this small campground in the Gifford Pinchot National Forest.

And yet, all those written memories can't and won't evoke the same knowledge for other readers; at best, it will hearken to their own memories of experience, their own tied knowledge and emotion and comforts, their own sense of their place within, and not apart from, the world. Perhaps that's one of the great challenges of writing about this: that words are so limited when used to attempt to evoke our connection to our world. It is easier to talk about our impact on the world or our views of the world or our beliefs about how to live in the world than it is to talk about actually being a part of the world. Words cannot replace experience and experience is the ultimate correction to separation. Words, then, cannot alone bring us back to the world—to nature, to creation, to whatever you want to call the community of lives and energy that make our existence—but can only serve as clumsy vehicles with which to try to theorize about and explain connection and experience. They can't replace the experiences themselves that actually do bind us back to our world, illuminating the connections that always exist but we too often forget.

If words are inadequate in evoking experience, place is assuredly not, for places embody the experiences themselves that are unique to them. Places are real: evocative of the senses and rooted in a physicality that words are not. Words may represent the place, but the place itself is the reality, and it's one that expands infinitely beyond the confines of words to embody—at least potentially—all our senses. Much as a video tour of a place may gain us a limited perspective of the sights and possibly sounds, it cannot express the entire experience. It cannot express even the full scope of visual experience to be had through an actual visit, let alone provide the full sensory experience such a visit would entail. It is limited and flattened, yes, but even beyond that it is not just a poorer experience, it's a *different* one. Isolate one or two senses and divorce them from all the rest, then attempt to provide those same stimuli within a completely different context than they originated, and you have created something that is only barely, tangentially related to the original source you hope to evoke.

This is why my descriptions of Panther Creek at the beginning of this essay may seem far thinner to the reader than they do to me, for they're a very poor representation of the full experience of the campground and surrounding landscape.

The Panther Creek I know and love is a collection of senses and stimuli and joy and connection. It's a sensation of being tied to an endless array of creatures and energies and raptures—of flowing water and trees and shrubs, dirt and rock and fire and stars deep in the nighttime sky, slugs and trickling trailside springs and endless expanses of ferns. It's an echoing, expansive, calming web of interaction and dependencies, of a sense of something mysterious and elemental flowing through me even as it flows through everything else, binding us into one existence that is, at the same time, an infinite number of unique existences. And that, frankly, cannot be put well into words. It has to be felt.

In other words, Panther Creek is an experience. It can't be sufficiently explained, though attempts can be made. What I think that means, though, is that I cannot *know*—the way we commonly interpret that word—what the place is. I can know it when I'm there, and that knowledge can echo, diminished, in the days and weeks and months after I leave the place. But I doubt I can truly know it when I'm not there. I can only evoke something akin to it through the skewed memories of sensations and, more importantly, with the memory of how I *felt* there. Thinking of the place often brings me a sense of peace and happiness, of joy. It also brings a corresponding longing that exists only in my separation from the place, never in my presence there. All those feelings represent the place for me, too, and—aside from the longing—are an echo of my feelings while there. They derive out of my experiences of the place.

The more I think of this, the more I believe that those feelings are the closest representation I have to what Panther Creek is, and it's in that realization that the reason the place never seems to change may become clear. When the floods of 1996 roared through the mountains, churned Panther Creek into something more along the lines of a turbulent river than a lazy creek, altered its course and at the same time changed permanently the land around the creek, the evidence and remnants of those changes surprised me the next summer. They caught my attention. However, they did not change the *sense* of the place. Yes, some trees were gone, as were sand bars I had grown familiar with; yes, a new island formed where it had not been before; and yes, no doubt innumerable other changes—some I recognized, some I did not—manifested in the disruption. However, the essence of the place did not. The next summer, when I arrived with my father for our annual camping trip there, the changes I discovered surprised me and even, in some ways, brought a brief disquiet as they proved one more piece of evidence of the way the world can change at a moment's notice. But my experience of Panther Creek remained much as it always had. I felt joy and connection, tied into the natural world around me, lifted by all the evident life and a sense of holding my own small place within it. That had not changed, despite the ways in which the land had been altered. And in the continuance of that particular experience—the very essence of what I identified

Panther Creek with—the place was the same. It looked different, but it wasn't *changed*. The feeling of it remained, and as the closest thing to a true identity that I know of for Panther Creek, that feeling assured me that I had arrived in the same place as I did every summer. I had, as always, come home.

Other changes have taken place over the years, but none so dramatic that they could eliminate the quiet, lifting sense of connection that I so strongly identify with the campground and all around it. It has not burned, nor been logged to nothing. The creek has not dried up, the trees have not died, the land hasn't gone barren. I don't know what degree of change would be necessary for my experience of the place to be lost, but such change has never come close to occurring. No doubt every time I arrive there, it is dramatically different in a thousand different ways, as well as much the same in a thousand more. Yet the life found there—the community of living things that I am able to settle into being a part of, if only for a brief few days—remains strong enough for me to find the peace and happiness that Panther Creek affords. I settle into the sensation that I am a small piece of something very big and very mysterious but, most of all, *welcoming*. Home. A place that not only have I been made a part of, but that I am a part of as my birthright—that *all* living things are as their birthright.

I hope that never changes. I suspect in some ways that feeling could be lost, though I believe it would by necessity have to show up elsewhere. (I suspect it is by necessity *everywhere*, though I so often do not feel it.) But I want it always to be there at Panther Creek, waiting for me whenever I might find the chance to arrive. Even as life and energy, matter and element continues to cycle through that landscape and all its living things, I hope that the sense of being a part of it and the deep joy and satisfaction and calm that it brings will always be available there for me. In the way that matters—in the only way that is the closest thing to a truth of Panther Creek—I hope that the place never changes. I want always to arrive there and feel at home and to remember just how much I belong on this planet; just how much I am a part of it, and it a part of me, and never truly separate no matter how often I may fool myself, momentarily, in believing so.

— Portland, Oregon
August 20, 2017

Into the Ruins is published quarterly by Figuration Press. We publish deindustrial science fiction that explores a future defined by natural limits, energy and resource depletion, industrial decline, climate change, and other consequences stemming from the reckless and shortsighted exploitation of our planet, as well as the ways that humans will adapt, survive, live, die, and thrive within this future.

One year, four issue subscriptions to *Into the Ruins* are $39. You can subscribe by visiting intotheruins.com/subscribe or by mailing a check made out to Figuration Press to:

Figuration Press / 3515 SE Clinton Street / Portland, OR 97202

To submit your work for publication, please visit intotheruins.com/submissions or email submissions@intotheruins.com.

All issues of *Into the Ruins* are printed on paper, first and foremost. Electronic versions will be made available as high quality PDF downloads. Please visit our website for more information. The opinions expressed by the authors do not necessarily reflect the opinions of Figuration Press or *Into the Ruins*. Except those expressed by Joel Caris, since this is a sole proprietorship. That said, all opinions are subject to (and commonly do) change, for despite the Editor's occasional actions suggesting the contrary, it turns out he does not know everything and the world often still surprises him.

EDITOR-IN-CHIEF
JOEL CARIS

ASSOCIATE EDITOR
SHANE WILSON

DESIGNER
JOEL CARIS

WITH THANKS TO
SHANE WILSON
JOHN MICHAEL GREER
OUR SUBSCRIBERS

SPECIAL THANKS TO
KATE O'NEILL

Contributors

As a child, **Al Sevcik** lived in a rural Hawaiian river community. After graduation from Hilo High School, he earned degrees in technology and business. After two years in the Air Force, Al moved to a career in business. He has lived in Denver, Los Angeles, New York City and Houston. Al now lives and writes in Tampa, Florida.

Joel Caris is a gardener and homesteader, occasional farmer, passionate advocate for local and community food systems, sporadic writer, voracious reader, sometimes prone to distraction and too attendant to detail, a little bit crazy, a cynical optimist, and both deeply empathetic toward and frustrated with humanity. He is your friendly local editor and publisher. As a reader of this journal and perhaps other writings of his, he hopes you don't too easily tire of his voice and perspective. He lives in Oregon with an inspiring, generous, beautiful woman whom he is so close to marrying.

W. Jack Savage is a retired broadcaster and educator. He is the author of seven books, including *Imagination: The Art of W. Jack Savage* (wjacksavage.com). To date, more than fifty of Jack's short stories and over seven hundred of his paintings and drawings have been published worldwide. Jack and his wife Kathy live in Monrovia, California. Jack is, as usual, responsible for this issue's cover art.

At the centre of **Alistair Herbert's** writing is a northern city which has walled itself off from the rest of the world. The city is part myth, part memory: a focal point for stories which interrogate our culture's ideas about community, place, and identity. It is also falling apart. Alistair studied creative writing at the University of Manchester, and now writes from Todmorden in West Yorkshire. He has previously published work with Manchester's Comma Press.

Born in the gritty Navy town of Bremerton, Washington and raised in the south Seattle suburbs, **JOHN MICHAEL GREER** started writing about as soon as he could hold a pencil. He is the author of more than forty nonfiction books and six novels, including the deindustrial novels *Star's Reach* and *Retrotopia*, and has edited four volumes of the *After Oil* series of deindustrial science fiction anthologies. He also wrote the weekly blog "The Archdruid Report" for eleven years. These days he lives in Cumberland, Maryland, an old red brick mill town in the north central Appalachians, with his wife Sara.

At 62 years of age, **JEANNE LABONTE** is a lifelong resident of northern New Hampshire. Her day job is with a small mail order business (to pay the bills) but her main interests are writing, drawing, gardening, reading and publishing personal observations about them, as well as about the beauty of the local environment, in her blog New Hampshire Green Leaves, located at jeannemlabonte.com

RITA RIPPETOE is author of *Booze and the Private Eye: Alcohol in the Hard-Boiled Novel* and *A Reappraisal of Jane Duncan: Sexuality, Race and Colonialism in the My Friends Novels*, both published by McFarland & Co. Rita received a PhD in English from the University of Nevada, Reno; a M.A. in English from CSU, Sacramento; and a B.A. in Anthropology from UC, Davis. She is a member of Mystery Writers of America and Sisters in Crime. Although she has lived as far afield as Los Angeles, Hawaii, Colorado and Vancouver, BC, she currently lives in the suburbs of Sacramento, California with two box turtles and a desert tortoise.

C. SPIVEY spent eight years as a meteorologist with the US Navy in Europe and Asia. He now teaches English as a foreign language while working on a rice farm during the spring planting and fall harvest. His fiction has appeared in *The Moon Magazine*, *SQ Mag*, *Fantasy Scroll*, and *Perihelion*.

LETTERS TO THE EDITOR

Editor's Note: In early July, I asked in a blog post on this magazine's website how readers stay grounded in the midst of the decline taking place around us. The initial three following letters are responses I received. The fourth letter, from Jon Andreas, is a response to my posed question from the last issue of what readers hope for in the face of decline. The two letters beyond that are not in response to any particular imposed question, but are a joyous examination of intriguing future business opportunities by our own G.Kay Bishop. Enjoy!

Dear Editor,

I have become more grounded by turning away from what used to be an obsession: reading about, tracking, and studying our various predicaments (to use your words). Only intermittently do I now tune in to media accounts of "the news" and even then, only via brief visits to a handful of alternative media sites that have earned my trust. By focusing on bigger pictures, the narratives or myths that frame the information fed to us and drive what's left of our civilization ever-closer to the cliff edge, I refuse to let the trees distract my attention from the forest, the natural world apart from "humans and (their) myriad artifacts," so evocatively described in your article. Simultaneously, I focus on another bigger picture, one which puts the natural world into even larger context. This is the spiritual journey which, I am thankful, remains a live option for me, although it has understandably become a dead end for many others. The centerpiece of that journey is an unorthodox devotion to the "historical Jesus" and his radical message about the kingdom of god, a myth starkly juxtaposed to those that pervade and permeate our sick society and ecocidal world order. For me, these bigger pictures come together in a universal, elemental value that I struggle to embody and which sustains me, what Schweitzer called "reverence for life."

Newton Finn
Waukegan, Illinois

Dear Editor,

My weekly shift at a local "soup kitchen" helps me stay grounded. I know that a few hours of my week have been spent in useful service to the community, and I enjoy the crew I work with. Everyone is cheerful and polite; most of our customers are as well. The chief cook sets the tone for us; he could have been a ghostwriter for Norman Vincent Peale, the way he preaches and practices his positive outlook. "It's a great day," he'll say from time to time. "I'm doing what I love, and glad to be here doing it." We thought we'd lost him two years ago, when he was hospitalized with a tumor on the spine. But he was back in a few months, a little unsteady on his feet but cheerful as ever.

Bob Wise
Merritt Island, Florida

Dear Editor,

I use daily meditation and Heartmath breathing as techniques to help me stay grounded and calm. Practicing forgiveness of myself, others, and events has helped a lot a well. Also, as I work in my garden and walk around my community, I enjoy observing the activity of insects on the flowers. I've reconciled to the fact that our "civilization" will pass away at some point, but remain curious and fascinated by the details. An ecologist by training, I'm inspired by the web of life and cycles.

Stephen Treimel
Carrboro, North Carolina

Dear Editor,

Even as we bumble and bump our way down the backside of the American Empire, I hold out hope for two of the greatest loves in my life: books and music. Both can be low tech and have stood the test of time. Some of my favorite authors, like Lao Tzu and Pelagius, have been around for a long time, and there's no reason why more recent ones, like Le Guin and Kingsolver, can't be hand-copied if needed. John Michael Greer sketches a secret book society in his novel, *Star's Reach*; I would enjoy the challenge of being part of such a network.

My violinist mother raised me around string quartets and our German-American friends' violin shop redolent with woodiness and Old World craftsmanship. My cello is two-and-a-half centuries old; why wouldn't it last again as long with such calloused hands to care for it? From Mozart to Celtic fiddle, the spirit of music will not be diminished. A few centuries from now, MP3 will be short for Musicians Playing a Trio.

Singing under the cottonwood,

Jon Andreas
Chino, California
www.ecodreamer.net

LETTER THE FIRST

DUKE, DUKE, DUKE, DUKE OF OIL

Dear Editor,

If Duke Power [*ed. note:* officially known as Duke Energy and headquartered in Charlotte, North Carolina] wants new revenue streams, why have they not put research-&-development dollars (R&D$) into a line of products designed to harvest methane from pig dung? There are more pigs than there are people in this state, and if Wisconsin dairy farmers can harvest methane from their cows' dung, power their own farm and thirty-five surrounding households from captured cow-fart gas, why not us? Not to mention selling sacks and sacksworth of odorless solids as rich, high-quality soil fertilizer. Now, right off the bat, there's two revenue streams that SUPPORT North Carolina pig farmers instead of trying to Yankee-fleece them, or nickel-and-dime us to economic death.

I mean, come on: This is not rocket science, boys. Biogas digesters are used in African and Indian continent villages run by basically illiterate and innumerate farmers. Why isn't Duke Power smart enough to make this happen here? Same for PSNC [Energy]—don't they have any real live engineers on board?

Or perhaps it is just the people at the tippy top who are the jumbo-dumbos: the ones without any vision, scope, genius and true intelligence. They say stupid people only make money fast; it takes smart ones to make money last.

Look at all the potential revenue streams Duke Power could be pulling in right now: gas-powered mini-generators, lagoon-balloons, solar/self-powered hydro-filters for off-gassing effluents, fertilizer brick frames, fans for piped waste heat to dry the odorless bricks, and self-powered sacking and labeling equipment.

That's just for starters: there are thousands of other revenue- and job-creating options they could be pursuing with their monopoly-extracted utility dollars.

How about locally-made and sold products such as small-to-medium-scale pipelines?

How about a trained, part-time workforce of contractors who survey, plumb, and install new systems?

How about on-going work for older systems, upgrading as technology improves, but in the meanwhile, protecting air quality as they seal and reseal lines as part of routine circuit-rider inspections for safety.

Hey? How about that? And that's all at the one level of operations. Similar infrastructure could be appropriately-scaled and sold at price points suitable for different levels of buyers: single farms, farm collectives, small market-towns, large urban neighborhoods, campus or government buildings, and whole municipalities.

Not to mention selling courses of training in local-scale pipeline maintenance and advanced training for folks seeking licensing certificates or moving up the scale ladder to larger or more complex power station models.

Instead of ruining young people's lives by burdening them with student debt or playing piratical protection rackets on the poor, Duke could be selling education resources to help people to help other people keep safe, warm, and powered up. Practical abilities meeting real needs. Each day leaving the environment a bit cleaner than the day before. And making money doing it. I mean, duh. . . .

Now let us talk about war and refugee preparedness. As climate change worsens (and it will, guys, it most definitely will) which methane-centered suite of technology is more likely to be disabled by aerial or ground-based enemy attacks, and crippled by criminal siphoning?

A) A huge, easy-to-map network of unprotected interstate pipelines;

B) A small, locally-produced and consumed product transported a few hundred feet from the residences of locals who constantly oversee and patrol their property?

If you answered anything but B), well, I have some stocks and bonds located on Mars that I would like you to buy. Yeah! It's a wonderful investment in the future. My future, not yours. Pay in cash.

Now, as I understand it, pig dung is too hot in potassium to be marketed directly. So why does Duke Power not use its OTHER waste product—namely, coal ash—to mix with the pig dung solids and make a NEW product that is better than ever? Don't they have any chemists on their staff? Do they not know that loss of organic material in soils is a worldwide problem, hence a world-wide opportunity to actually serve humanity while making smaller, slower, steadier, surer profits? Any technique, technical procedure, or technology they develop could make oodles of money in China, in India, in Africa as it is perfected for export.

And what they do for pig dung today, they can do to humanure tomorrow. It's called long-tail marketing. No pun intended.

Believe me, fellas, if you want a truly renewable resource there is nothing more reliable than shit. It took billions of years to convert whole dinosaurian ecosystems into pools of sweet crude; whereas you can power your own place plus a local village with what your pigs plopped out just yesterday.

The effluence of flatulence = munificence.

What can't ol' Duke duly do with doo-doo?

Boys, thar's gold in that thar brown.

So why exactly does Duke Power love pennies and hate people? Why do they go oogle-boogle after bucks while pig-sticking the farmers' pocketbooks? Where do they think they are going to get food from when they have heavy-metal fracked the land, poisoned the water, and acid-rain killed the trees?

Don't they have ANY sense?

No. Don't answer that question.

I'm afraid I already know the answer.

G.Kay Bishop
Durham, North Carolina

LETTER THE SECOND

The Duke Stoops to Profit: Further Thoughts on New Revenue Streams for Duke Power

Dear Editor,

In a word: parts and services. Yes, I know, how old-fashioned and unroyally ordinary. Instead of glamorous, kingly speculation in glittering gold and silver, establishing more solid metallic worth in the shape of cast iron, steel, and copper tubing—aluminum and stainless pipe-fittings. Creating a network of small farm-sized biogas installations, servicing them as parts wear out. What with solar PV and solar thermal, goats, pigs, dairy cattle, alpacas, and llamas, with each small plant powering its nearest neighbors, North Carolina could become the first energy-independent state in the nation.

Of course, this would require doing the actual work of manufacturing, stocking and maintaining parts. Training service people. It would require the Duke's most loyal and trusted liveried servants to rub their nice clean shoulders with us lowly smelly farming folk. Ewww! Maybe even touch our dirt-encrusted hands. But hey, *noblesse oblige* as they say in Latin, or is it French? One of those furrin lingos, anyway.

No, raahlly, the sacrifice should be slight enough. After their duties are done, they can repair to the Duke's solar-thermal supplied bathhouses and His methane-powered laundries. They need not turn up their noses so far that they get lost in the clouds. Perhaps an exclusive perfumery for the Duke's most-favored lot would sweeten the temporary loss of prestige and help maintain the proper respect for rank.

Should the Duke's people ever decide to condescend from their most monopolistic and holy highnesses to mingle with us peasants and peons by providing an honest-to-God public service, then they really ought to begin RIGHT NOW to decentralize methane capture and gear up for the long haul by supplying maintenance parts and training services departments.

The fact that other uses can be made of long hollow tubes of metal and jointing devices may not have occurred to their Most Monopolized Graces: bike frames, for instance. Pumping equipment. Portable air compression-driven tool-suites for roofing and construction sites far from power outlets. Stocking parts and servicing these additional metallic masses can supply a modest but not insignificant profit stream.

At each stocking locale, methane/acetylene welding and soldering stations. Welders on site. Sort of like the blacksmiths of the Elder Days, so similar to these ever-so-modern times of extreme wealth-and-power disparity.

To be sure, the consequence of setting up such a network of smaller, more durable profit centers might prove a little embarrassing. The wealth and power of the Dukedom might become less concentrated in the Manor

Proper and be shared more diffusely throughout the whole of the Estate. Peasants will have their price.

But the Duke must not think this a shameful outcome. A stout, sturdy, and healthy peasantry, together with a widespread yeomanry of skilled biogas pipefitters is worth much more than gold in the hard times that are sure to come. A grateful people who gladly accept the advice and guidance of their Most Monopolistic Majesties by purchasing costly pressure regulation gauges from His Shoppes and obeying His Rules for leak prevention will be far less likely to revolt against the Palace or set up wildcat power and explosive fertilizer sites wherever manure piles are to be found.

Then, when the glittering speculative orgies of the Kings of Wall St. come to their sudden and inevitable end, the Duke will be sitting pretty. He and His may not have so fine a set of crystal chandeliers as their Royall New Yorkist Peers, but He may be less likely to see the business end of a guillotine in action.

G.Kay Bishop
Durham, North Carolina

Into the Ruins welcomes letters to the editor from our readers. We encourage thoughtful commentary on the contents of this issue, the themes of the magazine, and humanity's collective future. Readers may email their letters to editor@intotheruins.com or mail them to:

Figuration Press
3515 SE Clinton Street
Portland, OR 97202

Please include your full name, city and state, and an email or phone number. Only your name and location will be printed with any accepted letter.

Author's note of corrigendum for "The Wizard of Was," published Spring 2017, Issue #5:

Dear Readers,

I should not have troubled the generous readers and honorable subscribers of this notable Organ with an account of my remissness had not my reputation as an unreformed pedant and remorseless curmudgeon not been at stake.

Your own modernity and comprehensive understanding may lead you to dismiss this revelation as unnecessary; however, I demand it of your justice.

To wit: the only two sentences that ought to be written or uttered containing the phrase "data is" are as follows:

"Data is a plural noun; the singular form is datum."

or,

"Data is on the holodeck, pretending to be human."

I exaggerate, of course, but my agonized feelings on this subject are otherwise inexpressible. By permitting an instance of the singular use of data in a work bearing my name, I have been grievously at fault.

The error is entirely mine; I failed to proof the "blues," so to speak, carelessly trusting to the more modern grammatical sensibilities of our comma-aware and punctuation-precise editor.

To compound this breach of my customary usage, I went out of my way to invent the word "zeronationing" as a substitute for the incorrect use of "decimation" to mean "killing large numbers of" rather than "killing one out of every ten." For me to then turn around and issue the grammatical fart of "data was entered" was contrary to all civilized converse, abhorrent to speakers of Latin, and an insult to fellow pedants everywhere. I most humbly apologize.

If there is a Mr. Collins in the house, I yield the floor to his more durable powers of apologetic continuance; I must leave you all to recover some degree of composure; at present, my spirits are quite overcome.

Sincerely,

G.Kay Bishop
Durham, North Carolina

STORIES

The Reactor, the Witch, and Higashi-dori

by C. Spivey

Kana had never seen the witch. The cursed woman living within the smoldering ruins by the sea was a tale told to all the village children. Finish your chores, help your neighbors, stay away from Higashi-dori. Lest the witch drag you inside and feed you to her devouring reactor. Like all menaces preached unseen to children, Kana had paid it little mind.

Still, when Kana saw the woman on the far side of the mountaintop chain-link, she knew exactly who she was. Abandoning her forage among the swaying bamboo around her, Kana crept toward the fence for a better look.

Higashi-dori's plume wisped upward before bending inland in the crisp autumn air. The smoke from the burning nuclear plant was a constant reminder of the old world for the hundred or so people scratching out an existence in the Aomori countryside. The sea beyond the decrepit power plant burned gold in the sinking afternoon sun.

She certainly didn't look like a witch, not in her powder blue coveralls and scuffed white hard hat. She carried a satchel over her shoulder not unlike Kana's. As Kana watched through the fence, she heard a chirping sound. The witch removed a black gadget from her pocket and shook her head. As if roused by some alarm, the woman sprinted down the mountain slope, her satchel sliding to the ground as she ran. Kana watched her vanish into the cedars surrounding Higashi-dori.

The discarded bag drew Kana's gaze. What would a witch be gathering in these woods? What exotic mushrooms and herbs bloomed on that forbidden side of the fence? Shrugging aside the danger drilled into her over the years, Kana slipped through one of the many holes in the rusted chain-link, and retrieved the witch's satchel.

Kana frowned after picking through its mundane contents. A few mushrooms and mountain yams identical to the ones Kana had foraged herself. Feeling an all too familiar disappointment, Kana made her way home.

A warm breeze blew off the sea as Kana descended the hills, heavy with salt and moisture. It cooled her sweat while dragging a stickiness with it. She dropped the two satchels in her bicycle's tiny trailer, and removed one of her only treasures from beside them. So innocuous was it that she feared no theft, leaving it in the trailer to soak up sunlight during her hours of forage. The lone remaining gift from her long vanished and presumed dead father. Her neon orange, glow-in-the-dark, Duncan yo-yo.

"Hobbies that require no batteries are the best these days," her father had said. He'd given her the simple toy years ago. Before he'd departed their village of Odanosawa for Mutsu City and never returned. It was a constant comfort and Kana floated it to lazy spins before snapping it back to her left palm during the five kilometer bike ride home.

Wildflowers sprouted from the cracked asphalt at regular intervals, springing through the holes where people had long ago pried away the small reflectors. Few inhabited homes remained in Odanosawa. The place had been almost abandoned even when her parents had first moved, encouraged by some government cash program to help repopulate the countryside. Back when Japan *had* a national government. Now, most houses tottered beneath their overgrowth, their windows long since salvaged away for their glass along with anything else useful. Each lonely hulk creaked in the breeze, empty windows staring like vacant eyes. Fruit and nut trees crowded the gardens of each abandoned home. Planted long before by those that remained, their boughs were heavy as fall settled over the countryside.

Kana passed what few rice fields remained scattered near Odanosawa's rivers. The fields had long since been drained for harvest and the crops hung drying on lengths of wooden rail. Kana, alongside every other able-bodied villager, had helped in the harvest just as she had with the spring planting. She'd slogged through the muck alongside all the others planting the vital rice that fed their tiny village.

Several stars glittered in the purple sky when Kana arrived home. Vegetables crowded every centimeter of their half-hectare property alongside wildflowers--heavy on the lemongrass and marigolds in feeble attempts to ward off mosquitos. Kana passed through leafy rows of daikon, the gigantic Japanese radish she'd eaten beside her rice since she could remember. A curtain of plastic pet-bottles hung inverted from their porch. Tomato plants vied for space from each hanging container, a few red stragglers amidst the green leaves. She plucked one of the late-comers and popped it in her mouth. Not sure what to do with the witch's bag she stashed it on the side of the house.

Several aged solar lanterns glowed dimly from beside the front door where they'd charge during the day. She grabbed one before entering. Within the genkan, where Kana removed her boots before entering, several jars of vegetables and two pots of rice were stacked. That meant a trip to their neighbor's to cook.

"Not much," Kana said to her mother when she entered the kitchen. She upended her forage of mushrooms, yams and shiso leaves to the kitchen table. Kana always made sure to bulk her forage with the ubiquitous red weed. The boiled down leaves made for a tart yet pleasant juice. Her mother just nodded while peeling a daikon-radish with her small knife, carefully dropping the skin into a bucket for their compost. She wore a stained white apron over her black t-shirt. Her jeans were as faded as Kana's own, and boasted an equal amount of patches.

Their dinner was a cup of cold rice each alongside sliced cabbage and onion mixed with mashed daikon. They chopped and sprinkled some of Kana's foraged mushrooms over both dishes. Dessert was a few mealy apple slices while they each sucked a quarter of a halved lemon.

Kana's mother chewed the last of her food slowly, staring into the gloom outside as if looking for something far away. Finally, she said, "Kurosawa-San is making a fire tomorrow. It's our day to cook."

"I know," Kana snapped. Her mother was always reminding her of the obvious. She looked at Kana, the hurt obvious in her eyes even in the dark of the dying solar lantern. Kana looked away to hide her guilt but didn't apologize.

Their neighbor's land abutted a forested spur of the mountain, providing easy access to abundant firewood from the cedars. While bamboo increasingly displaced the native cedars each year, Kurosawa's sprawling orchards still retained hundreds of the trees in addition to those bearing fruits and nuts. He'd built a large, brickwork stove topped with a sheet of steel salvaged from somewhere. It made for easy cooking for the community to prepare their rice as well as any other boiling they required. Much easier to keep a large fire going during prescribed cooking days than dozens of smaller ones throughout the area. It was also a way for locals to keep in touch while trading surplus produce and forage.

"You can spend some time with Ryou."

Kana was glad for the darkness as she rolled her eyes. Kana liked Ryou just fine. The two had gone to the same school together, one of only six others. In a countryside already reeling from population decline, Kana's few classmates had shared a single room in the three-story school built for a student-body 20 times that size. Like all their world, the school was an echoing, empty place full of shadows and forgotten dreams.

"I don't see why you dislike him," her mother said. "He's a handsome boy."

Kana spooned daikon-mush around her bowl. Ryou *was* handsome. Tall and lean while friendly and kind, the two had always gotten along. But she suspected Ryou wasn't interested in Kana or *any* girl for that matter. Their previous clumsy explorations had proven that unspoken realization for the both of them. But this wasn't something either of them had ever shared. In a community where those younger than twenty could be counted on one hand, their aging elders seemed desperate for any future pairing.

After washing the dishes Kana took one of the dimming solar-lanterns to her room. She laid out her futon before pulling a box from beside her dresser. Remnants of the old world, the items were little more than trinkets now.

One in particular she liked to hold was her father's old smartphone. He'd taken care of it so that it remained clean and undamaged. Besides her Duncan--a ghostly orange glow in the dark beside her—the phone's unblemished glass seemed the only thing without flaw in Kana's crumbling world. She like to touch it, to feel its rounded corners and glass face.

She remembered the day her father had set off, accompanied by several other men and women his age. They'd piled an old flatbed truck with their best produce. Fruits, vegetables, rice, squash and pumpkins, anything they might be able to trade for medicines and tools from the city of Mutsu across the hills to the west. Having gathered the few mules left in the area, they tied them to the truck, and set out to waves and a few tears. They'd departed the Shimokita Peninsula through the massive Highway-seven tunnel connecting it beneath the mountains.

Kana squeezed her phone at the memory. None of them had returned. She'd heard whispers that the witch had forbidden any to leave the village, and her spells cursed all who tried. Yet her father and the others had risked it in hopes of procuring much needed supplies. And the witch had struck them all down.

At least that's what Kana had been told. The remaining men and women had been too frightened to investigate. Left to their own imaginations on what peril might have befallen them on that journey, everyone assumed it had been the witch, striking down those who defied her by leaving the village.

But seeing the woman today, in her coveralls and hardhat, with her boring satchel filled with mushrooms and yams, Kana wondered if she was really a witch at all and not just another story.

Kana wrapped the old phone in cloth, and carefully replaced it in the box. Staring at her Duncan's ethereal orange glow, Kana fell asleep, memories of her lost father following into her dreams.

"I saw the witch yesterday," Kana said as she plucked a fat caterpillar from a cabbage leaf and dropped it in her bucket.

Ryou was bent next to her, spreading the leaves of another cabbage in search of any bugs feasting upon it. "You did not," he said. He was a good head taller than Kana with a lankiness to him that made bending over the cabbage rows difficult. "She's not even real. No one could survive so close to Higashi-dori."

"I *did* see her. I even took some of her food."

Ryou stood, ruining the wings of a flitting white moth with a twist of his fingers before adding it to his own bucket of squirming insects. "You what?"

Kana explained how she'd pushed through the fence and retrieved the woman's bag of forage, causing Ryou to take a step back.

"That place is poison. You might be carrying it with you."

"They say she killed our dads for leaving. That it was her curse."

Ryou returned to picking amongst the leaves for bugs. Kana thought it might have been easier than thinking about his own father, vanished on that same fateful trip as Kana's. "No one know that's what happened to them," he said.

Kana looked to the wisp of smoke threading its way above the seaward hills. Curses and magic *did* seem pretty childish.

"Why don't we ask her?" Kana said.

Ryou stood, looking around as if to confirm no one was there to hear their conspiracy. The adults always left the two of them alone and the cabbage patch was quite empty. "You won't just get in trouble. You could die."

"Get in trouble from who?" she asked, staring hard at Ryou.

He shook his head and bent back to his work. Kana remained silent and did the same, picking bugs from the cabbage until the sun crept toward the horizon. After, they went to Kurosawa's chickens, overturning the buckets as the greedy birds feasted on the writhing insects.

They didn't say much as they approached the brickwork fire-pit at the edge of the orchard. The adults were finishing their cooking and canning atop the fire-pit's steel top. Kurosawa-san, with his gray hair and beard, leaned upon his stick beside those chatting near the fire. Kurosawa-san's property provided an easy gathering place to the dozen or so families in Kana's neighborhood. And while there was a monthly market within the village center to trade food in addition to soap, candles, and the few other crafted or refurbished goods in Odanosawa, most neighborhoods had a similar setup to Kurosawa's.

The families cooking that day had brought their hard, stale rice from the previous week. Combining it in a large pan, they'd added sliced onions, garlic, bell peppers, carrots and eggs, turning that almost inedible rice into tasty fried-rice. Kana and Ryou had shared in it for lunch before returning to pick pests from Kurosawa's cabbages. Now, as the sun fell to the horizon, the adults were finishing steaming the rice that would be breakfast lunch and dinner for the following week.

Still out of earshot from the others, Ryou said, "If you're going to see the witch, then I'm coming too."

Kana followed her mother home in silence, their two tiny trailers packed with cooked rice and jars of preserved vegetables. The lights from their bicycles provided the only illumination in the twilight coming alive with stars. At home, they plucked their dim solar lanterns from the porch, the meager things having charged during the day to produce what little light their LED's were still able to muster.

Her mother had steamed two pots of rice at Kurosawa's fire and boiled down A large pot of shiso leaves, providing them with two plastic bottles of the tart, red juice. Kana began labeling the jars of canned vegetables from their garden while adding them to the shelves of others that would be their winter fare. Her mother set about with dinner.

One thing Kana enjoyed about their weekly visits to the Kurosawa's was the hot rice at dinner. The rest of the week's meals would be served cold, but those first scoops after returning were always a soft, steaming delicacy that they savored in the dinner gloom. They drank a small cup of shiso juice each.

"Ryou and I want to go foraging tomorrow," Kana said into the darkness, their lanterns growing dimmer with each bite.

"That's good." The light glinted from her eyes as Kana's mother stared at something far away in the dark. "Watch the smoke from Higashi-dori. If the wind shifts, run straight home. It's dangerous."

"She was right here," Kana said the next day. She'd returned with Ryou to the same broken portion of fence within the stand of bamboo.

"Well, she's not here now," Ryou said. The sky was clear but for Higashi-dori's ever-burning plume. Sunlight glinted a thousand times from the ocean stretching beyond the plant to the horizon.

"Let's look for her." Kana pushed through the fence, carrying the woman's forgotten bag alongside her own satchel.

"Are you sure?"

"You can wait here if you want," Kana said, slipping through the chain-link. "I'm going to find the witch."

She wanted desperately for Ryou to accompany her, but she wasn't about to let *him* know that. She proceeded to sidestep down the hill, smiling when she heard him pushing through the fence behind her.

"Shit," he grumbled as he caught up with her.

There was less bamboo on this side of the mountain. And while they sprung up wherever the older cedars had died, there were still fewer than where Kana usually foraged. Still, the two of them made slow progress as they stopped to dig fresh yams to take home. Hunting witches might be exciting, but foraged food would always take priority.

They worked their way down the slope like this for nearly an hour, chatting and laughing to hide their apprehension at the building growing in size at their approach. Two towers rose above the trees, the one belching its perpetual smoke, the other clustered with antenna. Ugly, squat buildings rose beside these, visible through the thinning trees nearer the site.

"What are you doing here?"

They both jumped at the voice behind them. The woman wore the same baby-blue coveralls from the day before. Her white hair hung in a ponytail beneath a scuffed white hard hat. She looked alien in her attire, lacking the patches and wear of Kana's own.

"Don't you know it's dangerous here?" she said, eyeing the two of them with suspicion.

"C'mon, Kana."

Kana slapped Ryou's hand away and stepped toward the woman. She had her Duncan out. Snapping it from her grasp and back in quick, comforting motions. A strange energy filled Kana. So absent was any excitement in her dreary life that now, after the thrilling disobedience of crossing the fence, seeing the woman added spectacle to her adventure.

"I brought your bag." Kana pocketed her yo-yo before unslinging the woman's satchel.

The woman stared for a moment before snatching it away. She stepped back, looking inside it.

"We didn't take anything," Kana said.

"You came to bring this?" she asked in disbelief.

Kana shrugged. "It was yours."

The woman looked at the two of them for several seconds in silence before finally saying, "Well, would you like to come inside?"

"Kana, no!" Ryou seized her by the arm. "This is crazy. We're right under it." He pointed to the plume rising above them. "We could be getting sick right now."

"That's nothing," the woman said, her back to them as she departed toward the buildings ahead. "It's just steam."

The light within Higashi-dori was so bright that Kana had to shield her eyes upon entering. The crisp white glow from the bulb overhead was like nothing she'd seen. Most of the lights were dark, but the few that burned did so brightly.

"You have electricity?" Ryou asked, knuckling his own eyes as they adjusted to the room inside where the woman had led them.

"What do you think this place was built for?" She hung her hardhat on a peg near the door and led them further within. The room had once been an office, Kana guessed. Dusty computers sat lifeless despite the lights above. They passed through several similar rooms, lit with a single set of lights while others were dark. Eventually, they reached a room like something out of a storybook.

"What . . . what is all this?" Ryou stammered.

A hundred lights twinkled red and green across a sprawling console many meters across, climbing past glowing monitors all the way to a vaulted ceiling. A single high-backed chair on wheels sat before it while a cot stacked with blankets and pillows was tucked in the corner. Several smartphones were charging beside the wall, their many wires attached to a plug-strip.

"Control room," the woman said. She stood before the console for almost a minute, scanning several screens and readouts before nodding. "Okay. Sorry. I have to keep on top of this damned thing all the time. But everything is okay. Well, as okay as it will ever be. C'mon. Let's have some tea."

Slow to remove their gaze from the wondrous flashing panels, Kana and Ryou followed the woman deeper into the facility. They passed from the interior through halls crowded with pipes snaking away in all directions. The three eventually exited into the afternoon sun once more to an open area. Pots crowded every bit of the concrete. Containers of every conceivable size and shape sprouted beans, squash and other produce as well as several bright flowering plants abuzz with fluttering insects. Seaweed hung drying in lines, the sun lighting it like stained glass.

They entered another building to find an even brighter room. Not a single overhanging bulb was unlit in the cavernous space. Beneath the glittering white LEDs was a true garden. Tomatoes and eggplant hung fat on their vines beside beans climbing poles toward the ten-meter high ceiling. Herbs crowded an entire corner, filling the place with an assortment of invigorating smells beside the more mundane green of the leaves around them. The woman directed them to a table in a corner, removing dusty plastic chairs from a stack before bidding them to sit.

"Haven't had guests in . . . well, a long time." A sad look passed across her face as she pulled dried leaves from a pouch and filled a pot with them. She poured water from a jug into a carafe and switched it on, a bright orange light glowing at its base. "It takes a few minutes to heat. The leaves I grow myself. On the hills nearer the water. Not the best stuff but anything is better than nothing."

The two simply nodded, lost amidst the wonders of this place so near them with its unknown electric wonders.

"You've had all this the whole time?" Kana asked.

"I try to be discreet. I don't want to bring . . . unwanted attention to the village."

"No one has even *seen* you in Odanosawa," Ryou said, suspicion in his voice.

"There are those who know of me. But it's been agreed not to let others become aware."

"But you could share all this." Kana gestured to the abundance around them. "You could give us light and heat once more." She pointed to the warming carafe beside them.

"Trust me, I need what little power this place produces just to keep it from burning to the ground."

Kana and Ryou looked at each other in confusion.

"It's a long story." The woman shook her head. "Even if the power lines hadn't long fallen down or been cannibalized for their cabling, it would be dangerous to try and re-electrify Odanosawa. Not to mention if . . . others outside the peninsula saw lights glowing around us."

Kana now noticed how the many windows above were blacked out. Old newspaper with sooty black paint slopped over them revealed the ancient print in certain places.

No sooner had the woman poured steaming water into their mugs than some alarm sounded from within her pocket.

"Of all times," the woman complained while fumbling with a device. It looked quite similar to the one Kana kept by her bed. "All three?" she said, swiping across its brightly lit face. She pushed away from the table and sprinted for the door.

Not sure what to do, Kana looked at Ryou, who only shrugged before the two of them followed the fleeing woman.

"The pumps," she shouted ahead of them as they raced to catch up the woman, surprisingly spry despite her gray hair. "Damn things seize constantly." They crossed the outdoor area, weaving around the potted plants before entering another building on the far side. The woman ran along a length of silver piping indiscernible from the dozens of others choking the hallway. Kana and Ryou paused behind her as she checked a metal wheel tied with a tag.

"Okay," she said before giving it barely a quarter turn. She was soon sprinting to another wheel further down the line. She gave it a similar turn before pausing. "What am I doing?" She slapped her forehead before turning to them.

"How should *we* know?" Ryou said between heaving breaths.

"You." She grabbed Ryou's arm and dragged him to the wheel she'd just turned. "Wait here. When I yell, turn this as far as it will go to the left. You." She grabbed Kana and dragged her back the way they'd come, parking her in front of the first wheel she'd turned. "Same for you. Wait for my yell then turn as far as it will go." Without another word she sprinted past Ryou and vanished around a corner.

"Whats going on?" Ryou yelled to Kana from his post.

It was Kana's turn to shrug. She felt her Duncan through her pocket but refrained from removing it lest it interfere with her orders.

"Now!" came a shriek from far away. "Turn, turn, *turn*!"

Kana did, cranking the metal wheel as hard as she could until it would turn no more. Ryou gave her an "okay" sign when she looked toward him. When the woman returned, she was grinning.

"That would've taken me almost an hour on my own."

"To turn three wheels?" Ryou asked.

"The line has to be cleared at once. Close one section off too much and the whole thing will blow. Used to be automated. But the electronics haven't fared well here. You should see the cobbled mess that is my breaker panel."

Kana had no clue what a breaker was, but kept silent, her Duncan now spinning a soothing rhythm in her hand.

"You two are pretty helpful," the woman said. "I'm Kiyomi. How would you like to learn more?"

"Thought you were going to ask her about our dads," Ryou said as they returned home that day.

Kana kept silent. The woman was hardly a witch. Just another tale from their elders. They'd been too busy listening to Kiyomi's excited explanations of that place to ask much more. By the time they'd realized the late hour, Kana had almost forgotten she was supposed to hate the woman.

"You could always ask her tomorrow." Ryou pushed through the chain-link at the top of the hill.

Kana followed, the two of them pausing to look at Higashi-dori through the fence. An overcast sky had crept upon them while within the plant, turning the ocean beneath dull gray but for a few rays punching sunlight far on the horizon. Kana was thinking about how similar the woman's smartphone had been to the one she kept by her bed. The one that had belonged to her father.

"I liked learning about that place," Kana said finally.

"Me too." Ryou looked at her and smiled. "I want to learn more."

And so they did, the both of them hurrying through their daily chores to escape to Higashi-dori. Kana rose before the sun, hanging her futon from the balcony wall to air out before loading her bicycle trailer with watering cans to fill from the well. Her mother was still wiping sleep from her eyes while Kana saw to watering their garden.

The two told their mothers they were foraging, and made sure to bring back what little they could find on their hikes over the mountain. If their sacks weren't quite full despite their time away, the knowing smiles they received while bicycling past waving villagers reassured them. The locals were happy at their time together. Hope for a marriage was a welcome thing in the village.

What the two were doing instead was getting on-the-job training at a nuclear power plant.

Kana's Duncan skipped in place against the concrete as she walked the dog with her left hand while consulting notes on one of Kiyomi's smartphones with her right. She'd written several apps—a new word for Kana and Ryou—to monitor different areas of Higashi-dori using the station's own wi-fi network. Kana spent her days checking gauges, displays, and pipes and assisting wherever Kiyomi directed them.

Within Higashi-dori's walls, footsteps echoing beneath clear LED light, Kana was learning more about the old world than any of her teacher's had been able to share. She was gaining understanding of a complex system that few, even during the pinnacle of the past, had ever truly understood. She imagined herself pursuing some similar career had she lived fifty years before. When engineering existed beyond salvage and scrap.

"I was wondering," Kana said during one warm fall afternoon in Kiyomi's outdoor garden. They were pulling drying seaweed from racks and folding it carefully. "Could I charge this?" She showed Kiyomi her father's old phone.

"Sure. Is that yours?"

"It was my father's."

Their garden work was interrupted by an alarm. One of the pumps had seized and the three spent the next hour turning knobs and wheels to keep vital water running to the reactor while Kiyomi fiddled to get the pump operating. Back in the control room, the three sat before the sprawling control panel to ensure the pump remained running.

"It will take awhile to charge," Kiyomi said after they located a cable that fit it. "But we can look through it now."

She showed Kana how to operate it, stating she was lucky the screen wasn't locked. After a brief introduction, the three of them were soon bent over its screen while Kana hurriedly swiped through folders full of photos.

"Yokohama!" Kiyomi said with a beaming smile. Several photos showed a sprawling seaside area full of towering buildings and more people than Kana had ever seen. A massive Ferris wheel dominated the skyline, its lights chasing a rainbow of different colors in each photo. "Oh I used to love going there."

"What was it like?" Ryou asked.

Kana only halfway heard them, so entranced was she with the images of her smiling mother and father. He looked so different from her memories. Her mother so much younger and happier. All the people did. Every shot was filled with smiling strangers.

How could none of them know? It seemed strange people could be so oblivious to what awaited them. Then again, Higashi-dori spoke volumes to how little any of them had expected. A place built to last far longer than the society that created it.

Kana thought of her mother. Weeping nightly for her lost world of frivolous comforts. She'd been blind to the collapse in those photos. Her delicate clothes and makeup were testament to their blindness of the world creeping toward them all.

And now, at Higashi-dori, it was Kana's task to see that the ignorance of those like her mother didn't kill them all now.

"Can't you just turn it off?" Ryou asked Kiyomi once while sitting before the twinkling control console. "Then you could leave this place and come live in the village."

Kiyomi shook her head. "It's not that simple. The rods are radioactive—they stay hot—for a long time. Centuries. Even a reactor as small as this takes years, and a lot more resources than I have, to decommission."

"What if we asked the village?" Kana asked. "I'm sure they would help if we explained."

This time, she looked at her scuffed work boots when she shook her head. "Someone will come. The Chinese. The Americans. They *have* to."

Kana didn't know much English, but she'd long ago learned every word etched into her Duncan. The Made in U.S.A. had always intrigued her. Her little yo-yo had traveled further than Kana ever would. How absurd a world where yo-yos had traveled across oceans.

"How would anyone know about this place?" Ryou asked.

"We were in contact. *We*, meaning engineers in the nuclear community. Once we saw how bad things were getting with the rest of the world, a lot of us planned to one day deal with these reactors. The thing is, decommissioning requires more than strong hands. But even if it didn't, none of the village will come near this place. Not after what happened to the other reactors like it."

"What happened to the others?" Kana asked.

Kana had trouble following much of it. Apparently there had been similar reactors all over Japan. Once the oil dried up and the old world slowed to its current crawl, it was decided to shut down permanently all Japanese reactors before resources became truly scarce.

"We were low on a pretty long list," Kiyomi said, pouring them tea within her lush greenhouse. They'd relocated for a hot drink during the conversation. "There were a lot of larger reactors nearer bigger cities. They had priority."

"But what happened?" Ryou asked.

"Hamaoka happened."

They learned another new word. Meltdown.

"There had been a tsunami years before I was even born. So a lot of reactors had already been taken offline after the incident at Fukushima, but not permanently. It was too late when people got serious about it, when the world economies started falling like dominoes and people here realized they wouldn't have unlimited resources forever to tackles these reactors. The job at Hamaokoa was rushed. It was in

Shizuoka—that's far from us, near where Tokyo used to be. The plant was near several cities and the Japanese people demanded it be shut down for good. The government complied. It should have been decades of meticulous work to ensure everything was done safely." She stared into the dregs of her tea. "They tried to do it in months and paid the price."

"How many people died?" Ryou asked.

Kiyomi snorted. "Lots. Thousands right away. Who knows how many after. The fire burned out of control for weeks, dumping radioactive ash on six cities. Your parents fear the harmless steam above *this* place? You should have seen the billowing black monster that killed Shizuoka.

"After that, people were pulled from here to get to work on the other reactors. There were no other incidents. The government, in its last days as a national entity, took the job seriously enough to ensure each decomm was handled with all the care and time required. But by that point, the electricity had started failing.

"Japan was getting natural gas from Russia to make electricity back then. But shipments dried up like everything else. Communications went with it. After a few years, I was the only one left at Higashi-dori. What colleagues weren't poached for decommissioning work across the country simply left to return to their families. I wasn't about to leave this place to eventually burn like Hamaoka. But the damage was done. People everywhere feared nuclear power, and not without reason. They wanted nothing to do with me. It's also why nobody comes across the mountains to your village. And why no one is allowed to leave. They assume all of us are contaminated."

Kana was about to ask the meaning of contaminated, but something halted her, the Duncan tumbling to the end of its string and bouncing on the concrete.

"What do you mean, not allowed to leave?"

Kiyomi looked at Kana as though she'd revealed something dangerous. "Ever notice how no one leaves your village? The people in Mutsu City won't allow it."

Kana stood, knocking over her chair in her rush. She'd long abandoned the single question she'd wanted to ask the woman, letting it burn to a cinder from the flame it had once been. Now, it flared to blinding white within her. "So it *was* your fault?"

"My fault?" Kiyomi looked to Ryou. "What's she talking about?"

Ryou was staring thoughtfully toward the lush plants climbing toward the high ceiling. "It wasn't her, Kana."

"You *are* a witch!" Kana was trembling. "My father's *dead* because of you!"

"Your father?" Kiyomi's expression sunk with a sad realization. "I'm sorry. But it wasn't me."

Kana wasn't listening. She thought of her father, vanishing into that tunnel along with the others, never to return. She'd always suspected some violence had met them, known it in her heart that only death would have kept her father away. But his absence had been a great hole. Another mystery from a crumbling world that offered little comfort and less answers. Only now she had that answer. It was this forbidden place that had taken her father, no matter how tenuous the connection.

And her excitement for the place, for all that she'd learned, felt like a betrayal. As if she now conspired with whatever harm had befallen him.

She fled, stuffing her yo-yo in her jeans pocket before sprinting away despite Ryou's calls to wait. This place was forbidden for a reason. Stupid Kiyomi was a witch after all. And like those horrid creatures in the tattered books she'd read as a child, this witch had conspired to rob Kana of the one person in the world who'd understood her.

She ran out into the dimming afternoon sun, through the maze of pots and plants. Past the sheets of hanging seaweed. She ran away from that terrible place. Beyond the gate and fence toward the mountain, tears wetting her face as she ran right into another person.

She stumbled backward, wiping her eyes for a better look. It was Kurosawa-San, leaning on his stick. Standing beside him was Kana's mother.

"What were you thinking?" her mother shrieked while dragging Kana through the front door. She hadn't spoken much during the bicycle ride, saving her complaints for the privacy of their darkened home.

Kana snatched a solar-lantern from a pile still cooling from the day's sun and stormed to her room.

"What if you're sick?" her mother continued, stomping up the stairs after her. "You could be poisoned even now."

"There's no contamination," Kana said, pausing at the entrance to her room while searching her newly acquired vocabulary. "Higashi-dori never melted down."

"You don't know that."

"And so what?" She turned on her mother. "So what if I'm sick? What am I going to miss out on here?" She gestured around her. "A dark house with daikon mush and rice three meals a day. A village full of old people with neighbors who kill anyone who tries to leave? How healthy do I need to be for *that*?"

"Kill anyone? Who told you that?"

But Kana was done. She slammed her door, threw her futon to the floor, and collapsed atop it. She had her Duncan in hand but simply looked at it, playing her fingers over the embossed words, its meager glow mixing with the lantern's dim light. When the door opened a few moments later, Kana turned to her side, facing the wall.

"They think we're all contaminated," her mother said from beside her, the sadness in her voice clear even in the dark. "It's why no one tries to go to Mutsu anymore. Why no one even enters the tunnel connecting us to them. It doesn't matter what's real, just what people think."

"That's what happened to dad." Kana turned to look at her mother. "And the others. They killed them because of Higashi-dori."

"No one really knows. But we can guess. We were so desperate for medicine. Supplies. Anything Mutsu City might have had." She shook her head. "Still clinging to the old life. Your father and the others volunteered to go. To at least try and trade in Mutsu. After they never returned . . . when their cart was found burned with all the vegetables and rice still inside, we knew not to try and leave."

Kana remained still, the welling tears in her eyes likely to fall if she moved.

"What were you doing there?"

What to tell her? Learning about the world that her mother's generation had destroyed? Trying to understand old world extravagance that somehow young people like Ryou and herself had to suffer for? Teenage angst mixed with anger at an unfair collapse sifted angry responses to her tongue.

Instead, she felt the phone in her pocket.

"This," she said, swiping it to life, the crisp, false-light of its screen banishing the darkness.

"Where did you . . . how?"

Its ancient battery held out for mere hours so she'd taken to plugging it in each day. The little battery logo read 10% but Kana hoped it would be enough. She tabbed open the folder the way Kiyomi had shown her, and showed her mother the photos.

She gasped, one trembling hand at her mouth as she took the phone in the other.

"I haven't seen photos in so long. We never printed any. Though we took them all the time."

"Is that Yokohama?" Kana asked, remembering Kiyomi's recollection of the place.

"Yes." She choked back sobs as she spoke. She slid the photos aside, revealing smiling faces, oblivious to the encroaching end.

"There's so much light," Kana said, one more entranced by the colors and lights glowing all about the photos, the Ferris wheel dominating them all. Different shades chased their way about its spokes in each photo.

"What are you wearing?" Kana pointed to a ridiculous set of high-heels her mother wore.

"Those were thirty thousand yen shoes once upon a time." Her mother zoomed to the shiny black shoes.

Kana remembered those shoes. They'd ripped the wooden heels for kindling while slicing the leather into strips for their cycle-pads.

"They don't look very comfortable," Kana said in a sneering tone. Her mother tensed and Kana felt instant regret at spoiling the moment. "They're pretty, though," Kana said, squeezing her mother's hand.

"They *were* uncomfortable. You should see what they used to do to my feet."

They sat like that, swiping photos and chatting like two people Kana's own age rather than mother and daughter. They laughed and forgot their tears and anger until the battery warning messages finally gave way to the phone's death, returning them to a heavy darkness. Kana was blind for a moment, her night vision destroyed by the previous light.

"Kiyomi has power at Higashi-dori," Kana finally said. "She uses it to keep the reactor from melting down. That's what she was teaching us. To one day replace her. Until it can be shut down forever."

"I see." Her mother didn't sound convinced, but the anger—as well as the sadness—was gone from her voice. A knock at the front door turned both their heads. They hurried downstairs to the door.

It was Kurosawa-San, leaning on his stick, his white hair and beard glowing in the weak light of a solar-lantern.

"It was wrong of you to defy your mother," he said. "That place could have been dangerous."

Kana made to object but he raised a silencing hand. "I've spoken to Kiyomi—yes, I know her. I've known her for a long time. And she assures me the readings are as safe as they've always been."

"Don't you see, mom?" Kana pleaded. "This is our chance to do something. Something that *must* be done."

"No," her mother said. "I won't lose you, too. I *can't* lose you."

Kana rallied some stinging rebuke at her mother, but paused, a shoot of empathy pushing through the soil of her teenage self-interest. How much had Kana mourned her lost father? How much more had her mother? Seeing those old photos, her mother almost unrecognizable in her happiness, Kana had seen the world from which she came. The old world. Kana might have been born into a civilization of darkness and decay, but her mother hadn't. She hadn't just lost her husband, she'd lost her world. Surprising even herself, Kana put her arm around her mother, who quickly leaned into the embrace.

"If we don't do something," Kana said. "We'll lose a lot more people. We *have* to keep the reactor from melting down. At least until someone comes to decommission it. Kiyomi believes someone will. The Americans, the Chinese, *someone.*"

"I know," she said, taking Kana's hand in her own and lifting her head. "I remember the news. Of what those crumbling reactors can do. What they *did* do in Shizuoka." She turned to Kurosawa-San. "We've named her a witch for so long. Do you trust this Kiyomi?"

"Yes," he said. "She's remained at her post, alone, for all these years. To me, such dedication in sacrifice for others is all the trust I need."

Kana's mother nodded. "Alright. But you still need to do your chores."

Kana agreed as her mother resumed a more familiar tone.

"And don't think you can shirk your foraging either. Winter is winter and we'll need no less stockpiled food than before."

"Of course."

"Then you should probably get to bed, if you're going to help me in the morning before you go off to college."

Kurosawa-San laughed while Kana gaped. It *would* be like college, or what Kana had understood that word to mean before everything collapsed. Only instead of endless classes, they would have but one subject to learn. With many different aspects, but with a clear goal in sight. To keep Higashi-dori from burning until someone came to finally extinguish its flame forever.

She couldn't wait to tell Ryou.

Incident Near Hidden Creek

by Al Sevcik

The rope tightened and the baked clay bell rattled. Brian's eyes opened to darkness. He rolled, then scrambled across the straw mattress, across the empty space where there was no one to warm the covers and onto the floor, bare skin sensing the hard and cool wood. The clay bell rattled again. He crossed the room and yanked up a panel cut into the floor. A man holding a lantern stood on stairs leading up from a tunnel.

Brian stepped back. "Hi Joe. Trouble?"

Joe climbed up into the room. "Could be, Boss. The night watch reports a group, a dozen maybe, gathered over by the road." He paused. "Better get some clothes on. Folks are heading for your office." As Brian buttoned trousers, pulled a shirt over muscled arms and slid fingers through light brown hair, more lights flickered in the tunnel and then two women, rifles in hand, climbed the stairs. They nodded to Brian and went into two connecting rooms where they slid covers off rifle-sized openings in the walls.

Brian strapped his feet into sandals, grabbed his rifle, stepped into the trap door opening and down into the tunnel. The underground pathway connected twelve houses and the town's administrative building. The houses themselves were arranged for defense in a rough circle around a central open area. There were two other circles of twelve houses and a short main street for business. Shadows, sometimes dancing but tonight menacing, quivered on the tunnel walls from always lit vegetable oil lanterns.

He paused at a stairway beneath the admin building and climbed through the open trapdoor up into a brightly lit room with five people, each holding a rifle, standing around a dark wood desk. He nodded to the group, stepped to the desk and sat down. "What's going on?"

A woman turned to him, pushing a chair aside with her foot. "Glad you're here, Mayor. About a half hour ago, around four o'clock, the watch noticed a gathering under the trees by the old road. Maybe a dozen men and women, possibly some children. One wagon. Horses. It looks like they have guns but they haven't threatened. They know we're on to them, of course. They can see that we've lit up two or three houses." She paused. "Rose and Fred think that it's best for us to act quickly, and I agree."

Brian said, "Right. If we move first we may control the game." He looked at the others in the room. "Somebody get Doc. Also wake up Linda, this will give our volunteer police chief something to worry about."

At that moment a tall woman with brown eyes and short cut red hair emerged from the tunnel. She was dressed in a tan shirt and trousers and held a rifle in one hand. "Already here, Boss." She smiled. "And already worrying."

"Good timing, Linda. You can cover me. I'm going for a walk to meet our visitors and find out what they're after." He left his desk and lifted an iron brace off the outside door.

Linda nodded, then turned to the others standing in the room. "Rose, Fred, bring rifles and come with me. Be warned, everything is wet from rain a few hours back."

One of the others said, "Wait, Boss. Is this really your job? We don't want to lose our mayor."

Brian looked at the speaker. His jaw tightened.

The other took a step back. "Okay, Boss. Okay. But let me get you a white cloth to hold."

"I'll go without the cloth."

"They may prefer shooting instead of talking."

"Not likely if they've got kids with them." Brian opened the door onto a grassy field encircled by houses. He followed Linda, Rose and Fred through the open door. They stood quiet in ankle high grass until eyes adjusted and the stars became clear. A thin crescent moon hung low in the east.

He felt a pull from the past, remembering how in the fall and winter when farm work eased and dark came early a teenage kid lay in the grass for hours beneath the carpet of stars that twinkled, sometimes streaked, across the sky. But it was the moon he watched, all its phases, its shifting shadows, the flat plains reflecting the sun's light. He had pondered the stories of the moon colony abandoned without warning two centuries earlier when technology stopped working.

With a shake of his head he vanished the memory. The four of them walked through the ring of houses to a field of short grass five hundred feet wide bordered on the far side by scattered trees and brush. Linda motioned to Rose and Fred to stay in shadow with rifles ready. She stood in the open, plainly visible, rifle across her chest. Brian walked alone on open grass holding his arms wide and his hands spread.

Halfway across the field he paused, then stepped forward another six steps, implying a friendly wariness. At first there was no response from the mixed shadows in the grove, then someone stepped away from the trees and came towards Brian. Two figures holding rifles also left the trees, but were motioned back. In the starlight it looked to Brian as if the person approaching was a woman. That was soon confirmed as she came nearer, walking straight and steady. She was wearing typical hand spun work trousers and shirt. As she approached, he saw her clothing was blackened as if burnt, and torn. Her shirt was blotched with what looked like blood. A scarf partially covered brown hair. Without preamble, she said, "We ask for your help."

Under the trees there were seven women, three men and three children. Linda soon had sleepy farmers and wives awake and helping the strangers to a nearby barn. Residents carrying lanterns came out of their homes. Among them was a thin man with strands of white hair brushed over a balding scalp, followed by a teenage girl who surveyed the injured visitors with troubled black eyes. Her shoulder length black hair was gathered in back by a blue ribbon. The man said, "Kathy, first we'll decide who needs immediate care and who can wait. You write their names and I'll give you a priority. Grab a lantern."

Brian watched as Doc and Kathy moved from person to person, checking broken ribs, bullet wounds, bleeding cuts, one bad sprain and lots of burns and bruises. Then he looked around for the woman who he assumed was the group's leader.

"Mr. Mayor?" A voice behind him, soft but firm. She had removed the scarf from her head and draped it around her neck. When he turned to her, she brushed her fingers ineffectually across the blood stains on her shirt. "I'm guessing you're the mayor. Thank you for the shelter and your doctor's help."

"Call me Brian." She was younger than she had seemed earlier. Late twenties, he judged. Perhaps three years under his thirty. Her take-charge personality had softened. Blond hair, loose now, was cut just below her jaw line, framing her face: wide cheek bones, green eyes, and a dusting of freckles. Obviously she was forcing herself to stay alert. He said, "The folks here will find shelter for your group, and food is coming as soon as the cooks can manage. Are you the leader?"

She shook her head. "No. I just stepped up. My name is Stella. Stella Watson." She put a supporting hand against stacked bales of hay. "We have a settlement, a farm. It's an easy day's ride from here in good weather." Her lips tried a smile, then stopped. "We moved there from San Antonio almost a year ago. You must know of us."

"We knew somebody was there, but you didn't bother us so we left you alone. We're plenty busy just taking care of ourselves." He looked down at her burned and bloody clothing. "I want to help you, but I need to know what happened."

For a moment her eyes focused somewhere beyond the barn, on something beyond seeing. She took a breath and composed her features. "Yesterday evening when we saw dark clouds piling up in the northwest we knew rain was coming so we brought the livestock into shelter. When the sun set the dark came at once because of the fast moving clouds. We were still finishing our preparations when men on horseback charged into our settlement, shooting and throwing torches. I'm sure they wanted to kill all of us, but that's when the storm hit. A waterfall of rain, constant thunder and lightning. Some of our group found their guns and were shooting back, but the downpour blinded everyone. Even when lightning flashed you could only see rain. People were screaming and stumbling over each other. It seemed like forever but it was just a few minutes and the attackers were gone. I guess the storm messed up their plan. It happened so quickly. . . . But we couldn't have stopped them anyway. We're not fighters." She wrapped her arms tight across her chest and bent her head down, trying to control herself.

Brian took her arm and guided her to a corner of the barn, away from the others. "Here, we can sit on the hay bales." He waited for a minute until she looked up. "Please go on. I know it's hard to talk, but it's important."

"They shot our leader. He was standing next to me. There were others. The ground flooded and we couldn't see. Some of us found a wagon and horses. We took everyone we could find, put wounded in the wagon, and came here, the nearest settlement we knew of. We had to get through washouts in the road. It took all night. We stopped in the trees at your entrance. We knew you had guns pointing at us. Everyone was scared but somebody had to step out and speak to you, so I did." Obviously fatigued, she wiped the back of her hand across her forehead. "Mr. Mayor, Brian, I have to go back. In the confusion we left some people. They may still be alive."

He studied Stella for a moment, bone tired, running on energy reserves. "I understand. I'll get some people and go back with you, but it will take an hour to get ready." He waved Kathy over. "Kathy, please help Stella get cleaned up and a few minutes rest, if possible. Bring her back in an hour. Okay?" He looked at Stella. "By then the sun will be up. We'll ride faster in daylight."

Kathy took Stella's hand. "Come with me. My house is right over there."

Brian stood and looked around. It seemed that whatever needed to be done was being done. He walked back to the administration building and to his office. Linda was waiting for him. "Glad you're here Linda. I was going to send for you." Brian pointed to a chair, then adjusted his own behind the desk. He watched as the police chief positioned her chair, dropped into it, raised a foot and pushed against his desk to tilt back at an unstable angle. She looked at Brian. "Some of the survivors say they were attacked by the Meycan Mexican army." She thumped her chair's front legs back to the floor. "I'm thinking it was pirates."

Brian nodded. "I'm thinking like you, but I'm not ready to rule anything out. I told their leader that some of us will go back with her. We have to do that anyway for our own safety. Maybe we can figure out what really happened. There's probably no danger, but I'd like for you and some others to come with guns. We'll need a wagon. We'll also need Doc. Anyone we find there will probably need medical help."

Linda jumped up. "I'll get it organized. Won't take long. Meet me at the barn."

The rock and rubble road was edged on both sides by a mixed growth of oak, cedar and elm. Low bushes with clusters of early summer blackberries covered the forest floor. Tree branches bowed towards the ground, dripping from last night's rain. Where water had gullied the road the horses slowed to study the ground before proceeding.

Brian turned in his saddle and surveyed the nine others in the group. Kathy, Doc, Linda, and two volunteer police, a married couple in brown clothing who were carrying rifles. Stella had three settlers with her, two men and a woman, coming in spite of injuries. The policewoman preceded the group, sometimes by a quarter mile. Linda, also armed, rode a few steps ahead of the others. Two horses pulled a wagon. The policeman and one of the settlers followed but stayed in eye contact.

Stella brought her horse close to Brian. "Is this the only road that goes by your community?"

Brian said. "We call our town 'Hidden Creek.' That's because the water flows underground, out of sight, during dry spells. There are other roads through the forest. Some better. We like being away from the more travelled roads. We don't want folks to find us easily." He lowered his voice. "Stella, you said you left San Antonio a year ago. Why? Did you really want to start a new community? That's hard to do for a small group of what, about two dozen? What made you go?"

The question hung in the air. Stella looked down at her horse's mane. Then she tightened the reins and dropped back with the other riders.

Ahead, Linda slowed her horse and waited for Brian to catch up. "The sun's high and my police-lady scout says that there's a clearing a quarter mile ahead. We could pause there to eat. The nice folks at the food warehouse put plenty of bread and cheese in the cart."

Brian nodded, "I agree. We'll stop, but only for a quick minute. I'm thinking we have at least four more hours of travel, but that's a guess."

When he was handed his meal, Brian let his horse wander to the road's edge to munch on grass. Sitting in the saddle, he folded whole wheat bread around a chunk of white cheese.

Stella brought her horse next to his. "I didn't answer your question." She was silent for a minute. "Do you know San Antonio?"

"Not really," Brian said. "Store owners sometimes make the two-day trip to buy supplies. I understand the Church of Gaia has a big following there."

Stella shook her head. "That's the way it was a few years ago. These days San Antonio and the Church of Gaia are the same thing. The Church picks the mayor and the city council and most of the rest. It used to be that the Gaians tolerated other ways of thinking. Not anymore. Now it isn't allowed. Because we follow the philosophy of Luna we've felt growing pressure, and recently open hostility. Brian, we didn't leave San Antonio because we wanted to. We were asked to leave." She smiled. "'Asked' isn't quite the word. We had a week's notice." Her eyes teared. She wiped her cheeks, smearing wet over freckles.

Brian reached over and laid his hand on hers.

"We didn't have time to think or plan what to do. Some of our group had seen a small valley many miles from San Antonio where there was water and grass and good soil. It seemed a good place to go. A place where we wouldn't be bothered." She turned her hand over and locked his fingers with hers. "Brian, our small group never hurt anyone. We follow a philosophy of peace. We believe that universal forces we call Luna and Sun created all there is. We thank them for the earth and for life."

He looked into moist emerald eyes. "Stella, there are thirty-six houses in Hidden Creek. There's a grocery store and a store for fabrics and more. There's a blacksmith, and other craftsmen coming. We're growing but we need people. We have extra land. Everyone would welcome you."

Brian's attention switched to Linda, who spurred her horse and galloped ahead of the group to join the advance scout. She lifted her arm in a stop signal then put a finger across her lips and pointed. Ahead, where the road turned sharply, an ephemeral wisp of smoke hung in the air. The two women slid off their horses, cradled their rifles, and disappeared around a curve in the road. Linda soon reappeared waving her arm, signaling for everyone to come forward.

They counted ten humans lying in the charred and soaked ruins, and two horses that had been shot. In spite of the wet the blackened remains of a wagon still smoldered, the source of the smoke they had seen. Torn canvass that had once served as shelter lay limp on the ground. The doctor and Stella knelt by each of the bodies. To their surprise two of the men and a woman were breathing. Stella found dry canvas for cover and tried to comfort them while Doc attended to their wounds. Afterward Stella walked slowly around the site, stopping when she came to Brian. Blinking back tears she said, "Another wagon, a covered wagon is missing."

Together they walked back to the road. Brian pointed. "There. Those could be wagon tracks, but mostly washed away. Let's look." The two of them remounted and walked their horses further along the road. Around the next curve, half of the road had washed downhill into a wooded hollow. A wagon, its front axle broken, one wheel gone, lay in a heap of broken planks. Its canvass covering had been ripped away and was lying in a wad of half-burned cloth. A boy knelt beside the ruined wagon. Stella said, "It's Tony."

The boy looked up as they dismounted and kneeled beside him. He was holding the hand of a woman lying in the wagon ruins. A whisper: "She's my Mom." He turned his face away.

Brian touched the woman's neck. She had been dead for some time. He glanced at Stella. "How long have you been here, son?"

"Since last night. Men were shooting at us. We tried to get away and then it rained so hard we couldn't see anything. Lightening scared the horses." Frightened eyes searched their faces. "My Mom . . . I know it's bad."

Stella lifted the boy's right hand from the corpse and kept it clasped in hers. Tony moved sideways to protect his left arm which rested awkwardly in his lap. Brian said, "Tony, your Mom's not here any more. She left her body here, but she's gone now." Brian gripped the small shoulder as the boy dropped his head and his body shook silently. Brian said, "It's okay to cry. Men do that when they loose someone they love. It's okay."

Stella put her arms around Tony's chest and held him close. They waited until the boy's shaking eased. She handed him a handkerchief and gently brushed blond hair away from his eyes. "How old are you, Tony?"

He sniffled into the cloth. "Fourteen."

"Tony, you're going to be all right. You know me, and this man is Brian. He and I will take care of you. Do you want that?"

Tony nodded.

"Tony," Brian said, "don't move your left arm, leave it lie as it is. I'm coming around to take a look."

Tony whispered, "I think it's broken."

"Yes." Brian nodded, eyeing two reddening humps in the skin above the boy's left wrist. "Easy now." He touched the boy's arm, ignoring the gasp of pain. "Tony, the bones in your arm need to be put back together and the longer we wait the harder that will be. The bones are trying to mend themselves now, but in a bad way."

Tony's eyes widened.

"A doctor came here with us. He knows about fixing broken bones." His eyes locked on Tony's. "Stella and I will help you stand up. You will have to walk a little ways to the doctor. Okay?"

Tony nodded.

As they approached the rest of the group, Brian waved Doc over, then motioned for Kathy to come, too. "Kathy, this is Tony. He has a broken left arm. Help him sit on that log." As soon as Tony sat Doc knelt to examine his arm then met Tony's eyes. "I can fix your arm, son, but you need to give me permission. I'll have to pull your arm bone apart and fit the broken ends together in the right way. When I do that it will hurt really really bad for a short time. It's okay to yell but you must not pull your arm away before I'm finished. Will you let me?"

Tony turned his head to look at Stella. She met his look with a gentle nod. He turned back to Doc. "It's okay."

"Kathy," Brian said, "hold Tony's other hand."

Working quickly, Doc realigned Tony's arm. Tony's jaw muscles tightened and his face whitened, but he kept silent.

Afterward, Kathy tied Tony's arm to a board fragment salvaged from a broken wagon. Then she cut a strip of canvas and made a sling. "You were super brave, Tony, but I thought you were going to squash my fingers right off my hand."

Stella put her hand on Tony's shoulder. "It's time now to place your mom's body into the ground with her other friends. Is it okay if we do that?"

Tony nodded. A soft voice. "It's okay."

"You and Kathy can stay sitting here while Brian and I take care of it."

Linda stood near two men digging in a cleared area beside the road. One held up a shovel to show Brian. "We found two of these in the wreckage." Linda stepped close to Brian. "We found some other stuff, too, Boss. Come with me." She led Brian across the camp site, picked up a crumpled cloth and spread it open on the ground. Obviously a flag, it was divided into thirds colored red, white and green. Over it all, an eagle with spread wings.

Brian took a deep breath. "Meycan Mexico."

Linda nodded. "Yep. Apparently we're supposed to believe they came from Mexico, attacked the camp, then just by accident dropped one of their flags."

Brian kicked the cloth. "Obvious and amateurish. What this tells us, Linda, is that the attackers weren't trained military."

One of the grave diggers stuck his shovel upright into a pile of dirt then looked past Brian to the lowering sun. "Mr. Mayor, do you want to say something at the burial?"

Brian motioned to Stella. "They're ready." She nodded and went with him to stand by the three open graves, the bodies in them covered with scraps of canvas. Once the other adults gathered, she spoke softly. "Yesterday these were six men and two women, eight good people, our friends. Today there is an empty place in the world, our friends have been enfolded in Luna's arms. Now we return their material bodies to the earth. We want to ask why this happened. But we know that question has no answer. Their passing is part of the mysterious poem of existence. We can only ask Luna to comfort us." Her voice trembled and she took Brian's hand. "These close friends and this loving mother are already missed."

Seeing Brian nod, the two men with shovels filled in the graves. Brian led everyone back to where the wounded were lying. "If we start back now we'll be traveling all night. I don't think we should tackle this road in the dark with three wounded and the rest of us tired. We'll stay here. We'll put some food aside for breakfast and divide the rest of what we brought to eat now. One more thing: between now and sunrise three of us—" he pointed at Linda, the policeman, and then himself "—will take turns on watch. I don't think we'll be bothered."

Brian helped gather the driest sticks and wood they could find. He lit a fire near the wounded and cleared a space for food for the fourteen to share. As they ate, shadows lengthened until their fire was a lone light in a sea of dark. Some settled themselves for the night. Stella left the fire and walked back to the graves. She stood quiet, looking at the wisp of moon embedded in starlit infinity. In a few minutes Brian followed her.

She wiped her cheeks. "It's so awful. I can't believe it, Brian. My friends . . ." She didn't move as he put an arm around her shoulder.

"Stella, tell me about Luna, about what the moon means to you." He dropped his arm as she lifted her face again to the thin crescent.

"Some people call us Loonies or Lunatics, but that's because they don't want to understand. It's not a religion, and we don't expect Luna to work any miracles." She turned her head to look at him. "From the old writings that have survived we know that the Goddess Luna influences earth in many subtle ways. People who open themselves to her become more aware and more understanding of how everything is part of one thing." She paused. "And we wait for the descendants of the abandoned moon explorers to return to earth."

"Stella, they were abandoned two hundred years ago."

"Yes, I know, it's family lore that a great-great-something-grandmother of mine was one of the scientists left on the moon. She was an agriculturist, supposedly well known back then though I don't know her name now. She was sent to find out how plants would grow. Brian, the governments on earth sent their best scientists, smart people. They would have known how to grow food. They could have survived. Sometimes we see bright spots on the moon. We don't know exactly what the lights are but we think the descendants of the original scientists are living, that they found sources of energy and have saved the old technology. They could build a space ship to bring the knowledge back to earth." She searched his face for a moment, then said, "You're thinking I'm either weird, or weak in intellect."

Brian shook his head. "Neither. I'm too busy hoping you'll decide to stay, I mean that I'd like it if you came to live in Hidden Creek."

She glanced at him sideways. "I guess I have to. Didn't we both promise Tony that we would look after him? I'll have to stick around to do that." She turned back to the freshly covered graves. "But there's something else that I have to do, too. Even though I believe in the teachings of Luna, in the philosophy of peace and compassion . . ." She stood stiff and clenched her fists. Her jaw tightened. She looked at the sky, at the graves, at Brian. "The evil that happened here must be answered. I have to . . . I will revenge the murder of my friends."

At sunrise Brian divided the remaining food while Stella and Linda helped move the wounded to uncomfortable pads in the cart. Others saddled horses and after a quick breakfast the group started the trip back to Hidden Creek, with armed riders both ahead and behind. The mud wallows in the road had dried or shrunk so the horses were less concerned about their footing and walked faster than before. Brian eyed the sky, dotted with puffs of white from edge to edge. The weather, for today at least, would be a friend.

Stella rode in front of the group, ahead of the cart, but after two miles she dropped back to ride beside Brian. She said, "When are you going to contact the Meycan Mexico army? We have the flag as evidence. It had to have been renegade Mexican soldiers. We must demand that they be arrested."

Brian rode in silence for several minutes. "The flag isn't evidence of anything, Stella. It was probably thrown there on purpose to make us suspect the army."

"No Brian. You can't imagine how bad the storm was. Totally black except for lightning hitting the ground and exploding trees. Rain and more rain. Thunder so loud it hurt. In all that confusion they could easily have lost their flag."

"Stella, I have to say it to you straight. A tiny community of pacifist farmers huddled in a shallow valley. No real defenses. Your cattle, horses and personal treasures were bait. All there just for the taking." Brian reined his horse to a stop and reached over to hold Stella's saddle. "Just for the taking, Stella. Your settlement was raided by pirates. Probably a roving gang that stumbled onto you by accident. They don't mind killing. For sure the storm saved your life." He let go of Stella's saddle. "Real soldiers, Meycan Mexican soldiers, wouldn't have run from the rain."

"Well, we should tell the army commanders anyway. They could send troops to get the pirates. Punish them."

Brian shook his head. "For fifty years Mexican generals have salivated over Texas and they've kept trying to inch the border north so there's no longer an official line. Just an indefinite agreed-upon area. Their army is only a hundred miles away. Just south of Victoria. General Sanchez would love to receive an invitation from a Texas mayor to bring his soldiers into the country. They'd walk right over the handful of Texas troops at the border and we'd be part of Mexico long before the main army in Dallas could get organized and get here."

Giving him a cold look, Stella turned her horse away and moved to the front.

Brian slowed his horse and fell back to check on the others. As the road warmed and dried, the horses easily maintained their pace. Good, he thought, we'll be home by sunset. He allowed himself a brief smile when he noticed Tony and Kathy riding close together at the rear. Kathy was helping Tony, who was clearly frustrated by his left arm, strapped in a sling.

In mid-afternoon Stella moved her horse back alongside Brian's. "I've been thinking and tomorrow I'm going to send a message to the government in Dallas. President General Roberts should send the Texas army to get that gang of thieves and murderers. Jail them. Clean them out, and any other gangs, too."

"Stella, seven or eight years ago two settlements like yours were attacked near San Antonio. Might have been pirates or might have been Mexican solders straying over the Tex-Mex boundary. Doesn't matter. San Antonio pleaded with the government in Dallas for help and that turned out to be a bad idea. Groups of young gun-carrying Texan soldiers were sent into the countryside to find and capture bad guys. The Texan kids turned out to be as bad or worse. Thievery, murder, rape, the whole bit. It took three years to get them all back to Dallas. It's good that the threat of the Texas army keeps Mexican General Sanchez on his side of the border. But soldiers ranging in small groups . . . that's trouble."

Without comment, Stella rode away.

With little leftover food, the riders made a pause at midday near a wild blackberry patch. A troubled Doc called over to Brian. "Mayor, can we make this a really brief stop? These wounded need to get out of the cart and onto proper beds."

The sun was nudging the horizon when they reached the entrance to Hidden Creek. Caring hands brought hot food and made the wounded as comfortable as possible in the barn.

Brian found Stella arranging a place for Tony. He said, "The boy can stay with me."

"You're a kind man, Brian, but Tony has known me since he was little. He's almost grown now, of course, but I think he'll be more comfortable here in the barn tonight with the rest of our group."

"As you wish. I'll see you in the morning."

As he turned away Stella said. "In the morning . . . Brian, I'm not happy with what you said today. We have to talk."

Brian nodded. "I'll come and get you. We'll have something for breakfast in my office."

The sun was above distant trees but the morning shadows of bushes and buildings were still long across the grass when Brian appeared at the barn. Stella was waiting.

“Come.” She took his hand and led him inside. Families and groups of friends had established separate living areas throughout the barn, with a few younger people up in the loft. As he watched, Doc, followed by Kathy, came in to check wounds and bruises. Kathy quickly found Tony and took a long time adjusting his sling.

"Two days ago," Stella said, "We had a working settlement. We were twenty-five people, including three children and one teen. We had crops, cows, horses, what we needed. Today there are seventeen of us. Eight of us were murdered. The rest wounded." She turned to face Brian directly. "These are my friends. People I've known for years. I've worked with them, played with them. It's my family. Now everything is gone. We have no possessions, no home." Her hands balled into fists. “I can't accept this. There must be revenge. I will have revenge."

Around the barn people paused, their attention grabbed by Stella's raised voice. Two couples moved close.

Brian could feel Stella's anger. It made him hurt. He wanted to help her, but stood silent.

One of the men reached out to Stella. "We'll do it again Stella, a safe settlement. We'll be smarter."

Brian said, "You are all welcome here."

"No." Stella's voice had a hard edge. "That's not enough. Eight people murdered. Eight. It's wrong. We can't turn our backs to that."

One of the women spoke softly, "Stella, honey. It's just us. There isn't anyone to come and make things right."

Stella dropped her hands. She looked around the barn then she touched Brian's hand. Her voice was a whisper. "Can we go to your office? Please."

Neither spoke as they walked through ankle deep grass to the town's administration building. From the entry, Brian pushed open the door with the “Mayor” sign. He closed the door behind them and slid a bar into place. He turned to Stella just as she turned to him.

She came close, lifted her arms, put them around his neck, and wept.

The Rig and the Wave

by Alistair Herbert

The rig bobbed slowly between rocks in the little bay, its rise and fall caused by—but not synchronised with—the steady grey waves. It had broken its anchor decades ago and lurched back steadily to the coast. The waves here had once looked alien themselves, he thought, but the rig pushed them into the background. It was too slow, too irregular, too huge. He could only look at it for so long before turning away from the line of the little bay and looking back to the high field. The sea will reclaim it in pieces, he consoled himself, but not before I am gone.

When it first landed, the oil company had erected fencing to protect it, right out into the sea, but the locals had long since cut through, ignoring orange signs and puttering out in their boats to take whatever was left in the belly of the thing. It had been seventeen years since the company's last visit and no other was expected. It stood in the water as an unsteady monument to a different time.

He whistled the dog and they crossed the outcrop and clambered down to the cave. The low tide exposed its entrance for around five hours: plenty of time to do his work.

The river ran into the rocks somewhere inland and cut out through a tunnel at the back of the cave, scoring a deep channel down the centre of the hole and out into the sea. Nets arrayed along its length caught junk and precious metals, a series of eighteen filters with ever tighter mesh—to the point that the smallest nets looked like fine plastic sheets—catching mineral sands from the tunnel walls and blocking them from progressing down to the sea. They had been expensive—he had been required to sign for them, however long ago that was.

In his pockets he carried the notebook, plastic bags for collection and storage, a knife and caver's headlamp, and a hat, because it would be cold by the time he left. He donned his lamp, ready to disappear into the gloom, and the dog trotted off down to the waterline—well accustomed by now to his routine. It was trying to rain, sea spray and flecks of cloud had made him wetter than he had noticed, so he was glad to reach the shelter even if it was dim inside.

He took the middle nets first and flushed them of mud and sand and pebbles, then moved to the end filters to carefully transfer their contents to the bags. He weighed them by sight and noted each value before placing the bags at the entrance ready to be removed home. This had been the job, originally: nobody paid him for the measurements any more, and nobody collected the data from him, but he kept the records all the same. It was a habit, and it helped him feel better about scavenging here. Afterwards he checked all the fixings for signs of wear—it was hard work replacing the big metal struts but not so hard as replacing the whole thing if he ignored rust for too long. He doubted anyone could pay for replacement parts now if the thing ever fell apart. The whole operation took time if it was to be done properly, but only when it was finished did he allow himself to consider the big nets at the cave's end. If he knew they held something good he wouldn't be able to pay proper attention to the other work. He thought about his daughter scolding him when he returned home, clasping treasures, but had forgotten to take proper notes.

As he moved he felt something behind him and realised it had been there a little while: a shape at the entrance slightly reducing the incoming light. There were people there watching him, and as he turned to see them the foremost spoke.

"Joe Sutton?"

He didn't answer.

"Time to move you on, sorry. The Owner wants us working this place by the end of the week."

He should have kept his mouth shut, but didn't.

"The Owner."

The other man seemed to grow in confidence, having been acknowledged.

"Best to just do as we say," he said. "No sense making it unpleasant when it doesn't need to be." He was trying to sound cheerful.

Sutton turned back to his work, slowly accepting the inevitability of a fight but trying all the same to delay it.

"I work here by court order and formal contract. I've not been notified of any change."

"That rig'll have oil in it again sooner than your court'll care about anything this far out of town," the other man joked, not unkindly. "We're here now, notifying you."

It was hard to act as if he was ignoring them and indeed to truly ignore them at the same time, so he wasn't really doing anything useful as he moved around with his back turned. The top net held nothing special anyway: pieces of foil packaging and a couple of scraps of electrical cable in amongst the usual junk. Nothing special, but worth having all the same. Then he came to the next and found something which made him forget the intruders entirely for a moment: a small fish. A small, living, fish.

Living on the coast, working the river nets daily, he would have thought he knew whether fish still lived here. The boats didn't bother going out any more, and the farms inland had emptied the nearby waterways not long after. He looked up, remembering the men standing out front, and couldn't think what to say. It didn't matter that they were against him: this was a mystery which anyone could share. He pointed at it.

He watched it struggle. It was too large to slip through the gaps in the twine and too weak to swim back the way it came. It wouldn't last long. As far as he knew it was the only fish in the world. It wouldn't even need a name. Skin flashed pallid in the yellow light of his headlamp as it rose and sank in the gurgling water. He stood, leaving it while he decided what to do, the men returning to his mind as an afterthought. He suspected the fish wanted whatever it wanted more than these men wanted what they had come for. Making a decision, he scooped the fish into one of the measure bags, water and all, to carry home. Maybe it would die from the shock of change, or from confinement, or from neglect, but it would last longer than stuck here in the cave when the salt water rose.

"I work here an hour each day," he said, preparing to leave. "Don't interfere with the equipment if you come here when I'm not—unless you want an invoice from the Department for Managed Transition to cover whatever damage you end up doing."

As he said it, invoking a world of law which had once seemed more real than the rock at his feet, he felt almost that he was repeating some ancient ritual or password, some pagan rite whose meaning had been lost but whose power somehow remained. Today that power was fading. A couple of the men looked to be smirking at him.

The speaker raised his hands in a calming shrug.

"Maybe I wasn't clear," he began, but Sutton cut him off.

"You were clear," he said brusquely, moving forward. "Am I free to go, or are you looking to fight?"

The other man moved from his path. "As you like. We better not see you here again, though."

Sutton didn't answer. As he exited the cave the dog came padding up, looking somehow pleased with itself.

"Alright," he said in greeting as they trudged back up the slope. "Some help you were."

He didn't look at the rig on the way back home. He never did.

‡‡

The dog barked this time when they arrived, so he knew they were there before he saw them. He stepped away from his work and moved to see what was happening and found them there outside the cave, three men in a row a few yards out. The man from the other day wasn't with them.

He had taken the job because he wanted to be away from the cities when the trouble got worse—he always knew, somehow, that the trouble would get worse—and because he wanted his daughter to grow up in one place, and not undergo the trauma of relocation which had so completely cut him off from a real sense of home. He had never truly recovered from being uprooted as a child. And he had hoped that this place would be small enough to escape the notice of the big world, that they could just potter on with their lives and worry about small things like food, and enjoy the more intimate threat and promise of people they knew well. He hadn't expected to be raising his daughter alone, but otherwise the plan had worked. But now here was the big world stood outside with a raised hand, wanting in again. And why?

The rig, he thought. The rig had brought them. Probably nobody had even known this place existed for years, until it had maybe shown up in a report about damaged infrastructure, or they'd spotted the hulking thing from waterside, scouting the coast like pirates. And now here they were, and what was the rig going to do to help them with the trouble it had caused. Not a great amount. He waited for them to approach but they didn't, so he just continued working, and then when he'd finished his tasks he found some excuse of a task to keep him in the cave a little longer. But he knew by now that if they weren't coming in then he wasn't getting out. He couldn't guess if it was better to confront them or stay put. He probably didn't have a winning move at this point in the game. He regretted not telling the girl about their last visit. If he was gone too long, she would come looking for him. Every morning she promised to stay locked inside until he came home, and every afternoon he found her outside. Some people just can't be locked away, he thought, and I have one of them for a child. The thought filled him with pride and longing. She was too young for anything to happen to him.

The men waited, and eventually he gave in. There were no clever tricks or plans he could follow to escape what he'd landed in, so he followed his nature. He placed a hand against the cave wall and felt it cold and smooth, and granted himself a moment to become calm again.

"I love my daughter, I love my garden, I love my work. I do what I must." It was a prayer.

As soon as he committed to the decision he felt himself change. His arms were excited; somewhere in his chest or the back of his neck a strange thing grew, a looseness and a tension at the same time. He wanted to bounce on his feet and move. This, he thought. This is what it feels like to be actually alive—there's that whisper of death stirred into your every action, but that's just how it works. And if you're not risking your whole body in your work then you can't be a whole man. It felt almost normal.

Picking up his bags of findings and pocketing the book he set his face as if it were any other day and he was going to just walk through them and home, and he readied himself for the fight. The light was decreasing in the late afternoon but it still took his eyes a moment to adjust as he stepped out from the overhanging cave roof and under the cloud blanket. The men remained impassive at first but then subtly shifted inwards to demonstrate that his path was blocked. He stopped walking about twenty yards from them, only a couple of paces out onto the beach.

"So," he called.

"You leave it behind, or you stay inside 'til you starve," came the answer. "We'll wait." The owner of the voice was wide and healthy and gruff, slightly shorter than Sutton. He had none of the earlier visitor's humour. In a straight fight it would come down to who was cleverer—not that there would be any straight fight.

"Which is to say if I want to go home we're going to fight," he replied.

"Fight and you'll lose anyway."

"Then I'll lose."

He took a breath and started walking, and the men bunched in a little closer. And then he stopped again in doubt, looking past them. Something wasn't right. Against his will he felt the balance of his mind tilting and tipping away from the place he'd so deliberately put it as he scanned the horizon. He'd looked out at this horizon daily for almost fourteen years and yet he couldn't spot what was different about it now, but something was different. The men were advancing. He looked again. There was the sea, grey and huge, and the grey sky stretching back, and out north the corner of headland which hid the rig in the bay, and scanning south in the other direction the slight hint of a different colour grey which marked the line of the distant coast extending out into the water—and then he saw it. That slight hint of grey wasn't there: it was all water. The other coast was hidden by the sea.

Once he knew what he was looking at it was a lot easier to see. The wave was moving fast, rising and swelling towards them like snow before a broom. It pulled up on the shallows and a crest began to form, sucking water back from the beach to lift it. Even the air seemed to disappear into it.

He turned to run for the cave. He didn't look back for the three men. The next thing he knew the water had hit, and everything was changed.

With no back passage the cave acted as an air pocket, absorbing the first impact of the water with a strange woofing thud. And then the water came, plenty fast enough still to hurt. Sutton had run for the back and then been bowled over and smothered, his headlamp snuffed and pulled from his head as he fell, but he kicked out and reached until his hand hit a slithering wall. Everything was dark. Something hit his leg and dragged at him along his hip. He kept kicking, found the beginning of the roof again with his hands and followed its crease upward, back to where he knew the highest point waited. Finally he found it and kicked up frantically, panic beginning to make itself heard, and his arms hinged as his head rose and there was air, air in his lungs in the boiling blackness. He realised there was another body jostling against him—one of the strangers. Hands grasped and pulled him down and he kicked away instinctively, then reached out to find the arm again and pull it towards him. The other man's head broke the surface of the water with a choking howl of sucking air, and they kicked water beside each other. Another swell dragged at Sutton's legs and this time the other man pulled him back. The space at the cave roof wobbled.

There was no way to say how long it lasted. They kicked and waited, gulping air when they could and not knowing if the water might come higher. The corner of breathing space was wide but very shallow, and there was nowhere to hold onto anything in the dark except each other. The water roiled and spat and moved this way and that around him, engulfing him until he was no longer a person but simply the small part of the wave which kicked and spluttered and hoped not to be water.

Eventually the tiny space in the dark seemed larger, and he found there was a gentler surface at which he could tread water and bob without his head going back under every few moments and rediscovering that terror of the first hit. He drifted away from the other man a little, their arms separating. And they sank slowly further, the two men and the wave together, and at last a grey hole of afternoon showed through the water, a space between the sea and the rock, and soon he could touch the bottom.

As the wave disappeared he found that he couldn't stand without its support, and his body slowly sank to the floor until he was lying in the wet sand and breathing ragged breaths. And he thought: how strange not to be part of the wave.

The other man staggered out on the beach. When he could stand again he followed, struggling to control his shivering body as his clothes clung to his limbs. The wreckage of his work floundered in the retreating water, jagged corners of plastic and steel showing in black silhouette before the white sky. The sun hung low behind him over the opposite end of the horizon, hidden from view by the rocks. The wind was rising and on the breeze he caught the sound of distant dogs barking. The other man's friends were gone.

"It's just us, then," he said as they stood beside each other. The man nodded, slowly.

"Looks like."

"You still want to fight?"

The man turned to him thoughtfully, his immense head taking a few moments to register what Sutton had said. It struck Sutton that the way someone looks is just the way they look, and sometimes it's no real measure of what's actually going on inside their head. The man looked at him for a long time. Then he laughed, and put a hand to his head, still shocked. Sutton guessed at a temporary truce.

His hands were still feeling for the crevice of rock at the cave roof, even as they hung useless at his sides. This is what it feels like to be a snail, he thought: a snail or a limpet, waiting beneath a boot in a half cracked shell. All you can do is trust that the boot won't come down, the air won't run out, keep clinging and keep breathing. This is what's happening here. All I can do is keep breathing and clinging.

There was no way to rebuild the nets and filters and gantries. He might find his pocketbook if he looked, or he might find it washed up weeks later on some other tideline. But there wouldn't be anything more to write in it. They'd have to get used to things being a little harder again. His thoughts turned to home.

The hillside seemed empty. Everything was soaked and speckled with a perfect film of sand. The sheep were crying. The dog came trotting up from behind him, its fur soaked and matted, its tail high but its eyes saying something else, and together they began to walk. When they passed the corner of the rocks and looked down on the northern bay, the rig was gone.

The Road to Finx: Chastity's Tale

by Rita Rippetoe

Chastity's hand ached from letting Marie squeeze it when the pains came. But it was the least she could do while the midwife murmured encouragement. After another long pain, with Marie screaming like a wounded thing, Mrs. Branson stepped into the front room to talk to Oliver.

"You've got to ride for the doctor. She's been laboring ten hours and her womb neck is only open two fingers. That's not right. The baby's head isn't down where it should be."

Chastity glanced up. Her cousin looked confused and anxious.

"Look, Mr. Gutierrez, it's like when you put on a sweater with a tight neck. You pull it open with your hands." Ms. Branson held her hands over her head pantomiming stretching a tight sweater open. "That's the womb muscles working to open the neck up. That causes the pains. But putting on a sweater you also pull it down and let your head open it. That's like the baby, pushed by the womb muscles, pressing its way out. But suppose you laid your head to one side, like this." She tilted her head. "The sweater wouldn't go over. That could be our problem, the baby laying wrong."

"Are you sure? The doctor is awful expensive. I'm still paying for when Edward broke his leg falling off the hay loft."

"I'm so sure that I'll tell this you right now: If your wife dies, I'll go to the Council and charge you with 'Death by Neglect.'"

Amazed by the vehemence of her tone, Chastity looked up in time to see her cousin nod grimly and turn toward the door. Several minutes later she heard hooves pounding up the ranch road.

The doctor arrived three hours later on his fine Posse horse. It wasn't the fastest horse in the district, but the doctor always bragged on how it could go long distances at an even gait. The breed had originally been called Peruvian Pasos, bred by the Spanish to ride their big plantations way down in South America, back in the Before Oil times. "Yes, he cost me a bundle, but it's worth it to reach my patients in a hurry without having my bottom pounded up between my shoulder blades," the doctor would say.

Marie was in the midst of a labor pain when the doctor arrived. He quickly washed his hands and donned a clean smock. When the pain subsided he felt all around Marie's outsized belly before reaching inside to check the cervix. Then he listened at several places on her belly with his stethoscope.

"Ms. Branson, can you help Ms. Gutierrez turn over and support her on her hands and knees?"

"Certainly, Doctor." She moved to the head of the bed. "Give me a hand, Chastity."

Marie moaned and protested inarticulately as she was maneuvered into position. The doctor leaned in and pulled and pressed at her suspended belly. "Miss Chastity, put some rolled up blankets behind those pillows. We've got to keep her on her side with her back elevated, so the baby has slack to move."

Several hours later the doctor stepped back into the main room where Oliver was alternately pacing and sitting to twist his bandana between his work roughened hands.

"Mr. Guiterrez, I've got nothing but bad news. The baby is transverse lie. Sideways. It can't come out that way and I've tried every technique I know to turn it head down, or even breech, but it won't budge."

"Then how?" Oliver paused, not sure exactly what he was asking.

"The only way the baby has a chance is if I cut it out. Even then, I'm not sure. The heartbeat is bad."

"But that would kill Marie!"

"Not necessarily. I've done nine of what we call section births in my career, and two of the women lived. But without it they both will die. That baby can't come out, and eventually Marie will just be worn out. The human body can only take so much."

Four years later, Chastity, now sixteen, passed a dish of pickled wild cherries to her cousin's guest. Mr. Hudlin seemed like an old man to her, though he was only twenty-eight. But he was a successful rancher and dressed the part, with an actual tailor-made suit and a city-style tie held in place with a turquoise and silver stickpin. He was pretty good looking, though hours in the sun had already begun to put crow's feet at the corners of his blue eyes. His naturally fair skin showed for about an inch of forehead that was usually covered by his hat, and his blond hair was cut short and combed back neatly.

"Please, call me Corwin. When people say Mr. Hudlin, I look over my shoulder for my father."

"Alright, Mr.—I mean Corwin. Would you like a slice of cornbread with the pickles?"

After supper was over and Corwin had ridden away, Oliver asked Maria to sit down in the parlor.

"Mr. Hudlin came to talk to me on a serious matter, Chastity. He's been our neighbor for many years and watched you grow up here since your mother and father died in the flash flood and Marie and I took you in." He paused to cross himself at the mention of his family dead: his uncle Antonio, his aunt Rachel, and his wife Marie. And the unchristened baby that had died in her womb. He was no longer a Roman Catholic, having converted to the Meeting House when he married, but still had the habits. "Corwin likes you and asked my permission to court you. I told him that I respected his good manners in asking, and that he has my blessing, but that your heart and hand are your own to give or withhold."

"But Mr. Hudlin is twelve years older than me. I mean he's a good man and all, but almost as old as my father would have been."

"I know. But many couples have an age difference and are still happy. My grandparents had eight years between them. All I ask is that you give yourself a chance to get to know him. He has been a good neighbor, he has a good, honest reputation, and his ranch is doing well. After the help you've been with the boys since Marie died, I owe it to you to see you well established. It would be pure selfishness to keep you on as a housekeeper instead of seeing you set up in your own home. Especially since you left school to take care of Edward and William."

After a brief prayer, the reverend introduced the evening's speakers to the Meeting. "Brother Matthew Long, Sister Megan Maple. These fine folks are members of the Warners. They've come here with a message about the world outside of Sweetwater."

"Sanctuary," the black man said, letting the word hang in the air for a moment. "That used to mean something holy. It's in the Bible, God's Holy Book. The Israelites are told to set up sanctuary cities for those accused of murder, to prevent blood vengeance from destroying society.

"But now this word has been corrupted. So called Sanctuary cities are cesspool of sin. Corrupt officials set aside an area that is outside the Regulations. Oh, they'll send in their armed men to drag out a killer or a thief, a usurer or a rapist. Their citizens wouldn't stand for that sort to be sheltered and allowed to come and go, preying on the city. But these officials accept payment to give sanctuary to worse criminals than those that merely kill your body or steal your earthly goods. They give shelter to people who sell drugs that warp your mind. Drugs that make you question God and His ministers. They give shelter to heretics. Worshippers of false gods. People who teach lies about the real God. People who deny Jesus. People who have been driven out of good towns like Sweetwater."

Chastity shifted in her seat. When was she ever likely to be near some place like that? Sweetwater was her home and leaving it seemed as likely as seeing an Oil Time airplane fly overhead.

Now the lady spoke. "I am pleased to see young people here to learn about the hazards that lurk in the world outside of your township. The material that Brother Matt and I are about to discuss is of a delicate nature. Because of this, I am asking that the men present rise and follow Brother Matt out to the ramada. As they move out, the women will please move forward so as to hear me clearly."

The women and girls shifted their seats. Chastity noticed that the deacons had closed the shutters on the side of the building facing the ramada. Was that to keep the women from hearing the men or the men from hearing them?

Sister Megan began slowly. "First, I should say that the Sanctuary cities are not the only place that some of what I am going to talk about is found. You read your Scripture, so you ladies all know that whores exist and always have. You should know that they are not always found in places clearly labeled as whorehouses. Heck, every town bigger than a wide place in the road has at least one woman who is rumored to be careless of her virtue in return for a good meal or some small thing of value. Wherever they are, the men who are looking always seem to find them. And in most of the actual whorehouses the women are degraded and abused, imprisoned and regarded as less than human.

"No one wants a fate like that. The danger of the Sanctuaries is that they try to make it sound better. They say the women there make their own choices, reject customers that are too gross or dirty, have guards to protect them from crazy men, keep their own earnings. They say that in Sanctuary a woman can work as a whore and still be a respected person with rights to vote and walk around where she pleases, be addressed as 'Ms.,' shop anywhere she wants." She shook her head.

Chastity squirmed in her seat. Why tell us this? As if any woman who came to Meeting would ever stoop to being a whore.

"Now there are other things that women need to be educated about. You may have heard rumors or jokes, but plain facts are always better, even if they make us uncomfortable. Some women are different in their feelings. They want to be intimate with other women, not with men. Some of them dress as men and pretend to be men. Others look like anyone else, but in the Sanctuaries they can violate the Sodomy Laws and do things that would be severely punished under the Regulations. They can kiss and embrace and rub together naked and touch each other places only a husband should be touching. They can marry and live together as couples. I see some of you ladies blushing, so I won't go into more detail.

"Other women go to the Sanctuaries for something different. They like men and relations with them. But they don't want to bear child after child, so they go to find the means to prevent that. Turning down the Lord's bounty for their own reasons."

Chastity was amazed. Kissing other women. Who ever heard the like? Preventing children? That was possible? She thought only God decided that.

Sister Megan continued. "All you women and girls learned the Regulations in school. But you may never have seen a trial for Sodomy or know the penalties. First conviction, whipping: ten strokes, once a week during the three months in the Reformatory. Second conviction, life in the Reformatory with twenty strokes whipping once a month. Brother Matt is telling the men about the penalties for men, which are harder, and for a second conviction amount to a death penalty of being worked and starved on the work crew."

Whipping Chastity understood. A boy in her Sunday School class had been caught with a girl. They were fifteen and fourteen and her father caught them half naked together. The midwife certified that the girl was still virgin, so they each got only ten strokes and three months in Reformatory. After he got out, the boy moved away to an uncle's ranch down south. All the women and girls had been assembled in the Meeting House to watch the girl being whipped on her naked back. Then the men and boys were let in for the whole community to watch the boy's punishment.

"Now you're all wanting to know where these terrible places are. Are you likely to blunder into one of these dens of sin by accident? Brother Matt and I travel the Colorado Territory of the Texas Public. Our remit goes over to Lost Angels, up to Denner and Sallac, down to the Mescan border. It probably won't surprise you at all to know that there is a Sanctuary City near Lost Angels. It's called Samona and it is over on the coast. Auro, outside of Denner, is another. Sallac had one twenty years back. But the Great Mormon uprising put an end to that. The Mormons may be heretics, but they know how to drive sin from among their people. Finx, over to Zona has one, too. You may think you will never see those places, but sometimes we travel when we don't expect it. It could happen that your husband would move the family for business, or you be needed to help a family member in another town, or even travel on business your own selves.

"The main thing you need to know about Sanctuaries is that they are in a separate quarter of town. You can go to Auro or Finx without ever setting foot in one. They are fenced and patrolled. Anyone who comes to the gate has to acknowledge that they are setting foot outside of the Regulations and cannot complain in court if they see a violation. Anyone who, God forbid, wants to stay, must appeal to the Jeffe and the Madam. Anyone who dwells in a Sanctuary has to wear a badge if they go outside, and be back in the gates after dark. They aren't allowed to marry or live outside the Sanctuary unless they repent in front of the Elders and go to a Cleansing.

"So, on one hand, Brother Matt and I have come to warn you about the existence of these places of depravity. But on the other hand, we have come to reassure you that you can go about your business, buy, sell, and travel without fear. You could go to the evil, God forbid, but the evil cannot venture out to claim you." She paused, surveying them. "Thank you for your attention. Bless your days and your homes."

The Reverend's wife stood up. "Bless your steps, Warner Megan. If you follow me, I have dinner ready at the house."

Oliver didn't say anything about the Warners' meeting after he and Chastity rode back to the ranch. As head of the household it had been his duty to make sure his cousin learned about such things, but she didn't ask questions and he didn't see a need to expand on the night's talks. Neither of them answered the questions from Oliver's children. They would hear it when they were older.

Corwin visited again the following week. He brought a small gift for Chastity, a book of poems from his late mother's library.

"You mentioned that you missed reading poetry at school. This one is real famous from the Before Oil days. Elizabeth Barrett Browning. My mother told me that her husband was a poet too. They fell in love and eloped. Mother said it was a real life romantic story." Corwin pressed the book into her hand and smiled hopefully.

"Thank you very much. I wasn't expecting any presents. I hope a good dinner is repayment enough."

"Just time spent in your company is payment enough, even if you served me hardtack and water."

Chastity blushed before excusing herself to the kitchen to finish up the gravy. What was she going to do? This kind man was smitten with her, but she just didn't feel anything for him. Oliver was going to be disappointed if she turned Corwin down. She knew Corwin was offering Oliver some help with the ranch. Not a bribe. He wasn't like that, but she had overheard him saying "If we're going to be brothers . . ." She hadn't heard the rest as they walked into the barn.

"Big news in town. The Peddler's Train is coming through. Everyone with anything to sell down in Finx is getting it together, and people are putting in orders for supplies with the local merchants to be fetched on the next train coming back." Oliver sank into his armchair.

Chastity looked up from her darning. "I can't think of anything we need that would be special order. I need to start sewing new shirts for the boys. But Crobie's regular stock has all the material and notions I would need. Anyone from Sweetwater joining up?"

"I hear Smithers is sending his son Pedro with a load of brandy. Crobie always sends someone for the special orders and his regular supplies. And I heard that Benjamin down at the pharmacy may go out to study at the university. That'll be something, a pharmacist with real schooling. Mr. Alejandro is good but he admits he learned mostly by apprenticeship.

"The Train Master let it be known he's hiring wranglers, so there may be others. Lost a couple to a bar fight in Allbekirk. They busted the big mirror in the place and had to stay behind to work off the damages."

Train Master James Miller looked skeptically at the young man applying for the vacancy. Skinny, not too tall, but not a runt either, muscular arms sticking out of rolled up sleeves. A vest buttoned over the shirt. Ordinary canvas work pants. Scuffed up boots, looked a little big, probably hand me downs. Black hair in a worse-than-most home haircut. Grey eyes. Looked younger than the sixteen years he claimed. Not a trace of mustache coming in. But could be Indian blood; they didn't have much facial hair.

"Anyone to vouch for you?"

"No one in town knows me in particular. My dad's spread is up north in Narrow Neck Wash. We don't come in town much, but one of our neighbors had been in to see Doc Cairn, the dentist. Told Dad about you needing wranglers. Dad said if I really want to apprentice to an engineer over in Finx this is my best bet to get there. Get paid to travel instead of paying. He would have come with me, but our best cow is due to calf and Dad can't afford to lose her."

"It's not like being a traveler. It's work," Miller said. "Each man is responsible for four mules. Up early, feed the mules, check their feet, load them up. Walk along side them on the road. Feed them at noon rest stop. Unload and brush 'em down at end of day. You up to that? You get three squares, a bed roll, twenty-five cents a day, paid at the end of the trip. Any town we come to, one quarter of the wranglers can visit at a time. Others wait for the next town. No borrowing against your pay for the town visits. If you get sick or busted up we leave you in the nearest town with a doctor. Next Train picks you up. Hire you back on if you're fit to work or take you home if you're not, no charge."

"That sounds fine, Mr. Miller. I've worked with mules. We got two to plow. I mostly take care of the cows: milk, pitch hay, help Mom churn cause I got no sisters. I can do the work."

"Okay Charles, come back in the morning. If I haven't hired anyone likelier you can have the job. If you don't work out though, I'll pay you off in the next town to make your own way back."

"Don't worry sir; I'll work as hard as anybody. And just call me Chas, like everybody does."

‡‡

The Peddlers Train formed up in the stockade outside Sweetwater's town gates, a trio of its residents joining in with the procession. Benjamin Cassidy, the pharmacist's assistant, had his letters of credit from Mr. Alejandro in a rubber lined pouch in his inner vest pocket. His mother had packed him clean clothes and grooming supplies, to which Benjamin had added Mr. Alejandro's extra copy of the pharmaceutical formulary and writing supplies. He had about twenty dollars of his own in cash, as well; he had put half the money deep inside his packed goods and the other half in a bag secured to his belt. He turned to his mother for his goodbyes, promising to study hard and make the most of his opportunity. Pharmacy was a profession that would make her proud, and one that could set him up for a secure life and to do good for the town.

On the other side of the train, Pedro Smithers went through a similar scene with his father, solemnly shaking his hand before his aunt led the three of them in a prayer. Pedro repeated to his father the instructions about the kegs of peach brandy—he knew the price he should get, how to get a letter of credit to bring the money safely home, and what supplies he should purchase. Now that it was time to move out, he swung astride the riding mule the Train supplied and reined into line.

Further back and keeping a distance from both the boys, Chas loaded a small haversack of personal belongings aboard one of the mules in the group of four and, taking the foremost animal's lead rope, led the animals into place. This string was fourth in the line of pack mules, with the individuals who traveled with the Train for safety or to accompany their merchandise riding ahead to get less dust. Each string would rotate position each day so that no set of mules or men took the brunt of dusty, churned up paths every day. Chas wore a floppy brimmed felt hat jammed down low and concentrated on the animals, without glancing at the crowd watching the train's departure. Lifting the pack saddles, pulling cinches tight, and loading the bags, boxes, and kegs of merchandise and supplies onto each mule had already caused aching arms and shoulders. Chas didn't want Mr. Miller to notice the stiffness and have a reason to hire a replacement.

The first day was the hardest Chas had ever endured. Due to the late start, the train didn't take a morning break, so the work of loading the mules was followed by almost three hours of walking, leading the first mule in the string by the bridle while keeping an eye on the others for signs of lameness or cargo working its way loose. Chas was almost too tired to line up for lunch, but skipping a meal was a bad idea with this amount of work. After lunch, another two hours of travel, a half hour break, two more hours of walking and it was time to set up camp. Chas led the four mules to the center of the camp, where the carefully numbered sacks and crates were unloaded and left under guard. Once unloaded, the mules had to be watered and led to the portable corral to be fed and tied for the night. Only then could a bone-tired Chas line up for grub and collapse into a bedroll.

The head wrangler watched Chas hobble to the corral the next morning. "You're one of the new boys from Sweetwater, ain't you?'

"Yes sir."

"You look sore as a three-day-old boil." The man reached into his vest pocket. "I got some arnica pills here. They help with the aches. But don't have any coffee the rest of the day."

Chas was familiar with homoeopathic pills. Even the regular doctor used them for a lot of ailments. "Thanks. I appreciate it. I'm used to a day's work, but this is harder than I counted on."

"Oh, you ain't the first one to say that. It's a tough way to earn a living. But I consider that it beats sitting on a played out piece of land somewhere waiting for rain or wondering if the buzzards are circling the back pasture because your best cow just up and died."

The second and third days seemed worse than the first, but by the fourth day Chas was adjusting. Still exhausted at the end of the day, but without the beaten all over with a board feeling.

It was the fifth day out, about seventy-five miles down the trail from Sweetwater. Pedro was riding up the train to regain his place near the front after taking a necessity stop after lunch. Just before he passed one of the mule strings, its wrangler led them to one side and halted, kneeling to examine the lead mule's right fore-hoof. Pedro pulled up and swung off his mule.

"Need a hand?"

"Just keep the rest of the string from crowding me, is all," the wrangler said without looking up, staying focused on the mule's hoof. "Careful to not get kicked. Number three is a right bastard."

The wrangler dislodged a stone from the animal's hoof, lowered the foot to the ground and stood, staying focused on the mule. "I'm going to lead him a few feet; let the others follow." They both watched the mule take a tentative step then walk on without evidence of discomfort.

"Thanks for the hand," the wrangler said, glancing quickly at Pedro and then away. I'd better merge back in."

Pedro led his riding mule as he walked along beside the wrangler, surveying him, his curiosity piqued. "You look familiar. Didn't you hire on in Sweetwater?"

"Yeah," the wrangler said, voice short. "I'm Charles from Narrow Neck Ranch. We don't come in town much. You wouldn't know me."

Recognition dawned. "The hell I wouldn't," Pedro said, looking around to be sure no one else was in earshot. "You're no more Charles than I am. You're Chastity Gutierrez and your cousin Oliver Gutierrez farms the South Meadow Spread, which is nowhere near Narrow Neck. Just because it's been six years since we were in the upper grades together doesn't mean I forgot who you are."

Chas looked up with an expression of defeat. "Damn you, Pedro. Please don't give me away. I'm running away from Sweetwater."

"Why? Does Oliver treat you bad?"

"No, but he's dead set on me marrying Corwin Hudlin, who's near twice my age. Corwin's been courting me. He drops a lot of hints to Oliver about how once they're brothers they can share that fine new stud bull he got. Oliver says he wants me settled with a good man. He takes it for granted that a husband and children is what every woman wants. Says he wouldn't feel right keeping me as a housekeeper instead of letting me get my own home."

"That's no reason to push you on a man you don't want."

"It isn't that I just don't want Corwin. He's not a bad man. He's nice and considerate, and not bad looking for his age. But I don't want to marry anyone. Oliver's wife died trying to birth their third son. She screamed for two days, 'til she was too weak to whimper. The doctor said the baby was crossways of the womb and the only way was to cut it out. Oliver wouldn't let him because he thought that would kill her for sure. So she and the baby both died." Chas turned away and rubbed her eyes with a dirty sleeve.

"I wanted to run off behind the barn where I wouldn't have been able to hear, but Marie had been like a mother to me. I couldn't leave her with no one but the midwife that she didn't know real well to clean her and hold her hand and all. But I can't face that. I just can't. I think about a man putting a baby inside me and I go cold all over. I figure if I make it to Finx I can find some way to make a living on my own, without marrying and everything."

Pedro walked silently aside her for a moment. "I won't give you away," he said. "I promise. Anyhow, I don't think Mr. Miller would spare a man to send you back now we got this far."

"Oliver may have figured out where I went by now. But he doesn't have anyone to send after me. And I figure Corwin would be too proud. He wouldn't want the town to know the girl he wanted to marry would rather wrangle mules."

The work got easier, but the trip was still difficult. Chas trained herself to wake before the others so that she could get to the latrine trench before anyone else. When she couldn't stand herself any longer she would wake in the middle of the night and risk undressing enough to wash and change underwear. The strips of cloth she wound around her chest to flatten her breasts itched and sometimes slipped and had to be surreptitiously adjusted. But she fell into a routine. After the latrine visit she would roll her bedding and repack her duffel, then feed her mules before heading to the camp kitchen for breakfast. Whole grain porridge sweetened with honey, a hunk of cheese or cured sausage and a hot cup of chicory coffee were sometimes supplemented by fried eggs if they had recently stopped to trade. Lunch and dinner were equally filling: bread, cheese, beans, cured sausage, salt pork or dried beef, sometimes some chickens purchased along the way. The guards sometimes brought in game they shot while on patrol. Cured vegetables like sauerkraut or pickled radishes provided relish and vitamins. Potatoes or biscuits at the longer stops, fresh vegetables when available. Monotonous but nutritious and filling.

After breakfast it was time to take the mules to water, check their feet and put on the pack saddles. Saddles in place, each mule was loaded with a carefully balanced cargo, fifty pounds to each side. The first few days she could barely lift the sacks or crates, but she gradually gained strength and learned the easiest ways of swinging the loads from the ground to the saddle. She had told the truth about working with mules before. She actually liked the animals and three of them were fairly friendly. Number three was the exception, but she learned to work around his bad temperament.

However the work was not as bad as the thinking. There was plenty of time for that as she plodded along at a mule's pace. Was she doing the right thing? Other women knew the dangers of childbearing and still got married. Maybe she should have just told Oliver and Mr. Hudlin how she felt. But she could never have had that conversation with Oliver. He had been devastated by the loss of his wife. His sorrow was increased by knowing that some people thought he should have let the doctor operate. Informing him that Marie's death was ruining his orphaned cousin's life as well would have been too cruel.

The Train traveled slowly. On rough or hilly stretches, the men and mules could make ten miles a day at most. On the long stretches of former Highway 60 they could average fifteen. But each stop at a town to trade meant at least a day of downtime. A few towns were off the main road and added more miles. It was a pretty average trip. A few places where a rock fall or a washed out area meant delay or detour. A few stops where water had to be rationed because the spring or creek was lower than normal. Old timers sat around the fires at night and told tales of storms, floods, bandits, wild animal attacks, bad water, and other perils they had endured on earlier trips. Trails were usually best near settlements. Towns wanted trade, so they would put some effort into maintaining the road—repairing the remaining bridges, filling the worst holes, making sure the water sources were protected from overuse by herdsmen.

‡‡

A small gang of bandits attacked just past the old state line. Chas followed the whistled and shouted orders to close up with the other mule strings while the guards formed a perimeter to fight off the attack. She struggled to control her mules in the noise and confusion. One of the bandits slipped through the outriders and got near enough to try to grab her lead rope, but she cut him across the face with her stock whip. The Train guards had rifles, but Chas was astonished to see that the bandits carried crossbows and long knives as their only weapons. The attack was over in a few minutes, with the attackers fading back into the rocks and brush on either side of the trail.

After the bandits were driven away a head count was made. One mule had been killed, another wounded too badly to walk. Their loads were redistributed and the cook team butchered the bodies for that night's supper. Mule meat wasn't favored, being stringy and sort of sweet, but it was meat, and fresh meat at that.

One man had been thrown from his horse and suffered a broken collar bone. Mr. Miller strapped his arm in place.

"There's a doctor at the next stop. Two days away. If you think you can stand it, I'll have a couple of outriders take you ahead at a faster pace."

"Thanks. I'd rather hurt more for less time and get this set properly." The man grimaced as Miller tightened the bandage. "But are you sure it's safe?"

"Bandits are after the merchandise or the mules. They seldom risk going after riders. They know if you were carrying gold you would stay with the Train."

The scouts brought in one of the bandits who had been knocked unconscious in the fight and abandoned by his gang. Miller asked whether any of the Train crew or passengers could identify the man. Chas spoke up.

"I'm pretty sure he's the one tried to grab my lead rope. See the mark on his cheek? I hit him in the face with my whip handle."

"I saw him too. He dropped down out of the big oak over there. He started to cut through the lead on my rear mule but got a kick for his pains." This from Randolph, the rangy blond man who led the string immediately ahead of Chas.

"Anything to say for yourself?" Miller lifted the young man's chin to look him in the eye. "Got a name for us to post up in the next town?"

"No. No name. I don't want my family to know I died a bandit. Better they never know what happened to me."

"Okay. Your choice. You know the law."

Miller stepped up on a nearby boulder to address the gathered Train. "As a duly licensed Train Master it is my duty to administer the Law of Trail. You are all witnesses that we are outside the jurisdiction of any settlement and more than a day's ride to the nearest Territorial Office. This man has been taken captive in the course of defending a Train against a bandit attack. He has been identified as one of the attackers by two separate witnesses. He will be executed by gunshot and his body left as a warning to others." He pointed out two of the guards. "Take care of it, men. The rest of you, let's get on the road."

The guards took the man away and it wasn't long before a gunshot rang out. Chas risked a look back as she led her mules into position and saw the guards tie a rope around and under the arms of the man's limp body, then haul it up to hang from a tree next to the trail. A piece of brown paper pinned to his shirt displayed a simple capital B. Anyone who passed would get the message: *We execute bandits*.

Tried by the execution and her role in it, Chas began to cry softly as she walked alongside her mules. Caught up in her guilt, she noticed too late that Benjamin had worked his way back to her position. He dismounted to walk beside her, and she stared at the mules to try to avoid his gaze and not be recognized by him.

"Chastity," he whispered. Startled, she looked him straight in the face, no secret left to be kept. "Pedro told me," he explained. Then he hastened to add, "Don't be mad at him. I thought I recognized you from Sunday School and asked him about you. He told me your situation. I won't tell anyone else, I promise."

She nodded. "Thank you."

He paused, then asked, "Why are you crying?"

She gestured back toward the dead man. "He wasn't much older than us, Benjamin. I looked him right in the eye when I hit him. When Mr. Miller asked if anyone recognized him . . . I didn't know he would be killed on my say-so, and Randolph's. That's a heavy thing to think about."

"It's a hard law. But I guess without it no one would be able to travel. We'd all have to hunker down in our towns like hunted animals." Benjamin patted Chas's shoulder awkwardly. "I'm sorry it was you that saw him. That *is* a heavy thing."

The road turned from northwest to due west and those with sharp eyes or binoculars could see tall buildings in the distance.

"We're still miles out, but you can see those buildings because they're taller than anything you've seen before," one of the other wranglers told Chas. "They have so many floors it takes a day to climb up and down."

"Why'd they build them so tall?"

"I don't know. Just to show they could? Oil Time people did a lot of stupid stuff. I've seen pictures of fountains shooting water up in fancy shapes. Just wasting it in the air. It's always been a desert in these parts but making it worse was pure dumb."

As they traveled toward Finx, the road got busier. Local traffic increased, composed of people going between the clusters of settlement. Official traffic started to appear, like a bio-diesel patrol car carrying local guardsmen. People on foot and on horses or mules were supplemented with buggies as they reached roads that were in better repair. There were even some bicycles.

The next morning Mr. Miller told the Train that they would arrive in the Finx

South Transport Stockade by the end of the day. He gave the wranglers instructions about unloading their mules and collecting pay and reminded the merchants where to file claims on lost or damaged merchandise and how to transfer to a Train to Lost Angels or the Border.

Miller rode back through the Train.

"Howdy, Chas. I've been watching you. You do good work. Like that." He gestured to an improvised pad that Chas had used to cushion a pack saddle that had rubbed a raw spot on a mule's back. "If the apprenticeship doesn't work out, look me up, I'll gladly sign you on again."

"Thank you, sir. But I'm not going back. Family problems back in Sweetwater, so I'll just see what I can do for myself out here."

"I thought as much. Well, take care, Chas."

Pedro and Benjamin were riding together. Pedro looked around to see if any of the older men were listening. "Listen, remember the Warners and what they said about the Sanctuary? Danged if I wouldn't like to just look inside that place, just to see." He glanced at Benjamin to gauge his reaction.

"Well, as long as we didn't get into any trouble," Benjamin said. "I have to get tested and enrolled in the university."

"I've got work, too, selling the brandy and buying supplies. How about we plan to head over there our second afternoon if our work is done?"

"What do you suppose Chas plans to do now she's here?"

Pedro thought a moment. "Well, it seems to me that a woman that doesn't want to have babies might want to visit the Sanctuary her own self."

Two days later the three friends stood in the shadow of a building across from the Sanctuary gates. Men and women wearing palm sized patches of bright green on their left shoulder were passing freely in and out of one side of the gates. On the other side of the gate, visitors were being quizzed, patted down for weapons, and made to read a large sign posted on the gatehouse before entering.

"Well, here goes nothing," declared Chas, and walked across the twenty feet of dusty plaza to the gate. She didn't look back, but knew that Benjamin and Pedro were behind her, trying not to gawk at the people on either side.

"Business?"

"Sanctuary," Chas proclaimed boldly.

The guard nodded and passed her onto a pair of guards behind him. "Who do you want to search you?"

"What difference does it make?"

"Women usually prefer to be searched by a woman, men by a man. Your choice."

Chas stepped in front of the woman guard, took off her hat as directed and handed over her haversack for inspection. The woman patted her down with quick, professional motions and pulled a folding knife from Chas' front pocket.

"No weapons. Sign for it here."

"Sorry, I think of my knife as a tool, not a weapon. Being a farmer's kid and now a mule wrangler."

"Read the notice."

> VISITORS MAY NOT CARRY WEAPONS: KNIVES, SWORDS, GUNS, BOWS, CROSSBOWS, EXPLOSIVES, CLUBS OR ANY OTHER OBJECT OR SUBSTANCE JUDGED DANGEROUS BY GATE CONTROL.
>
> PERSONS OF ALL RACES, RELIGIONS, LANGUAGES AND CUSTOMS ARE WELCOME IN SANCTUARY.
>
> PERSONS OF ALL GENDER EXPRESSIONS ARE WELCOME IN SANCTUARY.
>
> REGULATIONS AGAINST THEFT, PERSONAL ASSAULT, MURDER, KIDNAPPING, SEXUAL ASSAULT AND FRAUD ARE IN FULL EFFECT IN SANCTUARY. VIOLATORS WILL BE HANDED OVER TO THE CITY GUARD. BEING OFFENDED BY THE IDENTITY, CUSTOMS, IDEAS OR GENDER EXPRESSION OF A VISITOR OR RESIDENT WILL NOT BE CONSIDERED EXTENUATING CIRCUMSTANCES.
>
> REGULATIONS AGAINST CONSENSUAL SEXUAL RELATIONS, EXPRESSION OF NON-CONFORMING GENDER IDENTITY, AND REPRODUCTIVE FREEDOM ARE NOT IN EFFECT IN SANCTUARY.
>
> REGULATIONS AGAINST THE USE OF FORBIDDEN DRUGS ARE NOT IN EFFECT IN SANCTUARY. LEAVING SANCTUARY WITH SUCH PRODUCTS IS AT YOUR OWN RISK.
>
> REGULATIONS AGAINST TEACHING OR DISCUSSION OF ANY TOPIC, INCLUDING RELIGIOUS HERESY, POLITICAL IDEAS AND FORBIDDEN INFORMATION ARE NOT IN EFFECT IN SANCTUARY. LEAVING SANCTUARY WITH PRINTED MATTER IS AT YOUR OWN RISK.

By this time Pedro and Benjamin had been passed through the guard post, after declaring themselves visitors, and were reading the notice also.

"What the heck is gender expression?" queried Benjamin.

"What I've been doing since we left Sweetwater. Dressing up and pretending to be a man. Same the other way around; if you put on one of my old dresses and padded up your chest. You know that's against the Regulations, except for fun, like a costume party. If anyone had turned me in I could have been whipped and put in the Reformatory."

"The rest is the stuff the Warners talked about. The way I read it, if you get friendly with a lady and then realize she is really a man all dressed up, you can't get mad and hurt him, like you might back home," commented Pedro.

They each signed their agreement to abide by Sanctuary rules, then the two young men walked into town.

A middle-aged man wearing a badge beckoned to Chas. "You the one asking for sanctuary here?"

"Yes, sir. My right name is Chastity Gutierrez. My cousin wants me to marry a neighbor he is friendly with. I don't want to marry at all."

"Sounds like a tale you need to tell the Madame. Follow me."

The Madame was a wiry woman of about forty dressed in a full, mid-calf skirt of bright blue velvet, a loose cotton blouse of the same color and a large broach of green enamel.

"I need to ask one thing before I tell my story, Ma'am. No offense intended, but some people say that all the women in Sanctuary are, well . . ." Chastity paused.

The Madame interrupted. "They say we're all whores. I know that. But it isn't true. Some women are, and they get as much respect for what they contribute to the community as the women who do the laundry or cook the meals or run the shops. But nobody is forced to be a whore or not to be one. Except for age; you look too young to sign on, unless you have already been doing it on the outside. Now let's hear your story."

Chasity poured out her tale: orphaned, taken in by her cousin. She cried some recounting Marie's death and mumbled her shame at rejecting a marriage that would have given her security and also helped her cousin. "Then I heard about the Train coming through and decided on taking the chance of getting away."

"Well, young lady. You have put considerable thought and determination into running away from your situation. Hard work, too." She picked up Chastity's hand and gently traced the calluses.

"I admire your perseverance. You are running away from a marriage with a man not of your choosing; a situation in which you seem to owe an indefinite amount of unpaid work to your cousin in repayment for your room and board; and your fear of childbirth." She dropped Chastity's hand and smoothed her skirt.

"But have you considered what you are running toward? What are you hoping to find here in Sanctuary other than escape?"

"Well, there was a lot of time to think while leading those mules down the track. But it's hard since I don't really know what you have to offer, or what I have to offer that is worth anything to you folks." Chas ticked off her points on one hand. "I know how to do most farm chores, but I don't see any farms around." She lowered one finger and continued. "I know basic cooking, simple food that satisfies kids and working men. I know how to put up fruit and vegetables, make pickles and such, salt down pork, jerk beef. I can do laundry and ironing, basic sewing, a few fancy stitches, crochet, knit, darn socks. My cousin had a guitar, so I learned a few tunes. I've done my schooling up to eighth grade. I can read and write, do arithmetic and keep simple books. I nursed my little cousins through the childhood ailments. That's about it." She dropped her hands into her lap.

The Madame nodded. "The first thing you should know is that if fear of bearing children is the only thing keeping you from marriage, we have people here who sell herbs and devices to keep a woman from conceiving. We also know how to end an unwanted pregnancy. Of course these things are illegal out in the rest of the Territory, although we are working on ways to get them where they are needed.

"But if you are serious about staying we have a boarding house for new Sanctuary applicants. You can stay there for six months, learning our ways and doing your share of work for the community. The rest of the time you will be assigned to half days of internships or classes to learn about our ways and about the work we have available. You get paid, and that money is yours for personal things like clothing or books. During the six months you wear a yellow badge. You don't wear it if you leave the Sanctuary. That way you can learn about the rest of the city without being branded, as it were. We want you to make a free choice."

"That sounds real reasonable, Ma'am. Do I start now? I should say I have some money that I earned as a mule wrangler. But I feel like I should send some of it to Oliver to pay for the clothes I took when I left."

"You can settle all that with our novice mistress. Follow me."

After two months of attending the morning classes that explained how the community worked, Chastity was beginning to understand what she was trying to become a part of. The community itself was laid out in several sections. The area nearest the gate housed businesses that were regularly visited by outsiders but did not provide anything that was illegal in the outside world. Visitors came for good food in the restaurants, entertainment in the bars, theaters and music halls or to buy luxury items, such as tailored clothing, fine dresses and millinery, imported or specially manufactured food and drink and objects of art. These businesses were centered in Sanctuary because many of the people who worked in them were not welcome outside. Religious heretics, persecuted minorities such as the few remaining Muslims in the Texas Public, the sexual outlaws Chastity had heard about from the Warners, and runaways made the majority of the population and workers.

Tucked safely away from the gaze of respectable townspeople shopping for new hats or enjoying the latest stage play were the businesses that catered to the "vices" of outsiders. Brothels serving every taste, purveyors of pornography, sellers of illegal drugs and bookstores stacked with seditious or heretical works occupied an area further from the gates. Housing for Sanctuary citizens was scattered in both zones: apartments behind or above shops, some family houses, some apartments or dorms for singles and newcomers.

The rest of the territory was taken up with factories, warehouses and workshops. Among other things, Sanctuary was famed for its fine liquors, laces, and rag and hemp paper. Making paper, or trading for it with other Sanctuary sites was a practical necessity, as outside suppliers would often refuse to supply the production of illegal printed matter. Making liquor cut out the middlemen and gave higher profits to the entertainment sector. Lace making and other needlework was a good trade for women and girls who had fled abuse or enforced servitude. These women could feel safe and sheltered in occupations that kept them in private spaces.

Sweetwater had not been an Anti-Sci settlement, so Chastity had learned basic biology, ecology, math up to algebra, and the rules of basic sanitation. She was amazed to learn that her roommate, from an Anti-Sci religious settlement, had no idea that bacteria caused disease or why it was necessary to wash one's hands and utensils before handling food. But even Chastity had something to learn from the human sexuality classes. She learned anatomy; not that taking care of two small boys had left her ignorant of the male body. She learned about homosexuality and gender variations and of the tolerance demanded of Sanctuary inhabitants. She learned of the possibility of and the methods for contraception and prevention of sexually transmitted disease. And she learned that there were ways to eliminate the possibility of pregnancy permanently. However, she would have to be eighteen and convince the doctors that she fully understood that there was no going back before she could apply for the operation.

She also discovered that, with the exception of certain entertainment area jobs, there were no restrictions on what jobs she could apply for or seek training in. Job descriptions were matter of fact: ability to lift a given amount of weight; good vision, if it was needed; normal hearing, likewise; skills; and technical knowledge. As a newcomer with no specialized skills she spent her community work time making beds or cleaning rooms at the hotels, washing dishes in restaurants or peeling potatoes and cutting up ingredients in the mess hall kitchen. But she could have chosen tasks usually assigned to men, such as chopping firewood, cleaning stables or unloading wagons.

Chastity did her twenty-five hours a week of work cheerfully. Even monotonous tasks like ironing sheets were made lighter by companionship. More interesting were the trial apprenticeships. She was given a list of openings, allowed to tour the workplace and talk to the manager and workers before committing to a trial. She tried a stint in the brewery and another in the pickle factory, since the work seemed as if it would be familiar. Then she took a trial in one of the sewing workshops. She was amazed to find that instead of individual treadles, the sewing machines ran from a central drive shaft powered by wind turbines. The operators started and stopped their machines by engaging and disengaging a set of gears. A second set of turbines sent energy to a flywheel for use when the wind dropped.

"Drat, it's jammed again." Chastity raised her hand to summon the machine tender. "I think if you tightened that piece over there it will keep the gear from slipping," she told the young man when he arrived with his tool belt.

"Umm, looks like you're right. I should have seen that last time it jammed." He looked at her appraisingly. "You seem to have an instinct for machines. Ever worked on them?"

"Not really. Just keeping things clean and greased around the farm. We didn't have much machinery."

"Well, if you're planning any more work trials, why don't you give the Gadget Group a look? It's more interesting and pays better than sewing collars on all day. Tell Mr. Cooper that Leo sent you."

At first glance the Gadget Group was a whirring, buzzing confusion. One entire end of shop was filled with whole or fragmented machines of various sorts. Next to that area were several rows of labeled bins filled with part: nuts, bolts, bearings, wheels and gears of various sizes and materials. The far wall housed a drive shaft like the one in the sewing workshop. But instead of a row of identical machines there were a variety of different devices hooked up. The center of the room held workbenches and stools lit by a skylight and occupied by dozens of men and the occasional woman intent on the work in front of them.

Mr. Cooper acknowledged Leo's recommendation and walked Chastity around the workshop. Then he sat her at an empty bench, showed her the various tools stored on and in it and presented her with a hand crank can-opener. "Take this completely apart, then put it back together." He watched without comment as she twisted and turned the device before selecting a screwdriver and beginning to dismantle it. Two hours later the test was complete. He shook Chastity's hand and introduced her to the other workers.

By the end of her two-week trial, Chastity had found her niche. She would be on probation until she made her final pledge to Sanctuary, but now that she was officially apprenticed she no longer had to work in the general labor pool. She had learned that, unlike the brewery, the pickle factory and the sewing workshop, the Gadget Group was not a production workshop. They scavenged devices from abandoned towns and farms. Some could be refurbished and sold. Others could be converted from engine power to water- or wind-supplied energy. Others were disassembled for parts that could be reused. There was a certain amount of routine work, but every worker was encouraged to tinker: trying to redesign existing devices or to invent new ones for the changing times. Some eventually left the Group to set up repair shops or to work for other workshops, as Leo had done in the sewing workshop. But there was a definite future for Chastity once she had discovered her talent for working with machinery.

When her six months of probation were up, Chastity had no hesitation signing the pledge to the community. The Madame pinned the green enamel badge on her dress, the Jeffe shook her hand, and her co-workers and dormmates applauded. That evening, she sat down and wrote a long letter to Oliver explaining why she had run away and thanking him for his care. A shorter letter apologized to Mr. Hudlin and wished him well. She finished both letters with: "I am proud to be an apprentice engineer. I miss you and the other folks in Sweetwater. But Finx Sanctuary is my new home and I think I can build a good life here."

The Doctor Who Went Over the Mountain

by Jeanne Labonte

A FLOCK OF BIRDS EXPLODED FROM A THICKET several meters ahead of Abram Dubois as he walked up the uneven grassy sward that passed for a road. Quail, he decided, though he wasn't yet fully versed in the North American bird life which filled the landscape wherever he looked, confounding his original expectation of a land depleted of wild creatures (how his New Bostonian hosts had laughed about that!). He listened carefully for any further sound but heard nothing. Whoever was following him had inadvertently startled the birds but was clearly trying to keep him from suspecting he was being trailed. The only question of course was who it was and what were his, or perhaps their, intentions.

The young Essene doctor rubbed his dark beard, thinking back on his last conversation with the Harzaberg town archivist (or librarian scholar as they were referred to in both the New York and New Bostonia Commonwealths). The stooped-shouldered, lanky Benwillum Smitt had been very helpful in giving Abram information on what to expect when he started his overland journey from the far west border of the New York Commonwealth southwards towards the Ginia Republic.

"You'll not want to go too far to the east," drawled the librarian, rubbing his thinning grey hair, as he studied the maps. "They're pretty mean-hearted down there, those damned Christos, always have been. Not too many folk, I'm guessing because of the radiant spots there but nobody I think you'd want to meet up with."

"Is that where the Old U.S. Capital was?" asked Abram, his eyes following Benwillum's ink-stained finger tracing over the map. He had been assured these maps were all current, not based on older charts that didn't always show the changes in the coastline after centuries of sea level rise.

"Oh yes," replied Benwillum laconically. "Nothin' much to see though, from what little I know. All the old stuff's long gone or torn up for salvage, anything not under water that is. That's likely how the rad poison got out. Some poor soul busting open a place he shouldn't have or maybe something nasty washed up in a storm that should've been left alone. No one knows for sure what happened. The Christos got a bad habit of crucifying nosy people so that kinda discourages anyone trying to find out. Got some drawings round here somewhere of how the old city used to look. Wished I could have seen it."

"What about over here?" Abram pointed at a hilly region west of the Old Capital.

Setting his spectacles higher on his nose, Benwillum squinted closely at the area Abram had indicated.

"Well, the old main road peters out about Gettys, but this one goes by to the west of it. Not used often anymore but it's far enough so you don't have to worry about running into any Christos people. In fact, don't think anyone lives there now at all that I know of. Old records say the plague swept through long ago and anyone who survived left. Nowadays nobody really wants to move back there. It's a bit too close for comfort to the Christos for one thing and the area's got a reputation for being haunted by ghosts from the old Gettys battle fought a ways back. Way before my time." He said this last part with a broad wink. Evidently the battle actually happened over a millennium ago but listening to local residents you would think it had just barely been fought. Folk memory was surprisingly strong here.

Abram was more concerned about bubonic plague than ghosts. Several centuries had passed since a severe outbreak in Europe back home. The Essene order, with its rich store of preserved medical knowledge, had diligently educated people on how to keep vermin clear from their dwellings and the importance of cleanliness in staving off sickness. The result was now only an occasional plague case that the Essenes always quickly isolated and treated as best they could. Sadly, without the antibiotics the ancients had access to, little could be done save pray the victim had enough resistance to fight off the illness.

"Sure you won't take a clipper instead? It's faster by water." Benwillum's eyes twinkled.

"Surely not!" replied Abram, shuddering. It had been two years since he had made the Atlantic voyage but the memories of his nearly non-stop vomiting remained fresh. It had been frustrating that none of the relaxation or breathing techniques he had learned was even remotely effective in warding off his seasickness. Mal-de-mer was allegedly not fatal but certainly felt that way by the time Abram wobbled unsteadily off the boat at New Boston.

The truth was, his curiosity bump itched ferociously. Looking at the map, he listened as Benwillum described how the land south of the two Commonwealths had once overflowed with people but cruel civil wars, famine and disease emptied them out centuries ago. But Abram couldn't help wondering if there were people, perhaps long isolated, still living deep in the wilds. What knowledge did they still have, if any? Would a doctor be recognized as such and welcomed? Only one way to find out, of course. It was early June, the chilly winter rains still months off, so he had the summer to do a bit of exploring.

Well, if he was in danger now, he had only himself to blame. He had already been forced to detour from the Gettys road Benwillum recommended. While walking along the ancient way, the harsh sound of voices where he hadn't expected any awakened some inner sense of danger. Hiding quickly in the brush, he watched three men, unmistakably Christos, walk calmly up the road. Abram was suddenly glad he had worn his dark tan traveling robes instead of the traditional conspicuously white Essene healer garments. Carrying spears, laden with fierce looking bows and long arrows, the trio made a grim sight, with bright white crosses embroidered up the front of their padded clothing, their faces long, ugly and pinched, one missing an eye from some old fight. They chattered amongst themselves, their version of Old English mostly unintelligible to Abram, though he managed to recognize a word here and there. Evidently they were on patrol.

This was an unpleasant development to be sure. He had been led to believe the Christos didn't come this far west. Were they expanding their territory? Their casual mannerisms suggested they felt secure using the old road. Abram delved back in his memory for the other routes the old scholar had shown him. Several would require him to backtrack, which was clearly out of the question. There was an ancient road just a short ways further on that ran westward on the map and eventually turned southwards. But he had no way of knowing if neglect over the centuries had left it impassible. He finally decided to chance it. Hopefully he could locate it without encountering more soldiers. Being crucified for interloping was a fate he devoutly wished to avoid.

He located the road without incident, finding a gravel path wide enough for several wagons, though no marks showed anyone had used it recently. That was a relief, as it meant the Christos probably didn't bother with it. More likely they were trying to probe into the New York Commonwealth, directing their efforts northward. Westward should be reasonably safe. An odd faint growling sound in the far southern distance made the hair on the back of his neck stand up. It faded quickly but left him deeply uneasy. An angry bear? A pack of dogs straining on the leash of some Christos? Best not to find out the hard way. He started up the detour.

As the coarse uneven dirt rapidly ended, replaced by patchy grass over thin dark soil, the land grew steadily wilder in appearance, huge trees towering overhead. It was clearly centuries since lumbering had been done. Any downed trees appeared to be the work of wind or age rather than human hands. The rich scent of growth filled his nostrils, insects buzzed about their business and birdsong sounded in the treetops. The mosquitoes weren't bad, though he knew the farther south he went, the greater the risk of yellow fever, malaria and dengue. He would have to make it a point to start using the netting he brought with him. There was rodent life too, but the sight of hawks circling overhead was reassuring. As long he exercised caution, there was likely little risk of the plague.

Though he knew appearances could be deceiving, what he had seen of the local ecosystem so far showed nothing but good health. Some areas of both Commonwealths still bore the ugly scars of ancient industries even after a millennium. But here at least it was gratifying to see how well the land had recovered in spite of centuries of abuse by the ancients. Perhaps the former locals had had enough respect for their land to avoid ravaging it beyond repair. It never failed to awe him how the enormous vitality of the earth energies refused to be smothered by human hands.

One sign humans rarely if ever ventured here came in the form of a curious young spotted wildcat, with tufted ears and a short stump of a tail. It watched him walk along, peering from the brush but making no real effort to conceal itself, orange eyes wide with astonishment. It ran ahead after he went past, so it might keep an eye on him. It finally turned back, presumably once he was past its territory. The incident left him chuckling for a long time afterwards.

He found the crumbling remnants of ancient buildings amidst the foliage, lonely moss-covered wall fragments jutting up, framed by gnarled tree trunks, nothing to indicate what purpose they might have served, whether public buildings, businesses, or schools. They reminded him of similar ruins in his own native land of Wallone, filling him for a while with a brief intense stab of homesickness. The road itself dwindled to a leaf-strewn gap, the forest relentlessly colonizing what had probably been heavily paved highways and sidewalks.

He spent several days at one spot where two walls drunkenly leaned against each other, creating a shelter while he waited out a spell of torrential rain showers, passing the time praying and meditating. At night, wolves howled in the distance but nothing troubled him in the small niche he had found. His knowledge of plants and herbs kept his little cooking pot filled with edibles, and his slingshot brought down a fat partridge to roast over a small fire once he had apologized to its spirit for the necessity of killing it. When the weather cleared, he cleaned away traces of his presence and continued on his way. It was on the sixth day, when he became aware he was not alone.

It had been subtle at first: persistently rustling leaves off to one side following him as he walked. A feeling rather than the sound of quick movement as whomever it was, hurried alongside the road in an effort to keep ahead of him. In many ways it reminded him of the wildcat but he was quite certain he detected the pattern of two legs, not four. He had no immediate sense of danger suspecting his shadow or shadows were not Christos but something more interesting. Well, he thought to himself, he had come out here to see if anyone lived in these out of the way places. If they had had any contact with Christos, no doubt they were being sensibly cautious. But how to reassure them he was harmless? After musing a bit, he laid down his rucksack and sat on the mossy remnants of a wall.

Fishing around in the depths of his robe, he pulled out his little mouth harp. After making a great show of cleaning and inspecting it, he placed it in his mouth and made a few experimental twangs. Then he began to sing, confident this would produce a reaction, as he had it on good authority from all he met that he had a perfectly dreadful singing voice. He just hoped it wouldn't be in the form of rocks.

"The Spring-time Song of Mother Magdalen" seemed a good choice, as that had plenty of high notes. It didn't take more than a few verses of his cracked-voice rendition to bring out the muffled sound of giggles from behind the bushes. More than one then, youngsters from the sound of them. He paid no attention to their laughter, continuing with several more verses interspersed with twangs from his mouth harp until the sound of hilarity grew impossible to ignore.

He turned in the direction of the giggling with what he hoped was a long faced hurt expression. It was unlikely they would understand but he spoke using the creole Road Talk used on the east coast as a common language.

"I try to make beautiful music but you only laugh at me. Why is that?"

Two buckskin-clad boys, grinning broadly, promptly emerged from the bushes. He judged their ages to be roughly twelve and nine. To his astonishment, the elder answered him in broken Road Talk.

"You make birds unhappy, is why. Is our job make stop with bad sing and bring harmony back."

"Oh, dear," sighed Abram with much glumness. "I suppose I must stop now. Not good to make bad harmony." As he spoke, he inspected the lads. They were barefoot, their buckskin shirts and leggings well sewn, decorated with bright colored beads and feathers. Each had little knives thrust into their woven belts and carried small bows with arrows held in quivers slung over their backs. Their dark brown hair was long and tied back with rawhide. Their intelligent grey eyes inspected him in turn. The younger boy spoke to the elder. Abram was immediately intrigued. Whatever it was he said, it sounded nothing like Old English or any of its more modern dialects. Another language brought by ancient immigrants? Or perhaps some old creole long ago mutated into its own distinct tongue?

"My brother ask what that thing you had in mouth."

"Oh, you mean my mouth harp." He held it up for them to see and demonstrated its use to them, much to the youngsters delight. He then solemnly introduced himself.

"I am D'lan," replied the elder boy in return. "This my brother, Mohad. We watch for Christos. Bad trouble, they."

"You are right about that," agreed Abram. "I came up this road to get away from them."

D'lan received this information thoughtfully and immediately huddled with his brother in earnest discussion. After a bit he turned back to Abram with an invitation to their village which the Essene quickly accepted. Mohad ran ahead, presumably to let the adults know they were coming. While he and D'lan walked, the boy peppered him with questions about the outside world, which Abram did his best to answer.

"How did you learn Road Talk?" he finally asked D'lan, after trying with only minor success to explain what an ocean was, not to mention a boat.

"From Mama. She was Christos but ran away so they not crucify her." At Abram's horrified expression, he added, "Because of her face. They kill people not looking right."

By now D'lan's village came into view. The forest, which before had loomed over them, now gave way to a broad open expanse. Benwillum was clearly wrong about no one living here. Small log homes lined the clearing, gardens freshly planted with vegetables and amaranth grain in the center. Here and there were stumps, where trees had been girdled and felled so the land could be prepared for planting. In the midst of the fields a platform sat atop a tall tree trunk. Beside each home was a well-maintained compost pile. Chickens and turkeys ambled about, pecking the ground. Goats bleated in a nearby pen. Several brindle-colored dogs began barking energetically at the sight of Abram.

A crowd of men and women waited near the edge of the clearing, their faces open and welcoming. No xenophobia here, thought Abram with relief. Most of them wore buckskin like the boys but some had cotton homespun skirts or trousers and a few of the men had woolen vests woven in a flamboyant pattern of brown and white. A woman stepped forward. Abram immediately realized what D'lan meant about his mother.

Her face was malformed, her grey eyes extremely wide-set, one noticeably higher than the other, her mouth crooked as though part of it was trying to slide off her face. In spite of it all, her expression was curious and cheerful, her smile gently shy. No doubt they had selected her to speak for them since she knew Road Talk.

"Welcome to Palachia, stranger. I am Nahomi. We greet you and ask you to make yourself at home. May the blessings of Father Jesu and the Great Dove be upon you."

"Thank you," replied Abram, bowing deeply, accepting the long strip of buckskin she handed him. It was decorated with beads and fragments of colored glass, likely salvaged from somewhere. With a bit of prompting from Nahomi, he discovered he was supposed to drape it over his shoulders, much to the amusement of D'lan.

It wasn't long before Abram found himself the guest of honor at a feast the villagers promptly started preparing. Like D'lan, they were full of questions about the outside world, especially about what the Christos were up to. Evidently the incursion he had seen was something recent, and concerned them greatly, particularly Nahomi. As they ate, her story gradually came out.

Born among the Christos, she grew up in an insular rigid feudal culture ruled by an oligarchy of families. Listening to her account and asking questions, Abram was able to piece together what had happened prior to her birth. The radiant pollution was the result of ancient ruins being broken into for salvage, possibly an old power plant where waste was stored and then forgotten. If any signs posted to warn off the inquisitive still remained, no one comprehended them. The chunks of poisonous material were traded about before people realized the danger. Regrettably the radiant waste was either buried on the spot or thrown into rivers, as no one understood how to safely isolate it. Those who handled it either died or were left with their health shattered. Inevitably, malformed infants were born to those who suffered exposure but survived.

Abram recalled a similar tragedy in Europe nearly a century before. The Essenes, educated enough to recognize the symptoms of radiation poisoning, reacted quickly but scores of people including many of the doctors themselves were sickened, often fatally. By the time the waste was safely stored back where it had come from, nearly two hundred had died and many more suffered from lingering ailments. Numerous children were born malformed much like Nahomi.

But at least her deformities were mild. Except for her face, she seemed healthy enough. But the harsh version of Old Christianity the Christos adhered to interpreted her appearance and that of others like her as the curse of their God.

"They said my parents had sinned and my face was the sign of their wickedness. Every time something bad happened in the village, they would be blamed and have to do the Rites of Penance. We were singled out the most because my parents didn't try to hide me. I didn't get flagellated like they did but people would make fun of me or scream at me saying Yehovah would strike me dead soon because I was so ugly. Sometimes they would push me over or throw rocks at me." Her tone of voice was matter of fact but Abram's heart ached at the haunted look in her eyes as she recounted her torment.

"D'lan said you ran away because you were in danger of being crucified. What brought that about?"

"It was after my thirteenth birthday, the families of the Holy Congressional Covenant, those who rule over us, issued a pronouncement. Any infant born deformed had to be exposed. The rest of us were to be crucified. They said it was the only way to turn Yehovah's wrath away. "

Abram shook his head in disgust. It was sickening to think anyone would accept such a cruel decree but knowing no other way of life, people began obeying. To their credit, Nahomi's parents could not bear to have her killed. Instead, under cover of darkness, they slipped her out of the village they lived in, gave her a small sack of food and instructed her to go north.

"I tried going north like they told me but there were soldiers everywhere. I don't know what they were doing. It looked like some sort of fight had happened, so I had to go west instead. I hid all the time and my food ran out." She shook her head, her eyes brimming with tears. "I was so afraid. It was hard to think straight, my stomach ached so much. I kept going west but there had been a big forest fire the year before so there was nowhere to hide. Some soldiers saw me and started chasing. I ran and ran but finally I just couldn't run anymore and fell down. I thought it was the end. Then J'hann came."

Her future husband, then a young man of sixteen, was scouting near the Christos border and heard her screaming while the two soldiers beat her. He wasted no time killing them with his arrows.

"J'hann was so gentle with me. He was the first person besides my parents who didn't look at me with disgust. Do you know what he said to me later? He said that the men trying to hurt me were the ugly ones." Nahomi's face softened as she described the kindness of her rescuer, who carefully tended her injuries and then brought her back to his people in the hills. "They told me I could stay as long as I wanted. They were all so good to me. I felt like I was waking up from a long bad dream." The Palachians accepted her without question and it didn't take long for love to blossom between her and J'hann. Now years later, she was happily married with two strong healthy sons and a third child on the way.

Still, the past was rarely far from her mind. Though Abram was able to reassure her that her deformities had been caused by the radiant waste and not any sin on her parents' part, he was less able to tell her what the recent Christos activities signified. He suspected some ambitious strong leader had arisen, galvanizing them, possibly to expand their territory so people could move out of the contaminated areas, or maybe just to satisfy some yearning for conquest and fame. The idea of a latter-day Napoleon or Daesh chilled him. He could only hope the New York Commonwealth, already in the habit of keeping a close eye on their baleful southern neighbor, would be alert to any troublesome developments.

For now though he preferred enjoying the celebration. Dancing had started, with several men and women playing simple instruments; rattles, flutes, wooden clappers, drums, and a huge gourd hollowed out and fashioned into a lute-like instrument. Couples joyfully twirled about, stamping their feet and leaping into the air. One of the musicians chanted periodically and when he did, the dancers would change their rhythms or swap partners. It looked like such great fun Abram couldn't resist joining in. Since he didn't understand a single word the chanter was calling, it made for many missteps on his part but this only added to everyone's enjoyment.

With the sun settling near the horizon, the festivities started winding down. Several people gave the goats a final milking and the dogs were unleashed to begin patrolling the village perimeter guarding against bears and wolves. For the first time he noticed there was also a thorn hedge around the village and fencing ready to be placed to block the pathways leading in and out.

"Yes, it keeps the deer and other animals away from our crops." Said Nahomi. "The dogs help but the thorns work well, too." They both watched as the chickens and turkeys were shooed into a large thorny enclosure and eventually the goats into a similar pen.

"I don't see any horses, cattle or sheep." Noted Abram. "Are these all the domestic animals you have?"

"Oh no, there are donkeys to carry things long distance and many of the other villages have alpacas. Their hair makes good wool." Nahomi chuckled. "When I first came here, I had never seen them before and thought they were some sort of strange deer."

With evening chores finished, Abram discovered the purpose of the elevated platform. An older man, one of the village elders, wearing a long dark robe climbed up the tree. Once on the platform, he waited while everyone gathered solemnly before their homes. Then the man cupped his hands over his mouth and Abram heard the unmistakable call to prayer he had often heard in scattered villages in Catalonia and Espania. As there, the Islamic influence was intermingled with local beliefs. The villagers below raised their voices in song, pressing their hands together Christian fashion. Once the exchanges of prayers were finished, all crossed themselves. Abram discovered the prayers, addressed to Father Jesu and the Great Dove, were mostly thanksgivings for good weather, growing crops and of course the delight of having a new face in their midst. He found himself blushing a bit to think he was the object of prayers.

There was no morning repeat of the call to prayer, which seemed to be only for the end of the day. As soon as it grew light, villagers began moving about, checking the fencing and preparing early meals. Using a clay pot, Nahomi cooked a simple but flavorful amaranth porridge accompanied by fresh picked strawberries just coming into season.

"This is very good," said Abram, appreciatively smacking his lips. Nahomi offered him some goat cheese, which he accepted, though he had to dodge both D'lan's and Mohad's hands also reaching for the cheese. They had already finished their bowls and like most growing boys were still hungry. Their mother admonished them to leave some food for their guest, but Abram spotted Mohad out of the corner of his eye, sneaking another spoonful of porridge while his mother's back was turned.

"Ho, hey, there!" The sound of someone hailing them in Road Talk while they ate made Abram look up to see a tall rangy grey haired woman approaching, her round face creased with a generous smile.

"Greetings, Ida!" Called out Nahomi, a smile brightening her face. Abram could see others also smiling at the sight of Ida. Evidently she was a welcome visitor.

"Is this the newcomer? Folks said an outland fellow showed up who said he was a healer."

"That would be me," replied Abram, rising to his feet.

"The blessings of Father Jesu and the Great Dove be with you. I'm the healer in these parts," said Ida, seizing Abram's hand and shaking it vigorously, a North American custom he found hard getting used to compared to the tradition of bowing back home. "I do midwifing, doctoring, and help fix up people's sick animals. If you're looking for any special roots or herbs, I can tell you where to find them."

Forthright and garrulous, Ida proved to be well traveled by the standards of her people. Her worn, patched buckskin robe twinkled with a variety of glass, bone and wooden charms and amulets sewn into the garment. She even had a Saint Appleseed scapular, acquired on a trip she had made south. Her rucksack, very similar to Abram's, was full of dried herbs and other tools of her trade. He was intrigued to see she had a crude book, made from animal skins and bound together with rawhide. Using an ink made from berries and other substances, she created illustrations of the herbs she harvested. What especially delighted Abram was the writing she used. The Palachians were illiterate but her former teacher years ago had heard about writing on one of the rare trips he made outside their land. Inspired by the concept, he devised a simple pictogram script of his own which he had taught to Ida. She expanded it, teaching it in turn to her own students (two of whom were her grandchildren). Abram wondered if he was seeing the birth of a new system of writing.

Ida cheerfully granted Abram's request to accompany her on her rounds. Once she had tended the two patients she had come to see, they set out for the next village. He had noted the general robust health of the Palachians, not finding any indication of nutritional blindness, scoliosis or any skin diseases, though he had seen a few goiters. When asked about it, Ida indicated this was a serious concern of hers.

"We were always able to get dried fish and seaweed from the ocean through trade with the south folk before," she complained. "But some of the routes have been cut off by the damned Christos people so it's harder to get. The other healers and I make sure the pregnant women and little ones get what they need, but if all our trading gets cut off, I don't know what we'll do."

"The New York Commonwealth to the north has access to the ocean. I could help you in setting up trade with them. They're good people and don't like the Christos any more than you do. I'm sure they'll be glad to help."

"Don't know much about the north folk but if you say they'll help, that will take a big load off my mind." She nodded her head towards the village they were approaching. "Now I've got to see how that fellow with the bad burns is doing. He says he got them when the Devil Bird flew over and spit fire at them."

"The Devil Bird?" Abram stared at her baffled. "What do you mean?"

"Well, this spring, some strange bird folks had never seen before flew way high overhead. From the east, they said, growling the whole time. Kind of circled once and went off. Then just over a week ago, I reckon, it came back. I didn't see it but it was flying lower this time. They had a hard time describing it to me, but said it was damned weird. Depending on who I talked to, it spit or pooped and when the stuff hit the ground, it started burning." Ida shook her head, exasperated. "The silly fool tried to put out the fire with his hands and of course he got burnt. The burns look pretty nasty, not like other burns I've seen."

The hair on Abram's neck prickled as Ida spoke, recalling the growling noise he had heard early in his journey. An engine? It didn't seem possible.

He had seen the simple airplanes, their small engines using ethanol fuel, which both the New York and New Bostonia Commonwealths had built, based on preserved diagrams of the earliest aircraft from a millennium before. Only a handful had been created, with the idea of border surveillance in mind particularly against the western raiders. It was thought to be more advantageous than the hot air balloons more commonly used, since unlike balloons planes could move about under their own power. But being very dangerous to fly and even more difficult to maintain they were used only when necessary. Abram had chanced to see a flight last year, and had been utterly overwhelmed by the sight of the machine in the air. It seemed incredible to think the ancients had routinely used more complex versions of these marvels and thought nothing of it. Now that he considered it, the Palachians who knew nothing of machines would easily mistake an airplane for a strange demonic bird. But who had sent it? Could it possibly be the Christos? Abram didn't think they had any industry but now he wasn't so sure.

A quick look at the man's ugly burns confirmed his fears. No conventional fire made these. They were clearly chemical burns. He had seen similar burns back in his homeland on chemists experimenting, attempting to recreate various substances the ancients had used. Whatever had been in the "droppings" was likely something flammable, possibly phosphorous. After they had cleaned and rebandaged the man's injuries, Abram explained his suspicions to Ida. She had enough knowledge of the outside world to understand some of what he was talking about.

"Well, it's got to be the Christos," she declared. "They've been getting pretty troublesome lately. You say the Commonwealth folk don't even know about us so it can't be them. Somehow the Christos have figured out how to build one of those flying things and are trying to scare us with it."

Abram had no doubt her terse assessment was likely the correct one. Somehow he would have to get word of this development to the Commonwealth. The only good thing in all this was that if the Christos had somehow managed to build a plane it would be every bit as dangerous for them to use as it was for the Commonwealths. The fear factor would have more power than the plane itself. Once people understood it was a thing humans had created and not a demon, much of the shock value would likely disappear.

Their next stop was a young woman, heavily pregnant, her time of lying in not too far off. It was here Abram witnessed a curious technique. Ida had the mother-to-be lie down so she could carefully massage her abdomen.

"What are you doing?" asked Abram, though he was beginning to suspect.

"Why moving the babe of course, so its head's down proper. I do it regularly with all the mothers I visit." Ida looked surprised at his question. "Learned it from my old mentor, Haddad. You mean your healer folks don't do this?"

"No, I've never seen this before," replied Abram excitedly. "Oh, please you must teach me. Finding new healing ways is why I came to this land."

"Be happy to." Ida smiled at his eagerness to learn, and then added proudly, "Ain't had a breech birth yet doing this."

So over the next four days they tramped up and down the surrounding hills, visiting a total of seven villages with nearly two dozen pregnant women, giving plenty of learning opportunities. Ida was well liked, so Abram was easily accepted as one of her apprentices. She also began tutoring him on how to speak Palachian.

Finally they completed the round back to Nahomi's village. As they walked along, they talked about the bubonic plague, which Ida called the "black swells." She knew nothing of bacteria but did understand the source of the sickness, the fleas carried by rodents, and the importance of keeping homes and people clean. They were discussing possible improvements to further reduce the nuisance of vermin in the villages, when they became aware of a strange growling sound in the sky. With a stab of terror, Abram realized it could only be one thing.

Suddenly it soared overhead, flying just above the trees, the noise from the engine deafening. It was low enough so Abram could see a white cross painted on the tail and the pilot strapped into a basket-like arrangement, gripping what he supposed were the controls guiding the plane. It looked like a very bad copy of the Commonwealth aircraft. Abram looked at Ida, her face so white with fear, he thought for a moment she was going to faint. But she was made of stern stuff.

"It's headed towards the village!" they both shouted at the same time, breaking into a dead run. Years of climbing hills had made Ida so fit she reached Nahomi's village just ahead of Abram.

They arrived to a scene of utter pandemonium. Adults and children screamed in terror, dogs ran about in confusion barking. The pilot had already tossed one of his small bombs, striking a wicker frame meant for squash to climb up, setting it ablaze. D'lan and others frantically splashed water from gourds onto the flames.

Abram shouted at them to throw dirt but had to repeat himself because in his fright he forgot to use Road Talk and spoke in his own native tongue instead. Wide-eyed with fear himself, D'lan had managed to keep a cool enough head, so he was able to grasp what Abram was saying and, throwing aside his gourd, began scooping up handfuls of dirt, instructing his companions to do the same.

Abram glanced around at the panicky villagers and spotted Nahomi. She must have seen the white cross on the plane. The look of haunted terror on her ashen face was gut-wrenching. He suddenly felt a white-hot, very un-Essene-like rage ignite in his chest. From what he could see, the plane was circling to make another pass. He spotted his slingshot sitting on a flat rock by J'hann and Nahomi's cabin. Mohad must have been practicing with it. Abram snatched it up along with a stone and sprinted towards the prayer platform.

He climbed frantically to the top, hoping he wasn't being impious in doing so. The plane was already beginning to make its run, swooping down like the Devil Bird the locals had called it. Commonwealth planes generally could only stay in the air a few hours before they had to go back for fuel. Assuming it was the same for the Christos plane, it would likely make just a few passes before it returned home. This meant Abram would only have one chance.

Everything seemed to slow to a crawl. He could see the pilot, one arm already raised, holding a small bomb while clinging to the controls with his other hand. His attention seemed focused on the people below, so there was a good chance he was unaware of Abram. The Palachians fired arrows at the terrifying apparition bearing down on them, but their weapons meant for close hunting in the woods simply didn't have the range to strike their flying attacker with any force. Abram could feel sweat streaming down his face and back as he aimed and released his stone while the pilot dipped low, only meters above him, tossing his bomb.

The rock ricocheted between the wings and the wicker seat, startling the pilot enough so he involuntarily raised both hands to shield his head. In that moment he was lost. The plane, now with no hands guiding it, suddenly tilted and nose-dived. With a sickening thud it rammed into the ground while people below frantically dodged it. Abram could see small bombs escaping from a basket the pilot had beside him, bouncing on the ground but thankfully not enough to burst.

After climbing back down, Abram approached the crumpled remains of the plane. No one on the ground had been hurt. The only casualty other than the squash plants crushed by the plane was the pilot, who lay where he had been thrown from his seat, goggles dangling from his face, his neck at a horrible angle, plainly dead. Abram's adrenaline high faded as he looked at the Christos. He was very young, barely eighteen from the look of him, short and spindly. He had likely been chosen to fly the plane for his light weight.

A sick feeling came over Abram, hot tears of shame burning his eyes as the impact of his actions sank in. What had he done? He was an Essene, doctor of the ill and injured, of an ancient holy order dedicated to the ways of the Divine Healer, preserving and disseminating healing knowledge and wellness both physical and spiritual. Only hours before, he had experienced the indescribable joy of feeling an unborn child move under his hands with Ida's wrinkled hands over his, guiding him in the careful nudging necessary to move it into the proper position for birth. Now this. An ancient admonition echoed through his mind. *Abstain from doing harm.* As a ragged sob began working its way up his throat, he felt a gentle hand on his shoulder. He turned to see Ida's kindly face looking into his.

"Father Jesu and the Great Dove know what truly lies in your heart. You didn't do this for evil's sake but for the living. If that fellow had gotten back to his people, they'd know they could scare us easy whenever they wanted to, with no one to stop them. The attacks would get worse. We'd never know peace again." Abram swallowed with difficulty. She was right, though that knowledge didn't make him feel any better. After later reflection, he realized it wasn't supposed to.

The villagers cautiously gathered around, while Abram examined the plane. He could see Nahomi standing to one side clutching her sons close to her. The aircraft was a hodge-podge of wicker, cloth and wood with scrap metal melted and reshaped to create the frame and a wooden propeller hooked up to the engine. Now close up, he could see how fragile it actually looked. He was amazed it had been able to stay in the air. The engine was largely intact, though its fuel tank dribbled ethanol from a crack. It was so well made Abram was not surprised when he found the metal forger's mark on it, showing its place of manufacture to be the New York Commonwealth.

"They must have stolen the engine." He told them, recalling news circulating during his stay at Harzaberg. The plane hangars located at Lincaster had been set ablaze along with several other buildings. It was thought at the time to be the work of rogue salvagers trying to steal scrap metal to melt down and resell, using the fire to cover their tracks. It was now apparent who the true culprits were.

"Will they try to get another one?" asked Nahomi.

"Maybe," replied Abram. "But we need to warn the Commonwealth. Do you know of any other roads that go north? I don't think it's safe to use the one I came on."

Once his words were translated, the Palachians quickly suggested other routes they were confident only they knew of. J'hann said he would get some donkeys, so they could carry the engine back to the Commonwealth. Some of the villagers, their fear having evaporated, were already cleaning up the plane wreckage and had covered up the pilot with a blanket. Ida told him later the body had been buried deep in the woods and charms set up around the village to ensure his ghost did not return to haunt them.

Eight days later, Abram was in Harzaberg again, showing the engine along with the little bombs to the men and women of the town governing council. They were visibly shocked by this proof of the growing brazenness of the Christos. As the Commonwealth had radios, this news would spread quickly, hopefully circumventing another theft attempt.

"We'll step up patrols along the south border," said Tomas Dunn, head of the council. "I don't think anyone realized the Christos knew about planes. We don't fly them very often, mostly just to watch for horse raiders from the western plains."

"I've no doubt they must have seen them once or twice," remarked one woman who was examining the engine. "But you would think they'd just believe it was some sort of devil we were in league with. You know how they're always accusing us of being ungodly." Most of the council members nodded their heads, rolling their eyes.

"A woman who fled them told me the oligarchy is literate, even though the plain folk are not," replied Abram. "They must have old records, with enough information so if they saw a plane, they would have realized what it actually was. They would certainly have coveted one."

"There was printed material for repairing planes at the hangers. I'll wager they have spies among us," said the councilwoman, suddenly straightening in alarm. "How else would they have known where to go and what to take? I think we've been underestimating the Christos. They're obviously literate enough to get information from them for building a plane. "

"And have enough industry to make one," added Tomas, darkly.

"That would explain the reports we've been getting of increased scrap raiding by the Christos," spoke up another council member. "They must have been gathering materials to make a plane."

"Possibly," replied the councilwoman. "I can't believe they've developed the forging craft to make an engine, though. I'm sure they'll try to steal another one."

"Well, we'll make damn sure they don't get another," growled Dunn.

Abram returned to the Palachian hills along with Ida, after helping her set up the trade needed for seafood. He wound up staying not only for the summer but through the fall and winter as well, mastering the technique of child turning, exchanging knowledge on healing and nutrition and acquiring a decent smattering of the Palachian language.

Very early on a chilly mid-November morning, after the villagers moved into a lodge they used during the winter, Abram had the great delight of helping Nahomi safely deliver a baby girl. The infant's eyes were wide-set though not abnormally so and she bellowed loudly in protest at being thrust into the world from her mother's warm body. J'hann and Nahomi held their daughter close, while D'lan and Mohad peered in fascination at their new sister. The joy radiating from Nahomi's face made her beautiful.

The Solstice celebration had a familiar practice: the raising of a large evergreen before the lodge decorated with wood and bone ornaments. Stories were told of the birth of the Winter Child Moses to his parents Father Jesu and the Great Dove. In the summer would come the birth of his brother Mohamut. Abram listened in amusement as the children were entertained on winter evenings with tales about the brothers, many of which involved them quarrelling in various ways about what the correct direction for praying was: west or east? The arguments of course were never completely resolved and provided different lessons for the children on life and how best to live it.

Spring came, the cold winter rains and occasional snowstorms giving way to warmer rains and the sight of geese migrating. Ida, back from her latest trip north, brought news. The Christos had indeed made another more aggressive attempt to get an engine but been fiercely repulsed. Many of them had been killed in the battle, including what appeared to be their leader. Abram knew it wasn't proper but he felt secretly relieved. The loss would likely leave the Christos in disarray for some time to come. Nahomi and her adopted people could continue living in peace.

His curiosity bump was itching again, so he knew the time had come to move on. The news that he was departing was greeted with sadness by everyone but they extracted a promise from Abram to visit again when he came back north, which he was more than happy to give. He had come to love these proud, generous hill folk.

D'lan and Mohad accompanied him to the southern edge of the Palachian territory. During the winter, D'lan had suddenly sprouted, now nearly as tall as Abram. His voice was beginning to crack as well; something Mohad needled him constantly about, calling him "Froggie." But Mohad himself was growing too, becoming more thoughtful. He had begun asking Abram many questions about the herbs Ida and he used and accompanied them a few times on gathering expeditions. It looked like Ida would soon have a new student.

"When you come back, I will have my manhood tattoos," said D'lan, puffing himself up a bit. Abram knew the young man-to-be would also get circumcised, and be required to undergo a vision quest, so he suspected there was a bit of anxiety under the bravado.

"Do you think you'll have a beard like mine?" teased Abram.

"If he does, I'll call him Hairy!" chimed in Mohad impishly, but quickly grew solemn. "My curiosity bump itches too. Someday I'll go with Ida to see what the world looks like."

"Learn everything she teaches you and one day you will." Abram assured him.

They embraced one last time, then as the boys stood watching, Abram walked down the path that Ida had outlined to him on a crude map leading to the Warm Springs land. Beyond was the Ginia Republic. D'lan couldn't resist calling out one last time.

"Don't sing too loud! We don't want the birds falling out of the sky."

"Unless they are good to eat," added Mohad quickly.

Abram laughed and waved. As he traveled the path, he could see green hills receding into the distance and an eagle soaring high above. Reaching into his traveling robes, he found and pulled out his little mouth harp. After twanging it a few times, he sang the beginning of a children's song he had heard back in the Commonwealth. When no admonishing rocks came his way, he continued.

"The bear walked over the mountain, the bear walked over the mountain, the bear walked over the mountain, to see what he could see . . ."

Don't miss a single issue of Into the Ruins

Discover the First Year of Into the Ruins

Thank you for reading!

Made in the USA
Middletown, DE
31 August 2017

Wildlife of the Eastern Caribbean

WILDGuides

Steve Holliday and Gill Holliday

PRINCETON
press.princeton.edu

Published by Princeton University Press,
41 William Street, Princeton, New Jersey 08540
99 Banbury Road, Oxford OX2 6JX
press.princeton.edu

GPSR Authorized Representative: Easy Access System Europe - Mustamäe tee 50, 10621 Tallinn, Estonia, gpsr.requests@easproject.com

British Library Cataloging-in-Publication Data is available

ISBN: 978-0-691-19981-8
ISBN (ebook): 978-0-691-26991-7
Library of Congress Control Number: 2024944625

Editorial: Andy Swash and Jacqui Sayers
Design: D & N Publishing, Wiltshire, UK
Cover Design: Rob Still
Production: Ruthie Rosenstock
Publicity: Caitlyn Robson-Iszatt and William Pagdatoon

Cover image: Barbados Anole © Jenny Daltry
Title page image: Brown Boobies © Gill Holliday

Printed in China

10 9 8 7 6 5 4 3 2 1

Contents

Preface

This book is inspired by the amazing biodiversity found on a string of small tropical islands in the Eastern Caribbean, an area stretching from the Virgin Islands south through the Lesser Antilles to Grenada. Along this arc, where the Caribbean Sea meets the vast expanse of the Atlantic Ocean, a unique range of flora and fauna has evolved in relative isolation on seventeen island groups. More than 30% of all the species included in this guide are endemic to the region, found nowhere else on earth.

Exploring the region's wildlife will take you from beautiful sandy beaches and bays, many of which provide traditional nesting sites for sea turtles, past mangroves and brackish ponds rich in waterbirds and crabs, into low-lying scrub and dry forests, with their distinctive and characteristic birds, reptiles and butterflies. High on volcanic peaks, trails lead deep into lush rainforest and, on some islands, even into mist-shrouded elfin forest. These precious forest habitats can hold the entire world population of particular birds, bats, amphibians, reptiles and dragonflies. Many species are common and easy to find; others require a little more effort and determination! More widely, the islands are vital links along the migratory flyway for thousands of waterbirds and landbirds that breed in North America; small offshore islets and cays attract internationally important numbers of breeding seabirds; and the rich seas provide breeding and feeding grounds for whales and dolphins.

This is the first photographic identification guide to bring together all the birds, mammals, amphibians, reptiles, land crabs, dragonflies and butterflies that are likely to be seen in the Eastern Caribbean. Over 420 species are covered, illustrated with high-quality images and with their key identification features highlighted. In addition, more than 150 species that are rare or highly restricted in range, such as those only found on small offshore islands, are listed for completeness.

The wildlife of the Eastern Caribbean faces many conservation challenges: more than 100 of the species included in this guide are globally threatened, some being on the brink of extinction. In response, governments throughout the region are working alongside island-based and international conservation organizations to protect vulnerable species and to conserve or restore their fragile habitats.

We are grateful to many people for their help and support when researching and writing this guide. We hope that it will encourage a wider appreciation and understanding of the wildlife of the Eastern Caribbean; there is still much to discover and learn!

Steve and Gill Holliday
January 2025

Map of the Eastern Caribbean region

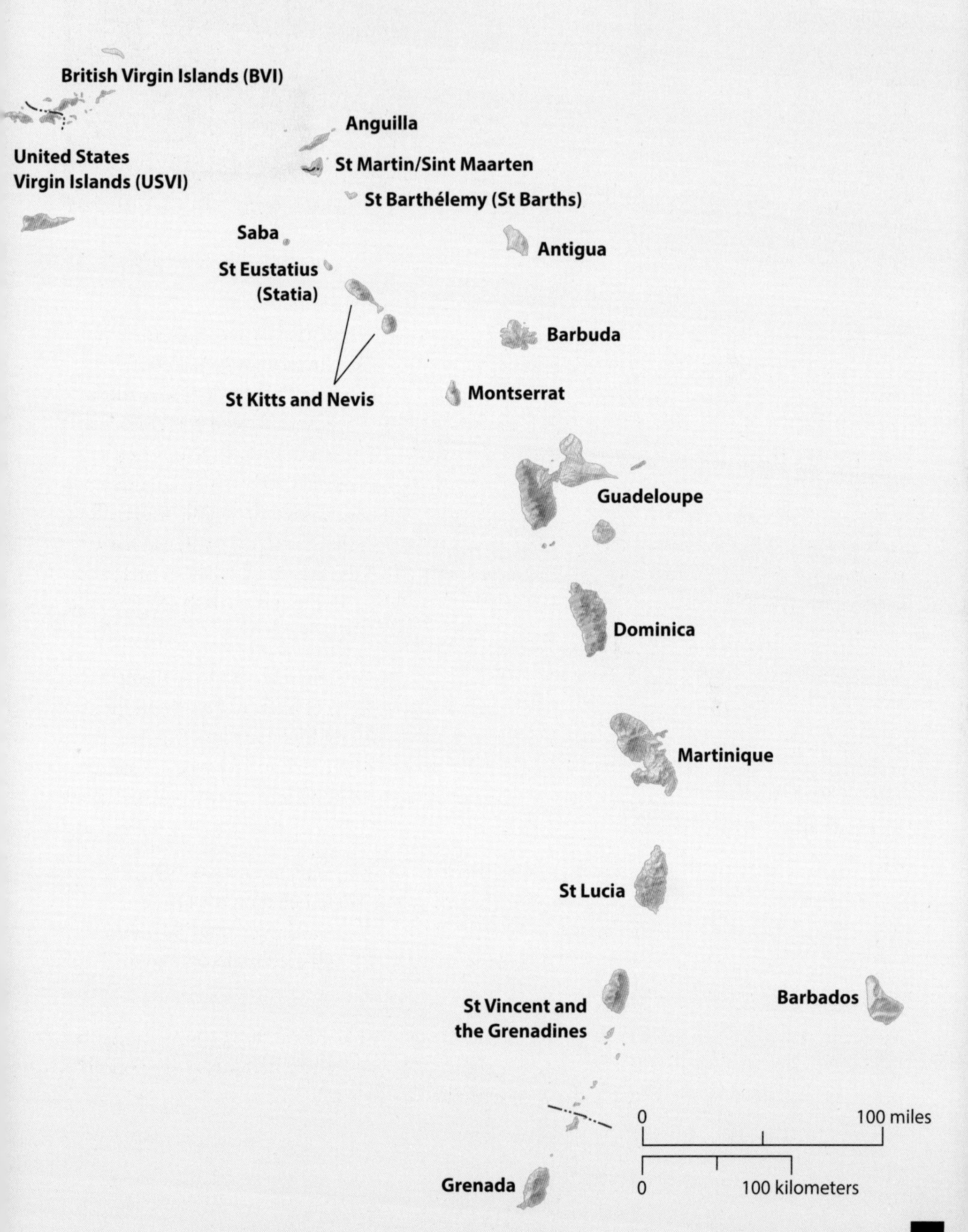

The Wider Caribbean

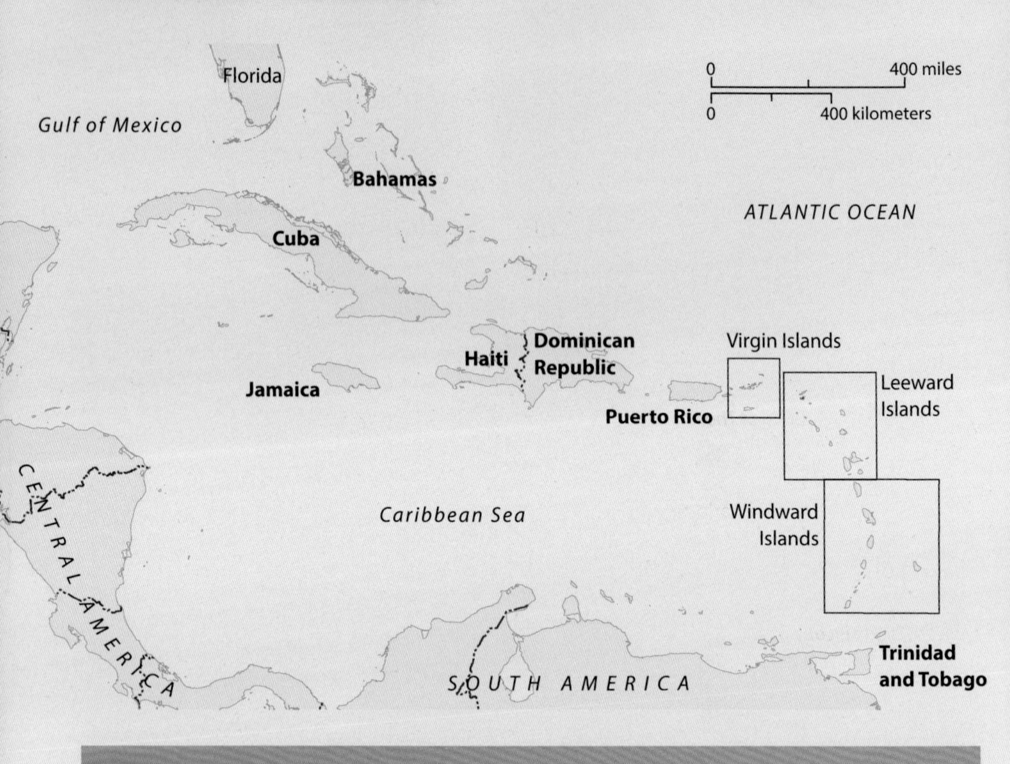

The archipelago of St Barthélemy (St Barths) in the Leeward Islands.

The Virgin Islands

Anegada

British Virgin Islands

Culebra

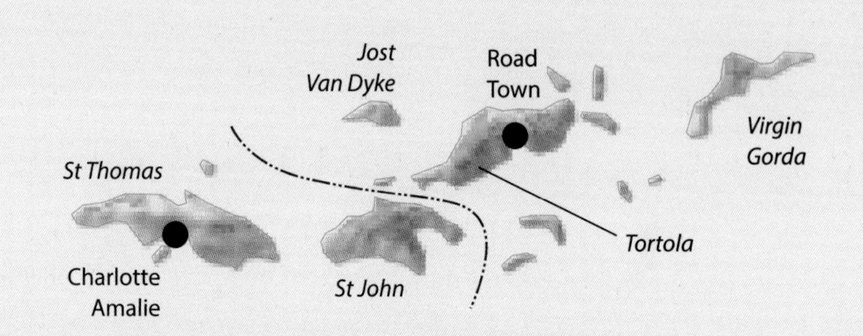

Vieques (Puerto Rico)

United States Virgin Islands

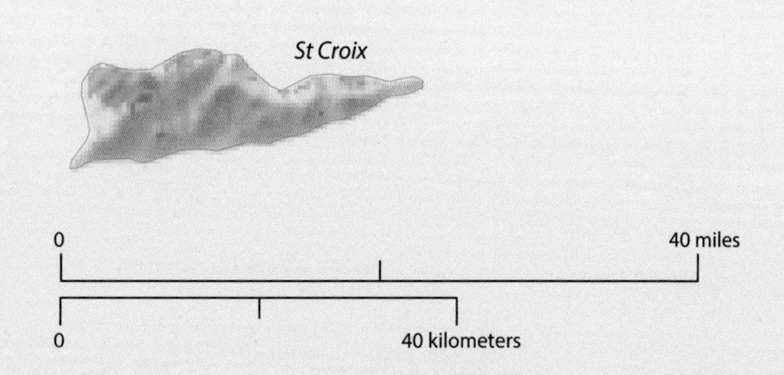

Leeward Islands: Anguilla to Guadeloupe

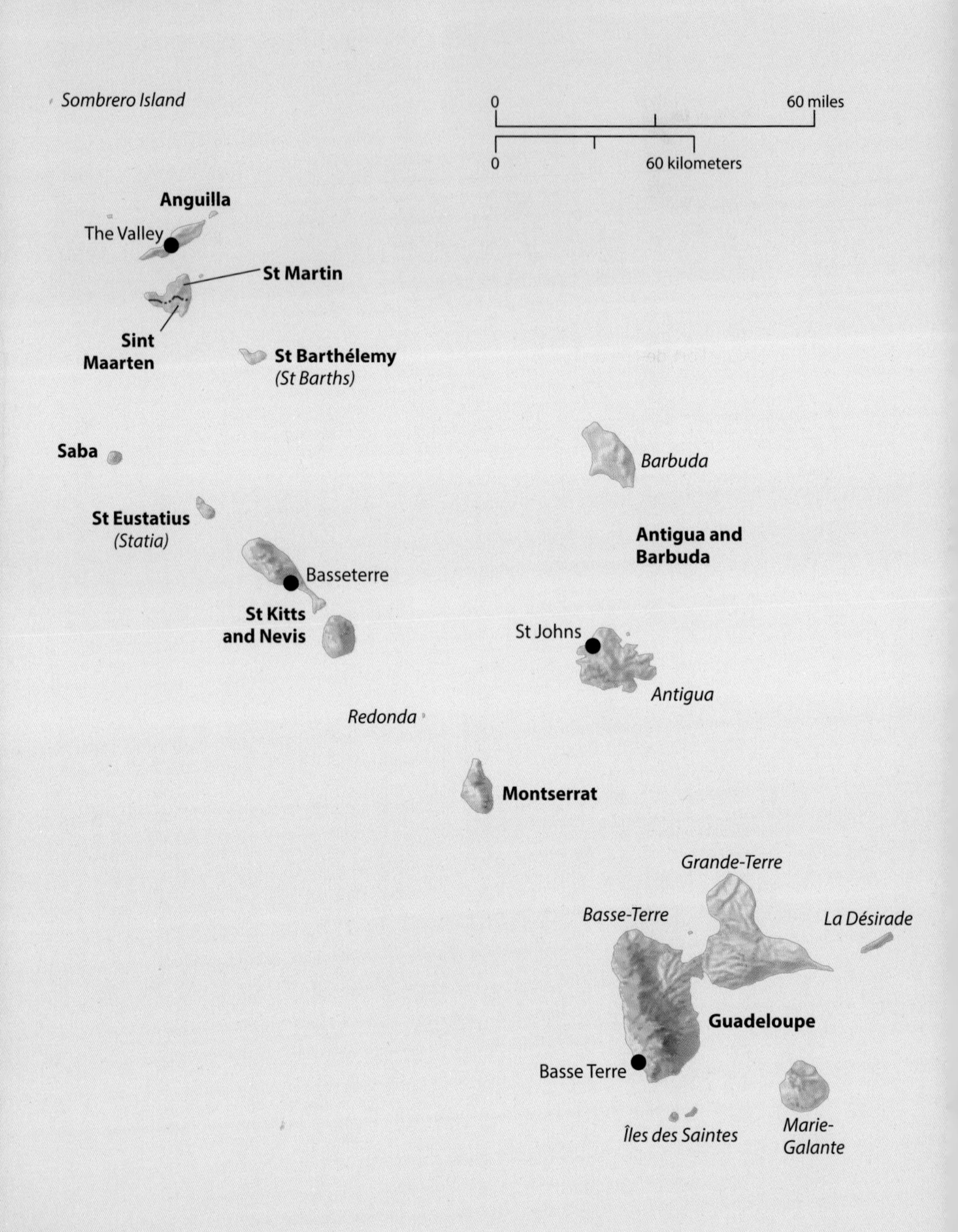

Windward Islands: Dominica to Grenada

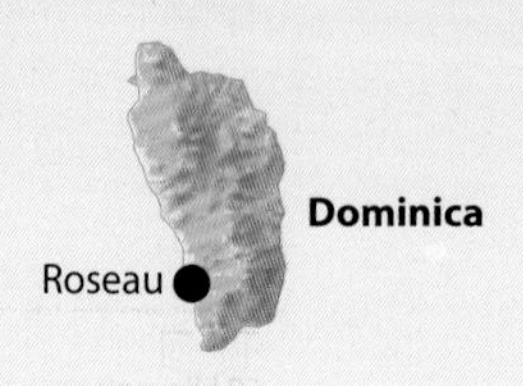

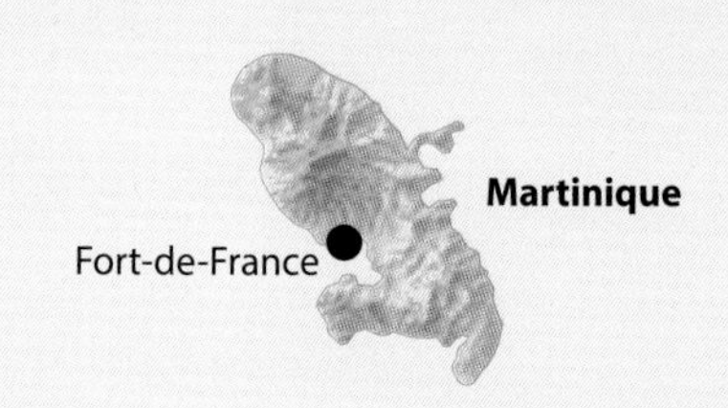

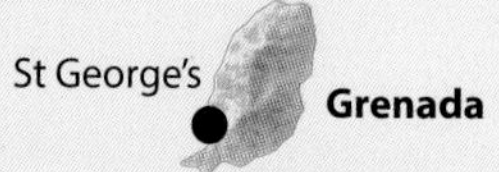

0 60 miles

0 60 kilometers

Introduction to the region

The islands of the Eastern Caribbean stretch over 800 km (500 miles) from the Virgin Islands to Barbados and Grenada and have a combined land area of 6,573 km² (2,538 sq. miles), 3% of the total area of all Caribbean islands. They range dramatically in size. The smallest—Saba, St Barthélemy and St Eustatius—each have a land area of under 26 km² (10 sq. miles). The largest—Guadeloupe, Martinique and Dominica—all exceed 775 km² (300 sq. miles) in land area. The islands are geographically close: apart from the greater distances between the Virgin Islands and northern Lesser Antilles (167 km/103 miles), and between St Lucia and Barbados (174 km/108 miles), the next island is never far away, its distinctive outline often visible on the horizon.

The geological history of the Eastern Caribbean is long and complex, resulting from volcanic activity over many millions of years. The islands in the region vary in age and can be separated into three broad groups.

The oldest rocks, at around 100 million years, are found in the Virgin Islands. Here the geology tells of past periods of volcanic activity and more recent limestone deposits. Continuing erosion has left a series of islands with low hills and peaks—the exception being Anegada, which is a low, flat limestone island that lies to the north of the main archipelago.

The volcanic islands of the Lesser Antilles farther east were formed as the Atlantic tectonic plate subducted under the Caribbean plate. These comprise two broad arcs of activity:

The oldest arc curves from Anguilla through St Martin/Sint Maarten, St Barthélemy, Antigua, Grande-Terre and Marie-Galante (Guadeloupe) and Martinique. These islands are up to

St Kitts from St Eustatius.

Limestone coast, Anguilla.

Virgin Islands looking north from St John.

40 million years old and were formed along a line of past volcanic activity. Their volcanic landscapes and rocks have been eroded and reduced to lower, gentler hills or have been overlain with limestone deposits; these islands are sometimes referred to as the Limestone Caribbees.

The most dramatic landscapes, characterized by cone-shaped volcanic peaks, are found on the younger, inner arc from Saba to Grenada, including Basse-Terre (Guadeloupe), which formed within the last 10 million years. Volcanic activity continues here, with the most recent major eruptions on Montserrat in 1997 and St Vincent in 2021.

The geological origin of Barbados is much more recent—thought to be less than a million years ago. It was formed when ocean sediments were scraped up through tectonic plate activity and subsequently covered by reef corals; the resulting limestone landscape is flatter with gentle slopes.

Soufrière Hills stratovolcano, Montserrat.

Reptile distribution provides evidence that some islands and their offshore islets were connected as 'island banks' when sea levels were lower. An example is the Anguilla Bank, comprising Anguilla, St Martin/Sint Maarten and St Barthélemy. These islands are separated by relatively shallow seas and share the same species of groundlizard, anole, dwarf gecko and racer snake. Similar evidence of island banks can be found throughout the region, but the more southerly Lesser Antilles are separated by deeper channels with smaller island banks.

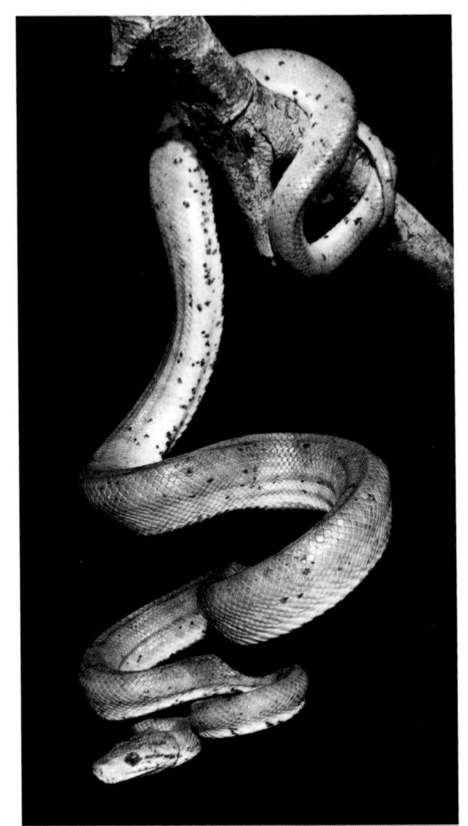

Grenada Treeboa *(p. 220)*
Eighteen out of 21 species of snake are endemic to the region, and a further three are only found on the Virgin Islands and Puerto Rico.

The ways in which the wildlife of the region arrived over time is the subject of much biogeographical study. The islands' oceanic origins meant that any colonizing animals had to cross expanses of open sea, which limited the arrival of terrestrial species and those not able to fly. Many must have arrived on flotsam carried by ocean currents, dispersal on the wind or displacement by climatic events. By whatever means they arrived, a distinctive range of plants and animals subsequently evolved in geographic isolation. Of the 578 species referred to in this guide, 171 (30%) are endemic to the region, most of which are only found on a single island or island bank. There are 35 species of endemic birds, but the highest rates of endemism are found in native amphibians (12 of 15, or 80%) and reptiles (106 of 127, or 83%). In addition, there are several species endemic to the Caribbean that only occur on the Virgin Islands and Puerto Rico.

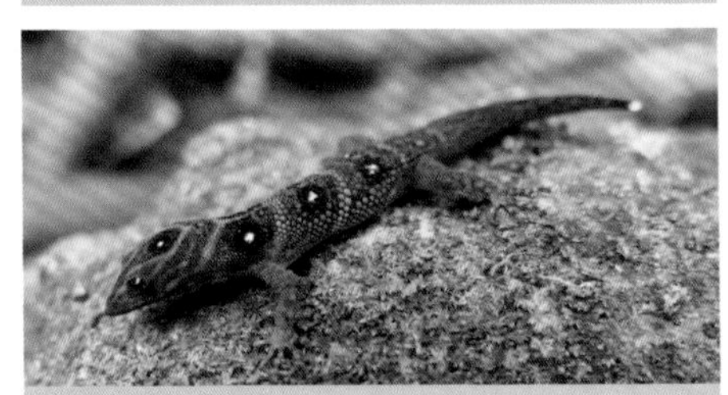

Union Island Clawed Gecko *(p. 213)*
Eighty-three percent of all Eastern Caribbean reptiles are endemic to the region.

Recent and ongoing studies, including DNA analyses, are contributing to a better understanding of species and their relationships, resulting in some revisions and differentiation. For example, Antillean Euphonia, a forest bird, has been recently recognized ('split') as three distinct endemic species: Hispaniola Euphonia, Puerto Rican Euphonia and Lesser Antillean Euphonia, with the latter becoming a new endemic for the Eastern Caribbean. Accordingly, the region's list of endemic species is likely to increase in the years ahead.

Climate

Cloud cover on the high slopes of Mont Pelée, Martinique.

The tropical climate of the Caribbean has 7–8 hours of daily sunshine, and temperatures that average between 24–30°C (75–86°F), moderated by the prevailing Atlantic trade winds from the east, which provide constant breezes. Seasonality is much reduced in the tropics and is broadly determined by rainfall. December to May is recognized as the dry season, during which the weather is more settled and benign. Rainfall is usually sporadic and localized, often in short sharp showers, and some islands can experience periodic droughts. In the wet season, between June and November, temperatures are at their highest, the weather is more unsettled, and the region experiences heavy showers and thunderstorms. As the seas warm into September and October, tropical storms and hurricanes can develop over the Atlantic, bringing destructive winds and flooding, which can be devastating to any islands in their path.

Rainfall is an important variable that affects vegetation and wildlife, as well as people. At low elevations, annual rainfall averages 1,000–2,000 mm (39–78″), but at high elevations it can be well in excess of 4,000 mm (157″). Even on sunny days the highest peaks can be lost in clouds as warm humid Atlantic air is forced upwards, cooling to fall as rain or form the mists that envelop elfin forests. Geography and aspect within the islands are often expressed in terms of 'windward' and 'leeward'. On some mountain ranges the windward slopes intercept much of the moisture, leaving drier conditions or rain shadow on the leeward side. As a general rule, seas are rougher and slopes wetter on the exposed windward Atlantic coasts, with calmer seas and less rainfall on the sheltered leeward coasts.

The future is uncertain, with climate change a serious and increasing threat to the region. Predictions are for rising temperatures, rising sea levels and the potential for more intense weather events.

Tropical storms can bring strong winds and heavy rainfall.

Habitats and vegetation

Forest regeneration around the ruins of former plantation buildings.

On these small Caribbean islands, the sea is never far away, the clear blue inshore waters often pierced by rocky outcrops or surf breaking over coral reefs. Coastlines vary from cliffs and scrub-covered headlands to shallow bays edged with pristine sandy beaches. On some low-lying coasts, dense stands of mangroves fringe a variety of wetlands, from wide and open coastal lagoons to small, brackish ponds. Moving inland there are low windswept bushes and cacti in exposed locations; these give way to denser scrub and dry forest. Land at lower elevations may have been cleared for development or agriculture, creating open and modified habitats. On the more mountainous islands, luxuriant rainforests cover the high slopes and streams tumble through ravines (locally known as 'ghauts'). On the highest peaks, often lost in swirling cloud, stunted elfin forest can be found. There are trails on some islands that can take you from the beach to the rainforest in a matter of hours.

Most habitats are easily recognizable, but forests, which predominate throughout the region, are complex and difficult to interpret on the ground, requiring knowledge of characteristic plant communities. Vegetation varies with altitude and is heavily influenced by rainfall and exposure to wind, and further modified by soil type and depth. Broadly, forest habitats can be described as:

- **Scrub and dry forest** at lower elevations, with some deciduous tree species, a distinct dry season, low rainfall and low humidity.
- Transitional, moister **semi-evergreen and evergreen forests** at mid-elevations (although this may be the highest point on some islands, such as the Virgin Islands and Antigua). Here rainfall and humidity increase, especially on windward slopes. From a wildlife perspective, some species in these transitional forests may also be found in either dry forest or rainforest—or both.
- **Rainforest and elfin forest** at higher elevations, with high rainfall and humidity.

In this guide, for simplicity, forest types are referred to as either **scrub and dry forest** or **rainforest and elfin forest.**

Each habitat type has its own dominant or characteristic plant species. Plant diversity is remarkable throughout the wider Caribbean with more than 11,000 species, 72% of which are endemic. The Critical Ecosystem Partnership Fund recognizes the region as one of 36 Global Biodiversity Hotspots and considers it a global priority for nature conservation. In the Eastern Caribbean there are typically more than 1,000 species of plants on each of the larger islands and over 300 on the smaller islands; all island groups have their own endemic or regional endemic species. The number of introduced plant species is increasing: some were brought as crops, others as decorative plants. For example, spectacular trees, such as the Flamboyant Tree or Royal Poinciana *Delonix regia* (originally from Madagascar), is now widely established throughout the Caribbean and wider tropics. Some plants are invasive and detrimental to native flora and fauna: this can present huge conservation challenges, such as with the Coral Vine or Coralita *Antigonon leptopus*, which can smother native vegetation.

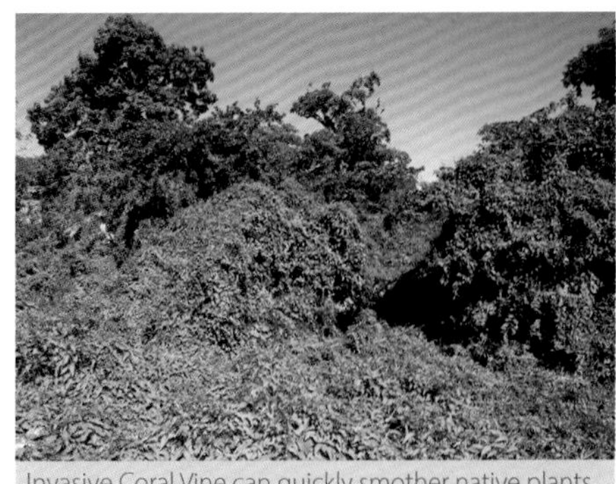
Invasive Coral Vine can quickly smother native plants.

To some extent, all habitats have been altered by humans. The biggest changes by far came with European colonization and the forest clearances that followed. Timber was used for construction and fuel, and extensive areas were cleared for plantation agriculture. Dry and intermediate forests at lower, more accessible, elevations were cleared first, but deforestation continued, pushing higher into rainforests, leaving only relatively small areas of pristine forest. As some agricultural production was abandoned from the beginning of the 19th century, forests were largely left to regenerate, with small areas used for commercial forestry. Today, the presence of former crop plants such as cocoa, coffee and cotton, along with derelict stone walls and buildings, are signs of secondary or regenerating forest.

The main habitats, together with some of their characteristic wildlife, are described in six broad groups:

- **Coasts and inshore waters**
- **Mangroves**
- **Wetlands**
- **Modified land**
- **Scrub and dry forest**
- **Rainforest and elfin forest**

Low coastal scrub with cacti and frangipani.

Coasts and inshore waters

The region's beautiful and often dramatic coastlines are surprisingly varied. They are fantastic places for wildlife and the mainstay of regional tourism.

Warm, shallow waters teem with vibrant marine life. Coral reefs are especially diverse and rich in fish, crustaceans, shellfish and other wildlife. These fragile ecosystems provide a natural buffer against strong seas but are threatened by climate change and pollution.

Close inshore, Green Turtles feed among beds of sea-grass, and seabirds plunge for fish. Offshore, in deeper water, whales and dolphins breed or pass through on migration.

There are many remote small islands and cays where the typically sparse vegetation is able to withstand strong winds and salt spray. Many are 'seabird' islands, with cliffs and open areas of rock providing safe nesting sites for important numbers of terns, tropicbirds and boobies. Endemic groundlizards, skinks and other reptiles have evolved in small isolated populations in the absence of ground predators.

Rugged, heavily fissured cliffs provide nesting sites for tropicbirds and a safe retreat for iguanas, with natural sea-caves holding some of the largest bat roosts in the region. Seabirds and shorebirds such as American Oystercatcher feed and find undisturbed

Windward coast, St Martin.

Fraser's Dolphins (*p. 162*), a specialty of the region.

Hawksbill Turtle (*p. 232*) foraging over a coral reef.

Offshore islands: St Barthélemy, with Île Frégate Nature Reserve (*middle*).

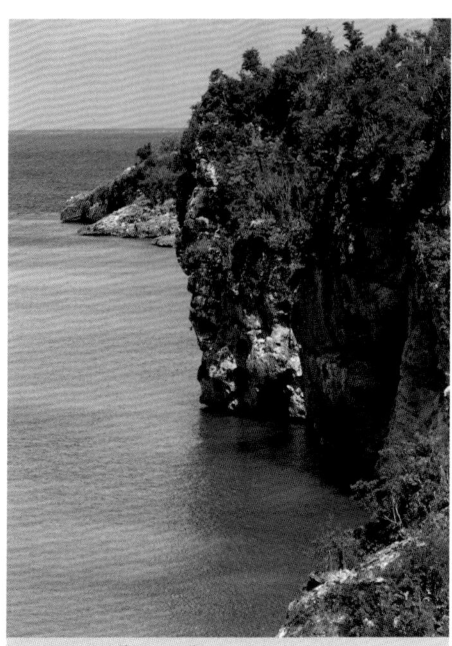
Limestone cliffs, Anguilla.

roosts along low rocky coasts. Sally Lightfoot Crabs can be common on wave-swept rocks.

Caribbean islands are famous for their beaches and sheltered bays. Ruddy Turnstone, Sanderling and other shorebirds feed along the tideline and will forage on the occasional influxes of sargassum seaweed. Sea turtles seek out quiet, unlit beaches for egg-laying, and small holes and tracks in the sand are signs of the impressive Atlantic Ghost Crab.

Atlantic Ghost Crab (*p. 240*) on an undisturbed beach.

Sheltered bay, Tortola, British Virgin Islands.

Mangroves

Mangrove trees form swamps and green fringes to many shorelines and saline lagoons. Four species are found in the Eastern Caribbean: Red, Black and White Mangroves, with Buttonwood on the drier, landward margins. Mangroves withstand varying, often tough, conditions: high levels of salinity; periodic inundation from storms; freshwater flows from rivers and rainwater; waterlogged and oxygen-poor sediments; constant drying winds; and seasonal, parched, drought-like periods.

Mangroves are a vital but vulnerable habitat. They occur in patches around many islands, but the UN Food and Agriculture Organization reported that between 1980 and 2005 the region's mangroves were reduced in area by 17% to 7,813 hectares (19,306 acres). Often undervalued, mangroves were lost through coastal and urban development, infilling, dumping and over-extraction of timber. In the face of climate change their value in coastal resilience is increasingly recognized, and there are a growing number of protection and restoration projects.

Mangroves are beneficial habitats, creating a natural buffer against waves and storms. Their elaborate root systems trap sediments and nutrients from inland run-off, protecting coral reefs and marine habitats. They provide a refuge and nursery ground for fish, making them commercially important; fallen mangrove leaves and detritus are the base of a food web that includes fish, shrimps and other crustaceans. Their value for wildlife tourism is increasingly recognized, with a growing number of sites providing access through boardwalks or boat trips.

Mangroves support an array of specialist wildlife. Pelicans, egrets and herons nest and roost in mature trees, and a wide range of birds forage among the tangle of roots, including Yellow-crowned Night Heron, Sora and Northern Waterthrush. The burrows of Blue Land Crabs can be obvious on the muddy floor, and fiddler crabs, sometimes in huge numbers, can be found along the more open margins.

Mangrove swamp, Antigua.

Red Mangrove *Rhizophora mangle* grows on the 'front line', where waves meet land, aerial prop roots providing stability.

The short, pencil-like roots ('pneumatophores') of Black Mangrove *Avicennia germinans* grow vertically from the main submerged root system to act as 'breathing roots' above the oxygen-poor sediment.

White Mangrove *Laguncularia racemosa* has thick, leathery leaves and small, inconspicuous flowers and seed-pods.

Buttonwood *Conocarpus erectus* grows along drier, landward margins. Leaves are narrow and pointed, flowers and fruiting heads growing in more obvious clusters than mangroves.

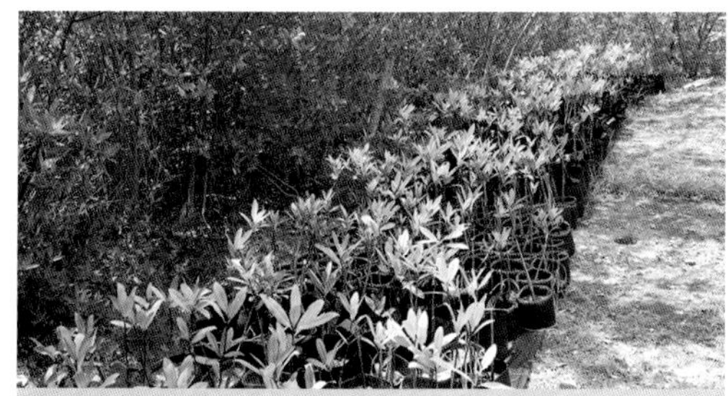

Young mangrove plants ready for planting at a restoration project.

Colony of Blue (Great) Land Crabs (*p. 242*).

Juvenile Yellow-crowned Night Heron (*p. 96*).

Wetlands

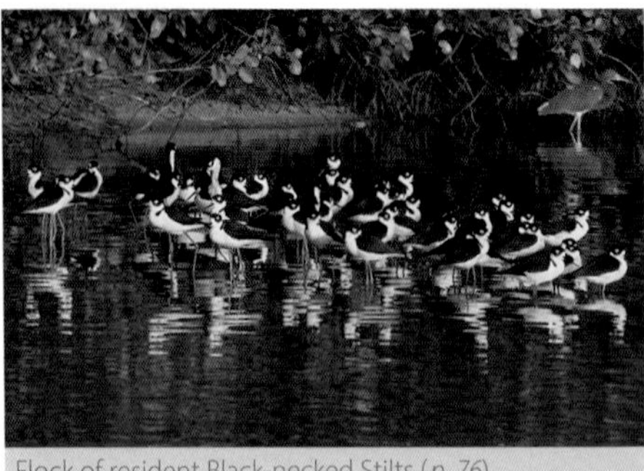

Flock of resident Black-necked Stilts (*p. 76*).

Salt-pond walls.

The wetlands of the Eastern Caribbean are varied and dynamic. Together they form a vital network for breeding and migratory waterbirds, and the marginal or fringing vegetation that surrounds most wetland habitats attracts reptiles, amphibians, crabs and dragonflies.

Shallow brackish wetlands occur on many low-lying coasts and are mostly separated from the sea by mangroves, beaches or dune systems. Saline lagoons, which are connected to the sea or periodically inundated by storm surges, tend to be larger and more open. Some were used as salt-ponds; lines of low walls are a sign of former salt production. Many ponds are seasonal, with water levels and salinity fluctuating through rainfall and evaporation. These important wetlands can teem with flies, shrimps, worms and crustaceans, which provide food for a wide range of fish, crabs and waterbirds.

Freshwater wetlands can be scarce but include low-lying marshes, spring-fed or seasonal ponds, crater lakes in rainforests, man-made reservoirs, irrigation ponds and ditches. Many have emergent and floating vegetation and are rich in invertebrates, attracting dragonflies and waterbirds, especially ducks and grebes.

Saline lagoons attract large numbers of waterbirds.

Rivers and streams are a feature of mountain rainforests, often plunging over spectacular waterfalls. They flow through gullies ('ghauts') and valleys, where bats and dragonflies forage over pools and along bankside vegetation. In some catchments they are intercepted to provide vital drinking water. At lower elevations short stretches of slow-flowing river ultimately reach the coast, often in forest swamps and sandy, brackish estuaries.

Crater lakes are some of the largest freshwater wetlands.

Wetlands provide flood alleviation and water storage following storm surges and heavy rainfall. They help protect marine environments through filtration, and by intercepting silt, run-off and pollutants. They serve as fertile spawning grounds for fish, shellfish and crustaceans, and are an attraction for wildlife tourism, with many providing accessible opportunities for close-up views of waterbirds.

Temporary rainwater pools often form on grassland, drawing in dragonflies, Western Cattle-Egrets and flocks of migratory waterbirds—especially American Golden-Plover and Pectoral Sandpiper.

Despite their benefits, wetlands are often undervalued, and many remain vulnerable to direct loss through infilling, pollution and especially coastal development, including conversion of coastal lagoons to marinas. Invasive plants such as Common Water Hyacinth *Pontederia crassipes* block precious freshwater ponds and watercourses, reducing flow with adverse impacts on native wetland species.

Rainforest stream.

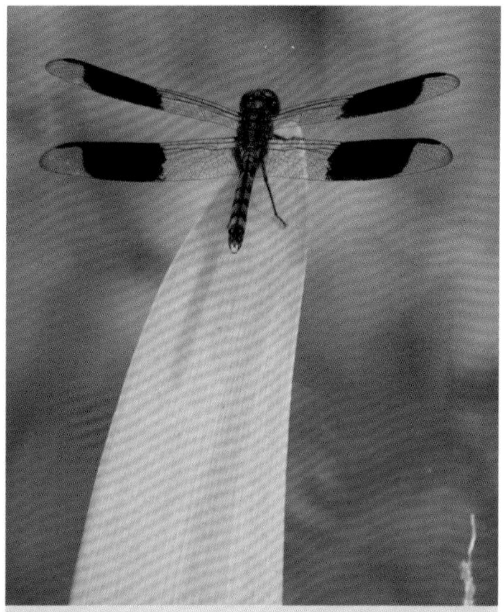

Band-winged Dragonlet (*p. 256*), one of the most common and familiar dragonflies.

Modified land

Natural habitats have been modified over many centuries. Indigenous people from South America established the first settlements and brought the first crops, but the most dramatic changes came with the early European settlers, who cleared extensive areas of forest for agriculture and building materials. The most significant recent and ongoing changes include increases in built development, infrastructure and amenity grassland.

Agriculture is often small-scale for personal consumption and local markets, but some larger islands have more extensive areas in agricultural production, mainly for sugar, bananas, citrus fruit and spices. Livestock farming is largely restricted to cattle, goats and sheep, which often range freely in scrubby habitats. Irrigation ponds, ditches and grassy or flower-rich field margins provide a range of seeds and nectar sources that attract doves, finches, reptiles and invertebrates, including butterflies and dragonflies.

Natural grassland or savanna is generally scarce but can occur on hills and in hollows with dry conditions and shallow soils. More widespread are low-cut, managed grasslands, including airfields, sports fields and golf courses. These grasslands, which can be rich in soil invertebrates, attract ground-feeding birds such as Western Cattle-Egrets, doves, Carib Grackles and Shiny Cowbirds, while flycatchers, mockingbirds and introduced finches readily use perimeter fencing as vantage points.

Built-up areas, especially around ports, provide opportunities for pigeons, gulls, small rodents and other scavengers. A number of reptiles, amphibians and birds, such as House Sparrow, have been accidental introductions, with many establishing localized populations.

Gardens and hotel grounds with native planting, fruit trees and a range of flowering plants attract hummingbirds, fruit-eating bats, lizards and amphibians, as well as dragonflies, butterflies and a range of other invertebrates. Mature botanic gardens with a mix of formal and informal planting are among the best and most easily accessible places to see a wide variety of wildlife.

Small-scale agriculture.

Commercial banana crop.

Large-scale sugar production.

Shiny Cowbirds (*p. 144*).

Development around busy port.

Well-established botanic gardens are on many islands.

Julia Heliconian (*p. 288*), Martinique.

Scrub and dry forest

Scrub and dry forest habitats range from open, sparsely vegetated, rocky ground, through low, often thorny shrubs and trees to moist closed-canopy forest. They form in areas where there is an extended dry season and low annual rainfall. In response many tree species are deciduous, and wildlife has adapted to seasonal differences. On low-lying limestone islands these habitats form the climax vegetation, and on mountainous islands they cover the lower slopes. Many of these forest areas are secondary forests, naturally regenerating following historic clearance.

On rocky ground, especially along exposed Atlantic coasts, cacti and low-growing plants are able to tolerate thin soils, sea spray and drought. In some areas littoral forests occur along the coasts: here trees and shrubs are short and sculptured by constant drying winds.

Away from exposed coasts and bare rock, scrub thickens and can become impenetrable. Deciduous trees and shrubs create leaf litter where groundlizards and dwarf geckos forage for invertebrates. Clearings and margins can be rich in flowering plants, attracting hummingbirds and nectaring butterflies. Antillean Nighthawk is a specialty species that breeds in this habitat.

Closed-canopy dry forests with taller trees are found in sheltered valleys and on lower slopes. There are subtle variations in tree and plant communities, influenced by altitude, exposure, soil and especially rainfall, which is heavier on the windward side of an island (*p. 13*). The forest floor is often thick in leaf litter and rich in invertebrates, attracting lizards and forest birds such as quail-doves and thrashers. Forest butterflies and dragonflies can be common along sunny open trails and in clearings.

Scrub and dry forests are often undervalued despite their specialist wildlife interest. Many endemic species, such as the Critically Endangered Grenada Dove, are now restricted to small or discrete areas. Habitat loss and fragmentation through development, predation by invasive mammals and overgrazing by goats remain serious conservation threats to both the habitat and its wildlife.

Most islands have areas of coastal scrub and mature dry forest.

Vegetation is sparse along windswept rocky coasts.

Leaf litter on semi-deciduous forest floor.

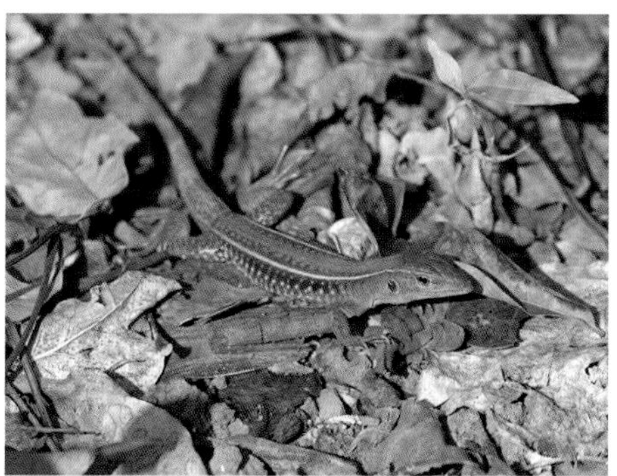
Common Puerto Rican Groundlizard (*p. 190*) foraging in dry leaf litter.

Many islands have well-managed trails through dry forests.

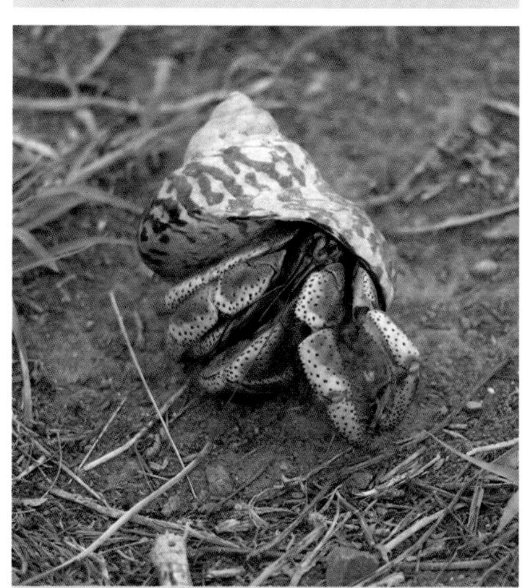
Caribbean Land Hermit Crab (*p. 240*) crossing a trail.

Grenada Dove (*p. 104*) is categorized as globally Critically Endangered.

Rainforest and elfin forest

Elfin (cloud) forest, a rare habitat found only on the highest peaks.

Tropical rainforests with towering trees, a high canopy, luxuriant vegetation and shady forest floor can be awe-inspiring. They cover the high volcanic slopes and are rich in plant and animal species, many found nowhere else on earth. Where clouds form and catch the highest peaks, elfin (cloud) forest develops. Here, ferns, grasses and stunted trees grow in the cooler, windier conditions and, shrouded in mist, create a rare and atmospheric habitat.

Majestic trees reaching 30 m (98 ft) or more form a closed canopy, restricting sunlight below. The hot and humid conditions enable epiphytic ferns, bromeliads and orchids to thrive. Foraging fruit- and pollen-eating bats help with seed dispersal and pollination.

The mid-story is often a tangle of shrubs, climbing vines and trailing roots. Where gaps occur from fallen trees, shafts of sunlight trigger prolific new growth. Forest birds, snakes, lizards, land crabs, dragonflies and butterflies are all seen from trails but can be elusive.

Ferns and mosses dominate the damp forest floor, and plant and animal matter is quickly recycled by invertebrates and fungi. Tree roots run along the surface or rise as impressive buttresses.

Rainforest covers the mountainous interior of many islands.

Pristine (primary) rainforest is incredibly rich in biodiversity but substantially reduced by historic clearance. Much of what remains is secondary forest, which continues to regenerate following agricultural abandonment and periodic damage from hurricanes and volcanic flows.

The importance of rainforests is widely recognized. They are essential freshwater catchments on many islands, and the forest structure slows water run-off, which reduces flooding, soil erosion and landslides, especially during intense rainfall. Most islands with extensive forested areas have Forestry or National Park departments working on conservation programs, and access is often provided through a growing number of visitor trails and facilities. The rainforests' amazing biodiversity contributes to an expanding wildlife tourism sector.

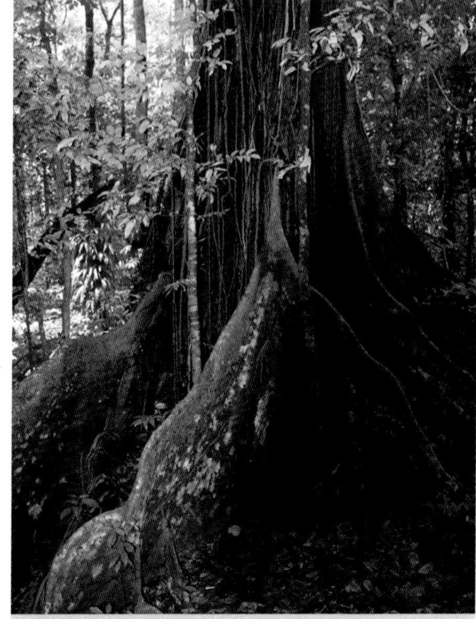
Huge trees include *Sloanea* spp. With impressive buttress roots, they are rainforest giants.

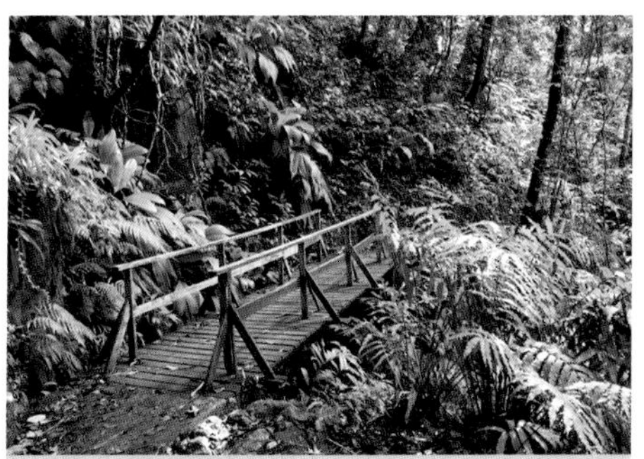
There are impressive and dramatic rainforest trails on many islands.

St Lucia Dwarf Gecko (*p. 213*).

Prolific growth on the rainforest floor.

The endemic Yellow Land Crab (*p. 243*) can be an unexpected sighting in a rainforest.

Conservation

The islands of the Eastern Caribbean make up only 3% of the total Caribbean land area but hold a remarkable number of endemic birds, bats, amphibians, reptiles, invertebrates and plants. Goal 15 of the UN Sustainable Development Goals aims to: "Protect, restore and promote sustainable use of terrestrial ecosystems, sustainably manage forests, combat desertification, and halt and reverse land degradation and halt biodiversity loss." These objectives bring their own particular challenges to the Eastern Caribbean:

- Land areas are small; a tiny rocky outcrop can hold the total world population of a globally threatened species of lizard, and the entire range of some bird species may be limited to a few small forest fragments.
- Invasive, non-native plants and animals are becoming established at an alarming rate and exert massive and adverse impacts on native flora and fauna.
- Habitats are being lost or fragmented and damaged as a result of new development, the unpredictable effects of climate change including hurricanes and storm surges, and periodic localized volcanic activity.

Historic events have had significant impacts on the wildlife of the region. Changes were slow at first with the arrival of indigenous people from South America approximately 4,000 years ago. They moved between islands by canoe and were initially hunter-gatherers, but subsequent arrivals established villages and cleared land to cultivate crops, including Cassava. It is thought that they introduced Common Red-rumped Agouti and Red-footed Tortoise as food sources, and possibly other species.

Towards the end of the 16th century the first European settlers arrived, starting a process of extensive forest clearance for commercial crops and buildings. Livestock and domestic animals—including cattle, pigs, goats, chickens, dogs and cats—were introduced; rats and mice were accidental arrivals off sailing ships. By the late 19th century Small Indian Mongoose had been deliberately introduced to many islands to control rats and snakes; similarly, South American Cane Toad was brought in to control invertebrates in sugar plantations. Collectively, the effects on native wildlife have been devastating. Habitat loss and the newly introduced predators resulted in a wave of extinctions, especially among reptiles. Small Indian Mongoose,

On Antigua, McKinnon's Salt Pond Important Bird and Biodiversity Area (IBA) is one of the most important and easily accessible sites for waterbirds in the Lesser Antilles.

in particular, is implicated in the population reduction or total extinction of many species.

Island-restoration projects are benefiting seabirds and reptiles such as Redonda Anole (*p. 200*).

The range and variety of non-native plant and animal species that have become established in the region have increased considerably in the last 50 years. Some species arrived accidentally among imports of exotic plants for landscaping or shipments of building materials. Birds and reptiles, in particular, have been brought in through the pet trade; many have either escaped or been released. Several of these introduced species are now considered invasive and a threat to native wildlife and habitats.

Recent changes in land use have seen increases in infrastructure, leading to some habitat loss and fragmentation, and the growing tourism sector has put particular pressure on coastal habitats.

The region is responding to these challenges. Many forest reserves and National Parks have been created that are managed by government forestry departments or National Park Trusts. Some forests are protected as essential catchments for freshwater, which is in limited supply on many islands. In addition to local reviews and designations, a rigorous scientific review led by BirdLife International identified 112 Important Bird and Biodiversity Areas (IBAs) across the islands, covering 202,742 hectares (501,000 acres). A number of Marine Protected Areas (MPAs) have been established in coastal waters—with more proposed—for the protection of fish, marine mammal and sea turtle populations, coral reefs, sea-grass beds and mangroves.

Many species in the region, including more than 100 in this guide, are listed as globally threatened by the International Union for Conservation of Nature (IUCN) on the Red List of Threatened Species (iucnredlist.org). This global inventory provides the conservation status for species around the world. It is used to help set international and national conservation priorities and provides a framework to monitor their status and to develop action plans. In this guide the IUCN status is indicated for all species under global threat.

The scale of many of these conservation challenges is huge. Cooperation between governments, local and national conservation organizations, international non-governmental organization (NGO) partners and research bodies including universities is tackling species recovery and habitat restoration, backed by vital funding. Examples of current conservation projects include:

- Mangrove restoration, where plants are grown locally and used to restore this vital habitat (*p. 18*) for the benefit of both biodiversity and local communities.
- Well-established and successful species-recovery projects, especially for parrots, amphibians and reptiles, which involve monitoring, captive breeding and translocation, together with education and awareness programs.
- The control of invasive plant and animal species.
- Island-restoration projects, which have been successful on smaller offshore islands and cays, removing feral goats and eradicating rats and mice, to the benefit of plant communities, rare endemic reptiles and important populations of breeding seabirds.

Wildlife watching

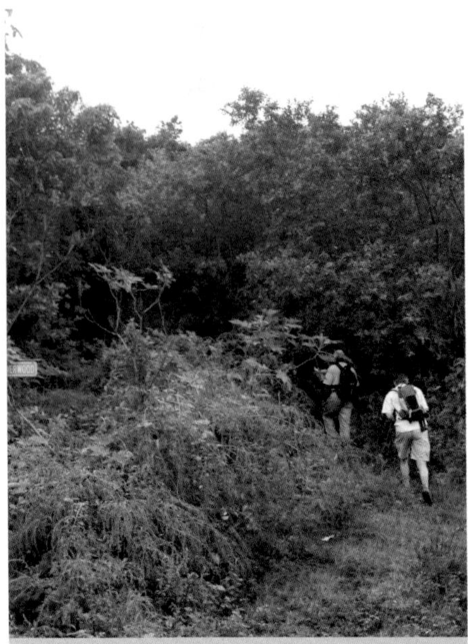

Experienced guides can be invaluable in navigating forest trails and helping to find elusive species.

Watching wildlife on these islands can be as straightforward as taking a walk along a beach or through any other natural habitat. You will come across seabirds in coastal waters, land crabs and waterbirds in mangroves and coastal wetlands, and a whole range of birds, reptiles and invertebrates in scrub and forest as you move farther inland. Species that are only found high in rainforests, however, take more planning and effort to find!

Be prepared and take precautions when spending time in the field, and always carry water and sun protection. Most trails at lower elevations are gentle and steady, but in rainforests they are usually steeper and uneven, and can be slippery. Tropical weather can be unpredictable, especially during the rainy season when there may be sudden heavy downpours. Mosquitoes and other biting insects can be a nuisance, more so after rain and at dusk, and especially around swampy wetlands. Snakes are rarely encountered and should never be disturbed; venomous snakes occur only on Martinique and St Lucia. Any snake bite is extremely rare but should always be treated immediately. A local guide can be invaluable for safely navigating trails and in helping to find the more elusive species.

Seasonality is particularly important for birdwatching. Between August and April migratory waterbirds and landbirds from North America can be found throughout the region, and there is always the chance of finding a rare visitor! Terns and other seabirds return to breed in April after wintering at sea and are reliably seen until September. Seabirds and cetaceans can be an unexpected sighting from any ferry crossing or sailing trip. Organized whale-watching trips are available on several islands and take place year-round, but the peak time for seeing both resident and migratory species is November to March.

We hope that this guide encourages you to get out and about to enjoy wildlife. Be sensitive in the field, try not to disturb any species, especially in the breeding season, and you can enjoy some amazing wildlife encounters. Try to support conservation wherever you can and be aware of illegal or damaging activities, such as buying or taking coral, or disturbing turtle-nesting beaches. Feedback on wildlife tourism is useful for hotels, NGOs, tourism and other government departments. There are volunteering opportunities for many conservation projects in the region, but by simply providing details of your sightings locally or through iNaturalist and eBird, you can make an enormous contribution to data, helping improve knowledge and understanding of the region's wildlife.

Introduction to the island groups

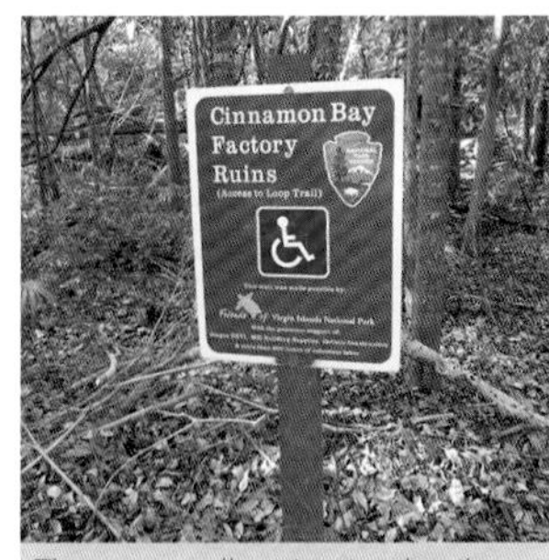

There are well-maintained trails on most islands.

Seventeen island groups are covered in this guide. For each there is a brief introduction to the wildlife highlights, with a list of endemic, restricted-range or specialty species. This is not comprehensive. For example, it may not include species found only on smaller, inaccessible islets and cays, which are listed within the relevant species accounts. Publicly owned or managed visitor sites on each island group are suggested: these cover a variety of habitats and provide opportunities to find a good range of species. Many are well-established National Parks or visitor sites with a range of facilities, including managed trails and boardwalks (some may incur a charge, as indicated by $). Note that visitor sites may be affected by naturally occurring weather events or volcanic activity. Access, especially for wheelchairs, can be particularly difficult in forest habitats. Where there is some level of accessibility, this is indicated by ♿, but it could be limited and should be checked. The Caribbean Birding Trail (caribbeanbirdingtrail.org), developed by Birds Caribbean, gives information on other sites that are good for birds and a whole range of wildlife, along with details of local tour guides. More information on accessible sites can be found on their Birdability pages.

Wildlife hikes are organized on several islands.

For up-to-date information and details of guided walks or events, check with local tourist boards and nature conservation organizations, including National Trusts, Forestry Departments and National Park services.

Accessible boardwalk through mangrove-fringed lagoon.

The Virgin Islands

USVI—347 km² (133 sq. miles), Crown Mountain, St Thomas 474 m (1,555 ft)
BVI—151 km² (58 sq. miles), Mount Sage, Tortola 523 m (1,716 ft)

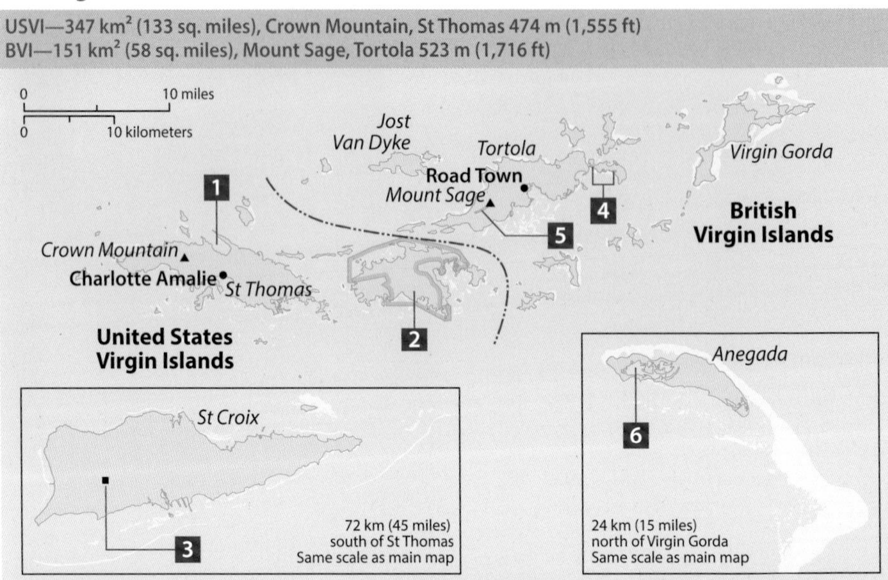

The US and British Virgin Islands comprise a single archipelago with good inter-island ferry services. Fifteen species of seabird breed, many of which can be seen over inshore waters, and extensive wetlands and mangroves attract large numbers of waterbirds and dragonflies. Scrub and dry forests hold endemic amphibians and reptiles, several shared with Puerto Rico, together with some butterflies and migratory warblers that are uncommon in the Lesser Antilles.

Single-island endemics	Anegada Rock Iguana CR, St Croix Anole, St Croix Dwarf Gecko EN
Restricted-range endemics	Puerto Rican Owl, Puerto Rican Mango, Puerto Rican Flycatcher, Adelaide's Warbler, Puerto Rican Red-eyed Frog, Antillean White-lipped Frog, Common Puerto Rican Groundlizard, Puerto Rican Crested Anole, Puerto Rican Anole, Puerto Rican Spotted Anole, Puerto Rican Eye-spotted Dwarf Gecko , Virgin Islands Dwarf Gecko EN, Virgin Islands Boa EN, Virgin Islands Miniracer

Virgin Islands archipelago.

UNITED STATES VIRGIN ISLANDS (USVI)

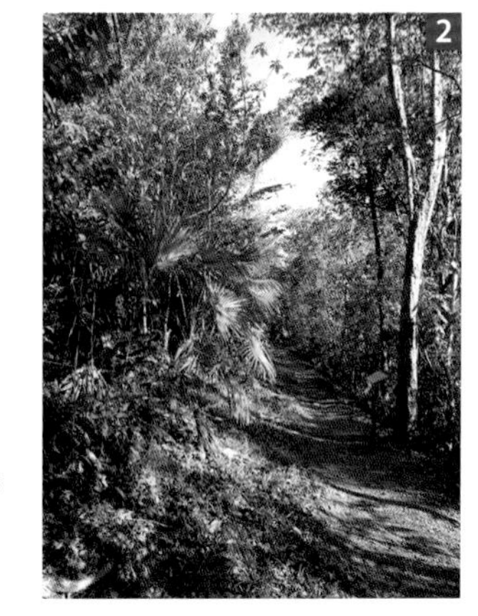

$ 1 **Magens Bay, St Thomas** (Public/private ownership and management) Secluded bay and beach with visitor facilities. A boardwalk and well-managed trails take you through mangroves and dry forest, then up into moist semi-evergreen forest, providing opportunities to see a wide range of birds, reptiles, land crabs and butterflies. Also, seabirds can be seen close inshore.

2 **Virgin Islands National Park, St John** (Managed by the US National Parks Service) A network of well-managed trails and boardwalks through a range of habitats from coastal wetlands to forests, with an impressive range of wildlife. This extensive National Park covers over 60% of the island, and the National Park Service runs a program of activities. Information can be found at the centralized Cruz Bay Visitor Center.

$ 3 **St George Village Botanical Garden, St Croix** (Managed by local trust) A 6.5-hectare (16-acre) historical site with easy access and a wide range of visitor facilities. Trails lead through extensive plant collections with formal ponds and gardens that are especially good for St Croix Anole, dragonflies and butterflies.

BRITISH VIRGIN ISLANDS (BVI)

Tortola Wetlands (Public/private ownership) Mangrove-fringed brackish wetlands include Josiah's Bay Pond and the more accessible Beef Island ponds 4, which have some good perimeter viewing. Together the wetlands hold impressive numbers of waterbirds, fiddler and mangrove crabs and dragonflies.

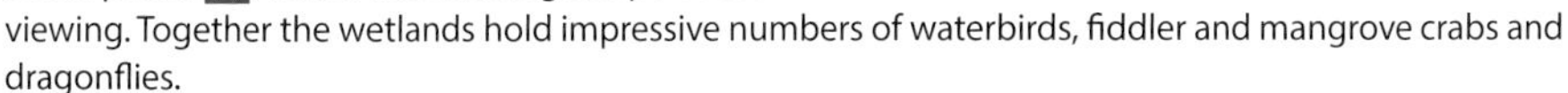

$ 5 **Sage Mountain National Park, Tortola** (One of several sites managed by National Parks Trust of the British Virgin Islands) Visitor center and trails through scrub, dry forest and areas of moist evergreen forest at the highest point of BVI. Good for a range of forest birds and butterflies.

6 **Anegada** Low-lying limestone island with scrub, dry forest and some of the most extensive and undisturbed areas of mangrove and brackish wetlands in the region. This is one of the best places to see migratory waterbirds. Specialties include a colony of American Flamingo, Anegada Rock Iguana and endemic butterflies.

Anguilla

91 km² (35 sq. miles), Crocus Hill 65 m (213 ft)

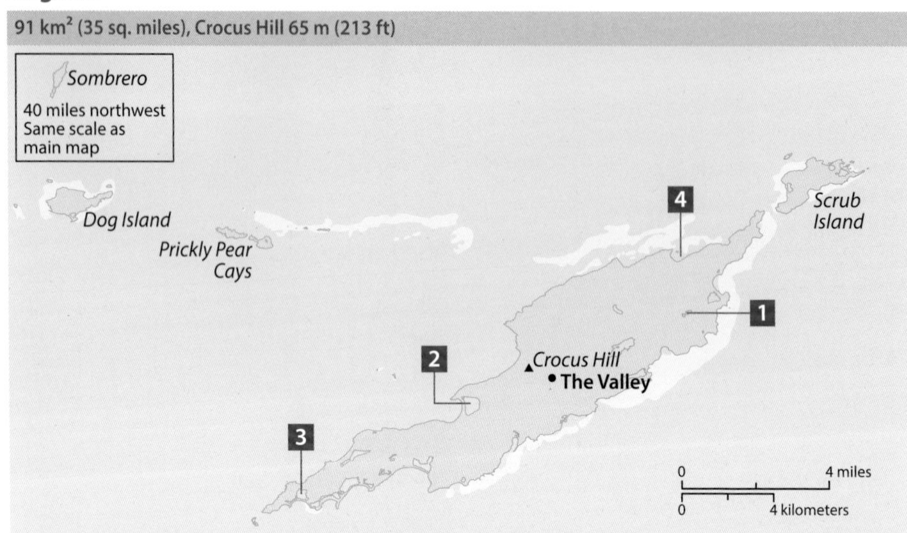

A low-lying island with extensive areas of limestone scrub and more than 20 large freshwater and brackish wetlands, which make it one of the best places in the Eastern Caribbean for close-up views of waterbirds. Smaller offshore islands hold internationally important numbers of breeding seabirds and rare endemic reptiles.

Single-island endemics	Reptiles on offshore islands
Restricted-range endemics	Lesser Antillean Iguana CR, Anguilla Bank Groundlizard, Anguilla Bank Tree Anole, Anguilla Bank Dwarf Gecko, Leeward Banded Dwarf Gecko, Anguilla Bank Racer EN
Specialty species	Snowy Plover NT, Red-footed Tortoise, Green Turtle EN

Anguilla wetlands (Public/private ownership) Some of the most varied wetlands in the region: many have accessible perimeter viewing. Waterbirds include White-cheeked Pintail, Black-necked Stilt and migratory shorebirds.

1 East End Pond (Managed by the Anguilla National Trust) A seasonal wetland with marginal vegetation and hillside scrub.

2 Road Salt Pond Shallow former salt-pond with sea channel, sandbanks, marshes and hillside scrub.

3 West End Pond Former salt-pond bisected by a causeway road, with areas of mud and fringing mangroves.

4 Island Harbour and northern coastline Inshore waters and sheltered bay with sea-grass beds that are good for a range of seabirds and attract foraging Green Turtles. Rugged cliffs and rocky cactus scrub along the northern coast can be difficult to access but hold populations of reptiles, including Lesser Antillean Iguana.

1

2

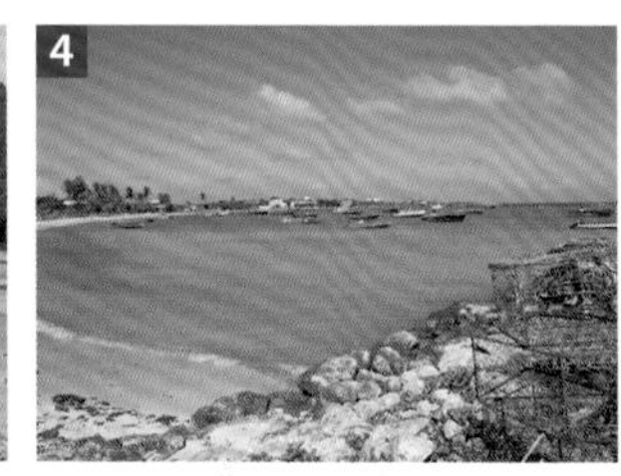
4

St Martin/Sint Maarten

87 km² (33 sq. miles), Pic Paradis 425 m (1,394 ft)

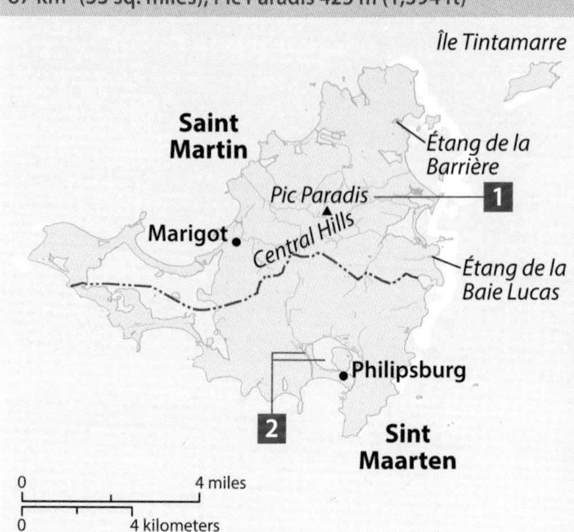

Part French, part Dutch, both sides of the island have areas of scrub, dry forest and some easily accessible coastal lagoons and ponds, which are great places to see reptiles, crabs and a range of waterbirds. Seabirds breed on the rocky islets and offshore cays and can be seen feeding over inshore waters.

Single-island endemics	Anguilla Bank Bush Anole, Sint Maarten Thick-tailed Gecko
Restricted-range endemics	Anguilla Bank Tree Anole, Anguilla Bank Groundlizard, Anguilla Bank Dwarf Gecko, Leeward Banded Dwarf Gecko
Specialty species	Breeding seabirds, including Least Tern

St Martin wetlands (Public/private ownership) Series of brackish wetlands with fringing mangroves and scrub, including **Étang de la Barrière** and **Étang de la Baie Lucas**, both managed by Réserve Naturelle de Saint-Martin. Some accessible viewpoints and boardwalks.

$ **1 Pic Paradis** and central hills, **St Martin** (Public/Private ownership) Tracks and trails through scrub and dry forest for a good range of forest birds including Scaly-breasted Thrasher, reptiles and butterflies. Can be reached by public road or trail from Loterie Farm.

2 Great Salt-pond and Fresh Pond, Sint Maarten (Public/private ownership) Large, expansive ponds with mangrove; fringes attract a variety of waterbirds, including Black-crowned Night Heron. Limited perimeter viewing.

Wetland with cactus scrub.

Étang de la Barrière.

St Barthélemy (St Barths)

21 km² (8 sq. miles), Morne Du Vitet 286 m (938 ft)

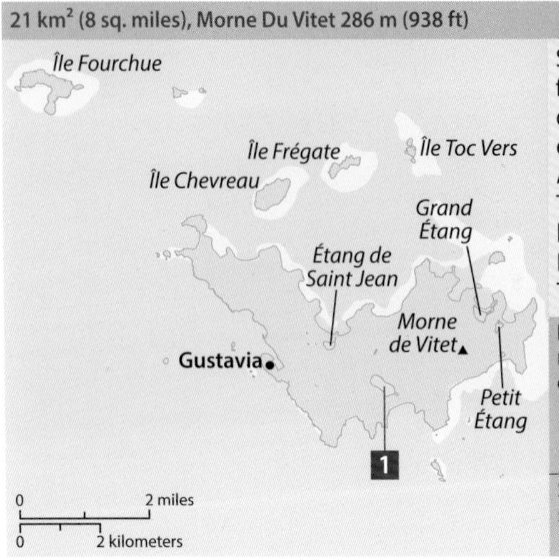

Small, low-lying island with mangrove-fringed wetlands and areas of grassland, dry scrub and forest, which hold some easy-to-see populations of Lesser Antillean Iguana and Red-footed Tortoise. The many small islets and rocky outcrops have breeding populations of tropicbirds, Brown Booby, Laughing Gull and Royal Tern.

Restricted-range endemics	Lesser Antillean Iguana CR, Anguilla Bank Groundlizard, Anguilla Bank Tree Anole, Anguilla Bank Dwarf Gecko, Leeward Banded Dwarf Gecko, Anguilla Bank Racer EN
Specialty species	White-tailed Tropicbird, Red-billed Tropicbird, White-crowned Pigeon NT, Red-footed Tortoise

1 Étang de Salinas Large salt-pond with perimeter viewing, which attracts breeding Least Tern and migratory waterbirds. Adjoining beach, dunes and scrub are good for Anguilla Bank Groundlizard and butterflies.

Other brackish wetlands with limited perimeter viewing include **Grand Étang** (Grand Cul-de-Sac), **Petit Étang** and **Étang de Saint Jean**, which has recently benefited from extensive restoration and the installation of a new boardwalk.

Grassland and hillside scrub.

Cactus scrub, offshore islands and St Martin in the distance.

Saba

13 km² (5 sq. miles), Mount Scenery 887 m (2,910 ft)

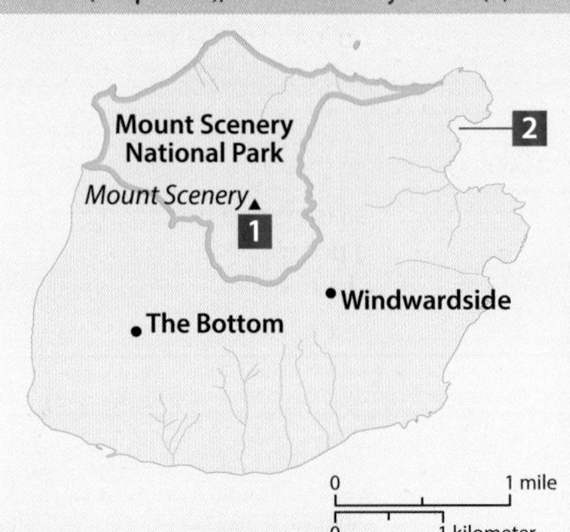

Small volcanic island with spectacular cliffs, which are one of the best places in the region to see Red-billed Tropicbird. There is an impressive network of managed trails, including to the peak of Mount Scenery, where you can experience mist-shrouded elfin forest. Saba Anole is widespread, and Caribbean Black Iguana can be seen around mature gardens and forest margins.

Single-island endemics	Saba Anole NT
Restricted-range endemics	Caribbean Black Iguana CR, St Kitts Bank Dwarf Gecko, Red-bellied Racer VU
Specialty species	Sargasso Shearwater, Red-billed Tropicbird, Scaly-breasted Thrasher

1 Mount Scenery (Managed by Saba Conservation Foundation) A steep trail climbs through rainforest to elfin forest and includes 1,064 steps! On the way look for Ruddy Daggerwing butterfly and forest birds, including Brown Trembler and Purple-throated Carib.

♿ **2 Cove Bay** Spectacular cliffs and rocky hillsides with low-lying scrub and accessible viewing from the roadside. A great place to see displaying Red-billed Tropicbirds. Saba Anole can be found on surrounding rocks.

St Eustatius (Statia)

21 km² (8 sq. miles), The Quill 602 m (1,975 ft)

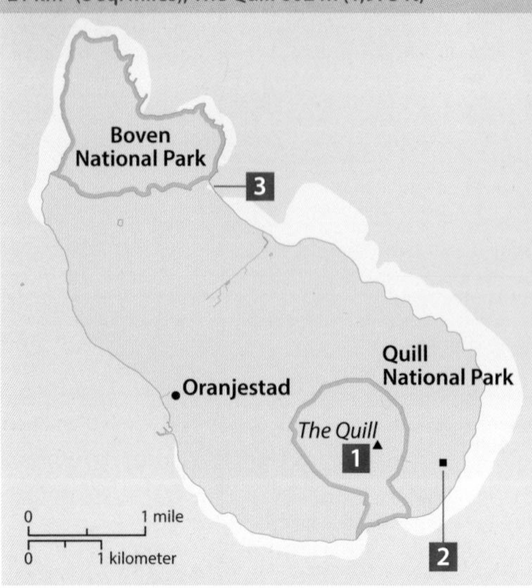

An island of contrasts, from arid grassland, cactus and acacia scrub on the rocky northeast coast of Boven National Park to dense forests on the slopes of The Quill. The National Park Visitor Center provides details of events and local wildlife. Lesser Antillean Iguana can be seen around the seafront at Oranjestad, and seabirds occur close inshore, especially breeding Red-billed Tropicbird.

Restricted-range endemics	Lesser Antillean Iguana CR, Red-faced Groundlizard NT, St Kitts Bank Bush Anole, St Kitts Bank Tree Anole, St Kitts Bank Dwarf Gecko, Leeward Banded Dwarf Gecko, Red-bellied Racer VU
Specialty species	Red-billed Tropicbird, Red-tailed Hawk, Scaly-breasted Thrasher

Seafront at Oranjestad.

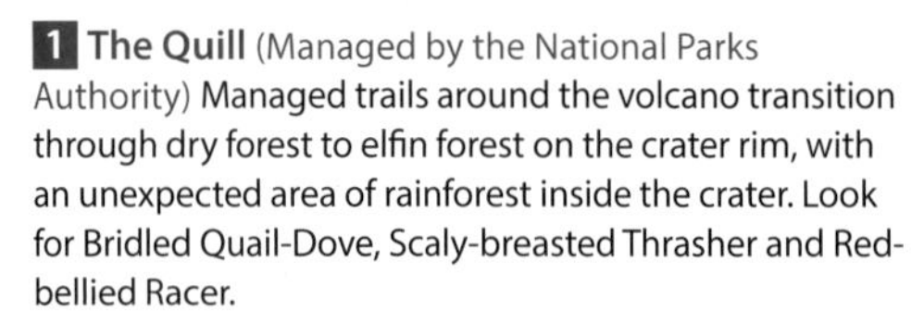

1 The Quill (Managed by the National Parks Authority) Managed trails around the volcano transition through dry forest to elfin forest on the crater rim, with an unexpected area of rainforest inside the crater. Look for Bridled Quail-Dove, Scaly-breasted Thrasher and Red-bellied Racer.

♿ 2 Miriam Schmidt Botanical Gardens (Managed by the National Parks Authority) Paths through informal gardens with native flora, dry forest and sea views. Good for a range of wildlife, including hummingbirds, Red-faced Groundlizard and anoles.

3 Zeelandia Beach and Cliffs Walk along the top of the cliffs for displaying Red-billed Tropicbirds. Migratory shorebirds can be seen along the beach, which is an important protected area for nesting sea turtles.

St Kitts and Nevis

St Kitts—168 km² (64 sq. miles), Mount Liamuiga 1,156 m (3,793 ft)
Nevis—93 km² (35 sq. miles), Nevis Peak 985 m (3,232 ft)

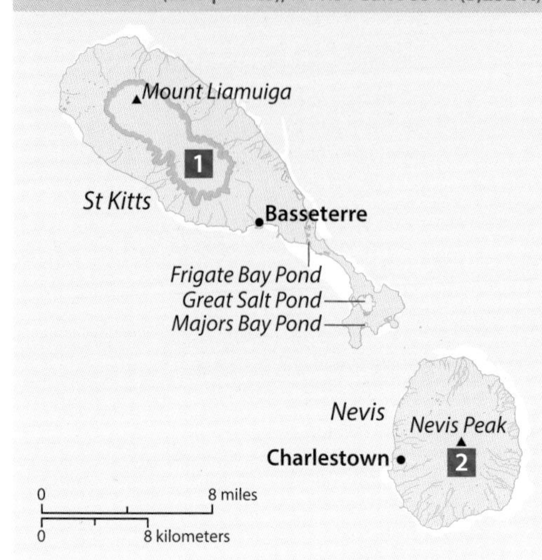

St Kitts, the larger of the two islands, has extensive wetlands that provide opportunities to see a wide range of waterbirds, including White-cheeked Pintail. Seabirds and Green Turtles can be seen from the regular ferry crossing to Nevis. Both islands have dramatic volcanic peaks with managed trails through dry forest and rainforest where endemic reptiles, forest birds and butterflies can be seen.

Restricted-range endemics	Lesser Antillean Flycatcher, Brown Trembler, Red-faced Groundlizard NT, St Kitts Bank Bush Anole, St Kitts Bank Tree Anole, St Kitts Bank Dwarf Gecko, Leeward Banded Dwarf Gecko, Red-bellied Racer VU
Specialty species	Wilson's Plover, migratory waterbirds

St Kitts Wetlands (Public/private ownership) This series of saline and brackish ponds fringed with mangroves and scrub include **Great Salt Pond, Majors Bay Pond** and **Frigate Bay Pond**, which are good for breeding and migratory waterbirds, including Black-crowned Night Heron and Wilson's Plover. Some accessible track and roadside viewing.

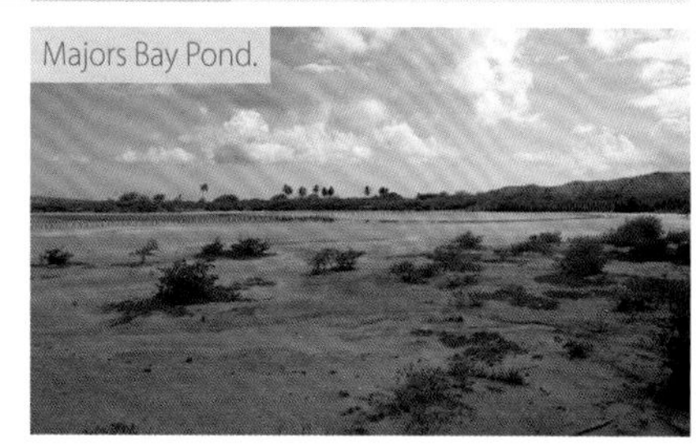
Majors Bay Pond.

1 Central Forest Reserve National Park, St Kitts (Public/private ownership) Managed rainforest trails take you to the crater rim of Mount Liamuiga. This is a steep and difficult climb at higher elevations, and a guide is recommended. Near the base of the trail, look for Lesser Antillean Flycatcher, Brown Trembler and endemic reptiles.

2 Nevis Peak (Public/private ownership) Several managed but difficult rainforest trails on and around Nevis Peak, including Golden Rock Trail; guides are recommended. Highlights include Lesser Antillean Flycatcher, Scaly-breasted Thrasher and Zebra Heliconian butterfly.

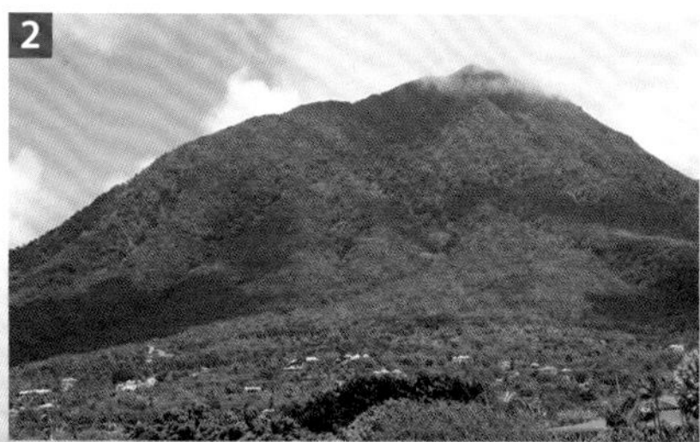

Basseterre: leeward coast looking towards the Central Forest Reserve.

Antigua and Barbuda

Antigua—280 km² (108 sq. miles), Mount Obama (Boggy Peak) 402 m (1,318 ft)
Barbuda—161 km² (62 sq. miles), high point 45 m (148 ft)

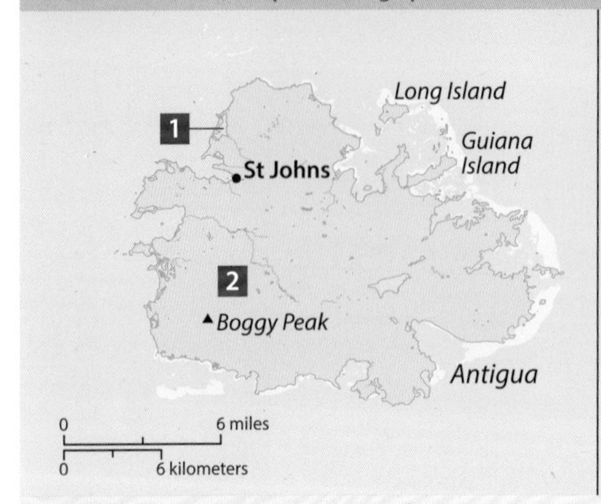

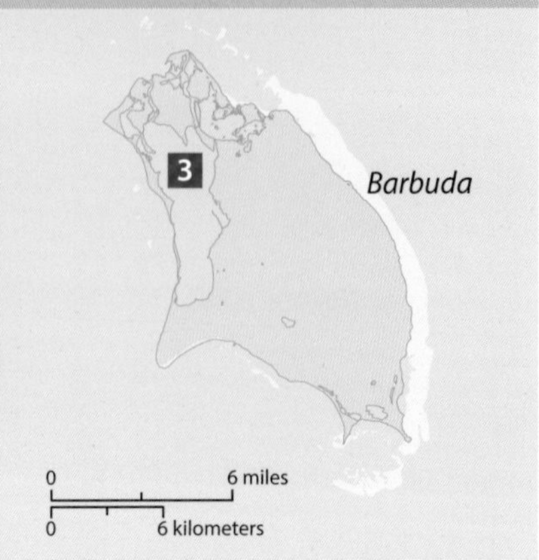

Antigua has areas of scrub and dry forest on the eastern side and pockets of evergreen forest on the highest ground in the Shekerley Mountains. Impressive numbers of breeding and migratory waterbirds can be seen on a range of wetlands and coastal lagoons. The extensive limestone scrub that covers most of Barbuda is home to the endemic Barbuda Warbler, and the Magnificent Frigatebird colony on Codrington Lagoon is one of the Caribbean's finest wildlife spectacles.

Endemics: Antigua and Barbuda	Barbuda Warbler (Barbuda only) VU, Antigua Groundlizard NT, Antigua Bank Bush Anole, Antigua Bank Tree Anole, Antigua Bank Dwarf Gecko, Antiguan Racer CR
Specialty species	West Indian Whistling-Duck NT, White-crowned Pigeon NT

Shekerley Mountains.

1 McKinnon's Salt Pond, Antigua (Public/private ownership) Large brackish wetland, mangroves and scrub with accessible viewing from the causeway and perimeter road. Look for breeding and migratory waterbirds, including West Indian Whistling-Duck, dragonflies and butterflies.

2 Christian Valley, Antigua (Public/private ownership) A series of trails through agricultural land and dry forest in the Shekerley Mountains take you to the summit of Boggy Peak. The valley is good for forest birds, Broad-winged Hawk and both endemic anoles.

3 Codrington Lagoon National Park, Barbuda Extensive lagoon, mangroves, sand dunes and surrounding scrub woodland. Boat tours visit the largest frigatebird colony in the Caribbean. Look for Barbuda Warbler in the scrub and dragonflies on nearby seasonal pools.

Montserrat

102 km² (39 sq. miles), Soufrière Hills (Chances Peak) 914 m (3,000 ft)

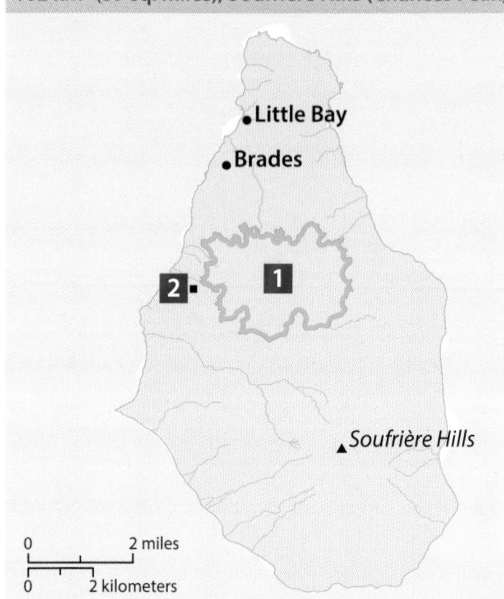

The Centre Hills provide a rare chance to experience the transition from coastal scrub through dry forest and rainforest to elfin forest. Enjoy spectacular views north to the more open Silver Hills and south to the smoldering Soufrière Hills volcano, in an exclusion zone since the 1997 eruption. Look for Montserrat Oriole, endemic reptiles and forest butterflies. Red-billed Tropicbirds nest along the rugged cliffs, and Brown Booby, Brown Pelican and Royal Tern can be seen over inshore waters year-round.

Single-island endemics	Montserrat Oriole VU, Montserrat Groundlizard NT, Montserrat Galliwasp CR, Montserrat Anole NT, Montserrat Racer NT
Restricted-range endemics	Forest Thrush NT, Mountain Chicken Frog CR, Caribbean Black Iguana CR, Southern Leeward Dwarf Gecko

Jack Boy Hill Trail.

1 Centre Hills Trails (Public/private ownership) Series of eight managed forest trails; local guides are recommended especially for Katy Hill and the higher slopes. Highlights include Montserrat Oriole and other forest birds, Montserrat Anole, Montserrat Racer snake and butterflies, including Red Rim.

$ ♿ 2 National Trust Botanical Gardens (Managed by the Montserrat National Trust) Small but interesting gardens, with visitor facilities, maintained by the National Trust. Tropical plant collection includes scarce native species, which attract hummingbirds and butterflies.

Soufrière Hills stratovolcano

Guadeloupe

Guadeloupe 1,479 km² (571 sq. miles), La Soufriere 1,467 m (4,813 ft); Marie-Galante 155 km² (60 sq. miles), Morne Constant 204 m (669 ft)

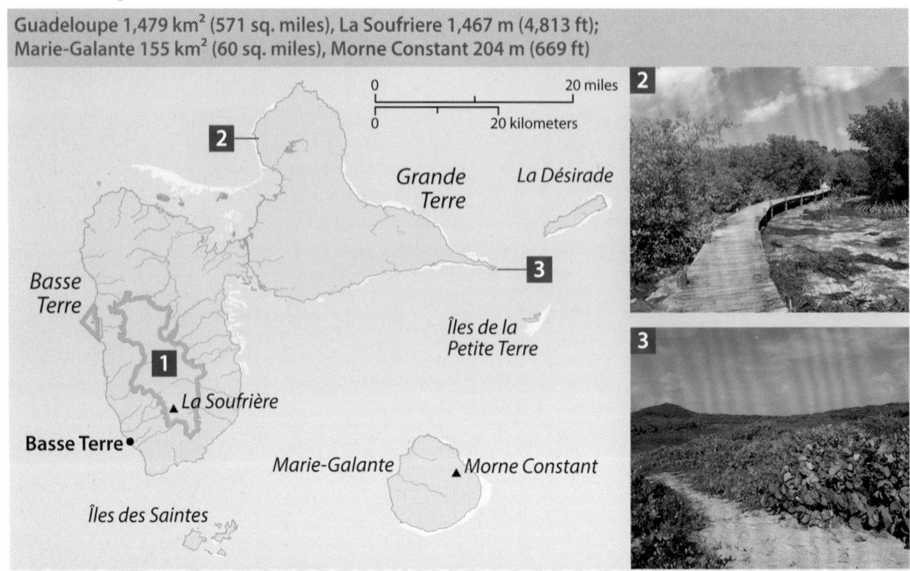

The largest island in the Eastern Caribbean with the greatest variety of birds (over 280 species recorded within the archipelago), butterflies and dragonflies in the region, with cetaceans off the leeward coast. Well-managed trails, some accessible, can take you through wetlands and mangroves or high into spectacular rainforest. The offshore islands and cays are important for seabirds; Marie-Galante, La Désirade and Îles des Saintes each have one or more endemic reptiles.

Single-island endemics	Guadeloupe Woodpecker, Guadeloupe Stream Frog EN, Guadeloupe Forest Frog EN, Guadeloupe Anole, reptiles on offshore islands, Guadeloupe Threadtail
Restricted-range endemics	Forest Thrush NT, Plumbeous Warbler, Southern Leeward Dwarf Gecko, Leeward Ground Snake NT
Specialty species	Ringed Kingfisher

1 Parc National Guadeloupe (Managed by the Parcs Nationaux de France) Rainforest, mountain streams, waterfalls and lakes, including Grand Étang, with an extensive network of trails, plus visitor facilities. Look for Guadeloupe Woodpecker, Forest Thrush, Plumbeous Warbler and endemic dragonflies.

1

2 Marais de Port-Louis (Managed by Conservatoire du Littoral) Extensive area of mangrove, marsh and dry forest with accessible trails and boardwalks. Good populations of fiddler and mangrove crabs, and dragonflies.

3 Pointe des Châteaux (Public ownership) Series of trails through coastal scrub with cliffs, saline lagoons, salt marshes and views of small islets. Resident and migratory seabirds and waterbirds can be found in the bay and lagoons with reptiles and butterflies in the scrub.

Dominica

751 km² (289 sq. miles), Morne Diablotin 1,447 m (4,747 ft)

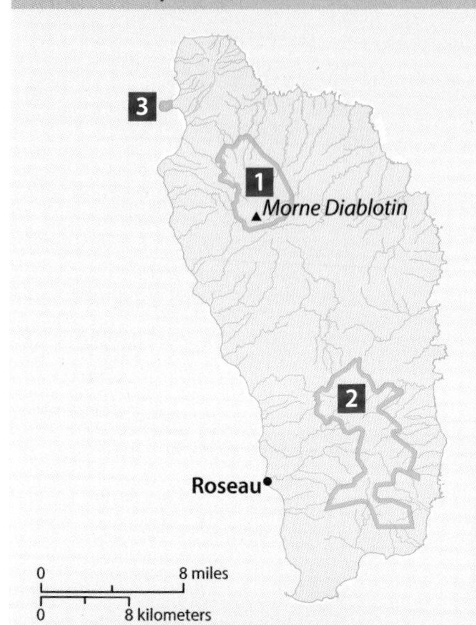

The mountainous interior has some of the most dramatic pristine rainforest in the Eastern Caribbean—home to endemic parrots, reptiles and butterflies. Spectacular fast-flowing streams with waterfalls and pools high in the mountains become slower and wider towards the coasts and are good places to see crabs, dragonflies and Ringed Kingfisher. Cetaceans in the deep-water channel include dolphins and breeding Sperm Whale.

Single-island endemics	Red-necked Parrot VU, Imperial Parrot CR, Kalinago Wren, Dominica Frog EN, Dominica Groundlizard, Dominica Anole NT, Dominica Skink, Dominica Boa, Dominican Hairstreak, Dominican Snout
Restricted-range endemics	Blue-headed Hummingbird, Plumbeous Warbler, Martinique Frog NT, Mountain Chicken Frog CR, Southern Leeward Dwarf Gecko, Northern Martinique Dwarf Gecko, Leeward Ground Snake NT

Trafalgar Falls.

♿ 1 **Morne Diablotin National Park** Several managed trails through large tracts of rainforest, including Syndicate Trail and visitor center. One of the best places to look for Red-necked and Imperial Parrots, Blue-headed Hummingbird and endemic reptiles.

$ 2 **Morne Trois Pitons National Park** Managed trails through rainforest and elfin forest. Visitor centers include **Freshwater Lake** and **Emerald Pool**. Look for Forest Thrush, Plumbeous Warbler, Rufous-throated Solitaire, dwarf geckos and forest butterflies.

♿ 3 **Cabrits National Park** Managed coastal trail through wetlands, swamp and dry forest with visitor center. Good for waterbirds, Dominica Groundlizard, Dominica Racer and dragonflies.

All sites are managed by the Forestry, Wildlife and Parks Division.

Martinique

1,129 km² (436 sq. miles), Mont Pelée 1,397 m (4,583 ft)

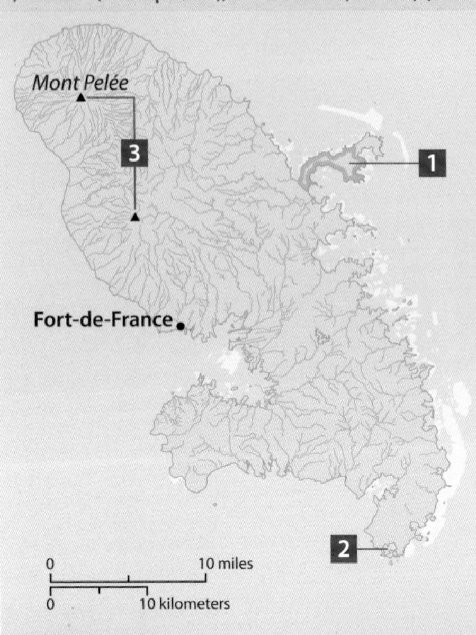

The impressive mountainous north of the island has extensive areas of rainforest, with elfin forest on the highest peaks, where rare frogs, endemic reptiles and a wide range of forest birds can be found. In the lower-lying south and east there is a mix of large-scale agriculture, dry forest and scrub, where specialty species include Martinique Thrasher and Dominican Leafwing butterfly. A range of wetlands and coastal lagoons with mangroves attract migratory waterbirds and hold large populations of fiddler and mangrove crabs.

Single-island endemics	Martinique Thrasher EN, Martinique Oriole VU, Martinique Volcano Frog CR, Martinique Anole, Martinique Lancehead EN
Restricted-range endemics	Blue-headed Hummingbird, Gray Trembler, Martinique Frog, Northern Martinique Dwarf Gecko, Southern Martinique Dwarf Gecko
Specialty species	White-tailed Nightjar

1 Réserve Naturelle de la Caravelle (Private/public ownership, partly managed by Parc Naturel Régional de la Martinique) Trails and boardwalks through mangroves, grassland and extensive dry forest. Look for Martinique Thrasher, Lesser Antillean Saltator, Martinique Anole and butterflies.

2 Étang de Saline Boardwalk and trails encompassing salt-pond and scrub, enabling close views of breeding and migratory waterbirds, fiddler crabs and mangrove crabs.

3 Pitons du Carbet and Mont Pelée (Public/private ownership) A network of managed trails take you through grassland then rainforest into elfin forest; access can be difficult at higher elevations. Good for Martinique Oriole, Blue-headed Hummingbird and Gray Trembler, plus endemic reptiles and amphibians, including the rare Martinique Volcano Frog.

St Lucia

616 km² (237 sq. miles), Mount Gimie 950 m (3,117 ft)

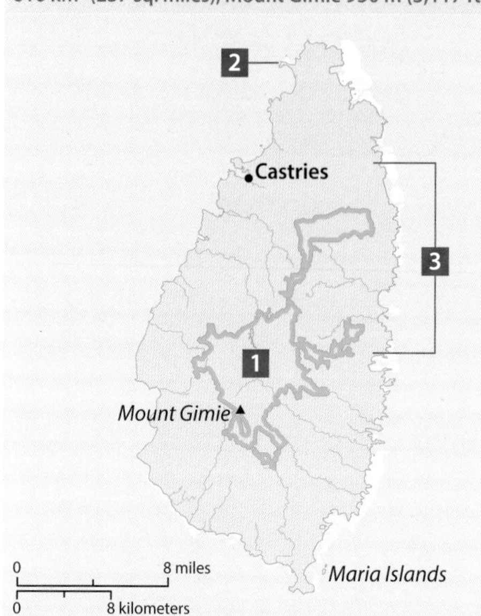

The landscape of St Lucia is dramatic, with mountainous peaks, dense rainforest, fast-flowing streams and waterfalls. The Central Forest Reserve holds an impressive number of endemic birds and reptiles, Yellow Land Crabs and scarce dragonflies. The often-overlooked dry forest and scrub on the east coast is worth exploring for specialties such as St Lucia Thrasher. Rare reptiles occur on offshore islands.

Single-island endemics	St Lucia Parrot VU, St Lucia Wren, St Lucia Thrasher EN, St Lucia Warbler, St Lucia Oriole EN, St Lucia Black Finch EN, St Lucia Anole EN, St Lucia Dwarf Gecko NT, St Lucia Boa EN, St Lucia Pit Viper EN, reptiles on offshore islands
Restricted-range endemics	Lesser Antillean (St Lucia) Pewee, Gray Trembler, Southern Lesser Antilles Horned Iguana
Specialty species	Rufous Nightjar

1 Central Forest Reserve (Public/private ownership) An extensive network of trails (Des Cartier, Millet and Soufrière), some with visitor facilities, leads deep into the rainforest to look for St Lucia Parrot, St Lucia Black Finch, St Lucia Boa and Lesser Antillean Threadtail. Guides are recommended.

$ ♿ 2 Pigeon Island (Managed by St Lucia National Trust) Historic site with visitor facilities and trails through grassland, scrub and dry forest. Look for hummingbirds, Spectacled Thrush and St Lucia Anole in the scrub, and for seabirds offshore.

3 East coast dry forest Entry points can be difficult but include tracks to Grande Anse beach. Guides are recommended. Highlights include St Lucia Thrasher, Rufous Nightjar and Orion Cecropian.

2

1

3

Barbados

430 km² (166 sq. miles), Mount Hillaby 343 m (1,125 ft)

An island with gentle slopes, open agricultural landscapes and small pockets of remnant forest, often nestled in gullies, such as Turner Hall Woods. The rocky windward coast is wilder in character, with cliffs, exposed stretches of grassland and low scrub. Its isolated location, over 161 km (100 miles) east of St Vincent, makes Barbados an important landfall for birds on migration. Large numbers of waterbirds drop in to rest and feed on wetlands between August and November, and rare or vagrant birds and insects can occur from as far away as Africa and Europe.

Single-island endemics	Barbados Bullfinch, Barbados Anole, Barbados Leaf-toed Gecko CR, Barbados Threadsnake CR
Specialty species	Black-bellied Whistling-Duck, Masked Duck

$ ♿ 1 **Andromeda Botanic Gardens** (Managed by Barbados National Trust) Mature gardens with visitor facilities and partially accessible paths lead through an extensive collection of tropical plants and water features. Hummingbirds, Barbados Bullfinch, Barbados Anole, and a good range of butterflies and dragonflies can easily be seen.

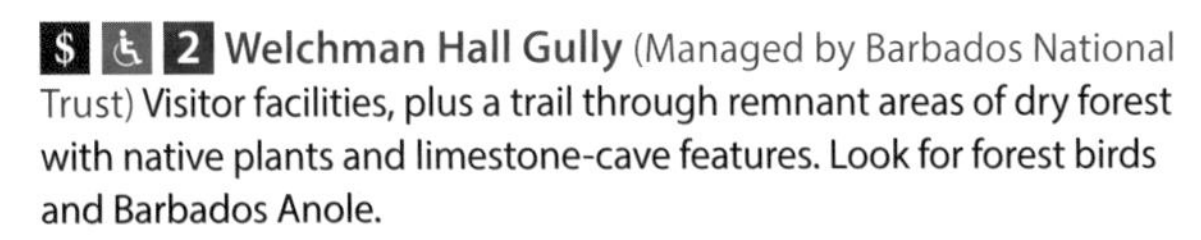

$ ♿ 2 **Welchman Hall Gully** (Managed by Barbados National Trust) Visitor facilities, plus a trail through remnant areas of dry forest with native plants and limestone-cave features. Look for forest birds and Barbados Anole.

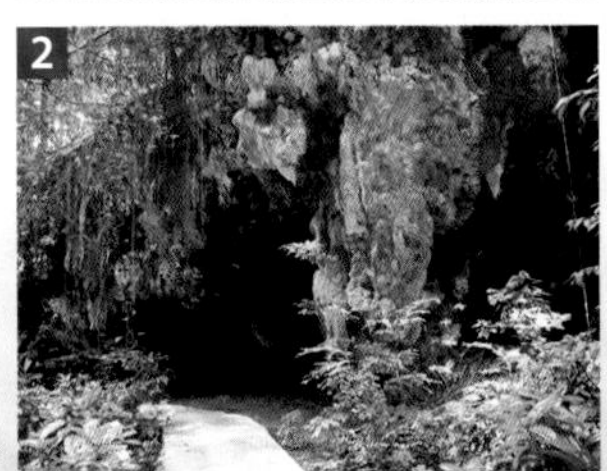

3 **Barbados wetlands** (Most under private ownership) A network of wetlands, some seasonal, attract a remarkable range of migratory waterbirds. Some have viewing from a perimeter road or beach, but there is uncertainty over public access, which should always be checked.

Rocky scrub on the windward coast.

St Vincent and the Grenadines (SVG)

388 km² (149 sq. miles), La Soufrière 1,234 m (4,049 ft)

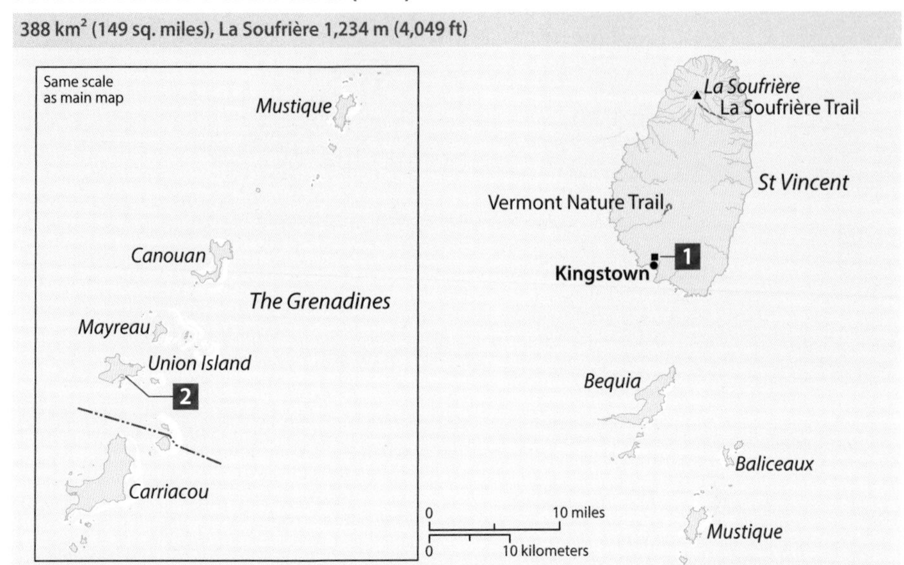

This large volcanic island has a heavily forested, mountainous interior that is home to endemic reptiles and birds, including St Vincent Parrot. The Grenadines are lower lying, with scrub, dry forest and coastal wetlands that attract a range of waterbirds. Beaches and rocky cays are important for nesting sea turtles and seabirds, including Red-footed Booby, with cetaceans offshore.

Single-island endemics	St Vincent Parrot VU, St Vincent Wren, Whistling Warbler EN, St Vincent Frog EN, St Vincent Bush Anole, St Vincent Tree Anole, Union Island Clawed Gecko CR, St Vincent Treeboa, St Vincent Coachwhip (Black Snake) CR, St Vincent Hairstreak
Restricted-range endemics	Grenada Flycatcher, Rufous-throated Solitaire, Lesser Antillean Tanager, Southern Lesser Antilles Horned Iguana, Antillean Ameiva, Southern Martinique Dwarf Gecko, Windward Tree Racer

$ National Park trails: Vermont Nature Trail and La Soufrière Nature Trail (Managed by the National Parks Authority) Visitor facilities and well-managed trails through rainforest, with elfin forest on the La Soufrière trail; some sections are steep and difficult. Look for St Vincent Parrot, Whistling Warbler, Rufous-throated Solitaire, endemic reptiles and Yellow Land Crab.

Vermont Nature Trail Visitor Center.

$ ♿ 1 SVG Botanic Gardens, Kingstown (Managed by the National Parks Authority) Mature formal gardens, with visitor facilities, that attract Common Black Hawk, the all-black form of Bananaquit, anoles, butterflies and dragonflies. The St Vincent Parrot captive breeding program is on site.

La Soufrière Trail.

1

♿ 2 Ashton Lagoon, Union Island An inspiring habitat restoration project, with walkways, trails and an impressive suspension bridge. The lagoon holds migratory waterbirds, crabs and dragonflies. Seabirds and sea turtles can be seen offshore.

Grenada

344 km² (132 sq. miles), Mount St Catherine 840 m (2,756 ft)

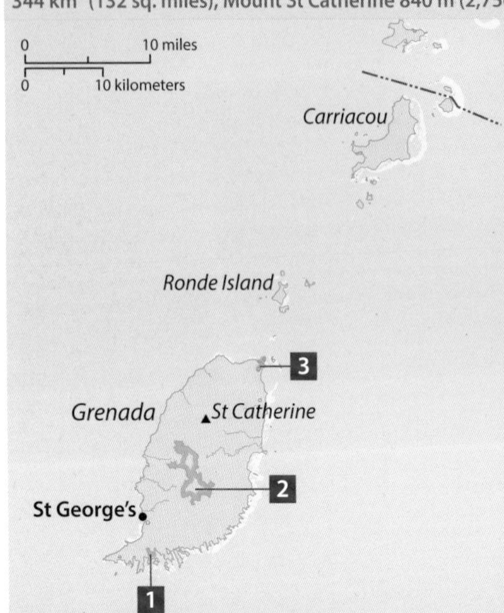

A heavily forested volcanic island with three distinct National Parks that hold the whole range of endemic birds and reptiles. Dry forest is especially important to the critically endangered Grenada Dove, one of the rarest birds on earth. Several bird and bat species from South America reach Grenada but are rare or absent farther north. The offshore Grenadines have areas of scrub and dry forest, accessed by trails including the High North Peak on Carriacou: these are important for breeding seabirds and nesting sea turtles.

Single-island endemics	Grenada Dove CR, Grenada Wren, Grenada Frog CR, Grenada Tree Anole, Grenada Bush Anole, Grenada Treeboa
Restricted-range endemics	Grenada Flycatcher, Lesser Antillean Tanager, Antillean Ameiva, Windward Tree Racer
Specialty species	Hook-billed Kite, Rufous-breasted Hermit, Fork-tailed Flycatcher

1 Mount Hartman National Park Visitor center and trails through dry forest bordering mangrove-fringed coastal lagoons. One of the last two remaining areas for Grenada Dove. Look for Hook-billed Kite, Grenada Wren, Fork-tailed Flycatcher, endemic reptiles including Grenada Treeboa, land crabs and butterflies, including South American Mestra.

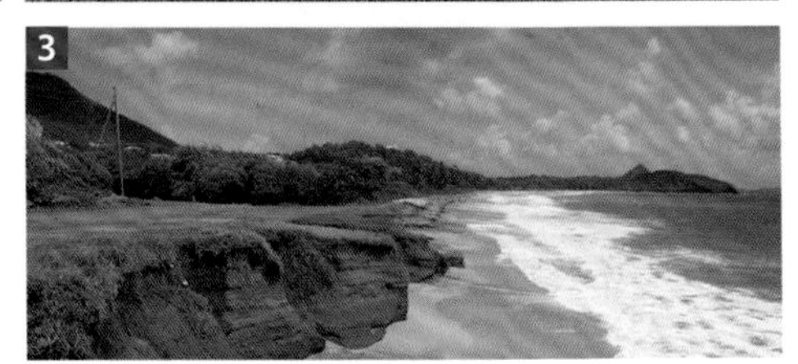

2 Grand Etang National Park Freshwater lake and rainforest with trails, accessible viewpoints and a visitor center with formal garden. One of the best sites for Rufous-breasted Hermit, Cocoa Thrush, Lesser Antillean Tanager, endemic reptiles and forest dragonflies.

3 Levera National Park Rocky windward coast and beaches with information center and a large, mangrove-fringed lagoon with a boardwalk and observation tower. Look for seabirds and Green Turtles offshore, with migratory waterbirds and mangrove crabs around the lagoon.

All sites are managed by the National Parks and Forestry Department.

How to use this guide

Each species account includes the following information:

Names: common and *scientific* names are given for each species. Recent research has led to some taxonomic revision and reclassification, affecting both names of several species, particularly reptiles. Where taxonomy is unsettled, this is indicated; for clarity, some former common and scientific names are included in parentheses.

For consistency, names are aligned with the American Ornithological Society's *Checklist of North and Middle American Birds* (used by eBird), the American Society of Mammologists' *Mammal Diversity Database*, and for amphibians and reptiles, Caribherp and *Reptiles of the Lesser Antilles* (Thorpe, 2022). For the remaining groups, the most current and widely accepted common and scientific names are used, largely based on iNaturalist.

IUCN Red List Status is given for all globally threatened species (see box at right).

IUCN Red List Status

- **EX** Extinct
- **CR** Critically Endangered
- **EN** Endangered
- **VU** Vulnerable
- **NT** Near Threatened
- **DD** Data Deficient

Endemic species are indicated to identify those species unique to the region. All other species occur more widely in the Americas:

- **E** Species endemic to the wider Caribbean
- **E** Species endemic to the Eastern Caribbean
- **e** Subspecies endemic to the Eastern Caribbean (may be more than one)

Distribution gives an indication of presence and is always listed north to south from the Virgin Islands to Grenada. Data for some species and/or islands are limited.

- **Throughout** Found on all the main islands; may be absent from smaller offshore islands.
- **Widespread** Found on most of the main islands.
- **Limited or restricted** Found within a specific geographic range, either contiguous (*e.g.*, "found from Anguilla to Antigua") or discontinuous (*e.g.*, "only on Dominica and St Lucia").

Relative abundance for a species can vary between islands, and with both habitat and seasonality, and is allocated to one of four broad categories:

- **Common** Occurs in high densities; can be easy to see in its main habitats.
- **Locally common** Occurs in high or moderate densities but can be limited to discrete areas of habitat.
- **Uncommon** Occurs in low densities, often in discrete areas of habitat.
- **Rare** Occurs in very low densities or as an occasional visitor, often highly localized in particular habitats.

Identification (ID) At least one measure of **size** is given for the adult of each species; an approximation is used for the few species where data are not available:

- **L** Total length, including tail.
- **HB** Head and body length.
- **HS** Height at shoulder.
- **WS** Wingspan.
- **FW** Forewing length.
- **CL/CW** Carapace length/width.

Species are described with **key identification** features **highlighted** together with images. Similar species are grouped on a page where possible, so are not always presented in systematic order.

Voice (*i.e.*, calls and/or song) is described phonetically where helpful for identification.

Rare and highly restricted-range species that are difficult to see or found only on offshore islands, together with introduced species, are not always fully described. Most are included, often in tabular form, for completeness.

Birds

Over 300 bird species have been recorded in the Eastern Caribbean, of which 36 are endemic. Rare and vagrant species are not included here but are widely covered in some excellent field guides to birds of the West Indies (*see* "Further Reading", *p. 301*). Birds Caribbean regularly updates *The Complete Checklist of the Birds of the West Indies* (birdscaribbean.org), which also includes island checklists.

For ease of use, birds are separated into three sections, based on habitat: seabirds; waterbirds and shorebirds; and landbirds.

Species are resident and present year-round unless indicated through one of the following categories:

- **Breeding visitor** Mainly April to September; migrates to wintering areas elsewhere.
- **Non-breeding visitor** Visits for part of the year, typically August to April.
- **Passage visitor** Visits briefly during migration, which is mainly southbound between August and November, with fewer northbound between March and May.

Identification (ID) describes the plumage that you are most likely to see. Differences between male (♂) and female (♀) are given; juvenile or immatures are described where these can be confusing:

- **Adult plumage (ad,** ♂ [male], ♀ [female]) All resident species with little or no change year-round.
- **Breeding plumage (b)** Mainly between April and July/August.
- **Non-breeding adult plumage (n)** Mainly between September and April.
- **Immature (i)** Non-adult plumages. 1st-winter is used for birds that have undertaken a first partial molt from their juvenile plumage (mainly terns and gulls).
- **Juvenile (j)** First plumage.

Black-necked Stilts (*p. 76*)

SEABIRDS

The rugged coastlines, sandy spits and scattered islands of the Eastern Caribbean are fantastic places for seabirds. Some pass through on migration and can be seen off Atlantic coasts, but 17 species breed, several in globally important populations—such as Brown Booby and Red-tailed Tropicbird.

Royal Tern, Brown Booby, Brown Pelican, Magnificent Frigatebird and Red-billed Tropicbird are resident species and can be a common sight on some islands, often feeding close inshore. Terns, gulls and some boobies are breeding visitors, returning in April and May to small islands where they can safely breed. They form mixed colonies, noisy seabird cities full of action with courtship displays, aggressive interactions with neighbors, juveniles calling to be fed and the constant activity of adults flying to and from feeding grounds. By September young have fledged and colonies begin to empty as birds disperse; some to the coasts of South America, while pelagic species, such as Sooty Tern and Bridled Tern, head out to sea, often to unknown wintering areas.

Only a few species nest on the main islands, where they are vulnerable to disturbance, habitat loss and predation from introduced mammals. Least Terns breed in colonies along undisturbed coasts and around the edges of some salt-ponds and brackish lagoons. Tropicbirds find secure crevices and holes on inaccessible or remote cliffs, and Brown Pelicans nest in some of the larger mangrove forests.

Most of the major seabird colonies are recognized as Important Bird and Biodiversity Areas (IBAs), but many are vulnerable, with no formal protection. Introduced rodents that prey upon seabird eggs and chicks are one of the biggest threats. Rodent-eradication projects have been undertaken on several small islands, resulting in improved seabird breeding success while also benefitting populations of rare reptiles.

Adult breeding plumage is described for all species. For those species that overwinter or that may be seen on migration, non-breeding and juvenile/1st-winter plumages may be included.

Sooty Terns (*p. 52*) can form large colonies.

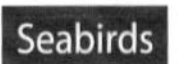

Terns

Terns are slender, streamlined seabirds, with **narrow, pointed wings** and a light, buoyant flight. Most have a long slender bill and **forked tail, although this is not always obvious.** They feed by hovering and dipping or diving to catch small fish on or near the surface, rarely settling on the water. Royal Tern is the only resident species; the rest occur as breeding or passage visitors, but adults in duller non-breeding plumage and immature birds may linger until November and can be tricky to identify!

Brown Noddy *Anous stolidus* L 39 cm (15½″) | WS 81 cm (32″)

Uncommon breeding visitor **throughout**; occasional records year-round. Breeds in scattered colonies, mostly on small, uninhabited islands, nesting on cliffs, rocky outcrops, and in bushes. Surprisingly rare off main island coasts, but loose flocks are occasionally seen feeding over inshore waters.
ID: A distinctive **chocolate-brown** tern, mostly seen in flight, where it appears all-dark with a striking **white forehead and crown**, and a **square-ended tail**. Immature similar to adult but with reduced white on head.
VOICE: A range of croaking and rattling calls, rarely heard away from breeding colony.

Sooty Tern *Onychoprion fuscatus* L 41 cm (16″) | WS 81 cm (32″)

Breeding visitor; can occur **throughout**. Easily the most numerous seabird in the region but is difficult to see away from breeding sites on small, often remote islands. The largest colonies are around USVI, Anguilla and St Lucia: some are in excess of 10,000 pairs.
ID: Black upperparts contrast with clean white underparts. Very similar to Bridled Tern, but obvious **white forehead** on black crown extends only to **top of the eye**, not beyond. Flight strong and steady, showing white edges to forked tail. Juvenile is sooty-brown with dark breast and **lines of pale spots** on upperwings.
VOICE: Characteristic three-note call "*wacky-wack*" or "*wide-awake*".

Bridled Tern *Onychoprion anaethetus* L 38 cm (15″) | WS 76 cm (30″)

Breeding visitor **throughout**, but difficult to see from the main islands. Nests in small, scattered colonies on remote, rocky islands, often with other seabird species but typically in less open situations among rocks and in crevices.
ID: Differs from Sooty Tern in having paler **gray-brown upperparts** with an obviously **black cap** and **longer white forehead** that **extends as a line behind the eye**. In flight shows white edges to **long forked tail**. Juvenile has **pale barring** on back and upperwings.
VOICE: Short nasal "*kek kek*" and softer trills.

1
2
3

BRIDLED TERN
BREEDING
p. 52
SOOTY TERN
BREEDING
p. 52
BROWN NODDY
BREEDING
p. 52
LEAST TERN
1ST WINTER
p. 56
LEAST TERN
BREEDING
p. 56
ROSEATE TERN
BREEDING
p. 56
ROSEATE TERN
JUVENILE—1ST WINTER
p. 56
COMMON TERN
BREEDING
p. 56
SANDWICH TERN
BREEDING
p. 56
GULL-BILLED TERN
BREEDING
p. 56

ROYAL TERN
BREEDING
p. 58
ROYAL TERN
NON-BREEDING
p. 58
ROYAL TERN
JUVENILE
p. 58
CASPIAN TERN
NON-BREEDING
p. 58
LAUGHING GULL
BREEDING
p. 58
LAUGHING GULL
JUVENILE—1ST WINTER
p. 58
LESSER BLACK-BACKED GULL
1ST WINTER
p. 58

1 **Least Tern** *Sternula antillarum* L 23 cm (9″) | WS 51 cm (20″)

Widespread but localized breeding visitor from the **Virgin Islands to Martinique**, passage visitor farther south. Forms small colonies, mostly fewer than 100 pairs, on sandbars, beaches, coastal lagoons and salt-ponds. The only tern that regularly breeds on the main islands.
ID: Tiny; the smallest tern. Neatly marked with **pale gray** upperwings, **black cap** and **white forehead**. **Bill bright yellow**, can show a small black tip; legs yellow. A thin dark line on the wingtip shows as a **dark leading edge** to outer wing in flight. Post-breeding adults and the browner, more marked juveniles, have a dark bill, speckled crown and, especially on juveniles, a dark bar at bend of wing. First-winter birds can be confusing, with large dark wedge on outerwing and **striking white panel** on rear inner wing. Flight is very fast, readily stopping to hover before splashing into water for prey.
VOICE: Very vocal: a shrill, chattering "*krit-krit*", often heard when birds are hard to see against the sky.

Roseate Tern *Sterna dougallii* L 37 cm (14½″) | WS 74 cm (29″)

Breeding visitor; can occur **throughout**, but more numerous in the Virgin Islands and northern Lesser Antilles. Nests in scattered colonies on low-lying offshore islands but is vulnerable when breeding; colonies are known to move between sites if disturbed. Occasionally seen over inshore waters, especially during migration.
ID: A **very pale gray** tern; can show a pale pink flush to white underparts, hence common name. Black cap; black bill, becoming **orange-red at base when breeding**; and bright orange-red legs. Long outer tail feathers **extend beyond wingtips** when perched, showing as long, forked tail in flight. Juvenile has dark V's on back and a reduced black cap. Flight is dashing and rapid, with angular shallow dives.
VOICE: A sharp two-note "*chiv-ick*".

Common Tern *Sterna hirundo* L 37 cm (14½″) | WS 76 cm (30″)

Uncommon breeding visitor from the **Virgin Islands to Martinique**, passage visitor farther south, rarely seen from the main islands. Similar to Roseate Tern, but upperparts are darker gray, with a broad dark trailing edge to wingtip (*pp. 54–5*).

Sandwich (Cabot's) **Tern** *Thalasseus sandvicensis acuflavidus*

L 43 cm (17″) | WS 86 cm (34″)

Uncommon breeding visitor to the **Virgin Islands** and **northern Lesser Antilles** but can be seen throughout on passage over inshore waters and coastal lagoons. Readily rests on buoys, jetties, beaches and salt-pond walls; nests in small colonies with other terns on sandy spits and cays.
ID: Upperwings and back **very pale gray**, underparts white: looks all white at distance. **Shaggy black cap**, much reduced post-breeding, long black bill with small but **obvious yellow or pale tip**, and black legs. Flight is strong with long narrow, angular wings and **short, forked tail**.
VOICE: Flight call is a characteristic and far-carrying, harsh, two-note "*kir-rick*".

(Common) **Gull-billed Tern** *Gelochelidon nilotica* L 42 cm (16″) | WS 85 cm (33″)

A rare breeding visitor to **Anegada** (BVI); occasional passage visitor elsewhere. Similar to Sandwich Tern but with **shorter and heavier black bill**, broader wings and shorter, lightly forked tail (*pp. 54–5*).

1j
1b
2b
2j
3b
3n

1 Royal Tern *Thalasseus maximus* L 49 cm (19½") | WS 104 cm (41")

The only tern **present year-round**. Found **throughout**, but more numerous on the northern islands. Nests in small numbers on sandy spits and small cays. A familiar sight on many islands over shallow bays, inshore waters and coastal lagoons: often seen resting on boats, salt-pond walls and rocky outcrops.
ID: The **largest** commonly seen gray tern. Distinctive with a **stout orange bill** and **shaggy black cap** (post-breeding, this is much reduced to dark band behind eye). Flight is strong and direct, showing long wings and shallow-forked tail. Upperwing has thin dark bar near trailing edge and a black wedge on upper wingtip, which shows as **dark trailing edge on underwing**. First-winter has more extensive dark markings to upperwings and tail.
VOICE: Rasping, high-pitched "*kur-rerr-ik*", often heard when bird is hard to see against the sky.

Caspian Tern *Hydroprogne caspia* L 55 cm (22") | WS 110 cm (43")

Uncommon to rare non-breeding visitor that can occur throughout. Similar to Royal Tern but is larger with a heavier, dark-tipped red bill and **large black patch at tip of underwing** (*pp. 54–5*).

Gulls

Laughing Gull is the only breeding species of gull, but several occur as rare or non-breeding visitors or vagrants. Numbers and sightings of larger gulls are increasing, especially on the northern islands. Lesser Black-backed Gull is the most frequent, but Ring-billed, Herring and Great Black-backed Gulls are all possible. All have a series of immature plumages, which can make identification difficult. Larger gulls can take four years to reach full breeding plumage.

2 Laughing Gull *Leucophaeus atricilla* L 41 cm (16") | WS 104 cm (41")

Breeding visitor **throughout**, with occasional records year-round: the only regularly occurring gull. Nests in colonies on sandy cays and low-lying islands. Noisy and gregarious, often gathering in large flocks over sandy coasts, inshore waters and coastal wetlands. Associates with other seabirds when feeding but, unlike terns, will settle on water, picking food from the surface. Tolerant of people: readily scavenges around ports and harbors.
ID: **Smoky-gray** upperparts with **black wingtips** and **obvious black hood**, much reduced with a whiter head post-breeding. Dark bill is slightly **down-curved at tip**. Juveniles, seen from June onwards, lack black hood and are dusky gray-brown overall, with a slightly paler belly and a bold dark band near tip of white tail, obvious in flight.
VOICE: Nasal, laugh-like calls are a familiar sound on many islands during the breeding season.

3 Lesser Black-backed Gull *Larus fuscus* L 53 cm (21") | WS 137 cm (54")

Non-breeding visitor, from the **Virgin Islands to Guadeloupe** and **Barbados**, with occasional records year-round: numbers appear to be increasing throughout the Caribbean. A surface-feeder typically seen over inshore waters, coastal lagoons and salt-ponds, but will readily scavenge around ports.
ID: **Large** (noticeably bigger than Laughing Gull), with a heavy bill. **Back and upperwings dark gray**, head pale, **bill and legs yellow**. Juvenile and 1st-winter birds are more common in the region: mainly dark gray-brown with heavy streaking, paler streaked head and dark bill.
VOICE: A variety of nasal calls and often repeated bark-like "*awoo*".

1b
1n
BREEDING TO NON-BREEDING
2
2
1ST WINTER
3n
3j

Tropicbirds and shearwaters

1 **Red-billed Tropicbird** *Phaethon aethereus* L 48 cm (19"), 99 cm (39") including tail plumes | WS 105 cm (41")

Resident **throughout**, but localized on remote headlands, cliffs and rocky islands. Largest populations are on the **Virgin Islands**, **Saba**, **St Eustatius** and **Guadeloupe**. Most easily seen when breeding (Jan–Jul): they nest in crevices and holes along cliffs but feed out at sea, where they hover at height before diving to catch fish and squid. These beautiful seabirds can put on an amazing show with their screaming calls and spectacular display flights.

ID: Mostly seen in flight, showing distinctive **long white tail streamers**. Adults are strikingly white with fine black barring on back and inner wings and **black edges to outer wings**. A **bold black line** runs from the **short red bill** through the eye. Juvenile lacks tail streamers; bill is paler, more yellowish.

VOICE: A range of rattling and screaming calls at breeding sites, including a harsh, extended "*keee-arrr*".

2 **White-tailed Tropicbird** *Phaethon lepturus* L 39 cm (15½"), 81 cm (32") including tail plumes | WS 93 cm (37")

Breeding visitor **throughout**, but less numerous than Red-billed Tropicbird. The largest populations are on the **Virgin Islands** and **Guadeloupe**. Nests along coastal cliffs and on rocky outcrops, where pairs perform wonderful synchronized display flights. Feeds out at sea, hovering before diving to catch fish and squid.

ID: Similar to Red-billed Tropicbird but with a **yellow bill** and a **bold diagonal black stripe on inner wing**, obvious in flight. Juvenile has coarse barring on back and hindneck; lacks tail streamers. Flight is fast with shallow wingbeats, typically at height over the sea.

VOICE: Deep nasal croaking and high-pitched "*kwit*".

3 **Sargasso** (Audubon's) **Shearwater** *Puffinus lherminieri* L 30 cm (12") | WS 69 cm (27")

Widespread but elusive resident in small scattered colonies along isolated cliffs and on offshore islands. Returns to nest sites at night and is difficult to see when breeding, but small groups fly past exposed headlands or gather to form rafts out at sea, where they are occasionally seen from boats and ferries. Makes shallow or surface dives for small squid and fish.

ID: Dark brown upperparts contrast with **clean white underparts**. **Head brown to base of eye** but can show thin pale eye-surround; lower face and throat white. Bill thin and dark, hooked at tip. Flight is characteristic of shearwaters: a few fast wingbeats interspersed with glides very low over water, when it shows **dark undertail** and white center to dark underwing.

VOICE: Silent at sea, but highly vocal around nesting colonies after dark. Calls include a soft rolling, repeated four-note "*pum-il-i-co*".

1
2
3

Boobies

Large seabirds, distinctive in flight with obvious projecting head, neck and bill; a pointed tail; and long thin wings. Boobies fly with stiff, shallow wingbeats, interspersed with glides, typically low over water, where they make angular dives for fish and squid. Three species occur. All nest colonially on small, often remote rocky islands. They can have an extended breeding season in the region.

1 **Brown Booby** *Sula leucogaster* L 74 cm (29″) | WS 145 cm (57″)

The most numerous and easy-to-see booby: resident **throughout**, with the largest populations on the **Virgin Islands** and **Anguilla**. Regularly feeds close inshore and can be confiding, resting on rocks, buoys, boats and jetties.

ID: Dark brown overall with a **sharply contrasting white belly** and white center to base of underwings. **Face, legs and large webbed feet are pale yellow**. Immature has a gray bill and is a paler, washed-out brown, with a **clearly defined line between darker breast and lighter belly**.

VOICE: Calls include a sharp, nasal honking, mostly heard at breeding sites.

2 **Red-footed Booby** *Sula sula* L 71 cm (28″) | WS 152 cm (60″)

Widespread resident with a fragmented distribution: the largest populations are on **USVI, the Grenadines** and **Grenada**. Breeds in scattered colonies, often nesting in low bushes and trees. Difficult to see away from breeding sites.

ID: There are **two main color phases**: all **white** or **buff-brown**. Both have dark brown-black outerwings extending to form a broad dark band along innerwings, and typically, a **buff-white tail**. White phase can show yellowish wash to head and neck. All have a **pale blue bill** and distinctive red legs and feet. Immature variably gray-brown with paler underparts, dark underwings, grayish bill and dull red feet.

VOICE: Calls include a harsh "*squawk*" and deep rattle.

3 **Masked Booby** *Sula dactylatra* L 86 cm (34″) | WS 165 cm (65″)

Localized resident, mainly around the northern islands, where the largest populations are on **USVI** and **Anguilla**. Breeds in small numbers in a few scattered colonies, with Brown Boobies. Adults make regular flights from nest sites to deeper water to feed and are rarely seen from the main islands.

ID: Strikingly white with **black tail** and outerwings extending to form a broad dark band along innerwings. Obvious **dark mask around yellow eye and bill**; legs and feet gray. Immature browner with strongly contrasting **white underparts and collar**, and a paler bill.

VOICE: Calls include a goose-like braying and whistles.

1

1i

1
DARK PHASE
2
2
LIGHT PHASE
3i
3

Distinctive, large seabirds

1 **Magnificent Frigatebird** *Fregata magnificens* L 102 cm (40") | WS 229 cm (90")

An iconic species of coastal waters, Magnificent Frigatebirds can be seen **throughout** but only breed in a few scattered colonies on small islands off **BVI, Anguilla, Antigua, Barbuda** and **Guadeloupe**. The largest and most accessible colony is in mangroves at Codrington Lagoon, Barbuda. Most often seen in small groups effortlessly circling high in the sky along coasts and inshore waters, they never land on water but rest and roost on mangroves, rocky outcrops or buoys. Also known locally as 'pirate birds' or 'man-o'-war birds', they aggressively chase other seabirds with great aerial agility, forcing them to drop their catch, and will swoop for flying fish and discards from fishing boats.

ID: Large and distinctive in flight with **long, thin, angled wings** and a **long, forked tail** that is often held closed. Male all black with a **red throat sac**, inflated in courtship display. Female is similar, but with a **white breast**. Immature has **white head and breast**. Both female and immature show paler panel across inner part of upper wing. **VOICE:** Typically silent at sea but highly vocal at nest sites with a range of guttural rattling calls and bill clicking.

♂ with inflated throat sac.

2 **Brown Pelican** *Pelecanus occidentalis* L 122 cm (48") | WS 215 cm (85")

Unmistakable, seen year-round along inshore waters, cliffs and coastal wetlands **throughout**, with smaller numbers south from Martinique. Nests in small, scattered colonies in mangroves and on sea cliffs. Their spectacular plunge-dives for fish are often close inshore and can even be among people swimming! They sometimes gather on ponds and form tight, surface-feeding flocks. Can be confiding when resting in mangroves and on rocks, trees, jetties and boats.

ID: **Huge and distinctive** with heavy body, short tail and **characteristic long bill with pouch**. Head and neck white, becoming more colorful when breeding, with yellow forehead and chestnut hindneck. Immatures drabber, with paler underparts and darker head. Often seen in flight, which is heavy with a few flaps and short glides; small groups fly in lines.

VOICE: Guttural grunts and squeaks with bill-claps, but usually silent away from breeding colonies.

WATERBIRDS

The varied wetlands of the Eastern Caribbean are vital habitats for waterbirds, from flocks of elegant Black-necked Stilts fringing a salt-pond to a solitary Yellow-crowned Night Heron stalking crabs in the deep shade of a mangrove swamp. Migration periods can be particularly dramatic, especially between August and November, when large numbers of plovers and sandpipers arrive, some just days after leaving their Arctic breeding grounds. The best places to see a range of waterbirds are the more extensive open ponds, coastal lagoons and mangrove swamps. Numbers of birds on any wetland fluctuate in response to rainfall and water levels: many shallow wetlands periodically dry out, and waterbirds respond by moving between sites or even between islands.

More than 50 species are resident or regular visitors, and identification can be challenging at a wetland teeming with unfamiliar ducks, herons, egrets and shorebirds. A good starting point, especially for shorebirds, is to compare size, leg length and bill shape and look for different feeding strategies. For example, some species probe in deeper water, some disperse around muddy or vegetated margins, and others feed together in tight flocks.

Most migratory species are seen in non-breeding plumage between September and March, so this is described. However, some birds arrive early in August or leave later in April/May, when they can be in breeding plumage or in transition between the two. Key features of breeding and juvenile plumages are given where these are likely to be seen or cause confusion.

Close views of waterbirds on a coastal wetland, Anegada, BVI.

Ducks and grebes

1 White-cheeked Pintail *Anas bahamensis* L 43 cm (17")

Widespread and locally common resident from the **Virgin Islands to Guadeloupe**, becoming scarcer farther south; often the only duck species present. A dabbling duck found on deeper freshwater and brackish wetlands, including salt-ponds, where flotillas of ducklings can be a common sight. Fluctuating water levels result in some local movement or dispersal.

ID: Unmistakable combination of **white cheeks, red bill patch**, boldly spotted brown underparts and **pointed white tail**. Brown and green bands on upperwing and white patch on underwing are visible in flight.

VOICE: A range of rasping quacks and whistles.

2 Blue-winged Teal *Spatula discors* L 39 cm (15½")

Non-breeding visitor **throughout**, with smaller numbers south from Guadeloupe: the only common migrant duck. Often in flocks, it can occur on any large freshwater or saline wetland, where it feeds by dabbling in shallow water and along wetland margins.

ID: Male finely spotted brown with **dark gray-blue head, obvious white crescent in front of eye** and white patch on flanks before dark tail. Female dull mottled brown, with **pale patch at base of bill** and thin dark line through the eye. In flight both show an obvious **pale-blue panel** on upperwing and **white center** to underwing.

VOICE: Mostly silent when in the region, but female has a bark-like "*quack*", male a thin repeated whistle.

Scarce and rare dabbling ducks can be found by searching through flocks of Blue-winged Teal. The most frequent are Green-winged Teal *Anas crecca*, American Wigeon *Mareca americana*, Northern Shoveler *Spatula clypeata* and Northern Pintail *Anas acuta*.

E 1 West Indian Whistling-Duck *Dendrocygna arborea* L 53 cm (21″)

NT **Endemic to the Caribbean**, with the main populations in the Greater Antilles and Bahamas. Only reliably found on **Antigua and Barbuda**, with occasional records elsewhere. Small flocks feed mainly at night on seeds and plants, often flying to grassland away from water. Can be difficult to see in the daytime when roosting around brackish lagoons, freshwater ponds and marshes. Habitat loss, predation by introduced species and hunting have all contributed to its decline: extensive conservation and public awareness programs are now well established.

ID: Large with **upright posture**, long neck and long legs. Mostly warm mottled brown with **boldly marked black and white flanks**; throat and neck pale, except for dark brown line down hindneck. Bill and legs gray. Shows **large pale patch on upperwing** in flight.

VOICE: A mournful, high-pitched whistle and brighter, rapid trilling.

2 Black-bellied Whistling-Duck *Dendrocygna autumnalis* L 51 cm (20″)

Uncommon resident on **Barbados** and increasingly seen on **Grenada**. A rare wandering visitor elsewhere. Localized on freshwater ponds and marshes, flying out at dusk to forage for seeds and plants in fields and grassland.

ID: A large, striking duck with a distinctive **black belly, white band across wing** and pale face with obvious **white eyering**. **Bill and legs** are a **bright pinky-red**. Juvenile duller overall with less black on belly. In flight shows black underwings and **broad white bar on upperwing**.

VOICE: Shrill trilling whistles and a sharp "*chit*".

3 Fulvous Whistling-Duck

Dendrocygna bicolor L 48 cm (19″)

A rare and transient non-breeding visitor to coastal marshes and wetlands. It can occur anywhere in small numbers but is most often recorded on **Barbados**, where possibly introduced.

ID: Dark brown upperparts, contrasting **warm tawny-brown** underparts with **white flashes on flanks** and **white undertail**. Bill, legs and feet are **bright blue-gray**. In flight **wings are all-dark** and **tail has obvious white band at base**.

VOICE: Wheezy and high-pitched "*pi-tuuu*" and rasping "*rruppp*".

1
2

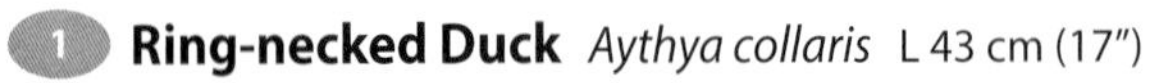

1 Ring-necked Duck *Aythya collaris* L 43 cm (17")

An uncommon and sporadic non-breeding visitor **throughout**. A diving duck found mostly on deeper freshwater ponds and wetlands, where it makes frequent short dives for plants and invertebrates.
ID: Male is striking with black upperparts and contrasting **pale gray flanks** with obvious **white band at the front**. A red-brown ring at base of neck explains its common name but is difficult to see. Female brown with paler head, white base to bill and **white eyering**. Both have a distinctively patterned **bill: gray with black and white bands at tip**.
VOICE: A short, deep barking quack.

2 Lesser Scaup *Aythya affinis* L 42 cm (16½")

Uncommon to rare non-breeding visitor. Can occur **throughout** on freshwater ponds and saline lagoons, where it dives for aquatic invertebrates.
ID: Male black with contrasting **white flanks** and **pale, finely barred back**. Female brown overall with paler flanks and obvious **white patch at base of the bill**. Both have bright yellow eyes and pale gray bill with **small dark tip**.
VOICE: Growling, low repeated "*rrrra*".

3 **Ruddy Duck** *Oxyura jamaicensis* L 39 cm (15½")

Non-breeding visitor **throughout**, but there are localized breeding populations on islands that have extensive freshwater wetlands with fringing or emergent vegetation. The most commonly seen diving duck, often found in small groups. Male has a distinctive courtship display, head-bobbing and rapidly tapping bill against breast, forming bubbles on the water surface.
ID: Compact shape with a large head and **long tail, often held upright**. Male is chestnut overall with striking **white cheeks** and undertail, and a **distinctive blue bill**. Non-breeding males are browner with a dark bill. Female dull brown with a darker cap, **dark line across pale cheek** and gray bill.
VOICE: Male display calls are repeated short popping and croaks.

4 **Masked Duck** *Nomonyx dominicus* L 33 cm (13")

An uncommon resident, restricted to **Guadeloupe, Martinique, St Lucia** and **Barbados**; rare visitor elsewhere. A diving duck, found on small ponds with thick emergent or floating vegetation, where it often stays in cover and can be difficult to see. Readily moves in response to varying water levels in local wetlands.
ID: Small and compact with a large head and **long tail, often held upright**. Male is red-brown with a **black face**, pale eyering and **bright blue bill** with a black tip. Female paler, mottled brown with **two bold stripes across the face** and a gray bill. In flight, both show dark tail and **obvious white patch** on upperwing.
VOICE: A sharp "*tek*" and run of whistles.

1 **Least Grebe** *Tachybaptus dominicus* L 24 cm (9½")

Resident in small numbers on the **Virgin Islands**; rare elsewhere. Highly localized on sheltered freshwater wetlands with fringing vegetation, where it dives for small fish and invertebrates. Mostly occurs singly or in pairs. Can be secretive and difficult to see. Vulnerable to fluctuating water levels and disturbance.
ID: Tiny: smaller and sleeker than Pied-billed Grebe. **Very dark gray** with black crown and throat in breeding plumage, becoming much paler overall when non-breeding. No obvious tail. Distinctive **bright yellow eyes** and **slender dark bill**. Juvenile paler with striped head.
VOICE: Rapid, high-pitched chatter and a squeaky "*beep*".

2 **Pied-billed Grebe** *Podilymbus podiceps* L 34 cm (13½")

Generally uncommon, occurs **throughout** as a non-breeding visitor, but there are some small scattered breeding populations on islands with suitable habitat (mainly freshwater wetlands, less often brackish ponds). Dives for small fish and invertebrates but can be elusive, readily swims to cover in emergent vegetation.
ID: Small and compact with dark brown upperparts and tawny underparts; looks grayer at distance. Eyes dark with **pale eyering** and **bold black band near tip** of **thick bill**. More striking when breeding, with black throat and more strongly marked bill. Juvenile paler with striped face and neck.
VOICE: A rapid, agitated chattering.

Coot

3 **American Coot** *Fulica americana* L 39 cm (15½")

Locally common **throughout** but less frequent south of Martinique. Scattered breeding populations are joined by non-breeding visitors. Dives to feed on plants and invertebrates in shallow, vegetated ponds or searches adjoining marshy and grassy areas. Gregarious, often noisy and aggressive when breeding, males chasing each other and flapping across water surface. **'Caribbean Coot'**, with a larger white shield extending onto crown, was formerly recognized as a separate species, *F. caribaea*, but is now included with *F. americana*.
ID: Unmistakable, **gray-black** with a **white shield** to forehead and **stout white bill** with broken dark band near tip. Juvenile has paler throat and underparts. Swims with jerking head movement, often showing white undertail patch. Out of water, **distinctly lobed toes** are obvious.
VOICE: A range of calls include throaty clucks and short, single "*pruk*".

Some Caribbean birds have an extensive white shield that may show some yellow.

Gallinules and rails

1 **Common Gallinule** (Moorhen) *Gallinula galeata* L 34 cm (13½″)

One of the most common and widespread waterbirds, resident **throughout** on a wide range of wetlands with emergent or fringing vegetation. Forages for plant material and invertebrates in ponds and on adjacent swamps and grassland. Surprisingly agile: will climb among low branches and vegetation.
ID: Dark gray and brown with **broken white line on flanks**, striking white edges to undertail, obvious **yellow-tipped, red bill** and **red forehead shield**. Legs and **long, thin toes** are pale yellow. Juvenile duller pale gray and brown, lacks red bill shield.
VOICE: Highly vocal with a variety of cackling and clucking sounds and a sharp "*kek*".

2 **Purple Gallinule** *Porphyrio martinica* L 33 cm (13″)

Appears to be establishing on freshwater wetlands and marshes at least on **Guadeloupe** and **Barbados**; rare elsewhere.
ID: Broadly similar to Common Gallinule but head, neck and underparts are **brilliant purple-blue, forehead shield blue-white** and legs bright yellow.

Clapper Rail *Rallus crepitans* L 37 cm (14½")

Resident in small numbers on the **Virgin Islands, Antigua and Barbuda**, increasingly on Guadeloupe; rare or absent elsewhere. Most active at dawn and dusk, it forages for crustaceans, invertebrates and seeds along vegetated and muddy margins of mangroves and brackish swamps. More easily heard than seen, its loud calls can ring out across a wetland and territorial disputes in males often lead to noisy, dramatic chases.
ID: The **only long-billed rail**; can look long-necked. Mottled gray-brown with buff underparts and **vertical, black-edged white barring** on flanks. Tail often angled upwards, showing white undertail with black barring. Gray face with **long, slightly down-curved orangey bill**; long pale legs. Juvenile paler and duller with browner bill.
VOICE: Single or excited runs of loud raucous "*kek-kek-kek*".

Sora *Porzana carolina* L 22 cm (8½")

Non-breeding visitor **throughout** but uncommon and localized. Secretive, most active at dawn and dusk, and may be under-recorded. Searches for seeds and invertebrates around vegetated and muddy margins of mangroves, and both brackish and freshwater ponds.
ID: The **only regularly occurring small rail**. Warm mottled brown upperparts with fine streaking, underparts gray with **subtly barred flanks**. Short tail is often angled upwards, revealing pale undertail. Distinctive **black face and throat**, stronger when breeding, and a **short bright yellow bill**. Juvenile browner, less well-marked, bill duller.
VOICE: A rapid trill, slowing and descending, and a clear, shrill, two-note whistle.

Shorebirds

Each year thousands of shorebirds stream in from North America to overwinter with resident species or make short refueling stops during long migrations to South America. Weather fronts can temporarily ground migrating birds in large numbers. Barbados, through its isolated location, provides a particularly important refuge for birds to rest and feed. Migratory species are mainly present between August and April, but there can be occasional records in all months. Many of the region's wetlands are easily accessible with close perimeter viewing, providing ideal opportunities to identify and become familiar with both resident and migratory species; you may find a rarity, even one that has crossed the Atlantic!

LARGE, DISTINCTIVE SHOREBIRDS

1 **Black-necked** (Black-winged) **Stilt**

Himantopus (himantopus) mexicanus
L 36 cm (14")

One of the most distinctive and familiar species of open brackish lagoons and salt-ponds. More common from the **Virgin Islands to Guadeloupe**, becoming scarce farther south. Wades through deep water to feed on invertebrates; rests in tight flocks, often on one leg with bill tucked away. Noisy and active when breeding, some birds are confiding and nest close to tracks or boardwalks.

ID: Unmistakable, slim, strikingly **black and white**, with a **long thin bill** and **very long pink legs**. Female and immature are browner on the back and wings.

VOICE: Highly vocal, including noisy and insistent "*wit-wit-wit*".

2 **American Oystercatcher** *Haematopus palliatus* L 48 cm (19")

Widespread but uncommon resident from the **Virgin Islands to Guadeloupe**, rare or absent farther south. Mostly occurs singly or in pairs along rocky coasts and on headlands, stony beaches and offshore cays; can be elusive and flighty. Feeds on invertebrates and shellfish, which it prizes open with its strong bill.

ID: Large and distinctive with **long red bill** and **yellow eye** with a red eyering. **Boldly marked** with dark brown upperparts, **black head and neck**, and contrasting white underparts. A broad **white wingbar** is obvious in flight.

VOICE: Short, high-pitched emphatic "*kweep*", often given in flight, and repeated fast chattering "*peep-peep-peep*".

3 **Whimbrel** *Numenius phaeopus hudsonicus* L 43 cm (17")

Uncommon non-breeding visitor, more frequent in the **northern islands** and **Barbados**, with fewer south of Guadeloupe. Small numbers return to overwinter in mangrove swamps and on brackish lagoons and freshwater ponds where there are good populations of small crustaceans and invertebrates. Can be seen around wetland margins, resting on perches such as rocks or low branches.

ID: One of the largest shorebirds. Mottled brown with some streaking and barring, but easily distinguished by its **very long down-curved bill** and long gray legs. Bold **dark stripes** run through the eye and along the crown. In flight shows **dark rump**, barred tail and underwings.

VOICE: Far-carrying run of high-pitched whistles "*pii-pii-pii-pii-pii-pii*".

1♂
1♀
2
2
3
3

PLOVERS

Plovers are short-billed wading birds that forage along beaches and drier wetland margins, or on grasslands. When feeding, they tend to spread out in search of small invertebrates, adopting a 'stop, look, run' approach. Each species has a distinct call, often given in flight. The smaller plovers all show **white wingbars** and dark markings on the crown, face and breast, typically darker or black when breeding, especially in males.

1 **Black-bellied** (Grey) **Plover** *Pluvialis squatarola* L 30 cm (12")

Non-breeding visitor from the high Arctic with occasional records year-round. Can occur **throughout**. Typically forms small flocks on coastal lagoons, salt-ponds and sandbanks, especially around the drying margins of seasonal ponds. Roosts on rocky outcrops, salt-pond walls or sandy areas.
ID: Large, heavy-looking with gray upperparts and mainly white underparts, **stout dark bill** and long gray legs. Juvenile similar but more speckled overall with light streaking on breast and flanks. Striking in breeding plumage with spangled black and white upperparts and **solid black underparts from face to belly**. In flight shows **white rump** and distinctive **black patch at base of underwing**.
VOICE: Mournful single- or three-note whistle "*tu-oo-ee*", mainly given in flight.

2 **Southern Lapwing** *Vanellus chilensis* L 35 cm (14")

Large plover from South America, increasingly recorded on **Barbados** and **Grenada**, occasionally on **St Vincent and the Grenadines**.

American Golden-Plover *Pluvialis dominica* L 25 cm (10")

Uncommon passage visitor mainly between August and November, with occasional records at other times; can occur **throughout**. Mostly overflies the region on route to wintering grounds in South America, but small flocks can be grounded by storms and weather fronts. Most often seen on seasonal wetlands and rainwater pools in short grassland, including airfields and golf courses.

ID: Very similar to the more common Black-bellied Plover, but slimmer and appears longer-legged, and is mostly found in different habitats. Large, mainly gray-brown with **speckled upperparts** and paler mottled underparts, **black bill** and long gray legs. An **obvious white stripe above eye** extends to forehead. Post-breeding adults retain varying amounts of gold spotting on upperparts and black markings on breast and belly. Juvenile has crisper, pale spotting on upperparts. In flight shows faint white wingbar and **gray underwings**.

VOICE: Soft, high-pitched whistles, "*wee-wer*" or "*wee-eet*".

NT 

Killdeer *Charadrius vociferus* L 25 cm (10")

Widespread resident and non-breeding visitor from the **Virgin Islands to Antigua**, rare or absent farther south. Nests in open grassy or stony areas around wetland margins but often forages for invertebrates away from water, on short grassland and disturbed ground.

ID: Mid-sized and long-tailed; the only plover with **two distinct dark breast bands.** Brown above, mainly white below, with an **orange rump and uppertail** and a boldly marked head. Eye is large and dark with an orange eyering; legs are pale. Shows bold white wingbar in flight.

VOICE: Vocal day and night; calls include a high-pitched extended trilling and drawn-out "*kill-dee*".

Semipalmated Plover *Charadrius semipalmatus* L 19 cm (7½")

Common non-breeding visitor **throughout** to beaches and coastal wetlands, with occasional records year-round; the most easily seen small plover. Gathers in small, loose flocks when feeding around muddy and sandy margins. Forms roosts on rocky outcrops, salt-pond walls or open sandy areas, often with other shorebirds.

ID: Brown upperparts, clean white underparts with obvious **white collar** and **single dark breast-band.** Head brown with white forehead and thin white eyebrow. Head markings and breast-band blacker when breeding, especially in male. Bill short and dark with **pale orange base. Legs yellow-orange**, toes partially webbed ('semipalmated'), but this is difficult to see. Juvenile upperparts have thin, pale feather fringes.

VOICE: High-pitched, short "*che-u*" and a sharp, repeated "*pyip*".

Wilson's Plover *Anarhynchus (Charadrius) wilsonia* L 20 cm (8")

Widespread but uncommon resident, rare or absent from islands without large coastal wetlands and mangroves. A solitary species that can be inconspicuous when resting in the open with its belly to the ground, but small flocks sometimes gather to roost. Uses its strong bill to exploit small crabs and invertebrates. Nests in coastal habitats where it is vulnerable to disturbance and encroaching development.

ID: Broadly similar to Semipalmated Plover but differs in having a **longer and heavier, all-dark bill**, and **pale gray-pink legs.** Forehead patch and broad breast-band blacker when breeding. Posture can appear flattened and slightly elongated.

VOICE: Repeated short sharp "*kwit*" and a softer "*chrrp*".

Snowy Plover *Anarhynchus (Charadrius) nivosus* L 15 cm (6")

Uncommon resident from the **Virgin Islands to Anguilla**, becoming increasingly rare or absent farther south. Found on sandy spits, beaches and dry areas around coastal ponds. Runs very quickly when feeding or alarmed. Numbers are in decline: threats include habitat loss, disturbance and predation.

ID: Very small. The **palest plover**; can be difficult to spot on white sand beaches. Pale gray upperparts, white underparts, **gray patch at base of neck that never forms a complete breast band. Face is white** with darker crown, cheek and neck patches (latter black when breeding, stronger on male). **Short, thin black bill and gray legs.**

VOICE: A soft rising whistle "*kuu-wi*", sharper "*trrp*" and a rolling trill.

NT Piping Plover *Charadrius melodus* L 19 cm (7½")

Rare visitor to the northern islands. Non-breeding birds are similar to Snowy Plover but have **pale orangey legs** and a short, stubby bill that is **orange at base in breeding plumage.**

Collared Plover

Anarhynchus (Charadrius) collaris

L 14 cm (5½")

A small plover, increasingly seen on **Barbados** and **Grenada**, rare elsewhere. Similar to Semipalmated Plover but smaller with **thin black bill, pinkish legs** and **chestnut markings** on crown and neck.

1n
1b
2n
2b
3n
3b

SANDPIPERS AND OTHER SHOREBIRDS

Several species of small shorebirds overwinter or pass through on migration, with occasional records year-round. They readily form small mixed flocks that wheel low over open ponds and lagoons. Many species appear superficially similar and can be difficult to separate; familiarity with Least Sandpiper and Semipalmated Sandpiper can be useful, as these are the smallest and most common species.

1 Ruddy Turnstone *Arenaria interpres* L 22 cm (8½″)

A common non-breeding visitor **throughout** to wetland margins, beaches and rocky coasts. Can be confiding around jetties and harbors. Gathers in small flocks, often with Sanderling, to forage along beaches or on washed-up sargassum seaweed. Flips rocks (and plants) with its bill when searching for invertebrates, hence its common name.
ID: Dark upperparts with contrasting white belly and **bold dark breast-patch**; short, sharp black bill; and **orange legs**. Juvenile similar, but pale feather-edging gives a scaly appearance to upperparts. Unmistakable in bright orange and black breeding plumage. **Strikingly patterned in flight**.
VOICE: Given in flight, a short low "*tuk*" or "*tuk-a-tuk*".

Sanderling *Calidris alba* L 20 cm (8″)

Non-breeding visitor to coastal wetlands **throughout**. One of the few species to forage on open sandy beaches, where it runs rapidly between waves, picking invertebrates from wet sand. Roosts on rocks and beaches in small flocks with other shorebirds, especially Ruddy Turnstone. Lacks a hind toe (unique among sandpipers).
ID: Very pale gray and white, with whitish face and a **dark crescent at bend of wing** (can be obscured). Breeding plumage much brighter, with rufous head and neck and more mottled upperparts. Short, straight black bill and black legs. Juvenile, which can be confused with other sandpipers, has white-edged dark feathers on upperparts and **faint streaking to sides of buff breast**. Shows white wingbar in flight.
VOICE: Typical call a high-pitched short "*kwit*".

Red Knot *Calidris canutus* L 27 cm (10½″)

Uncommon to rare passage visitor **throughout**, typically seen singly or in small numbers among mixed flocks of shorebirds on beaches and margins of coastal lagoons. Red Knot is always a special find, as the vast majority overfly the region on their long and amazing migrations from breeding grounds in the Arctic to wintering areas in southern South America.
ID: Stocky; one of the largest sandpipers. Gray upperparts, paler underparts with **fine gray spotting and barring on breast and flanks**. Obvious **pale stripe above eye**, stout black bill and short greenish legs. Juvenile is similar but has fine pale feather-edging on back and wings, giving a scaly appearance. Breeding plumage is much more colorful, with red-orange underparts from head to belly. In flight all plumages show thin white wingbar and **gray, finely barred rump**.
VOICE: A soft deep "*chup*".

1
2
3
1b
1n
2j
2n
1ST WINTER
3

NT 1 Least Sandpiper *Calidris minutilla* L 15 cm (6″)

A common non-breeding visitor found **throughout** on a wide range of wetlands, from small ponds to large coastal lagoons. Small flocks forage around muddy and grassy margins, where they can be unobtrusive.

ID: Tiny; the world's smallest sandpiper. **Brown upperparts**, pale underparts with some **streaking** to side of **brownish breast**. **Fine, slightly down-curved bill**. Distinctively **pale yellow-green legs** are short and often held at an angle, so birds can appear to be crouching. Darker in breeding plumage, with stronger streaking on breast and rufous fringes to upperparts. Juvenile has brighter more rufous upperparts with scaly feather-edging and buff sides to lightly streaked breast.

VOICE: Calls include a high-pitched, trilling "*tr-eep*".

NT 2 Semipalmated Sandpiper *Calidris pusilla* L 16 cm (6½″)

Common non-breeding visitor to a wide range of coastal wetlands **throughout**. Feeds in loose flocks, typically in shallow water and around muddy margins. Although the most numerous of the small wintering sandpipers in the Eastern Caribbean, its global population is in decline due to pressure on key wintering and migration sites.

ID: Very small. More **gray-brown** than Least Sandpiper, with diffuse streaking on side of breast and thin white stripe above eye. Short **black bill** is **straightish** and blunt-tipped. Black legs have **part-webbed toes** ('semipalmated'). Juvenile has pale feather-edges on back and wings, giving a scaly appearance. Upperparts darker in breeding plumage, with some rufous fringes and finer streaking on side of breast.

VOICE: Squeaky "*chrrp*". Flocks can be vocal with soft chattering calls.

VU 3 White-rumped Sandpiper *Calidris fuscicollis* L 19 cm (7½″)

Uncommon passage visitor **throughout**, found on muddy and shallow margins around coastal wetlands, occasionally beaches and flooded grassland. Mostly occurs in small numbers, often when grounded by storms and weather fronts, and can easily be overlooked among mixed flocks of shorebirds.

ID: Gray upperparts, white underparts with white throat patch and **gray streaking on head, neck and breast**; can look dark-fronted. Obvious white stripe above eye; short, **slightly down-curved black bill**; and dark gray legs. **Long wings extend beyond tail at rest**, giving a long-bodied appearance. Juvenile upperparts more rufous; white feather-edging forms loose lines on back. In flight, shows thin white wingbar and **distinctive white rump**.

VOICE: High-pitched twittering and squeaky "*tzeet*".

4 Western Sandpiper *Calidris mauri* L 17 cm (6½″)

Uncommon passage visitor. Can occur **throughout**. Very similar to Semipalmated Sandpiper and easily overlooked among mixed flocks of small shorebirds. Differs in typically having a **longer, fine-tipped and slightly down-curved bill**, and **longer legs**.

VOICE: An incisive, high-pitched "*cheeet*".

1n
1j
2n
2j
3n
3j
3
4j

1 Pectoral Sandpiper *Calidris melanotos* L 23 cm (9")

Uncommon passage visitor **throughout**, to muddy and shallow margins around coastal lagoons and freshwater ponds. Readily forages on flooded grassland, including golf courses, often in small flocks.
ID: Brown upperparts with pale feather-edging. In all plumages, distinctive **heavily streaked upper breast** (hence its common name) has a **well-defined border** with white belly. Pale stripe above eye and **slightly down-curved bill**, pale at base. Legs pale green-yellow. Juvenile is similar but brighter; pale feather-edging can form whitish V's on back. In flight shows thin white wingbar and white sides to dark tail.
VOICE: A lightly trilled "*trrrrrp*".

2 Spotted Sandpiper *Actitis macularius* L 19 cm (7½")

Common non-breeding visitor **throughout**, to a wide range of wetlands; the only shorebird species found from the coast to rainforest streams. Mainly seen singly, foraging on beaches, grassland and along the margins of streams and ponds, with a distinctive bobbing action.
ID: Plain brown with white underparts, **brown wash to side of neck** and fine white stripe above eye. Unmistakable in breeding plumage with **distinctive dark spotting on underparts**. Bill pale with dark tip, **legs pale yellow**. Juvenile is similar to non-breeding adult, but with extensive dark barring near bend of closed wing. Flies with characteristic bursts of **shallow, fluttering wingbeats** and short glides, typically low over water, showing obvious white wingbar.
VOICE: High-pitched "*weet*" or "*pee-weet*", typically in flight.

3 Solitary Sandpiper *Tringa solitaria* L 22 cm (8½")

Uncommon passage and non-breeding visitor **throughout**, mainly to freshwater wetlands, including temporary rainwater pools. Tends to migrate and overwinter singly or in small numbers. Walks with a characteristic bobbing action, although less obvious than Spotted Sandpiper. Flies quickly to height if disturbed.
ID: Darker upperparts than Spotted Sandpiper, with **fine white spotting**; underparts white with dark streaking on breast. White patch in front of the eye with **white eyering**, which can be obvious. Bill is dark gray, legs **pale gray-green**. When breeding, streaking is stronger on head and breast, and upperparts are more marked. Juvenile similar but with browner upperparts and more extensive spotting. In flight shows **dark center to barred white tail** and **very dark underwings**.
VOICE: Flight call is a high-pitched whistle "*pee-weet-weet*".

Spotted Sandpiper on a rainforest stream.

1j
2n
2j
2b
3j
3b

NT 1 Stilt Sandpiper *Calidris himantopus* L 22 cm (8½″)

Non-breeding visitor **throughout**, more numerous in the north and on Barbados, but less common south of Guadeloupe. Feeds around muddy and shallow margins of brackish and freshwater wetlands with a distinctive sharp, jabbing action, often leaning forward with head and upper neck under water. Gathers in tight flocks with other wading birds, especially Lesser Yellowlegs.

ID: Most easily separated from other small wading birds by **long, slightly down-curved bill** and **long yellow-green legs**. Upperparts gray-brown, underparts paler with extensive light streaking to side of breast and flanks, and obvious **white stripe above eye**. Juvenile paler overall with scaly feather-edging on upperparts. Much darker in breeding plumage, with heavily barred underparts. In flight shows **white rump patch**; feet project beyond tip of tail.

VOICE: Short "*trrrp*"; soft, whistled "*tuwee-tuwee*".

NT 2 Greater Yellowlegs *Tringa melanoleuca* and
VU 3 Lesser Yellowlegs *Tringa flavipes*

Common non-breeding visitors **throughout** on freshwater and brackish wetlands, Lesser Yellowlegs is more often found on small ponds and temporary pools. Very similar in appearance, both have distinctive yellow legs and are easily confused, especially if seen separately.

	2 Greater Yellowlegs	3 Lesser Yellowlegs
Size	**Larger** 36 cm (14″)	**Smaller** 27 cm (10½″)
Bill	Strong, longer, **slightly upturned**, often paler gray at base.	Fine, shorter, **straight**, mostly dark, can show small pale patch at base of lower mandible.
Non-breeding plumage	Upperparts gray-brown, finely spotted. **Underparts pale; fine streaking on neck and upper breast.**	Upperparts gray-brown, finely spotted. **Underparts pale; diffuse, less clearly defined streaking on neck and upper breast.**
Breeding plumage	Dark, more boldly marked upperparts and breast; **extensive barring on flanks that can extend to belly**.	Darker, more boldly marked upperparts and breast.
Juvenile	**Distinct streaking** on side of breast.	**Diffuse streaking** on side of breast; extensive fine spotting on back and wings.
Voice	High-pitched, typically **three- or four-note** "*tew-tew-tew*".	High-pitched and clipped but soft, often **single** "*tu*".
Feeding and behavior	Energetic; probes more actively and sometimes runs to catch small prey, often in deeper water. Mostly solitary or in smaller groups than Lesser Yellowlegs.	Restless; wades to pick invertebrates from surface or probes around margins. Readily forms flocks, often in large numbers.

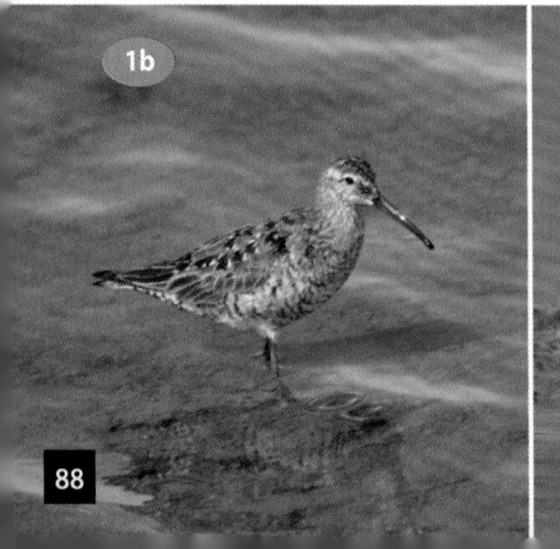
1b

2b

3b

1n
1j
2n
2j
3
NON-BREEDING
TO BREEDING
3j

 Willet *Tringa semipalmata* L 39 cm (15½″)

Resident from the **Virgin Islands to at least Guadeloupe**, occasional non-breeding visitor farther south. Individuals or breeding pairs can be elusive on brackish and freshwater wetlands, where they forage for small crustaceans and invertebrates in shallow water and muddy margins.
ID: Large and stocky with a **long, stout, straight bill** and **long pale gray legs**. Inconspicuously marked pale gray-brown with paler **gray wash to upper breast**, and white belly. Small pale patch in front of eye, bill gray with black tip. Darker and more heavily marked when breeding, with **extensive barring on neck, breast and flanks**. Striking in flight, **showing boldly marked black and white wings**.
VOICE: Sharp and repeated "*wik*" and "*weer*". When breeding, a rolling "*pill-will-willet*" (hence its common name).

VU 2 Short-billed Dowitcher *Limnodromus griseus* L 28 cm (11″)

Non-breeding visitor **throughout**, usually in small numbers on coastal lagoons, salt-ponds and mangrove swamps. Feeds with a probing, jabbing action around muddy fringes or in shallow water.
ID: Distinctive with **heavy body** and, despite its name, a **long gray bill**. Grayish overall with **bold white stripe** above the eye. Underparts whiter with **speckling on breast, flanks and lower belly**, and **fine white barring on undertail**. More colorful in breeding plumage, with orange underparts and feather fringes. Legs pale yellow. Juvenile browner than non-breeding adult, with orange-buff breast, obvious **dark crown** and strongly patterned inner flight feathers (tertials). In flight shows **white trailing edge to inner wing**, **thin white rump patch** extending to lower back, and finely barred white tail.
VOICE: A fast "*tee-tee-tee*" and soft, whistled "*wud-de-do*".

NT Long-billed Dowitcher *Limnodromus scolopaceus*

A rare visitor; can occur throughout. Very similar to Short-billed Dowitcher, but dark barring on undertail is broader and juvenile's tertials are plainer.

 Wilson's Snipe *Gallinago delicata* L 28 cm (11″)

Uncommon to rare non-breeding visitor. Can occur **throughout**. Often inconspicuous in vegetation around freshwater wetlands and marshes but will rest along margins, often in a hunched posture. Moves slowly with jerky motion when probing in soft ground.
ID: Very long straight bill and **short, pale legs**. Brown, **boldly striped head and back**; paler, heavily barred breast and flanks. If disturbed, rises quickly, flying with a zigzag movement, showing extensive barring to underwing.
VOICE: Harsh rasping "*k-reck*", given in flight.

1n
1b
2j
2n
3
3

Herons and egrets

Herons and egrets are a familiar sight in the region, readily gathering on wetlands where prey is abundant. Western Cattle-Egret, Snowy Egret, Little Blue Heron and Green Heron are the most widespread and easily seen. Some species wade patiently in deep water, stalking fish, while others dart for aquatic invertebrates around shallow margins. Egrets roost and breed in loose colonies in mangroves and large trees; flocks flying to and from feeding grounds can be an impressive sight. Migrant and winter visitors from North America augment the resident populations between September and April, especially on the more northerly islands.

1 Little Blue Heron *Egretta caerulea* L 63 cm (25")

Common non-breeding visitor **throughout** but becoming established as a breeding species on islands with suitable habitat. Most often seen singly on brackish and freshwater wetlands, rivers, small seasonal ponds and grasslands, but small groups will gather where prey is plentiful.
ID: **Gray-blue** with purple tones on head and neck (not always obvious) and long back plumes that extend beyond the tail. Distinctive **long, pale blue bill** with **obvious dark tip** and long, green-gray legs (darker when breeding). Juvenile is **all-white** and can resemble Snowy Egret, but the two-toned **bill** and leg color are distinctive. Immature can be a confusing and untidy mix of **white and blue-gray**.
VOICE: A deep, rasping "*crawk*".

2 Great Blue Heron

Ardea herodias L 119 cm (47″)

Regular but uncommon non-breeding visitor **throughout**, with occasional records year-round, including recent reports of breeding on the Virgin Islands. A solitary species of brackish and freshwater wetlands, it wades slowly or stands upright and motionless, looking for fish and invertebrates.

ID: The **largest** heron. Mainly blue-gray, with obvious **dark stripe** above the eye and **dark streaking on front of long neck**. Strong, **heavy yellow bill** and long gray legs. Juvenile can show pinker tones and has a dark crown, more heavily marked neck and a darker bill with a yellow lower mandible. Flight is slow, with wings bowed. Wings are strikingly two-toned: inner and central areas pale, outer and rear parts dark.

VOICE: Deep and hoarse "*fraank*", often given in flight.

2

2j

3 Tricolored Heron

Egretta tricolor L 66 cm (26″)

Uncommon to rare non-breeding visitor; can occur **throughout**. Stalks fish and invertebrates in brackish lagoons and freshwater wetlands, wading through deeper water, often up to belly feathers.

ID: Gray upperparts contrast **with clean white belly**. Neck long and sinuous, gray with white speckles on front. **Very long bill** is yellow with dark upper mandible, becoming blue with dark tip when breeding. Long, pale yellow-green legs. **Juvenile is red-brown** on head, neck and upperparts. In flight, white belly and **large white underwing patch** are obvious.

VOICE: A deep, rough "*craawk*".

3

3j

1 **Great** (Great White) **Egret** *Ardea alba* L 99 cm (39")

Locally common non-breeding visitor **throughout**, increasingly establishing as a breeding species. Mostly solitary or seen in small numbers on freshwater and brackish wetlands, occasionally on adjacent drier grassland. Wades slowly around pond margins, foraging for fish and invertebrates.

ID: The **largest egret**, all-white with **very long, thin neck; long yellow bill;** and **long black legs and black feet**. A bare patch of skin extends as a line below the eye. In breeding plumage, has wispy plumes on back and darker upper mandible. Long neck forms an **obvious deep bulge** in flight.

VOICE: Deep, harsh hollow-sounding "*craak*".

2 **Snowy Egret** *Egretta thula* L 61 cm (24")

Resident **throughout**, locally common on coastal ponds and lagoons. Can form large roosts, with localized breeding colonies in trees by wetlands, often with other species of egret and heron.

ID: Small, slim and **all-white**, with **dark legs** and **striking yellow feet**. Long black bill with bare **yellow patch between bill and eye**. In breeding plumage it develops spectacular plumes on head, neck, back and breast. In non-breeding adult and immature, dark legs are **yellow-green at rear**. In flight legs extend beyond tail, yellow feet clearly visible.

VOICE: A rasping, strong, deep "*raa-aarr*" or "*kaa-arr*".

3 **Little Egret** *Egretta garzetta* L 58 cm (23")

Small breeding population on **Barbados,** rare but increasing non-breeding visitor elsewhere.

ID: Similar to Snowy Egret, but **patch between bill and eye** is blue-gray (briefly red when breeding); lacks Snowy's rough, plumed crest, having **two longer and more clearly defined head plumes**. Non-breeding birds typically have all-black legs.

4 **Western Cattle-Egret** *Ardea (Bubulcus) ibis* L 56 cm (22")

A common and familiar resident **throughout** on open grassy areas, agricultural land, airfields, golf courses and around wetlands, but less frequently in water. Often associates with cattle and other livestock, feeding on the invertebrates and small reptiles they disturb. Nests and roosts in noisy colonies in mangroves and trees close to wetlands: small flocks flying to and from feeding areas are a highlight of a walk early or late in the day.

ID: The **smallest egret**. White with a **short neck, gray-brown legs** and **short yellow bill**. More colorful when breeding, developing buff-orange plumes to head, breast and back, a redder bill and yellow to bright orange-red legs. Immature has darker legs and bill.

VOICE: Short croaks and quacks.

4n

4b

TWO DISTINCT
HEAD PLUMES
1n
3
2b
2n
LEGS YELLOW AT REAR IN
NON-BREEDING PLUMAGE

1 **Green** (Green-backed) **Heron** *Butorides (striata) virescens* L 46 cm (18")

Resident **throughout**: one of the most common and easily seen herons in a wide range of habitats from coastal wetlands to forest streams, often away from water. Stands motionless on rocks and low branches, watching intently for fish and invertebrates; also wades slowly through shallow water.
ID: The smallest common heron; can appear **thick-necked** and **hunched**. **Gray-green** with **dark crown** and **brown-red underparts** with streaking on throat and breast. Strong, dark bill with yellow lower mandible, **yellow legs and feet**. Appears all-dark in flight. Juvenile more marked with **heavy streaking on neck and underparts**, and bands of fine pale spots on upperwing.
VOICE: A repeated "*kak-kak-kak*" and a loud, emphatic "*keowk*", given in flight.

2 **Yellow-crowned Night Heron** *Nyctanassa violacea* L 63 cm (25")

Resident **throughout**, locally common but in small numbers. Forages for crustaceans and invertebrates in mangrove swamps, on brackish wetlands and beaches, and even in gardens. Mainly nocturnal but often active at dawn and dusk; roosts in cover of mangroves and other trees.
ID: Stocky; can appear **short-necked** and hunched. **Gray overall**; head is black and boldly marked with a **white face patch** and **creamy-yellow crown** with short pale head plumes. **Stout black bill**; pale orange-yellow legs and feet (extend beyond tail in flight). Juvenile is gray-brown with finely streaked head and underparts and an **all-black bill**. Upperwing has rows of **small, pale, triangular spots**.
VOICE: Short, loud "*craark*" or "*cruuk*" in flight, often heard after dark.

3 **Black-crowned Night Heron** *Nycticorax nycticorax* L 66 cm (26")

Uncommon but **widespread** resident on ponds and along rivers; rare or absent from islands with few freshwater habitats. Stands motionless or slowly stalks prey, mainly fish and invertebrates. Nocturnal but often active at dawn and dusk, roosting by day in cover of mangroves and other trees.
ID: Stocky, looks **short-necked** and hunched when perched. **Pale gray** with distinctive **black crown and back** and two elongated white head plumes. **White face** with prominent **red eyes** and strong dark bill, green at base. Legs are pale yellow; feet extend just beyond tail in flight. Juvenile similar to Yellow-crowned, but rows of **pale spots on upperwings are more elongated**, and bill has a paler lower mandible.
VOICE: Short barked "*kwark*" in flight, often heard after dark.

4 **Least Bittern** *Botaurus (Ixobrychus) exilis* L 33 cm (13")

Uncommon resident on **Guadeloupe** and **Martinique**, rare visitor elsewhere. Unobtrusive, remaining hidden in marshy vegetation, most often seen making short, low flights when it shows distinctive large **pale upperwing-patch**.

1
1j
2
2j
3
3j

Flamingo, ibis, and kingfishers

1 American Flamingo

Phoenicopterus ruber
L 117 cm (46")

Reintroduced to **Anegada** (BVI) in 1992, where now well established, with subsequent reintroductions to other islands in the archipelago. Can be wide-ranging, with occasional records **throughout**, but restricted to coastal lagoons with high salinity. Wades with head upside down, filtering mollusks, crustaceans and other invertebrates through its remarkable bill.
ID: Unmistakable with **long neck, long legs** and **bright pink plumage**. Immature paler, more gray-white. Unusual bill curves sharply downwards. Flies with neck and legs outstretched, showing striking black and pink wings.
VOICE: Nasal "*honk*", a loud trumpeting call and a slightly mournful braying.

2 Scarlet Ibis

Eudocimus ruber L 63 cm (25")

Recently introduced to the BVI and now breeding. Sightings are increasing throughout the Virgin Islands on coastal lagoons, ponds and in mangroves.
ID: Bright **scarlet** with long, pale, down-curved bill. Juvenile drabber with brown upperparts and pale underparts.

3 Belted Kingfisher *Megaceryle alcyon* L 33 cm (13″)

Uncommon non-breeding visitor **throughout**, seen along rocky coasts in mangrove swamps and on coastal lagoons. Perches in trees and on wires, or hovers several meters above water before diving for fish. Can be elusive, often heard before being seen.

ID: Male has **blue-gray** upperparts, a **white collar** and white underparts with a **blue-gray breast band**. Female similar, with varying but limited **chestnut on lower breast and flanks**. Both have a **ragged head crest** and dark heavy bill. Often seen in flight, showing dark upperwings with obvious **white patch near tip**.

VOICE: Harsh rattling call often given in flight.

4 Ringed Kingfisher *Megaceryle torquata* L 41 cm (16″)

Resident only on **Dominica and Guadeloupe**; occasional records elsewhere. Uncommon and localized on lakes, rivers and rocky coasts, where it hovers and dives for fish or drops from a perch overlooking water.

ID: Large with a **strikingly heavy bill**, paler at base. Male has blue upperparts, white throat and collar, and **distinctive rufous breast and belly**. Female similar but has **white-bordered blue band** on upper breast. In flight **underwings** are largely **white in male, rufous in female**; both have **large white patch** on upperwing.

VOICE: Calls include a prolonged, even-pitched, staccato rattle.

LANDBIRDS

Take a stroll around a formal garden or through a patch of beachside scrub and you can quickly become familiar with some of the region's common landbirds, such as Zenaida Dove, Gray Kingbird and Bananaquit. Some landbirds are associated with agriculture, grassland and other open habitats. Carib Grackles and mockingbirds are often seen around airfields and cricket grounds, and an increasing number of escaped cagebirds have established populations and can be seen feeding along seed-rich grassy margins. To see a wider range of species you need to explore the forests. There are more than 30 species of forest birds found nowhere else in the world, and while some of these are widespread and easy to see, others are restricted to small discrete areas or a single island and can be tricky to find. Most landbirds are resident, but some North American warblers are passage or winter visitors, and although never common, they can be an unexpected highlight of a forest walk.

Landbirds are particularly vulnerable to habitat loss and degradation: several species are globally threatened. Imperial Parrot and Grenada Dove are Critically Endangered and among the rarest birds on the planet; Semper's Warbler, a Critically Endangered rainforest bird endemic to St Lucia, has not been reliably seen since 1961 and may now be extinct. Most species of landbird are inextricably connected to forests; habitat protection and regeneration are vital for their future.

Landbirds endemic to the Virgin Islands and the Lesser Antilles

Endemic to the Lesser Antilles; also occur on Virgin Islands and Puerto Rico	Endemic to the Virgin Islands and Puerto Rico
Antillean Crested Hummingbird	Puerto Rican Owl
Green-throated Carib	Puerto Rican Mango
	Puerto Rican Flycatcher
	Adelaide's Warbler

Endemic to the Lesser Antilles (light type) or to only a **single island** (bold type)	
Grenada Dove	**Martinique Thrasher**
Lesser Antillean Swift	**St Lucia Thrasher**
Red-necked Parrot	Brown Trembler
Imperial Parrot	Gray Trembler
St Lucia Parrot	Lesser Antillean Bullfinch
St Vincent Parrot	**Barbados Bullfinch**
Purple-throated Carib	**St Lucia Black Finch**
Blue-headed Hummingbird	Lesser Antillean Saltator
Guadeloupe Woodpecker	**Montserrat Oriole**
Lesser Antillean Pewee	**Martinique Oriole**
Lesser Antillean Flycatcher	**St Lucia Oriole**
Grenada Flycatcher	**Semper's Warbler**
Kalinago Wren	**Barbuda Warbler**
St Lucia Wren	Plumbeous Warbler
St Vincent Wren	**St Lucia Warbler**
Grenada Wren	**Whistling Warbler**
Forest Thrush	Lesser Antillean Tanager
Scaly-breasted Thrasher	Lesser Antillean Euphonia

The endemic Brown Trembler, only found in the Lesser Antilles.

In addition, several species are represented by endemic subspecies. Among these, taxonomy appears unsettled in some, including American Barn Owl, Lesser Antillean Peewee (St Lucia) and Rufous-throated Solitaire (St Vincent). In time, some could become full species.

Doves and pigeons

1 White-winged Dove *Zenaida asiatica* L 28 cm (11″)

Locally common from the **Virgin Islands to Guadeloupe**; range appears to be extending southwards. Found in lowland scrub, grassland and open habitats, where it forages on the ground but readily flies up to perch on overhead wires.

ID: Pale brown and grayish overall with **distinctive white crescent** at base of closed wings and white tips to tail, both **obvious in flight**. It has a bright **blue eyering** and a small dark line at base of throat, and can show iridescent green-gold on neck.

VOICE: A soft cooing, often a four-note phrase: "*cu-coo cu-coo*", which rises on the second note, then drops on the last two.

2 Eurasian Collared-Dove *Streptopelia decaocto* L 28 cm (11″)

Introduced, now established **throughout**, but tends to be localized in towns, gardens and open agricultural areas. Distinctive in display: flies up before gliding down on arched wings, calling loudly.

ID: Pale overall with pale brown upperparts and light gray head, neck and underparts. Distinct **black line forms a half-collar** at base of neck. Juvenile lacks dark collar. In flight shows **darker outer wings** and **broad white tips to tail**.

VOICE: A repetitive three-note song, with second note longer and emphasized: "*coo coooo cu*". In flight, a drawn-out nasal call.

1 Zenaida Dove *Zenaida aurita* L 27 cm (10½")

A familiar species **throughout** in dry forest, scrub, open grassland, agricultural land and gardens. Commonly known as 'Turtle Dove' on some islands, it readily perches on posts and wires and can be confiding and easy to see. Loose flocks gather to forage for seeds on the ground. Overlaps with the similar Eared Dove from St Lucia south.

ID: Warm brown above with distinct **dark spots on upperwing**, iridescent purple patch on neck and **short black line** below eye. Underparts pinky-brown, fading to white on belly. In flight shows obvious **white trailing edge to inner wing** and **white tips to outer tail feathers**. Wings clatter at take-off.

VOICE: Its muffled, soporific song is a familiar background sound on many islands: comprises two quick notes, rising on the second, followed by three slow notes: "*who-oo-ooo ooo ooo*".

2 Eared Dove *Zenaida auriculata* L 23 cm (9")

Locally common from **Martinique to Grenada**, including **Barbados**, with increasing sightings farther north. Small flocks forage on grassland and agricultural land for seeds and grain, mostly at lower elevations. Readily perches on open branches or overhead wires.

ID: Gray-brown with bold dark spots on upperwing. **Two short, dark parallel lines** run behind and below the eye. Male can show paler gray crown. Flashes **green-gold iridescent patch** on neck. In flight shows shortish tail and **pale rufous or white tips** to outer tail feathers. Juvenile is darker, with extensive pale feather-edging.

VOICE: Song a deep, low cooing, with the first note emphasized: "*hoooo hoo hoo hu-hu*".

3 Common Ground-Dove *Columbina passerina* L 15 cm (6")

Common **throughout** in dry forest, scrub, agricultural land, open grassland and even coastal dunes. Forages along trails and open ground for seeds and grain, mostly in pairs or small flocks. If disturbed, may fly a short distance ahead before landing to resume feeding.

ID: Tiny; **easily the smallest dove**. Pale gray-brown with **scale-like feather-edging** to head, neck and upper breast, and **dark iridescent spots** on upperwing. Legs and feet bright pink. Flies low with audible whirring wingbeats, flashing **rich chestnut wing-patches**.

VOICE: Song a repeated soft "*hoop hoop*" that is evenly spaced and rises at the end.

Eared Doves. Most species of dove gather on branches or wires.

1
1
2
2j
3j
3

Ruddy Quail-Dove *Geotrygon montana* L 25 cm (10")

Widespread from **Antigua to Grenada**, with occasional records elsewhere; absent from Barbados. Uncommon and localized in dense, shady areas of rainforest, less often at lower elevations. Forages on forest floor, searching leaf litter for seeds and invertebrates; will perch on low branches. Unobtrusive, more often heard than seen. If disturbed, walks quickly and quietly out of view, or flies low through trees.
ID: Male has **rufous-brown upperparts**, paler brown below with a **pale throat** and a white flash on side of breast (not always visible). Head brown with obvious **horizontal pale stripe below the eye**. Female similar but less bright.
VOICE: A repeated, slow, even-pitched "*hooo*", lasting a couple of seconds.

Bridled Quail-Dove *Geotrygon mystacea* L 30 cm (12")

Endemic to the Virgin Islands, Lesser Antilles and Puerto Rico; widespread south to St Lucia but absent from low-lying islands. Localized in dense areas of rainforest, less often in forests at lower elevations. Forages slowly through leaf litter for seeds and invertebrates; perches on low branches. Unobtrusive, more often heard than seen. If disturbed, typically walks into cover rather than flying away.
ID: Dark brown upperparts; paler underparts, especially lower belly; and a striking **horizontal white line below eye**. Metallic patch on neck and upper breast flashes shades of **vivid purple and green**. Pinky-red bill with obvious pale tip.
VOICE: Call is a far-carrying, deep and slightly mournful "*hoo-hooo*". Several birds may call simultaneously.

Grenada Dove *Leptotila wellsi* L 31 cm (12")

CR

Endemic to Grenada, now restricted to a few discrete areas of dry forest. **One of the world's rarest birds**: the most recent population estimate (2013) was 136–182 mature individuals. Secretive, lives totally within the forest and is more easily heard than seen. Forages for seeds, fruit and invertebrates on the forest floor; perches on low branches. At desperate risk from habitat fragmentation, development pressure and predation by Small Indian Mongoose (*p. 168*): a recovery plan is centered on Mount Hartman National Park.
ID: Unmarked **dark brown back, wings and tail**; forehead and crown paler. Underparts buff-pink with paler belly and **obvious white bar** at front of closed wing. A thin dark line runs between the dark bill and eye, which has a striking pale iris.
VOICE: A far-carrying, mournful repeated "*hooo*".

2

3

1 Scaly-naped Pigeon *Patagioenas squamosa* L 38 cm (15")

Common and widespread from the **Virgin Islands to Grenada**; mainly in rainforests, less often dry forests at lower elevations. Rare or absent from most low-lying islands but occurs more widely on Barbados. Small loose flocks can be seen flying over forests to roosts or favored feeding areas. Readily perches on bare branches and roadside wires but can be unobtrusive when feeding. Diet is mainly fruit, seeds and buds.
ID: Large; looks **all-dark** at distance. Slate-gray, slightly paler below with purple-brown neck and breast, and **distinctive scaly neck feathers. Red eye and eyering** with a dull yellow surround; pale-tipped red bill; and pink legs. Often takes flight with loud wing-clapping.
VOICE: An insistent and repeated three-note song, with an emphasis on the last: "*coo-cu coooo*".

2 White-crowned Pigeon *Patagioenas leucocephala* L 36 cm (14")

Widespread from the **Virgin Islands to Guadeloupe**; occasional wandering visitor throughout. Locally common in mangroves and dry forests but occurs more widely on St Croix (USVI) and Antigua. Can be elusive, especially when feeding, but may gather in small roosts. Recent population decline is linked to habitat loss, hunting pressure and introduced predators.
ID: Large. **Dark gray** with an **obvious white crown** and a scaly metallic-green neck-patch (visible at close range). Pale eye with a **white eyering** and a pale-tipped pink bill. Juvenile has a grayer crown.
VOICE: Strong, repetitive cooing song; three notes often with an uplift on the first: "*cwu-cu-cooo*".

3 Rock (Feral) Pigeon
Columba livia L 34 cm (13½")

Introduced, now established **throughout** but localized in towns and open habitats, readily nesting on buildings and other structures. Small flocks gather to forage for seeds on the ground.
ID: Ranges widely in color and pattern, from dark gray to brown or even white. Some resemble true Rock Pigeons, with two dark diagonal bands across closed upperwing and a white rump. Flight swift and direct.
VOICE: Repeated song a low, rolling cooing.

A dark gray Feral Pigeon.

1
2
1
2

Anis and cuckoos

1 **Smooth-billed Ani** *Crotophaga ani* L 33 cm (13″)

Found on the **Virgin Islands** and from **Montserrat to Grenada**; absent from Barbados. Localized in open habitats with scattered trees, agricultural land and forest margins. Gregarious, mostly seen in small (often family) groups that cross open spaces one at a time and can be inelegant on landing! Feeds on invertebrates, small lizards and fruit. One of the few species to build a communal nest where several females lay eggs. Surprisingly, it is a member of the cuckoo family.
ID: A distinctive **black** bird with untidy scaly feathering to head and neck; a **remarkable deep bill**; and **long, wedge-shaped tail**. Juvenile browner with slightly smaller bill. Flies with shallow flaps and glides; appears short-winged.
VOICE: A squeaky, rising "*dree-ah*", typically given in flight.

2 **Mangrove Cuckoo** *Coccyzus minor* L 30 cm (12″)

Widespread but uncommon from the **Virgin Islands to Grenada**; rare on or absent from Saba, St Eustatius and Barbados. Found in small numbers in mangroves, scrub, dry forests and rainforests at low elevations but can be elusive and is more easily heard than seen. Typically stays in cover, moving slowly through low vegetation or forest canopy in search of invertebrates and small lizards. Builds a nest, unlike some species of cuckoo.
ID: Slender. Gray-brown with pale **orange-buff underparts**, white throat and distinct **black patch behind eye**. Bill is down-curved with a **yellow lower mandible. Long tail**, dark on underside with obvious **large white spots**.
VOICE: A run of croaking notes, descending and slowing: "*gok-gok-gok-gok-gok-gow-gow*".

3 **Yellow-billed Cuckoo** *Coccyzus americanus* L 30 cm (12″)

An uncommon to rare passage visitor that can occur **throughout**, mainly September to November, more rarely April. Typically overflies the region on migration but may be grounded by weather fronts, when it can be a surprise find in coastal scrub and along forest margins.
ID: Similar to Mangrove Cuckoo, but with brown upperparts and **clean white underparts. Lacks black face patch** and has a distinct yellow eyering. **Yellow at base of bill extends just onto upper mandible**. Unlike Mangrove Cuckoo, can often be seen flying between areas of cover, showing **obvious rufous patch** on outer wing and bold white spots on undertail.

Shows rufous wing-patch in flight.

1
1
1j
2
2
2

Nocturnal species

e 1 Antillean Nighthawk *Chordeiles gundlachii* L 22 cm (8½″)

Uncommon breeding visitor, at least on the **Virgin Islands, Anguilla, Barbuda** and **Guadeloupe**; occasionally seen on passage elsewhere. Most often seen on the wing, hawking insects over undisturbed areas of scrub, open rocky habitats and grassland. Flight is light and erratic with stiff wingbeats.
ID: Cryptically marked: **mottled brown** with **pale line at base of throat**. Appears all-dark in flight except for **bold white patch on outer wing** (less distinct in female). **Wings slender and pointed**; long **tail has short notch at tip**.
VOICE: Distinctive calls given in flight. Four or five clipped notes: "*kara-be-be-be*"; also a repeated "*week*".

The similar **Common Nighthawk** *Chordeiles minor* can occur as a rare passage visitor but is very difficult to separate in the field.

e 2 Rufous Nightjar *Antrostomus rufus otiosus* L 28 cm (11″)

An endemic subspecies, restricted to **St Lucia**, where rare and highly localized in dry forest and scrub on the northeast coast. Outside the Eastern Caribbean, the species occurs more widely in Central and South America and on Trinidad.
ID: Similar to Antillean Nighthawk. In flight, wings are **rounded at tip and lack white wing-spots**; male flashes **white outer tail feathers**.
VOICE: A repeated mellow "*chup-wee-wee-wey*".

e 3 White-tailed Nightjar *Hydropsalis cayennensis manati* L 23 cm (9″)

An endemic subspecies that occurs only on **Martinique**, where rare and highly localized in dry forest and scrub. The species occurs more widely in Central and South America and on Trinidad.
ID: Similar to Antillean Nighthawk, but with a **pale buff band on nape**; pale throat and belly. Male has a band of **bold white spots on wing**. In flight shows **largely white undertail**. Female has weaker spots on wing and a barred undertail.
VOICE: A repeated two-note phrase: "*si-seeeer*", slightly falling away at the end.

3♂ photographed on Trinidad.

e 4 American (Common) Barn Owl *Tyto (alba) furcata* L 38 cm (15″)

An uncommon resident present in two endemic subspecies: *T. f. nigrescens* on **Dominica** and *T. f. insularis* on **St Vincent, the Grenadines** and **Grenada**. Hunts by flying low over open rough grassland and scrub, searching for small rodents, bats, birds and reptiles. Nests in caves, tree cavities and abandoned buildings. Also known as Lesser Antillean Barn Owl, and an ongoing review may lead to reclassification as one or two separate species.
ID: Much darker than American Barn Owls in North America and Western Barn Owls in Europe. **Dark brown upperparts** with **white spotting**; underparts paler brown with darker speckles and spots. **Heart-shaped face** is buff-brown with a darker center.
VOICE: Calls include a distinctive harsh, drawn-out shriek.

e Puerto Rican Owl (Screech-owl) *Megascops (Gymnasio) nudipes* L 24 cm (9″)

Endemic to Puerto Rico and the **Virgin Islands**, this small owl is found in forests and agricultural areas. Although now very rare, it is possibly still present on **St John** (USVI).

Look for bold white patch on outer wing.

♀ has weak white wing-patch (stronger in ♂).

Swifts

Four species breed; others occur as rare migrants or vagrants. All take airborne insects on the wing and are rarely observed to land, except when breeding. Black Swift is the most widespread and can be seen flying high over valleys and mountains, typically in small numbers. Smaller *Chaetura* species occur in chattering flocks low over the rainforest canopy, flying down to feed in more sheltered locations during inclement weather. They are difficult to identify, but most species do not overlap in range. Swifts often nest on remote cliffs, where they cling to rocks with their short legs and strong feet. Rapid wingbeats and long curved wings held and flicked at right angles to the body help distinguish them from swallows and martins.

VU

1 Black Swift *Cypseloides niger* L 18 cm (7″)

Widespread from **Guadeloupe to Grenada, including Barbados**; rare elsewhere. An uncommon resident or breeding visitor, mainly April–September.
ID: Large. All-dark with **long, pointed wings** and narrow tail with short **notch at tip. Flight slower** than smaller swifts.
VOICE: Calls include low "*chip*".

2 White-collared Swift *Streptoprocne zonaris* L 20 cm (8″)

Mostly occurs in small flocks on **Grenada**, where it is potentially a breeding species; rare elsewhere.
ID: Large. All-dark, with **striking white collar** on male (weaker on female, faint and difficult to see on juvenile). Long, sharply pointed wings; tail has short notch at tip.
VOICE: Calls include a loud squeaky twittering.

E

3 Lesser Antillean Swift *Chaetura martinica* L 10 cm (4″)

Endemic to the Lesser Antilles, from Guadeloupe to St Vincent. Locally common, typically seen in small flocks over rainforests.
ID: Dark, brown-gray upperparts and slightly paler underparts. **Broad, square-ended tail**. Flight fast with shallow wingbeats.
VOICE: A high-pitched, rapid twittering.

4 Short-tailed Swift *Chaetura brachyura* L 10 cm (4″)

Locally common resident on **St Lucia** and **St Vincent**; rare elsewhere.
ID: Dark gray-brown with contrasting pale gray rump and undertail. Long wings, distinctively **narrower at base. Very short square-ended tail**.
VOICE: Calls include a fast "*ter-ter-ter*".

5 Gray-rumped Swift *Chaetura cinereiventris* L 11 cm (4¼″)

Uncommon resident, only on **Grenada**.
ID: Slender. Dark brown with slightly paler throat and breast, and **obvious pale gray rump**. Short tail **narrows towards tip**; can look square-ended.
VOICE: Calls include a chattering "*chrrp*".

1
BLACK SWIFT
WHITE-COLLARED SWIFT
2
LESSER ANTILLEAN SWIFT
3
WINGS NARROW AT BASE
4
SHORT-TAILED SWIFT
5
GRAY-RUMPED SWIFT
5

Swallows and martins

1 **Caribbean Martin** *Progne dominicensis* L 20 cm (8″)

Locally common breeding visitor **throughout**. Prefers open habitats, particularly along coasts, where it readily settles on overhead wires and boat rigging. Mostly seen in pairs or small flocks circling and pursuing flying insects, often appearing briefly, then quickly moving on. Nests in open-sided buildings and other structures.
ID: Male is a glossy **dark blue** with contrasting **white belly and undertail-coverts**; obvious **notch** at tip of tail. Female more gray-brown, lacks blue. In flight, appears heavier and less streamlined than Barn Swallow.
VOICE: A rich deep *"chirrup"* and sharper *"twick-twick"*.

2 (American) **Barn Swallow** *Hirundo rustica (erythrogaster)* L 17 cm (6½″)

Common non-breeding or passage visitor **throughout**, along coasts or over wetlands and grassland. Typically gathers in small flocks that hawk aerial insects, often low to the ground, including over sargassum seaweed on beaches. Weather fronts can interrupt migration, causing large flocks to gather over suitable feeding areas or rest on overhead wires.
ID: Slim with **dark blue** upperparts, pale tan underparts and obvious **red throat**. In flight shows distinctive long, thin wings and **heavily forked tail with streamers** (longer in male). Fanned tail shows **white spots at base**. Immature has paler throat and short tail-streamers.
VOICE: A bright *"vit vit"*.

Uncommon migrant swallows occur in small numbers, often among flocks of Barn Swallows. The most regular are:

3 **Cliff Swallow** *Petrochelidon pyrrhonota* L 14 cm (5½″)

ID: Similar to Barn Swallow but with **pale collar, orange rump** and **slightly notched tail**, which can look square-ended.

4 **Bank Swallow** (Collared Sand Martin) *Riparia riparia* L 13 cm (5″)

ID: Small. **Upperparts brown**; underparts white with obvious **brown breast-band** and **short notched tail**.

1♂
1♀
CARIBBEAN
MARTIN
BARN
SWALLOW
2j
2♂
3
4j
SQUARE-ENDED
TAIL
CLIFF
SWALLOW
BANK
SWALLOW
4j
PALE COLLAR AND
OBVIOUS ORANGE RUMP
3

Hummingbirds

Tiny but dynamic, hummingbirds fly at incredible speed, are able to hover and can move backwards with great precision. They use their long bill and tongue to reach deep into flowers for nectar, in the process brushing against pollen and thereby playing an important role in pollination. In the Eastern Caribbean, they are essentially forest birds, although the three most common species also visit gardens. Hummingbirds regularly return to favored flowering plants and perches, often with a flash of iridescent color. They are territorial and aggressive, chasing other hummingbirds in noisy pursuit and even flying at passing predators, including American Kestrels!

E 1 Antillean Crested Hummingbird *Orthorhyncus cristatus* L 9 cm (3½")

Endemic to the Virgin Islands, Lesser Antilles and Puerto Rico. Common in all forest types: the only hummingbird found from coastal scrub to rainforest. Often noisy and conspicuous, can appear inquisitive, and may approach closely with *audible whirring wingbeats.*

ID: Tiny with a distinctive **short, straight bill**. Male has brilliant iridescent green upperparts, dark underparts (can show pale throat and upper breast) and a **pronounced crest** on forehead that flashes a striking metallic green or blue. Tail is short and dark. Female paler, underparts more gray-white, crest is less obvious, and tail has white tips to outer feathers.

VOICE: A short sharp "*tssp*".

E 2 Puerto Rican Mango *Anthracothorax aurulentus* L 11.5 cm (4½")

Endemic to Puerto Rico and **the Virgin Islands**, where now very rare and declining. Similar to Green-throated Carib, but male has a metallic green throat, black breast and belly, and lacks the Carib's blue breast-band. Female has pale gray underparts and narrow white tips to tail.

E 3 Green-throated Carib *Eulampis holosericeus* L 11.5 cm (4½")

Endemic to the Virgin Islands, Lesser Antilles and Puerto Rico. Locally common in dry forests and gardens, less often rainforests; typically has a coastal distribution on many islands.

ID: Upperparts, head and throat **iridescent green**; feathers can appear scale-like. Underparts dark with a striking **bright blue breast-band. Long thin bill** is **gently down-curved**.

VOICE: A thin, rapid twitter.

E 4 Purple-throated Carib *Eulampis jugularis* L 11.5 cm (4½")

Endemic to the Lesser Antilles, widespread from **Saba to Grenada**; occasional records elsewhere but absent from Barbados. Locally common in rainforests (where often one of the more visible birds along trails); less frequently encountered at lower elevations.

ID: All-dark but flashes a brilliant **purple throat** and iridescent **blue-green wings**. Long, **obviously down-curved bill**. At rest can look thick-necked, giving a hunched appearance.

VOICE: A sharp loud "*tep*", often repeated, especially when aggressively defending feeding territories from other hummingbirds.

1♂
1♀
1♂
2♂
3
3
4
4

E 1 Blue-headed Hummingbird *Riccordia (Cyanophaia) bicolor* L 10 cm (4″)

Endemic to Dominica and **Martinique**, where uncommon and localized in rainforests and along forest margins. Sites include the Syndicate Trail in the Morne Diablotin Range on Dominica and Mont Pelée in Martinique, but the hummingbirds can be elusive and difficult to see.
ID: Male is a stunning iridescent **green-blue** with a **striking blue head**; long, fine and straightish bill; and blue tail with slight notch at tip. Female similar to female Antillean Crested Hummingbird (*p. 116*): pale with **white throat and breast**; metallic green flanks; and bold white tips to outer tail feathers.
VOICE: Calls include a repeated shrill *"tic"*.

2 Rufous-breasted Hermit *Glaucis hirsutus insularum* L 12.5 cm (5″)

A subspecies found only on **Grenada**, and **Trinidad and Tobago**. Uncommon and difficult to see in rainforests: can be found along trails at Grand Étang. Regularly visits *Heliconia* flowers.
ID: The only hummingbird in the region with a rufous breast. Iridescent **brown-green** with **rufous underparts** and paler belly. Tail is rounded, rufous at base, with a black (subterminal) band and small white feather-tips. **Bill very long and down-curved** with **yellow lower mandible**.
VOICE: Call a thin *"tsip"*.

Woodpeckers

E 3 Guadeloupe Woodpecker *Melanerpes herminieri* L 27 cm (10½″)

Endemic to Guadeloupe: the only resident woodpecker in the Eastern Caribbean. Locally common in all forest habitats but more numerous in rainforests on Basse-Terre. Can be seen along several forest trails, where it forages high in the canopy for invertebrates, larvae, seeds and fruit.
ID: Black upperparts and tail with **deep purple-red throat, chest and belly** (not always obvious). Bill dark and sharply pointed.
VOICE: Call, a short rasping *"kaark"*.

Can be inconspicuous when feeding high in the canopy.

1♂
1♀
2
2
ROUNDED WHITE-TIPPED TAIL
3
3

Raptors (birds of prey)

1 Red-tailed Hawk *Buteo jamaicensis jamaicensis* L 48 cm (19″) | WS 122 cm (48″)

Resident on the **Virgin Islands, Saba, St Eustatius, St Kitts and Nevis**, with occasional records elsewhere. Uncommon in open areas and forest margins, often seen perching on trees, roadside poles or wires. Preys mainly on reptiles, small birds and invertebrates. No overlap in range with similar Broad-winged Hawk. **ID:** Dark brown upperparts; very pale underparts, typically with **dark markings on belly**. Tail **unmarked red on adult**, but pale and **finely barred on immature**. Soars on long broad wings held in a shallow V. Underwings pale with dark wing-tips, dark trailing edge and **distinctive dark bar** at front of inner wing. **VOICE:** A rasping *"keee-r-r"* call, falling away.

1i

1

FLIGHT PHOTOGRAPHS FOR 1 WERE TAKEN IN THE USA

e 2 **Broad-winged Hawk** *Buteo platypterus* L 38 cm (15") | WS 86 cm (34")

Resident on **Antigua, Dominica, Martinique, St Lucia, St Vincent** and **Grenada** in three subspecies; occasional records elsewhere. Locally common in rainforests and fringing open habitats; mostly seen circling at height or perched on trees, roadside poles or wires. Preys on lizards, invertebrates and small birds. In display, calls and stoops dramatically with closed wings. No overlap in range with similar Red-tailed Hawk.
ID: Dark brown head and upperparts; pale underparts with **chestnut markings**, often with dark throat and upper breast. **Tail broadly barred black and white**. Short hooked bill with yellow base; legs bright yellow. Immature has **darker streaking** on breast and **indistinct barring on tail**. Compact shape in flight with short, spread tail; soars on broad, rounded wings held in shallow V, showing **pale underwings** with a **thin, dark trailing edge**.
VOICE: Thin, high-pitched and extended *"keeeeeh"*, often given in flight.

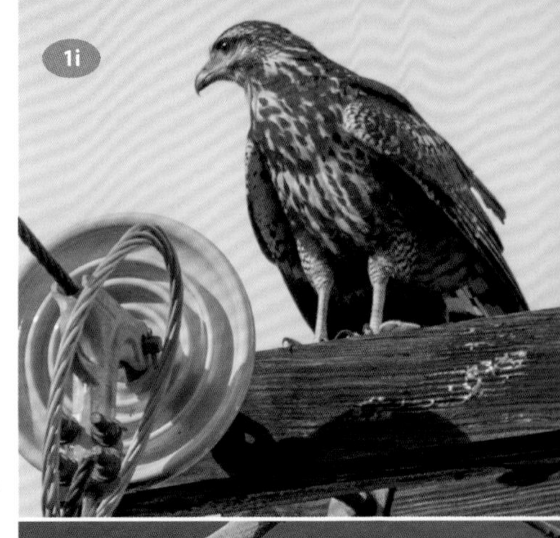

1 Common Black Hawk

Buteogallus anthracinus anthracinus

L 53 cm (21") | WS 117 cm (46")

Uncommon resident, occurring only on **St Vincent**; more widely on Cuba, Trinidad and Tobago and in the Americas. Mostly found in rainforests or along forest margins and river corridors at lower elevations. Often perches over a watercourse before dropping down to catch Yellow Land Crabs and crayfish. Sites include the Vermont Trail and the SVG Botanic Gardens.

ID: Black with **long, bright yellow legs and yellow bill** with black tip. Soars on flat, very broad wings, showing paler band along rear of wing and obvious **white bands at base and tip of short tail**. Immature pale with **heavily streaked underparts**, **finely barred tail** and **pale patch near wingtip** (obvious in flight).

VOICE: Repeated, high-pitched, piercing whistles: "*kee-kee-kee*".

2 Hook-billed Kite

Chondrohierax uncinatus mirus

L 41 cm (16") | WS 90 cm (35")

Rare endemic subspecies occurs only on Grenada; main populations of the wider species are in the Americas. Highly restricted to undisturbed areas of dry forest and coastal wetlands. Clambers among branches in search of snails, extracting them from their shell with its distinctive hooked bill. The population on Grenada may number fewer than 100 individuals and is under serious threat from habitat loss. Can be seen at Mount Hartman National Park.

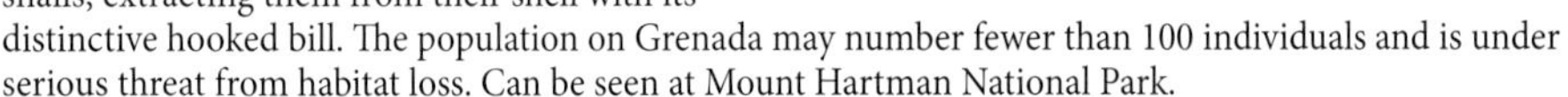

ID: Gray-brown with paler underparts. **Barring to breast and belly** is typically gray on male, red-brown on female and whiter (and less distinct) on juvenile. All plumages have **pale collar**, bold barring on tail, distinctive **yellow patch in front of eye** and yellow base to **strongly hooked bill**. Juvenile has a dark cap and pale face. Flies low through forest clearings with deep, loose wingbeats or soars high over the canopy. **Broad wings are pinched in near base**; underwings pale and finely barred.

VOICE: Calls include short bursts of a laughing rattle.

Images are of *C. u. uncinatus*, which is broadly similar.

3 Osprey *Pandion haliaetus* L 58 cm (23") | WS 160 cm (63")

Uncommon non-breeding and passage visitor **throughout**. The only fish-eating bird of prey in the region, typically seen soaring along coasts and over inshore waters and coastal wetlands. Hovers before making a spectacular feet-first plunge to grab fish with its sharp talons, and is often seen in flight carrying fish before landing on a nearby perch, typically a tree or utility pole.

ID: The **largest bird of prey** in the region. Back and wings **dark brown** with **contrasting white underparts**. **Head white** with **bold dark brown stripe through eye** and strongly hooked bill. Immature has pale feather fringes forming a scaly pattern on upperparts. Distinctive shape in flight: **long wings** held **slightly raised** at bend and **angled forward**. Underwings white at base with dark tip and **bar across inner wing**.

VOICE: Call a far-carrying, insistent "*chu chu chu*".

Ospreys take prey to a prominent perch.

1 **American Kestrel** *Falco sparverius caribaearum* L 23 cm (9″) | WS 56 cm (22″)

Locally common resident from the **Virgin Islands to St Lucia**; rare farther south. The most widespread bird of prey, with small numbers in open habitats, often around buildings. Perches on trees, posts, wires or buildings, dropping down to catch reptiles, small birds and invertebrates.
ID: Male has a colorful combination of a well-marked **rufous back**, contrasting **blue-gray wings** and long rufous tail with a **bold black band** near tip. Underparts paler with dark spotting. Female has rufous wings, more extensive spotting on underparts and a **finely barred tail**. Both have **two obvious vertical dark bars** on face. Flight is fast with shallow wingbeats and short glides, showing pale underwings with extensive fine barring and spotting.
VOICE: A high-pitched "*killi-killi-killi*", so the bird (a falcon) known locally as 'killy-hawk' and 'killy-killy'.

2 **Merlin** *Falco columbarius* L 25 cm (10″) | WS 61 cm (24″)

Uncommon to rare non-breeding and passage visitor **throughout**, mostly seen hunting over coastal wetlands and open habitats with scattered trees. Individuals can make a dramatic appearance—flying low and fast, twisting and turning in an often-extended pursuit of small birds. Will catch large insects, including dragonflies, in flight.
ID: Small and compact with **pointed wings** and long, obviously barred tail. Upperparts **dark gray in male, dark brown in female and juvenile**; all have a **thin pale stripe above the eye and heavily streaked underparts**.
VOICE: Rarely heard, especially away from breeding grounds.

3 **Peregrine Falcon** *Falco peregrinus* L 41 cm (16″) | WS 97 cm (38″)

Non-breeding and passage visitor **throughout**; uncommon to rare over offshore islands, rocky coasts and coastal wetlands. Preys on seabirds, waterbirds and pigeons, catching them mid-air during spectacular stooping flights and chases. One of the fastest-flying birds in the world.
ID: Large and stocky with **blue-gray upperparts** and contrasting **finely barred white underparts**. Head boldly marked with **dark hood, white throat** and **strong dark 'moustache' mark** below the eye, often obvious in flight. Eyering, base of bill, legs and feet are bright yellow. **Immature brown** with **heavily streaked underparts**. Flight is fast with shallow wingbeats; soars and circles with flat wings, showing relatively short tail.
VOICE: A repeated shrill and far-carrying "*kehk-kehk-kehk*", but mostly silent in the region.

1♂
1♀
1♂
2j
3
3

Parrots

Colorful and gregarious, parrots are among the most endearing but vulnerable of the region's rainforest birds. They are highly vocal, with complex social behaviors, and their screeches and squawks can often be heard from high in the canopy. The four endemic species are highly localized and can be difficult to see, so a local guide may be helpful.

Distinctive in flight—with a large blunt head, rounded paddle-shaped wings and short tail—parrots flash stunning reds, greens and yellows. Small noisy flocks can be seen, especially early morning and late afternoon, as they make local movements between roosting and feeding areas in search of seeds, fruit and berries.

All are threatened by habitat loss—especially the loss of the mature trees that provide nest sites—and there is still pressure from the illegal pet trade. Hurricanes can be devastating to nest sites and food resources; many birds are unable to survive the most intense conditions. Local and international conservation efforts continue for all species, including captive breeding and some imaginative public awareness programs. On the three islands where they occur, parrots are recognized as the national bird.

E 1 **Red-necked Parrot** (Amazon) *Amazona arausiaca* L 36 cm (14")

VU **Endemic to Dominica**, where uncommon in rainforests and, less frequently, forests at lower elevations. Locally known as 'Jaco'. The most accessible viewing is from the Syndicate Trail in the Morne Diablotin Range. In 2012 the population was estimated at fewer than 1,000 mature individuals.

ID: Bright green with **blue face**, **red throat-patch** and **pale bill**. In flight shows **bright red upperwing-patch**, bright blue-green on underwings and yellow tip to tail.

VOICE: Flight call is a harsh two-note "*arrk ack*", with a slight rise on the second. Flocks are often very noisy, with a range of calls, including trills and squawks.

E 2 **Imperial Parrot** (Amazon) *Amazona imperialis* L 48 cm (19")

CR **Endemic to Dominica**, where highly localized in rainforests. Locally known as 'Sisserou'. The most accessible viewing is from the Syndicate Trail in the Morne Diablotin Range. One of the rarest birds in the world, it has been particularly impacted by hurricanes through habitat loss and direct mortality. In 2019, fewer than 60 mature individuals were estimated to remain: urgent conservation measures are in place, including habitat recovery and protection.

ID: The largest parrot in the region. **Bright green** with **purple-blue head, neck and underparts**; feathers have a scaly appearance. In flight, wings are mainly green with darker wing-tips and **red patch at base of upperwing**.

VOICE: Variety of calls, including repeated emphatic and high-pitched squawks.

1

1
YELLOW TIP
TO TAIL
1
BLUE-GREEN
UNDERWING

2
2
2

St Lucia Parrot (Amazon) *Amazona versicolor* L 43 cm (17")

VU

Endemic to St Lucia, where widespread but uncommon in rainforests and, less frequently, forests at lower elevations. Main populations are in the central and southern forest reserves. They can be seen from managed trails, including Des Cartier and Millet. Population estimate in 2018 was fewer than 1,500 mature individuals; conservation work includes education and awareness programs.
ID: Bright green with **blue head** and **red breast**. Colorful in flight; shows bold blue patch on outer wing, small red patch on green inner wing, and **yellow-tipped tail**.
VOICE: Very vocal with a wide range of raucous squawks and squeaks.

St Vincent Parrot (Amazon) *Amazona guildingii* L 43 cm (17")

VU

Endemic to St Vincent, where uncommon in rainforests and along forest margins. Sites include the Vermont Nature Trail. Population estimate in 2008 was approximately 500 mature individuals, but habitat and population may have been impacted by volcanic eruptions in 2021. Conservation work includes a captive breeding program based at the SVG Botanic Gardens.
ID: Very colorful. Body plumage ranges from orange-brown to green, with blue on wing and at base of tail. **Whitish head and bill**, with light blue collar. In flight, shows obvious **bright yellow bar on outer wing** and **yellow-tipped tail**.
VOICE: Extremely vocal, with a variety of loud calls, including a high-pitched "*her-r-ick*".

INTRODUCED PARROTS

Brown-throated Parakeet

Eupsittula pertinax pertinax L 25 cm (10")

Introduced to **St Thomas (USVI)** in the 1800s; now well established but uncommon. Occasional records elsewhere in the **Virgin Islands** and more recently on **Saba**. Can be noisy when foraging high in the forest canopy for fruit, flowers and seeds.
ID: Bright green with paler underparts and **long pointed tail. Face yellow-orange, throat and breast brown**. In flight, shows blue on wingtips and trailing edge of wing.
VOICE: Very vocal: calls include a shrill repeated "*wiik wiik*".

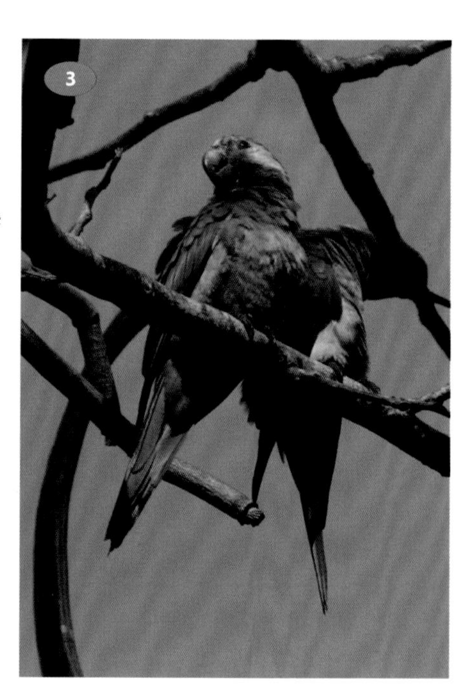

Parrots, parakeets and lovebirds have been brought into the region as pets. Many have escaped, and at least two species appear to be establishing breeding populations.

Rose-ringed Parakeet *Psitticula krameri* on **Martinique** and **Barbados**.
Orange-winged Parrot *Amazona amazonica* on **Martinique**, **Barbados** and **Grenada**.

1
1
2
2
2

Tyrant flycatchers (kingbirds, elaenias, pewees and flycatchers)

A diverse group of energetic, mainly insect-eating birds found in all habitats, from coastal scrub to rainforest. They all make characteristic darting flights to catch invertebrate prey, regularly returning to favored perches on branches, fences and overhead wires. Larger prey items are often beaten on a branch before being eaten.

1 Gray Kingbird *Tyrannus dominicensis* L 23 cm (9″)

Common and easily seen **throughout** in most open habitats, including scrub, grassland and gardens at low to mid elevations. Agile in flight, catches large invertebrates with a loud bill-snap. Often aggressive, particularly when breeding, and will chase away much larger birds, even hawks! Small groups gather during migration periods, suggesting some population movement through the region.
ID: The **largest**, most obvious flycatcher. Upperparts gray-brown; underparts **white** but can show a pale-gray wash. **Gray head** with distinctive **black mask** and **strong black bill**, finely hooked at tip; tail **slightly notched**.
VOICE: Highly vocal, with short rolling calls, leading to local names '*pipirite*' and '*chincherry*'.

2 Caribbean Elaenia *Elaenia martinica* L 16.5 cm (6½″)

The most widely distributed small flycatcher, found **throughout** in dry forest and scrub. Can be obvious and confiding on some islands but unobtrusive and surprisingly difficult to see on others. Feeds mainly on invertebrates but will eat small berries. Overlaps with Yellow-bellied Elaenia from St Vincent to Grenada.
ID: Subtle **olive-gray upperparts** with **two distinct white wingbars**; paler, gray-white underparts, sometimes with a light yellowish wash to belly. **Short crest** with white flecking (not always obvious) and a fine dark bill.
VOICE: Often vocal; calls include a short emphatic whistle and a cheery, repeated four-note phrase: "*chwee che chu chu*", the last two notes lower.

3 Yellow-bellied Elaenia *Elaenia flavogaster* L 16.5 cm (6½″)

Only on **St Vincent, the Grenadines** and **Grenada**; more widely, it occurs on Trinidad and Tobago and in Central and South America. Uncommon and localized in dry forest, scrub and gardens. Local name on Grenada is 'top-knot pippiree', referencing its crest and song. Overlaps with similar Caribbean Elaenia.
ID: Olive-brown upperparts with **two distinct white wingbars**. Underparts gray-white with **pale yellow belly (often faint)**. Raised crown feathers form a **long, untidy crest** with some white flecking. Short, fine dark bill.
VOICE: A harsh drawn-out whistle and short, hoarse-sounding, repeated song: "*peeperi peeperi pi pi*".

E 4 Puerto Rican Flycatcher *Myiarchus antillarum* L 19 cm (7.5″)

Endemic to the Virgin Islands and Puerto Rico. Now very rare on the Virgin Islands, the most recent sightings being from St John (USVI) and Anegada (BVI). Similar to Caribbean Elaenia but lacks any yellow in plumage.

1
1
2
3
3
4

E 1 Lesser Antillean Flycatcher *Myiarchus oberi* L 20 cm (8")

Endemic to the Lesser Antilles; only on **St Kitts and Nevis, Antigua and Barbuda, Guadeloupe, Dominica, Martinique** and **St Lucia**. Uncommon in rainforests and less often in forests at lower elevations. A largely solitary species, found along forest margins and in clearings; often seen from forest trails. No overlap with Grenada Flycatcher.
ID: A large flycatcher. Dark brown with **two pale wingbars** and some **rufous on wings and tail**. Underparts gray-white with an **obvious pale yellow belly**. Fine but strong dark bill.
VOICE: Short whistled calls include a two note "*pee-wheet*".

E 2 Grenada Flycatcher *Myiarchus nugator* L 20 cm (8")

Endemic to the Lesser Antilles. Occurs only on **St Vincent, the Grenadines** and **Grenada**. Locally common, mainly at lower elevations in mangroves, dry forests, scrub and open habitats (including gardens). Small parties will gather at dusk; a local name is 'sunset bird'. No overlap with Lesser Antillean Flycatcher.
ID: Very similar to Lesser Antillean Flycatcher: black bill has a slightly pale pink base to lower mandible.
VOICE: Short, sharp "*prip*"; also a series of three notes (the last rising slightly): "*prip-prip-ip*".

E 3 Lesser Antillean Pewee *Contopus latirostris* L 15 cm (6")

Endemic to the Lesser Antilles, it occurs in two subspecies: *C. l. brunneicapillus* on **Guadeloupe, Dominica** and **Martinique**, and *C. l. latirostris* on **St Lucia**. Uncommon in rainforests and less often dry forests; most easily seen along trails or in clearings, where it can be confiding, almost inquisitive. Upright posture when perched.
ID: Small and compact; appears large-headed and **long-tailed**. Olive-brown head and upperparts with pale fringes to upperwing feathers, paler throat and **orangey or buff breast and belly** (darker and more orangey in *C. l. latirostris*). **Short, lightly flattened bill** with a pale lower mandible.
VOICE: A soft, high-pitched "*pee*" or "*peet*", and a more emphatic, rising "*pree-e-e*".

4 Fork-tailed Flycatcher *Tyrannus savana savana*

L 30–41 cm (12–16") including tail

Uncommon non-breeding visitor (July to October) to **Grenada** and **the Grenadines**, occasionally elsewhere. Localized on open grassland and in scrub, dry forests and mangroves. Sites include Mount Hartman National Park, where small groups can be seen flying to roost at dusk. Breeding in South America, this is one of the few species to migrate north to the Lesser Antilles in the region's summer (the southern winter).
ID: Unmistakable, with **black head**, gray back and **clean white underparts**. A pale crown stripe can be difficult to see. Male has a forked tail with spectacular **long black tail streamers** (shorter in female and can be lacking in juvenile).
VOICE: Calls include a soft "*chup-chup-chup*".

Dominica

St Lucia subspecies has more orangey underparts.

Wrens, solitaires and vireos

Wrens occur as four separate endemic species, which formerly were all considered subspecies of House Wren *Troglodytes aedon*. There are differences in plumage and voice between species, but no overlap in range.

E 1 **Kalinago Wren** *Troglodytes martinicensis* DOMINICA L 11 cm (4½")
(Subspecies on Guadeloupe and Martinique now extinct)

E 2 **St Lucia Wren** *Troglodytes mesoleucus* ST LUCIA L 11 cm (4½")

E 3 **St Vincent Wren** *Troglodytes musicus* ST VINCENT L 11 cm (4½")

E 4 **Grenada Wren** *Troglodytes grenadensis* GRENADA L 11 cm (4½")

Uncommon in rainforests, dry forests and thick scrub, foraging for invertebrates in low vegetation and undergrowth; often seen around buildings.
ID: Red-brown to gray-brown upperparts with **faint barring on closed wings and tail**; underparts paler, gray-white to orange depending on species. All have a **pale line above the eye** and a thin **down-curved bill** with a yellow (or pale) lower mandible. **Short tail is often characteristically raised.**
VOICE: Very vocal. Loud warbling song with rapid trills. Calls include harsh scolding "*chit-it-it*" and softer "*tuc-tuc-tuc*". Some variation in song between islands.

e 5 Rufous-throated Solitaire *Myadestes genibarbis* L 19 cm (7½″)

Endemic to the Caribbean, occurring in six single-island subspecies only on **Dominica, Martinique, St Lucia, St Vincent**, Jamaica and Hispaniola. Uncommon and localized in rainforests, inconspicuous when searching through mid to lower canopy for insects, small fruits and berries. More easily heard than seen; its call is one of the most evocative of all the forest birds, giving rise to the local name of 'mountain whistler'.
ID: Dark gray upperparts; paler gray below with a bright **rufous chin, throat and undertail**. Small but obvious white lower eyering and **small white spot** at base of short dark bill. **Legs and feet yellow**. St Vincent subspecies *M. g. sibilans* has **blacker** upperparts.
VOICE: An arresting slow and mournful whistle, especially at dawn and dusk.

6 Black-whiskered Vireo *Vireo altiloquus* L 15 cm (6″)

Locally common **throughout** but may be absent from some low-lying islands. Found in all forest types and mature gardens. Typically seen searching for fruit and insects in mid and upper canopy but can be unobtrusive if not singing or calling. Will droop wings and raise tail.
ID: Olive-green above with gray-white underparts and **lemon wash to undertail-coverts**. Head well marked with gray crown, dark eyestripe and **pale eyebrow** with black line above. A **short dark line or 'whisker'** runs from base of sharply pointed bill but can be difficult to see.
VOICE: Song a repeated "*tee tu teo*". Calls include a harsh "*yeea*" and a thin "*tsit*".

Small black line or 'whisker' below eye.

Thrushes

Mid-sized forest birds; their clear whistled songs often ring out through the forest. All are long-legged with a short stout bill and readily forage through leaf litter for invertebrates or take berries from low bushes. They can be difficult to see but typically venture out from forest cover in the early morning and late afternoon, hopping briskly to feed in clearings or on roadside verges.

1 **Spectacled** (Bare-eyed) **Thrush** *Turdus nudigenis* L 23 cm (9")

Found from **Guadeloupe** to **Grenada** but absent from Barbados; range appears to be extending northwards. Uncommon in all forest types, agricultural land and gardens, mostly at lower elevations. Can be confiding at public sites: the easiest thrush to see within its range.
ID: Plain gray-brown upperparts with **paler buff** underparts, white lower belly and undertail. Pale throat with fine dark streaking and a **yellow bill.** A striking **yellow-orange area around the eye** gives the bird its common name. Juvenile has buff spots on closed wings, forming wingbars.
VOICE: Song is a series of short, precise, clear whistles. Calls include a squeaky, rising "*whee-eer*" and sharp "*tchup-tchup-tchup*".

2 **Cocoa Thrush** *Turdus fumigatus* L 23 cm (9")

Occurs only on **St Vincent** and **Grenada** but is present more widely on Trinidad and Tobago and in South America. Uncommon to rare in rainforests, more often at higher elevations, but can be elusive.
ID: Unmarked warm brown upperparts with slightly paler underparts, a lightly streaked throat and **creamy-buff undertail-coverts**. Dark eyes with **grayish eyering**; **dark gray bill**.
VOICE: Song is a series of repeated, soft, tuneful whistles. Calls include a harsh "*chak-chak-chak*".

e 3 Red-legged Thrush *Turdus plumbeus albiventris* L 27 cm (10½")

Endemic to the West Indies, ranging across the Greater Antilles and Bahamas, and occurring in the Eastern Caribbean only as an endemic subspecies on **Dominica**. (Taxonomy is unsettled and may change.) Uncommon in dry forests and scrub, less often in rainforests; it is mostly limited to the western side of the island.
ID: Slate-gray above, paler below with **bold white edges to black tail**. Throat streaked black and white; **bill, eyering and legs are bright orange-red**.
VOICE: Song is a series of slow, isolated chirps and a whistled "*ee-ooo*". Alarm call is a high-pitched, repeated "*tsweet tsweet*".

E NT 4 Forest Thrush *Turdus lherminieri* L 27 cm (10½")

Endemic to the Lesser Antilles. Occurs in four single-island subspecies on **Montserrat, Guadeloupe, Dominica** and **St Lucia** (although the latter is very rare, with no recent sightings). Uncommon to rare, most easily seen in the Centre Hills of Montserrat and on Basse-Terre (Guadeloupe), where birds forage in clearings and along roadside verges, especially at dawn and dusk. Threatened by habitat loss, nest parasitism by Shiny Cowbird and predation by introduced mammals.
ID: Upperparts **dark brown**; underparts white with **brown feather-tips, giving a distinctive scaled effect. Bold yellow eyering**, yellow base to bill and **long yellow legs**.
VOICE: Far-carrying repetitive song: "*tu-du-lu tee-u*". Calls include a harsh "*chuck chuck*".

Guadeloupe

Dominican subspecies has darker breast markings and whiter belly.

Thrashers

1 Pearly-eyed Thrasher *Margarops fuscatus* L 29 cm (11½″)

Common and widespread from the **Virgin Islands to St Lucia**; rare farther south. Found in a wide range of habitats, from mangroves to rainforests. Omnivorous and opportunistic, it forages for fruit, invertebrates and lizards but will also take eggs and young of other birds and, on some islands, even scavenges around restaurants! Overlaps in range with similar, but smaller, Scaly-breasted Thrasher.
ID: Brown with **heavily marked white underparts**, where darker feather edges can form V's on belly. Distinctive **strong pale bill** and **striking pale eye**, which gives the bird its common name. White-tipped tail is obvious in flight. Often seen on the ground in an upright posture, with wings drooped and tail slightly raised.
VOICE: Very vocal, calls include a single clear whistle and harsh raucous "*craar*". Song is typically a few isolated short whistles and chirps.

E 2 Scaly-breasted Thrasher *Allenia fusca* L 23 cm (9″)

Endemic to the Lesser Antilles: widespread from **St Martin/Sint Maarten to Grenada** but absent from some low-lying islands. Locally common in rainforests, dry forests and even gardens, where it forages for invertebrates and fruit. Often solitary, but several may gather on fruiting trees such as mistletoe and *Cecropia*. Overlaps in range with similar, but larger, Pearly-eyed Thrasher. The only species in its genus.
ID: Brown upperparts and head with **pale yellow eyes and dark bill**. Underparts paler with **dark 'scale-like' feather-edging** on throat and breast. Narrow white tip to tail, especially obvious in flight. Often perches with wings drooped and tail raised.
VOICE: Song is a slow series of short fluty phrases. Calls include a harsh squawk.

Until 2024, the following two endemic species were considered subspecies of the endemic White-breasted Thrasher *Ramphocinclus brachyurus*. There are subtle differences in size and plumage, but there are no overlaps in ranges.

E 3 Martinique Thrasher *Ramphocinclus brachyurus* MARTINIQUE L 20 cm (8″)

EN St Lucia Thrasher *Ramphocinclus sanctaeluciae* ST LUCIA L 23–25 cm (9–10″)

Rare and localized in dense areas of dry forest, especially along river courses. Sites include Presqu'île de la Caravelle on Martinique and the eastern dry forests of St Lucia. Can be difficult to see in thick cover, where they search through leaf litter for invertebrates, often flicking wings and bobbing tail up and down. Unusual cooperative breeding behavior, where offspring often help parents raise subsequent broods. Threatened by both habitat loss and introduced predators, the Martinique Thrasher population was estimated at 267 mature individuals, and the St Lucia population was estimated at 1,130 mature individuals (both 2016).
ID: Distinctive **sooty-brown upperparts** (darker on St Lucia Thrasher) and **striking white underparts** with darker flanks. **Bill black**, **slightly down-curved**; eyes dark red. St Lucia Thrasher is larger overall, with male larger than female. Juvenile paler with grayer underparts.
VOICE: Calls include a harsh drawn-out "*wheeshk*".

Martinique Thrasher

Mockingbirds

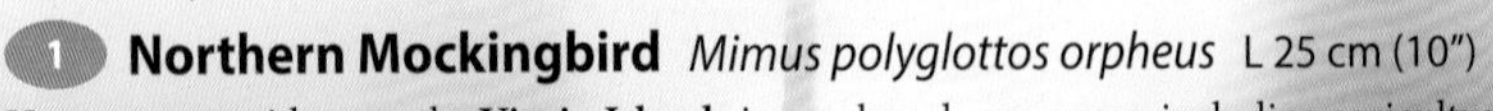

1 Northern Mockingbird *Mimus polyglottos orpheus* L 25 cm (10")

Uncommon resident on the **Virgin Islands** in scrub and open areas, including agricultural land, grassland and airport fringes. Can be conspicuous on open perches or when foraging for invertebrates and berries. Characteristically hops on the ground with wings drooped and tail raised.
ID: Soft gray upperparts, dark wings with **two white wingbars** and long white-edged tail. Paler gray-white underparts. A **weak dark line runs from eye to thin dark bill**. Juvenile paler with buff underparts and lightly spotted breast. Shows **large white wing-patch in flight**.
VOICE: A series of different repeated phrases and, as its name suggests, mimicry of other birds. Call a sharp "*tchack*".

e 2 Tropical Mockingbird *Mimus gilvus antillarum* L 24 cm (9½")

Locally common from **Antigua and Barbuda to Grenada**; absent from Barbados. Found in open lowland habitats, including parks, gardens and agricultural land, where it forages for invertebrates and berries. Large groups gather at productive food sources, such as newly cut grassland. Characteristically hops on ground with wings drooped and tail raised.
ID: Upperparts pale gray, wings darker with **two thin white wingbars**; tail is long and dark with white edges and tip. Underparts are **strikingly pale gray-white**. Pale gray head with **dark gray line through the eye** and faint pale **eyebrow**. Juvenile similar, but wings browner and breast lightly streaked.
VOICE: A series of repeated, varied phrases, including whistles, warbles and clear melodic notes. Calls include a sharp "*cheuk*".

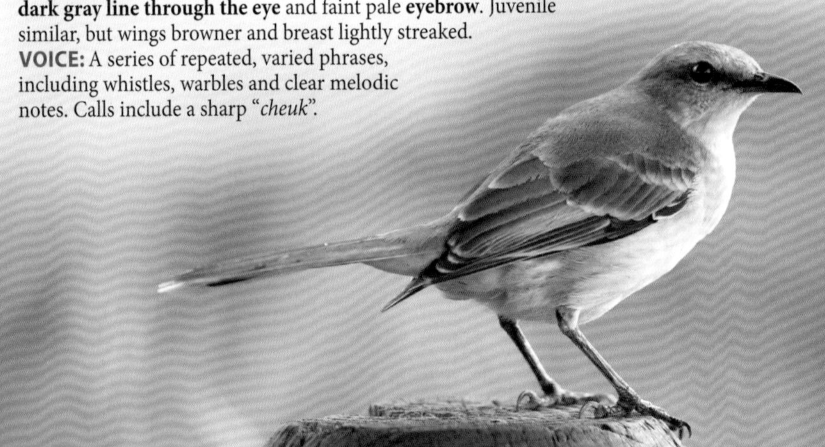

Striking and unmistakable, tremblers are found only in the Lesser Antilles. They have a remarkable habit of trembling with quivering wings when excited or alarmed—hence their common name. A highlight of any rainforest visit, tremblers move nimbly through trees, probing for invertebrates in dead wood and among epiphytes, typically perching with wings drooped and tail raised.

E 3 Brown Trembler

Cinclocerthia ruficauda L 26 cm (10")

Endemic to the Lesser Antilles: locally common on **Saba, St Kitts and Nevis, Montserrat, Guadeloupe, Dominica** and **St Vincent**.

ID: Warm **rufous-brown upperparts**, with paler underparts. Head and face gray with a **dark mask**, **bright yellow eye** and **long, slightly down-curved bill**.

VOICE: Song includes fluting melodic phrases and a smooth, fast trill.

E 4 Gray Trembler *Cinclocerthia gutturalis* L 26 cm (10")

Endemic to the Lesser Antilles, occurring in two single-island subspecies: *C. g. gutturalis* on **Martinique** and *C. g. macrorhyncha* on **St Lucia**. Uncommon to rare.

ID: Gray-brown with paler **gray-white underparts**. Head gray with **bold dark mask**, **bright yellow eyes** and **long, slightly down-curved bill**. Juvenile can show browner tones on wings and tail.

VOICE: Song is a series of fluting melodic phrases.

Orioles

Three endemic species are present, each confined to a single island and found in a range of forest habitats. Orioles forage for fruit and invertebrates, picking apart bark and vegetation with their sharp, slightly down-curved bill. They are closely associated with *Heliconia* and palms, weaving a suspended basket-like nest underneath their leaves. All are threatened to some extent by habitat loss, predation by introduced mammals, and brood parasitism by Shiny Cowbirds (where present), which lay their eggs in oriole nests and play no part in raising the young.

E 1 Montserrat Oriole *Icterus oberi* L 22 cm (8½")

VU

Endemic to Montserrat. Uncommon, now mostly restricted to the Centre Hills forests, where it can be seen from several trails. Volcanic eruptions in 1995–7 substantially reduced habitat, which led to a rapid decline in range and population. Extensive conservation efforts by local and international organizations have helped stabilize the population, estimated to be fewer than 500 mature individuals (2017).
ID: Male **black** with **yellow lower back, rump, belly and undertail-coverts**. Female is largely unmarked, lacking any black. Upperparts are **olive-yellow**, underparts slightly paler. Both have a **sharp gray bill**, paler at base.
VOICE: Song includes clear, loud, scratchy whistles. Calls include a sharp "*cht*" and harsh "*churr*".

E 2 Martinique Oriole *Icterus bonana* L 21 cm (8")

VU

Endemic to Martinique. Widespread in all forest habitats. Can be noisy when searching for invertebrates through bark and dried plant material on trees. Population is in decline, estimated at fewer than 15,000 mature individuals (2020).
ID: Male and female similar with mainly black upperparts, **browner head** and throat with bright **orangey wing-patch, rump, lower belly and undertail-coverts**. Sharp gray bill with **paler base to lower mandible**.
VOICE: Calls include a harsh, repeated "*keck*" or "*krrk*" and drawn-out whistles.

E 3 St Lucia Oriole *Icterus laudabilis* L 22 cm (8½")

EN

Endemic to St Lucia, where widespread but uncommon in rainforests, dry forests and along wooded margins. Often elusive but can be seen from several forest trails, including Millett. Population is in decline, estimated at fewer than 2,500 mature individuals (2020).
ID: Male **black** with **bright orange-yellow wing-patch, rump and undertail-coverts**. Female similar but less bright; patches are more yellow than orange. Both have a sharp gray bill, **paler at base**.
VOICE: Calls include frequent single harsh "*keck*".

3

1♂
1♀
2
3

Cowbirds and grackles

1 **Shiny Cowbird** *Molothrus bonariensis* L 19 cm (7½″)

Found from **Dominica to Grenada**, including **Barbados**, with occasional records elsewhere. Common in all open habitats; often in small flocks feeding on short grassland. A brood parasite, female lays eggs singly in nests of other species and plays no part in raising young. As such, the species represents a significant conservation threat to two globally threatened species of oriole.
ID: Male **black** with glossy purple-blue sheen; female **gray-brown** with slightly paler underparts and **faint stripe above eye**. Juvenile paler still, with pale wingbars and light streaking on buff-yellow breast. Short, **sharply pointed dark bill**; tail often characteristically raised when feeding.
VOICE: Varied song phrases, comprising rapid fluty bubbling whistles and trills. Calls include a repeated scolding "*tchk*".

e 2 **Carib Grackle** *Quiscalus lugubris* L 25 cm (10″)

Widespread in five subspecies from **St Martin/Sint Maarten to Grenada**; occasional records elsewhere. Common in lowland scrub, agricultural areas and grassland. Exploits a variety of food sources and even steals from unattended tables in restaurants! Gregarious, often foraging in small flocks and forming noisy roosts in palms and other trees. Nests can be parasitized by Shiny Cowbird; adult grackles are often seen feeding the smaller juvenile cowbirds.
ID: Adults have striking **yellow-white eyes** and a **stout black bill**. Male **black** with bluish sheen and **long tail**, often held in a characteristic **twisted or V shape**. Female coloration differs between subspecies—from pale gray-brown to wholly black (*Q. l. fortirostris* on Barbados). Paler forms have gray-brown head and underparts with faint stripe above eye. Immature male in molt can be an untidy, mottled black and gray.
VOICE: Calls include a harsh "*teck-teck-teck*", clear whistles and a series of notes that sound like a squeaky toy.

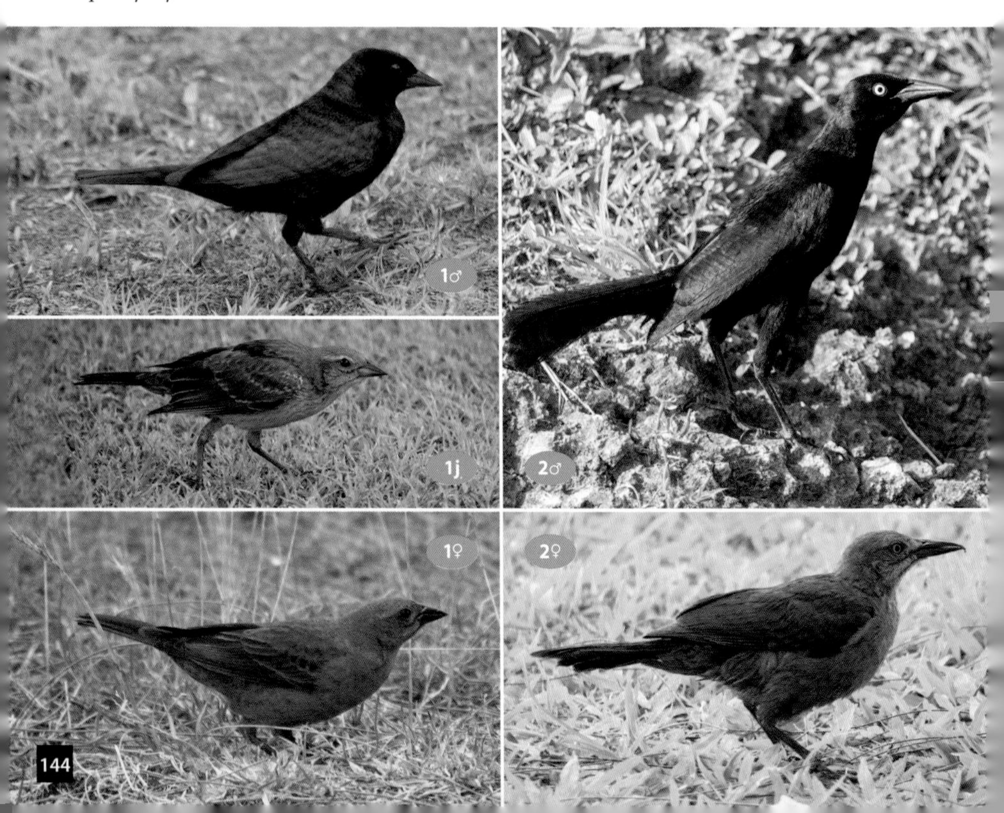

Warblers

Small, colorful and agile, warblers are found in all forest types, where they restlessly search through the canopy and understory, gleaning invertebrates with their short fine bill. There are only six resident breeding species, but over 30 species of North American migrant warblers have been recorded; a small number of these occur regularly and are described. Most of these are seen in non-breeding or 1st-winter plumage and can present identification challenges.

e 1 (American) **Yellow Warbler** *Setophaga petechia* L 12.5 cm (5")

Resident **throughout** in six subspecies; scarce on Saba. The most common and widespread warbler, found in dry forests, scrub and mangroves, often near water. Taxonomy is unsettled between the resident Caribbean populations, increasingly known as '**Golden Warbler**', and the North American migrant populations that can occur as rare visitors.

ID: Yellow-green upperparts and **bright yellow underparts** with varying amounts of **red-brown streaking** on breast and crown, more prominent in male. Some variability among subspecies, notably *S. p. ruficapilla* on Martinique, where male has a striking red head.

VOICE: Song is a short series of clear notes, accelerating at the end. Calls include a sharp "*tchit*" and harsh "*ter-ter*", which is often one of the most common bird calls in dry forests.

Martinique

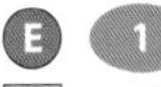

ENDEMIC WARBLERS

E 1 Barbuda Warbler *Setophaga subita* L 12.5 cm (5″)

VU **Endemic to Barbuda**, where uncommon in scrub and gardens. Population is in decline through habitat degradation, exacerbated by damage from Hurricane Irma in 2017. The number of mature individuals is estimated to be fewer than 1,700 (2020).

ID: Soft **gray upperparts** with **two weak white wingbars; bright, unmarked yellow underparts** with white undertail-coverts. Yellow face marked with **dark line through eye** and dark crescent below.

VOICE: A fast, strong, trilling song that fades towards the end. Calls include a short "*tchik*".

E 2 Plumbeous Warbler *Setophaga plumbea* L 13 cm (5″)

Endemic to Guadeloupe and **Dominica**. Widespread but uncommon, primarily in mountain rainforests and less often in dry forest and scrub. An active, restless feeder that moves quickly through the canopy, its tail often held slightly raised.

ID: Slate-gray upperparts with **two white wingbars**. Underparts slightly paler, with gray wash to neck and flanks. Obvious **white stripe above eye** and **small white crescent below**.

VOICE: Song a fast, clipped, rhythmic chatter.

E 3 St Lucia Warbler *Setophaga delicata* L 12.5 cm (5″)

Endemic to St Lucia. Widespread and locally common in forests and along wooded margins. Active and restless when searching for insects in trees and shrubs, it is most easily seen from tracks and trails.

ID: Brightly marked, **blue-gray** upperparts with **two white wingbars.** Underparts are **bright yellow** with white lower belly and undertail. **Head boldly patterned** with black crown-stripe, yellow face and black lines through and underneath the eye.

VOICE: Song is a loud clear warble that ends abruptly. Calls include a short "*tchik*".

E Semper's Warbler *Leucopeza semperi* L 14.5 cm (5¾″)

CR **Endemic to St Lucia**. Despite searches earlier this century, the last confirmed sighting of the warbler was in 1961, and its status remains uncertain. It was known from the rainforests high in the center of the island. The species may have suffered predation by introduced Small Indian Mongoose (*p. 168*), perhaps compounded by habitat loss.

ID: Gray-brown upperparts; pale gray-white underparts; pale legs and feet.

E 4 Whistling Warbler *Catharopeza bishopi* L 14.5 cm (5¾″)

EN **Endemic to St Vincent**. Rare and localized in rainforests. Sites include the Vermont and La Soufrière Trails. Secretive and more easily heard than seen; its loud whistled song rings out from forest cover. The only species in its genus.

ID: Unmistakable. **Gray-black** with obvious **white throat-band**, belly, undertail and strikingly bold **eyering**. Often perches with drooped wings and raised tail. Juvenile browner with indistinct markings and less obvious eyering.

VOICE: Song is a series of repeated whistles.

1
2
3
4

E 1 **Adelaide's Warbler** *Setophaga adelaidae* L 12.5 cm (5″)

Endemic to Puerto Rico but appears to be extending its range to the Virgin Islands, with recent records on **St John** and **St Thomas** (USVI).
ID: Blue-gray with two white wingbars. Throat and belly bright yellow with white undertail coverts. A bold eyebrow stripe is **yellow in front of the eye**, white behind, with a white crescent below the eye.
VOICE: Song is a high-pitched, accelerating trill. Call is a soft "*tswit*".

MIGRANT WARBLERS

Mainly found in **forests and mangrove swamps,** where they **forage for small invertebrates.**

2 **Northern Waterthrush** *Parkesia noveboracensis* L 15 cm (6″)

Non-breeding visitor in small numbers **throughout**, more easily heard than seen among tangled roots of mangrove swamps and wetland margins.
ID: Uniform **dark olive-brown** upperparts; **heavily streaked** creamy-white underparts, with **finer streaking on throat**. Obvious **pale stripe above eye**; dull pink legs. **Bobs tail** when foraging.
VOICE: Call a loud explosive "*chink*".

3 **Black-and-white Warbler** *Mniotilta varia* L 13 cm (5¼″)

Uncommon non-breeding visitor from the **Virgin Islands to Dominica**; increasingly rare farther south. Distinctive habit of working around trunks and along branches.
ID: Unmistakable: **boldly striped and streaked black and white** with **two broad white wingbars** and **dark spotting on undertail-coverts**. Face and throat black in male but white or grayish in female and immature.
VOICE: Call a slightly rasping "*tseek*".

4 **American Redstart** *Setophaga ruticilla* L 13 cm (5″)

Uncommon non-breeding visitor from the **Virgin Islands to Dominica**; rare or absent farther south.
ID: Male **black** with **striking orange patches** on breast, wings and base of dark tail. Female and immature much **paler overall** with **gray head**, green-gray back and wings, and **yellow (not orange) patches** on breast, wings and tail. All regularly flick wings and **raise and fan tail**.
VOICE: Calls include a soft "*tsip*".

5 **Northern Parula** *Setophaga americana* L 11.5 cm (4½″)

Non-breeding visitor from the **Virgin Islands to Dominica**; increasingly rare farther south.
ID: Small and well-marked. Male has a greenish back and gray wings with **two white wingbars. Head** is **gray-blue** with **small white crescents above and below eye**. Underparts gray-white with distinctive **yellow throat and breast**; may show **small rufous breast-patch or breast-band**. Female and immature duller, more olive-green, lack rufous breast patch. Short bill and tail.
VOICE: Call a sharp "*tzip*".

NT 6 **Blackpoll Warbler** *Setophaga striata* L 14 cm (5½″)

Passage visitor **throughout**, mainly in October and November, when large numbers may be grounded by storms during migration from North America to South America. Occasional records at other times.
ID: Gray-green upperparts with **two strong white wingbars**. Underparts paler with **yellow-green throat and (faintly streaked) breast**, and white undertail-coverts. Face subtly marked with dark stripe through eye and **pale lemon eyebrow**. Distinctive **pale orange legs and feet**. Adult male in breeding plumage has heavily striped back, boldly striped flanks, a black cap and white cheeks.
VOICE: Call a thin high-pitched "*tzeet*".

1
2
3
4♂
5
1ST -WINTER
6
1ST -WINTER
4♂

Small colorful forest birds

E 1 Lesser Antillean Tanager *Stilpnia cucullata* L 15 cm (6″)

Endemic to the Lesser Antilles, with two single-island subspecies: *S. c. versicolor* on **St Vincent** and *S. c. cucullata* on **Grenada** (treated as two separate species by some authorities). Widespread but uncommon in all forest types: can be unobtrusive and difficult to see in the canopy. Feeds on fruit including *Cecropia,* fig, mango and soursop: locally known as 'soursop bird'.

ID: Male colorful with **orange-yellow back and neck, blue-green wings and tail**. Underparts **paler** blue, sometimes appearing bright and iridescent; undertail-coverts orange. Obvious chestnut-brown crown, **paler** on St Vincent and **darker** on Grenada; both have black mask around eye. Female greener, lacking orange-yellow back. Colors of both sexes can appear much more subdued in shade of canopy. Bill short and stout.

VOICE: Call a sharp, forced "*tsweet*". Song a fast, twittery series of high-pitched notes: "*wit-wit-wit*".

E 2 Lesser Antillean Euphonia *Chlorophonia flavifrons* L 12 cm (4¾″)

Formerly considered a subspecies of *C. musica*, recently recognized as a new species **endemic to the Lesser Antilles**. It occurs from **Guadeloupe to St Vincent**, with sporadic records on Antigua, Barbuda and Grenada; rare elsewhere. Uncommon, mainly in rainforests, less often in dry forests. Feeds high in the canopy on berries, especially mistletoe *Phoradendron* spp.: a local name is 'mistletoe bird'. Secretive and, despite being brightly colored, can be inconspicuous so may be under-recorded.

ID: Small and colorful, with **short, dark stubby bill**. Male has dark green upperparts, paler yellow-green underparts, **bright yellow forehead and throat, black face** and **striking blue crown and nape**. Female similar but less bright, with greener underparts; lacks black face.

VOICE: Calls include a high-pitched, drawn-out whistle. Song is a rapid, tinkling twitter.

e 3 Bananaquit *Coereba flaveola* L 11.5 cm (4½″)

One of the most common and familiar birds in the Caribbean, resident **throughout** in seven subspecies. Widely known as 'sugar bird' for its attraction to nectar and sweet liquids: readily visits garden sugar-water feeders. Uses its short bill to pierce the base of long flower trumpets to 'steal' nectar without pollinating the plant. Untidy nests can be obvious in scrub, dry forests and gardens.

ID: Generally a distinctive combination of **black upperparts, bright yellow underparts and obvious pale eyebrow**. Throat color differs between subspecies and can be white, gray or black. All-black forms occur on St Vincent and Grenada. All have a **short, down-curved bill** with an **obvious red gape**. Juveniles are typically paler overall with yellower eyebrow.

VOICE: Usually noisy with buzzing calls, a sharp incisive "*tsst*" and a cheery "*tsee-tsee-tsee*". Song is drawn out and wheezy, with a rapid trill.

1♂
Grenada
1♂
St Vincent
1♀
Grenada
2♂
2♀
Anguilla
Grenada
3
3
Martinique
3

Endemic finches

e 1 Lesser Antillean Bullfinch *Loxigilla noctis* L 15 cm (6″)

Endemic to the Lesser Antilles, the Virgin Islands and Puerto Rico; absent from Barbados. Common and familiar in forests, scrub, gardens and open areas. Can be confiding around public spaces and will even nest on buildings. Forages for seeds and fruit, often on the ground, restlessly flicking wings and tail. Will 'pick' flower-heads, piercing the base to extract nectar. Some subtle plumage variation between males across the region's eight subspecies. Female can be confused with female Black-faced Grassquit (*p. 154*).
ID: Male **gray-black** with bright **orange-red eyebrow, throat and undertail-coverts. Stout conical bill** and **dark gray legs**. Female unmarked brown with **warmer brown wings**, paler underparts and **pale orange undertail-coverts**.
VOICE: Very vocal. Song is a fast repeated "*sweet-sweet-sweet*", with trills. Call is a sharp "*tsit*".

E 2 Barbados Bullfinch *Loxigilla barbadensis* L 15 cm (6″)

Endemic to Barbados: common and widespread in most habitats and can be confiding. Feeds mainly on the ground; diet includes seeds, fruit and small invertebrates. Male and female are alike; similar to female Lesser Antillean Bullfinch, but no overlap in range.
ID: Brown upperparts with **warmer brown wings**; paler brown-gray underparts with **orange undertail-coverts**. **Stout conical bill** and dark gray legs.
VOICE: Song a rapid, high-pitched trill ending with a buzzing wheeze. Calls include a shrill "*swit-wit*".

E 3 St Lucia Black Finch *Melanospiza richardsoni* L 14 cm (5½″)

EN

Endemic to St Lucia, where rare and secretive in all forest types. Forages on seeds on or near the ground among areas of thick understory but will venture onto trails early morning and late afternoon. Threatened by habitat loss and introduced predators, the population is declining: in 2020, it was estimated at under 1,000 mature individuals.
ID: Male **entirely black** with **heavy dark gray bill** and distinctive **pink legs and feet**. Female **browner** with paler underparts, **gray head** and **bill**.
VOICE: Song is a repeated short phrase: "*twiss-swiss-wissoo*". Calls include a slightly harsh "*tsweet-tsweet*".

E 4 Lesser Antillean Saltator *Saltator albicollis* L 22 cm (8½″)

Endemic to the Lesser Antilles, with two subspecies: *S. a. guadelupensis* on **Guadeloupe** and **Dominica**, and *S. a. albicollis* on **Martinique** and **St Lucia**. Locally common in dry forest and scrub, mainly at lower elevations, and found from ground cover to forest canopy, but it can be inconspicuous. Often moves in small groups, quietly picking large berries and fruit.
ID: Large and subtly marked with **olive-green upperparts**, gray-brown tail and paler underparts with **faint streaking on breast. Thin but obvious white eyebrow**, dark stripe on throat and **heavy, yellow-tipped black bill**.
VOICE: Strong, clear, repeated whistled song. Calls include a short clipped "*tsst*".

1♂
1♀
ORANGE
UNDERTAIL
Guadeloupe

2
3♂

4
3♀

Small finches

1 **Black-faced Grassquit** *Melanospiza bicolor* L 11.5 cm (4½″)

Common **throughout** and often easy to see, mostly at low elevations, but follows forest roads higher into hills. Forages for seeds in grassy areas along forest scrubby margins, often in small flocks.
ID: Male **olive-brown** with **black head, throat and upper breast**; **short, sharply pointed bill**; and pale legs. Female duller olive-brown and gray, with slightly paler underparts. Can be confused with female Lesser Antillean Bullfinch, but bill is smaller and it lacks orange undertail.
VOICE: Short, buzzing song phrase. Calls include a short "*tsip*" and a buzzing "*zee-zee-zee*".

1♂

1♀

2 **Blue-black Grassquit** *Volatinia jacarina* L 11 cm (4¼″)

Uncommon breeding visitor on **Grenada** but increasingly seen year-round. Male chooses an exposed perch for display, with a delightful habit of jumping 30–40 cm (12–16″) into the air with each song phrase, its wings spread and tail fanned; a local name is 'Johnny-jump-up'.
ID: Male **glossy blue-black** when breeding, can appear mottled blue-black and brown at other times. Female and immature are brown with paler underparts showing **gray streaking on breast and flanks**. Short, sharp gray-blue bill.
VOICE: Song is a sharp buzzing "*zzz-zzt*". Call is a short, sharp "*tsik*".

2♂

2♀

3 **Yellow-bellied Seedeater** *Sporophila nigricollis* L 11 cm (4½″)

Uncommon breeding visitor on **Grenada** but increasingly seen year-round; occasional records elsewhere. Mostly occurs at low elevations in grassy and agricultural areas, leading to a coastal distribution. Typically seen in small twittering flocks that often perch on grass stems picking off small seeds.

ID: Male olive-brown, boldly marked with **black head, throat and upper breast** and **pale yellow belly** (less obvious than its name would suggest). Female paler, olive-green above, with unmarked pale buff underparts and a whiter belly. **Short, stubby gray bill**, paler in male; legs dark.

VOICE: Song is a series of short, fast repeated phrases with clear notes and squeaky trills. Calls include a light squeaky "*dsee*".

4 **Grassland Yellow-Finch** *Sicalis luteola* L 12 cm (5½″)

Only on **Antigua, Guadeloupe, Martinique, St Lucia, Barbados** and **Grenada**, where localized in small populations along field margins and in open grassy areas, including airfields and sports fields. Often perches on low fences and bushes.

ID: Male upperparts heavily streaked brown with a **yellowy rump; face and underparts bright yellow**. Female duller, lacks yellow face. Immature has streaked breast. Small, stubby gray bill.

VOICE: Song is a series of fast buzzing trills. Calls include a soft "*tsit*".

Introduced species

A number of species from across the world have been introduced to the Eastern Caribbean, with several establishing breeding populations. Most originate from escaped cage-birds or are deliberate introductions (such as Red Junglefowl, which was probably introduced as a food source several centuries ago). Populations are usually small, highly localized and restricted to one or two islands. Their impact on native species and habitats is uncertain.

1 House Sparrow *Passer domesticus* L 15 cm (5¾")

Introduced and now long established **throughout** in small discrete breeding populations, mostly around buildings, especially ports and harbors. Often found in small noisy flocks, searching for seeds and food scraps on the ground.

ID: Male boldly marked **chestnut and brown** with **gray crown**, thin white wingbar and **black bib**; bill short and stubby. Female duller with pale stripe above eye, lacks black bib.

VOICE: Calls include a "*chirrup*" and an excited chatter.

2 Rufous-vented Chachalaca *Ortalis ruficauda*
Bequia, Union Island (the Grenadines)

3 Helmeted Guineafowl *Numida meleagris*
St Martin/Sint Maarten, Barbuda

4 Red Junglefowl *Gallus gallus*
Throughout

5 Channel-billed Toucan *Ramphastos vitellinus*
Grenada

6 Village Weaver *Ploceus cucullatus*
Martinique

♂

♀

7 Northern Red Bishop *Euplectes franciscanus*
Guadeloupe, Martinique, small numbers on St Croix

♂

♀

8 Orange-cheeked Waxbill *Estrilda melpoda*
Guadeloupe, Martinique

9 Black-rumped Waxbill *Estrilda troglodytes*
Guadeloupe, Martinique

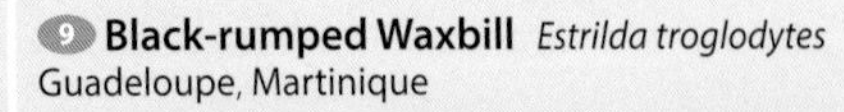

10 Common Waxbill *Estrilda astrild*
Martinique

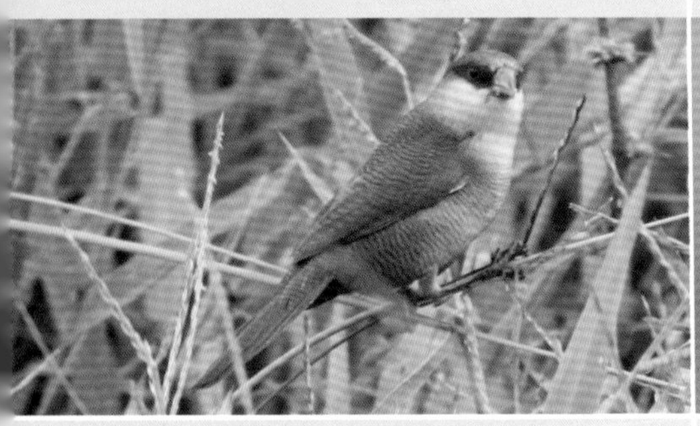

11 Red Avadavat *Amandava amandava*
Guadeloupe, Martinique

12 Scaly-breasted Munia *Lonchura punctulate*
St Kitts, Antigua, Guadeloupe, Dominica

13 Chestnut Munia *Lonchura atricapilla*
Martinique

14 White-headed Munia *Lonchura maja*
Martinique, recent record off Guadeloupe

Mammals

MARINE MAMMALS

A school of dolphins traveling at speed, or a pod of whales resting after a night feeding, must be among the most thrilling wildlife sights in the region. More than 20 species of cetacean have been recorded in the seas around the Eastern Caribbean: all occur more widely across tropical or temperate oceans. The most frequently seen are Sperm Whale, Short-finned Pilot Whale, Bottle-nosed Dolphin, Pantropical Spotted Dolphin and Spinner Dolphin, all of which have resident populations. The spectacular Humpback Whale regularly passes through on migration; some overwinter in the warm seas of the Caribbean, where they mate or calve. Other species have been recorded on migration along West Atlantic routes or as they wander nomadically through tropical waters. Their appearance in the region is both unpredictable and exciting.

Populations of marine mammals are much reduced globally through past exploitation and continue to be affected by pollution, marine debris, noise pollution and accidental fishing-related mortality. They remain vulnerable in the Caribbean. Many islands have designated Marine Protected Areas (MPAs), and new marine-mammal sanctuaries have been established around Saba, St Eustatius and Guadeloupe to protect cetaceans, along with sharks and rays. A further MPA is proposed to the west of Dominica for the protection of Sperm Whales.

Cetaceans are occasionally seen in inshore waters, but most sightings are from boats, especially organized whale-watching trips, which are available on several islands. These typically visit deep-water channels close to land and have gathered much of the available data. Despite increased awareness and co-operation, information and authenticated records are patchy. Further research is needed to learn more about the distribution, numbers and behavior of marine mammals in the region. Information can be found locally or from the Caribbean Cetacean Society (ccs-ngo.com).

Whale-watching trips should follow locally or internationally agreed operating guidelines to prevent disturbance. All cetaceans are protected by the pan-Caribbean Special Protected Areas and Wildlife (SPAW) Protocol 1990.

L is given as approximate mature length, but this may be exceeded by some individuals.

Whale blow, often the first sign that whales are present.

Pantropical Spotted Dolphin

Other marine mammals

Caribbean Monk Seal *Neomonachus tropicalis* formerly occurred in the region but is now considered extinct, with the last sightings in 1952.

West Indian Manatee *Trichechus manatus* is still found in the wider Caribbean but was extirpated from the Eastern Caribbean early in the 20th century. There are plans to reintroduce manatees to at least Guadeloupe.

VU

1 **Sperm Whale** *Physeter macrocephalus* L Male 18 m (59′), female 12 m (39′)

Resident in deep-water channels, at least off **Dominica** and **Guadeloupe**, but can occur as a migrant **throughout**, mainly between September and April. The largest of the toothed whales; small groups can be seen at the surface before making deep foraging dives, mainly for squid. Females form small nursery schools with their young.

ID: Impressive whale with **huge, square-fronted head** and thin inconspicuous lower jaw. Dark gray overall, **dorsal fin appears as a small triangular hump** towards rear of body, with distinctive **smaller bumps** between dorsal fin and tail, all visible when it dives. Flippers are small and inconspicuous; the wide triangular tail has **dark gray flukes and an obvious central notch**. The blowhole is on front left of head and angled; spray is typically low and broad.

2 **Humpback Whale** *Megaptera novaeangliae* L Male 14 m (46′), female 16 m (52′)

Widespread breeding visitor and passage migrant **throughout**, mostly November to April; largest numbers are off the **Virgin Islands**. An active species, known for flipper- and tail-slapping, and for spectacular breaches. Humpbacks are baleen whales, sieving large quantities of small fish and plankton out of the water through a series of comb-like plates that hang from the upper jaw. During the northern summer, the Caribbean breeding population moves to rich cold-water feeding grounds in the North Atlantic.

ID: Large, dark gray with **short, hooked dorsal fin set towards rear of body**; appears **hump-backed** when diving. Large, **flattened head** with **obvious fleshy lumps** (tubercles) on upper surface and long grooves on throat. **Flippers are long, thin** and **mostly white**. **Very wide tail** is briefly raised above water before diving, showing flukes with distinctive **white markings** on underside and an **uneven, serrated rear edge**.

3 **Short-finned Pilot Whale** *Globicephala macrorhynchus*

L Male 6.8 m (22′), female 5.5 m (18′)

Can be seen **throughout** with sightings year-round, mostly in deep-water channels. A member of the dolphin family, found across tropical and subtropical waters. A deep-diving species that forages at night, mainly for squid. Highly social, living in extended family pods of typically 10–30 individuals; will congregate with Common Bottlenose Dolphin and other dolphins.

ID: Stocky with **bulbous, rounded forehead** and **no obvious beak**; the genus name *Globicephala* translates as 'ball' or 'round head'. **Dark gray to black overall** with white markings on throat and belly. **Dorsal fin** (much broader in male) is **set towards front of body** and **slightly hooked**. Dark gray flippers are narrow and sharply pointed. The body flattens vertically before the tail flukes, appearing deeper when viewed side-on.

Dorsal fin and bumps visible when diving.

Wide triangular tail flukes with central notch.

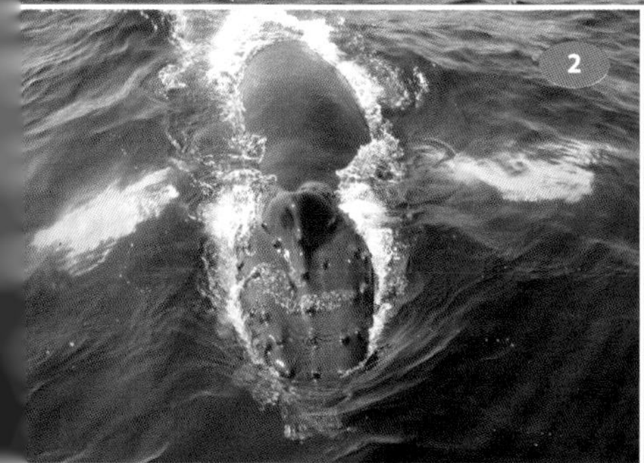

Head tubercles and white on flippers.

Wide tail with serrated rear edge.

3

Common Bottlenose Dolphin *Tursiops truncatus* L 4 m (13′)

Resident **throughout** in offshore and shallower inshore waters; the most commonly seen dolphin. An energetic species known for bow-riding and breaching high out of the water when traveling at speed. Usually seen in small pods (fewer than 30 individuals), but larger numbers may gather in deeper waters. Feeds on fish and squid; will hunt cooperatively to herd shoaling fish.
ID: Large and sturdy; uniform dark gray above, with slightly paler flanks and even paler belly. Distinctive head profile with bulging forehead and short stubby beak. Prominent long and strongly curved dorsal fin, positioned centrally on the back.

Fraser's Dolphin *Lagenodelphis hosei* L 2.7 m (8½′)

Widespread but most often seen from **Montserrat to Martinique**, and **St Vincent and the Grenadines**, especially in deeper channels. Found in tropical seas worldwide, but the Caribbean is among the best places to see this species. Often in large pods, dives deep for fish and squid but also feeds at the surface with a characteristic, energetic splashing.
ID: Stocky overall with very short beak; small, triangular dorsal fin; and small, dark flippers. Adults are dark gray on dorsal surface; throat and belly are off-white but can show pinkish flush. A key feature when present (typically on mature males) is a dark line on the face that continues along the flank, but this is usually weak on female and not visible on immature.

3 Pantropical Spotted Dolphin *Stenella attenuata* L 2.6 m (8½′)

Widespread resident from at least **St Martin/Sint Maarten to Grenada**, especially in deep offshore channels, where they forage for small fish. Fast, energetic swimmers, often leaping high out of the water; large groups form and readily congregate with other dolphin species, especially Spinner Dolphins.
ID: One of the smaller dolphins, slender and streamlined. Mostly pale gray, with contrasting **dark gray forehead and back** (cape) extending just beyond the dorsal fin. Adults and larger immatures typically have **distinctive white spots** (only visible at close range). Dorsal fin is tall and curved, flippers small and narrow. **Long thin beak has distinctive white 'lips' and tip**; a dark line from the base of the beak to the eye can extend to flipper.

Atlantic Spotted Dolphin *Stenella frontalis* L 2.3 m (7½′)

Uncommon resident, most often seen in deeper waters from the **Virgin Islands** to **Guadeloupe**.
ID: Similar to Pantropical Spotted Dolphin, but dark gray on back extends to tail and belly is whiter, developing black spots with age.

1
2
3

1 Spinner Dolphin *Stenella longirostris* L 2.3 m (7¾′)

Resident **throughout**; forms small pods in inshore waters but congregates in larger numbers in deep offshore channels. Named for its twisting action when breaching—may spin several times during a single breach! Forages, mainly at night, for small fish, shrimps and squid, which move upwards from deeper water. Often mixes with other dolphin species.

ID: A small, slender dolphin, subtly three-toned with dark gray back, light gray flanks and paler belly. Long, narrow beak (*longirostris* is Latin for 'long beak') with dark lips and tip. A narrow dark line runs between eye and flipper. Dorsal fin is tall and broadly triangular; flippers are short and curved.

Uncommon to rare whales and dolphins can occur throughout. The following records are from the Global Biodiversity Information Facility (GBIF) database and the Caribbean Cetacean Society.

Species	Recorded from at least …
Common Minke Whale *Balaenoptera acutorostrata*	Guadeloupe, Dominica, Martinique
Pygmy Killer Whale *Feresa attenuata*	Saba, Guadeloupe, Dominica, Martinique
Risso's Dolphin *Grampus griseus*	St Eustatius, Martinique, St Lucia, St Vincent, Grenadines
Killer Whale *Orcinus orca* DD	Can occur throughout
Melon-headed Whale *Peponocephala electra*	Guadeloupe, Dominica, Martinique, St Vincent, Grenadines, Grenada
False Killer Whale *Pseudorca crassidens* NT	Saba, Antigua and Barbuda, Montserrat, Guadeloupe, Dominica, Martinique, Grenada
Clymene Dolphin *Stenella clymene*	Guadeloupe, Martinique, St Lucia
Striped Dolphin *Stenella coeruleoalba*	Saba, Guadeloupe, Martinique
Rough-toothed Dolphin *Steno bredanensis*	Guadeloupe, Martinique, St Lucia
Pygmy Sperm Whale *Kogia breviceps*	Guadeloupe, Martinique, St Lucia, Grenada
Dwarf Sperm Whale *Kogia sima*	Guadeloupe, Martinique, St Lucia, St Vincent, Grenadines, Grenada
Cuvier's Beaked Whale *Ziphius cavirostris*	Guadeloupe, Dominica, Martinique, St Lucia

LAND MAMMALS

There are few terrestrial mammals in the Eastern Caribbean, other than bats. There is evidence of extinct rodents. For example, fossils of a giant hutia *Amblyrhiza inundata* have been found on Anguilla and St Martin/Sint Maarten. Several species of rice-rat persisted well beyond the arrival of humans, from at least Nevis to Grenada, although all are now extinct. Giant Rice-rats are known to have survived on St Lucia until the late 19th century and on Martinique until the early 20th century: Small Indian Mongoose has been implicated in their extinction. The last documented St Lucia Giant Rice-rat *Megalomys luciae* died in London Zoo in 1852.

Bats, as flying mammals, were well suited to colonize the islands and are widely distributed throughout. Robinson's Mouse Opossum, which occurs only on Grenada, could be a natural arrival from nearby Trinidad and Tobago. Other species have uncertain origins or are known to have been introduced, either accidentally or deliberately. Common Red-rumped Agouti was probably the earliest intentional introduction, taken by indigenous people from South America as a food source: populations still exist on several islands. European settlers in the 17th century brought with them a whole range of livestock and domesticated animals: pigs, sheep, goats, donkeys, cats and dogs have all since established feral populations. Rats and mice are presumed to have arrived accidentally with the first sailing ships. A few exotic species were taken as pets: some, such as Green Monkey, escaped or were released, and there are now established populations on several islands. There are occasional records of other introduced mammals, but it is not clear if any have become established: one example is the small number of European Hare *Lepus europaeus* on Barbados.

Native wildlife was highly vulnerable to many of these new mammals, some of which have been devastating and are now classed as invasive. Probably the most destructive is Small Indian Mongoose, which was deliberately introduced in the 19th century to control rodents in sugar plantations. They, together with rats and mice, are largely responsible for the local or even total extinction of some reptiles, amphibians and ground-nesting birds. Black Rat, House Mouse and Small Indian Mongoose all feature on the UN Global Invasive Species Database (GISD) list of 100 of the world's worst invasive species. The management and control of all invasive species is a major and ongoing conservation challenge throughout the region.

Robinson's Mouse Opossum (*p. 166*).

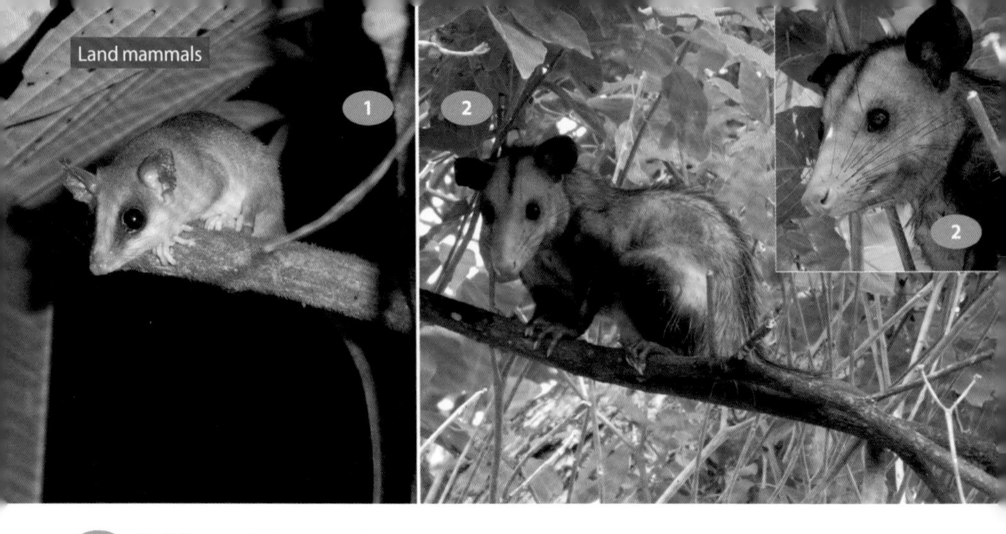

1 **Robinson's Mouse Opossum** *Marmosa robinsoni* L 42 cm (16½")

Only found on **Grenada** but occurs more widely on Trinidad and Tobago and in Central and South America. Uncommon in most forest types; nocturnal and difficult to find. Forages in the canopy for invertebrates and fruit, using its long tail to grip branches when climbing.
ID: Brown to gray-brown with pale underparts, a pointed snout and a gray mask around large, dark eye. Tail looks bare and is obviously longer than body.

2 **Northern Black-eared** (Common) **Opossum** *Didelphis marsupialis* L 69 cm (27")

Uncommon, found at least on **Dominica, Martinique, St Lucia, St Vincent, the Grenadines** and **Grenada**; occurs more widely in Central and South America. There is some debate about its status as a native or introduced species, although it has been present on some islands for centuries, being known locally as 'manicou'. Nocturnal, it is an adept tree-climber with a broad, opportunistic diet including fruit, plants, invertebrates, reptiles and birds.
ID: Large. Appears gray overall with darker legs and black, rounded ears. Face is pale with a dark line down center of forehead, prominent dark eyes and a long, pointed snout. It has a long, furless tail.

3 **Green** (Vervet) **Monkey** *Chlorocebus pygerythrus* L 130 cm (51")

Native to Africa. Established on at least **Tortola, St Martin/Sint Maarten, St Kitts, Nevis** and **Barbados** in forests, scrub and agricultural areas. Introduced, possibly as early as the 17th century, when it is thought they were kept as exotic pets. Primarily forages for fruit and vegetation but is omnivorous so readily takes invertebrates, reptiles, birds and their eggs. Considered an invasive species in the region; a threat to both biodiversity and agriculture.

4 **Mona Monkey** *Cercopithecus mona* (NT in native range) L 136 cm (53")

Native to West Africa, introduced to **Grenada** in the 18th century; now established and localized in rainforests. Small troops forage primarily for fruit, leaves and invertebrates.

5 **White-tailed Deer** *Odocoileus virginianus* HS 100 cm (39")

Native to North America, with introductions in the 18th and 20th centuries to **St John, St Croix, St Thomas** (USVI) and **St Kitts**. Wary, emerges early and late in the day, when it can be seen browsing trees and shrubs along forest margins, roadside verges and beaches; most easily seen on St John. There is growing concern about its impact on native plants and habitats, including mangroves, through grazing pressure.

3
4
5

1 **Common Red-rumped Agouti** *Dasyprocta leporine* L 64 cm (25″)

An introduced species, established on at least **USVI, Montserrat** and **from Guadeloupe to Grenada**, excluding Barbados; native to Central and South America. Active at dusk and dawn; can be seen along forest margins, where it forages for fruit, roots and vegetation. Lives in burrows or holes in rocks and tree roots.

Rats

Two species, similar in appearance, were accidentally introduced to the region and are now probably established **throughout**. They are mainly nocturnal but can be seen during the day, and are omnivorous, opportunistic feeders. They are now considered invasive, responsible for extensive predation of birds, reptiles and invertebrates as well as damage to plants and crops. Ongoing seabird and reptile conservation programs aimed at eradicating rodents from small offshore islands are proving successful.

2 **Black** (Ship/House) **Rat** *Rattus rattus* L 40 cm (16″) including tail

Originally from Southeast Asia. Often found in less disturbed areas, including high in rainforests, where they pose a serious threat to native flora and fauna. Recognized as one of the 100 worst invasive alien species in the world.
ID: Slender. Fur ranges from gray-brown to black, paler underneath. Eyes and ears larger, and snout longer, than Brown Rat. Tail longer than head and body.

3 **Brown Rat** *Rattus norvegicus* L 52 cm (20″) including tail

Originally from central Asia and China, now widely dispersed around the world. They probably occur on all the main islands and are most often seen around ports, buildings and in agricultural areas.
ID: Stockier and larger than Black Rat. Fur typically warmer or paler brown. Eyes and ears smaller, and snout shorter, than Black Rat. Tail shorter than head and body.

---

4 **House Mouse** *Mus musculus* L 20 cm (8″)

Introduced and established **throughout**. Found in all habitats, including buildings, but less common in rainforests. In addition to seeds, grain and fruit, readily takes invertebrates, small lizards and birds' eggs and as such is highly invasive; recognized as one of the 100 worst invasive alien species in the world.

5 **Northern** (Common) **Raccoon** *Procyon lotor* L 79 cm (31″)

Native to North and Central America, introduced to **Guadeloupe** (probably in the late 19th century), with occasional records from **St Martin/Sint Maarten** and **Martinique**; formerly on Barbados. Mainly nocturnal with an opportunistic diet that includes invertebrates, fruit, plant material, small amphibians and reptiles. Readily scavenges around buildings and picnic areas.

6 **Small Indian Mongoose** *Urva (Herpestes) auropunctata* L 94 cm (37″)

Native to Southeast Asia, introduced to the wider Caribbean in the 19th century to islands where sugar cane was grown; now widely established from the **Virgin Islands to Grenada**. Active by day, it feeds opportunistically in all habitats and is commonly seen crossing roads or scavenging around picnic areas. Responsible for the significant decline, extirpation and even extinction of several native species of ground-nesting bird, amphibian and reptile that had evolved in the absence of predatory land mammals. Recognized as one of the 100 worst invasive alien species in the world.

1
2
3
4
5
6

BATS

As dusk settles, darting silhouettes and twisting shapes in the fading light are signs of bats emerging from their daytime roosts. On most of the islands in the Eastern Caribbean bats are the only native land mammals; at least 30 species occur, 11 of which are endemic to the Lesser Antilles. Only ten species are widespread; the rest are rare or highly restricted in range. Bats are difficult to identify in the field, but groups can be broadly separated by habitat, diet and feeding behavior:

- Greater Bulldog Bat is the only fish-eating species in the region. It is widely distributed and can be seen foraging over watercourses, wetlands and coastal bays.
- Insect-eating bats consume huge quantities of night-flying insects, including mosquitoes. Pallas's Mastiff and Brazilian Free-tailed Bats can be seen in large numbers over forests and built-up areas and are distinguished from other bats by their fast and erratic flight.
- Fruit-, pollen- and nectar-eating bats range widely, visiting trees and plants to feed. This group plays a vital role in the ecology of forests and agriculture, pollinating plants and dispersing seeds. They are especially important in habitat regeneration on disturbed ground and in areas damaged by hurricanes or volcanic eruptions.

Bats have a variety of daytime roost sites. Some use trees, finding holes in trunks and branches, or hide away in dense foliage; others, especially the small insect-eating bats, squeeze into tiny crevices in caves or man-made structures, including buildings. The largest colonies are in natural caves with some traditional sites holding hundreds or even thousands of individuals, often of several species. Safeguarding cave-roost sites is critical for the future of bats and a vital conservation priority.

Data on local bat population trends are limited, although eight species are known to be globally threatened to some extent. The key threats are habitat loss and degradation, including through periodic hurricane damage, which affects both roost sites and food sources. However, folklore and superstition mean that bats are often misunderstood and not always tolerated. Through the work of individuals, government departments, university researchers, and local and international conservation efforts, the beneficial role of bats in controlling insects and helping maintain healthy forests is now becoming much more widely recognized and valued.

Some of the images used in the guide were taken of bats in the hand by experienced fieldworkers undertaking research. **Handling or coming into close contact with bats should be avoided, both to prevent any potential health risks and to minimize disturbance to the animals or their roosts.**

Cave roost of Antillean Fruit-eating Bat.

1 Greater Bulldog (Greater Fishing) Bat *Noctilio leporinus* WS 75 cm (30")

Uncommon **throughout**: the **only fish-eating bat** in the region. Mostly seen over calm stretches of watercourses, wetlands and coastal bays, typically singly or in small numbers. Detects ripples from fish and aquatic invertebrates using echolocation, catching prey with sharp claws or lifting tail membrane before trawling for fish by dangling long feet in the water. Occasionally seen along roads, where it hunts for invertebrates. Roosts in caves, hollow trees and rock crevices, where there may be a characteristic fishy smell from droppings.

ID: Largest bat in the region. Long wings, distinctive long legs and large feet with sharp claws. Fur ranges from orange to gray-brown and can show a pale central line from head to rump. Looks heavy-jowled with drooping 'bulldog-like' upper-lip. Ears very long and narrow. Flight is slow, mainly low over water.

Fruit-eating bats

1 Jamaican Fruit-eating Bat *Artibeus jamaicensis* WS 45 cm (18″)

Common and widespread from the **Virgin Islands to Martinique** and **Barbados** in forested and open areas, especially around fruit trees. Can be seen along trails, quiet roads and in gardens, often in small noisy flocks. Forages for a wide range of wild and cultivated fruit, pollen and nectar, carrying small items to feeding roosts, where it expels pellets of indigestible material, playing an important role in seed dispersal. Roosts in clusters within caves, rocks, old buildings and ruins, and also in foliage or hollow trees. Formerly considered to be present throughout the Lesser Antilles; ongoing analysis has so far identified that a congener, Schwartz's Fruit-eating Bat, also occurs, with a zone of hybridization at least on St Lucia.
ID: Large with short chestnut-brown to gray-brown fur with faint white lines on forehead and below eye. Head broad, with a distinctive large nose-leaf that has a wide spike. Wings short and broad; flight slow when foraging.

E DD Schwartz's Fruit-eating Bat *Artibeus schwartzi*

Endemic to St Vincent and several of the Grenadines. Similar to Jamaican Fruit-eating Bat and difficult to separate. Differs in having pale lines from the corner of the jaw to the ear and down the center of the forehead.

E 2 Antillean Fruit-eating (Antillean Cave) Bat *Brachyphylla cavernarum* WS 45 cm (18″)

Endemic to the Eastern Caribbean and Puerto Rico. Widespread and locally common from the **Virgin Islands to St Vincent and Barbados** in scrub, dry forests, gardens and rainforests. Loose flocks can be noisy when feeding. Forages for fruit, pollen and nectar, thereby playing an important role in seed dispersal and pollination. Roosts in caves, tightly packed in clusters that can number into the thousands.
ID: Large with pale gray to brown fur. Short snout with stumpy, circular nose-leaf (species is also known as 'Pig-faced Bat'). Ears small, slightly rounded at the tip with obvious but small, pointed tragus (a small, fleshy projection that covers the entrance to the ear). Flight is slow when foraging.

E 3 Lesser Antillean Tree Bat *Ardops nichollsi* WS 30 cm (12″)

Endemic to the Lesser Antilles: common and widespread from **St Martin/Sint Maarten to St Vincent** but absent from some lower-lying islands. Individuals or small flocks forage mainly for fruit in dry forests and rainforests, and play an important role in seed dispersal, especially for native fruiting trees such as figs. Roosts in dense tree foliage, including 'beards' of palm trees.
ID: Smallest of the common fruit-eating bats. Pale brownish-gray fur, with a white patch on each shoulder. Short, wrinkled snout with long, spike-like nose-leaf; small, bright yellow tragus (a small, fleshy projection that covers the entrance to the ear).

1
1
2
3
2
SMALL, POINTED
TRAGUS VISIBLE
AT THE ENTRANCE
TO THE EAR
3
PROMINENT,
SPIKE-LIKE
NOSE-LEAF

Insect-eating bats

E 1 **Lesser Antillean** (Gray's) **Funnel-eared Bat** *Natalus stramineus*

WS 25 cm (10″)

Endemic to the Lesser Antilles. Uncommon but widespread from **Anguilla to Martinique**, including Nevis but absent from St Kitts, mainly in dry forest and moist semi-evergreen forest. Maneuverable in flight; forages among vegetation, picking insects from leaves. Roosts in caves, where humid conditions possibly help prevent its thin, delicate, wing membranes from drying out.
ID: Small with pale brown to orange fur that appears fluffy. Broad-based ears reach base of short snout. Wings are broad with a long tail membrane; flight fluttery, moth-like.

2 **Brazilian** (Mexican) **Free-tailed Bat** *Tadarida brasiliensis* WS 30 cm (12″)

Locally common **throughout** but appears to be rare in the Virgin Islands and absent from Barbados. Flies high over open areas and forest canopy, feeding on insects, including moths and beetles. Highly colonial: mainly roosts in caves and abandoned buildings, from where large numbers may be seen emerging at sunset. One of the **fastest-flying** animals in the world: can reach speeds of up to 160 kph (99 mph).
ID: Small with warm brown velvety fur (some can be orangey); snout has 'dog-like' nostrils and wrinkled lips. Ears are large and blunt-tipped, with obvious ridges, and almost meet on the forehead. Wings are long, thin and pointed; a mouse-like tail projects beyond tail membrane, hence the common name.

3 **Pallas's Mastiff** (Velvety Free-tailed) **Bat** *Molossus molossus* WS 30 cm (12″)

Common **throughout** over towns, open areas and forests. Emerges at dusk, often in large numbers, to forage for insects, including beetles, moths, flies and flying ants. Roosts in roofs and walls of inhabited and abandoned buildings, squeezing into tiny fissures; also uses tree hollows and palms.
ID: Small with velvety brown fur. Short, pointed ears; sloping forehead; and a deep snout with smooth upper lip. Mouse-like tail projects beyond tail membrane. Wings long and thin; flight is fast and direct; can look swift-like (*p. 112*).

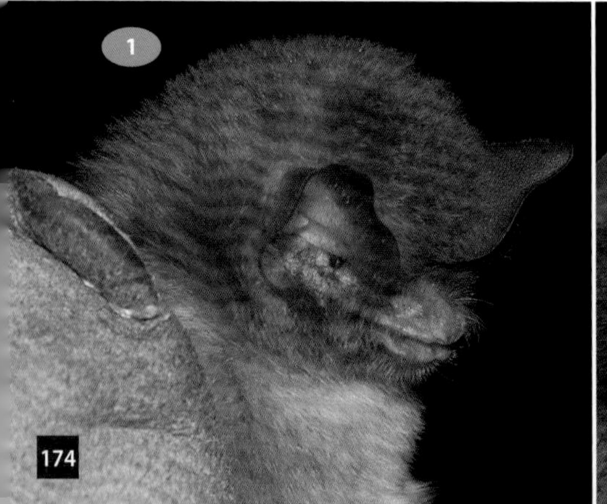

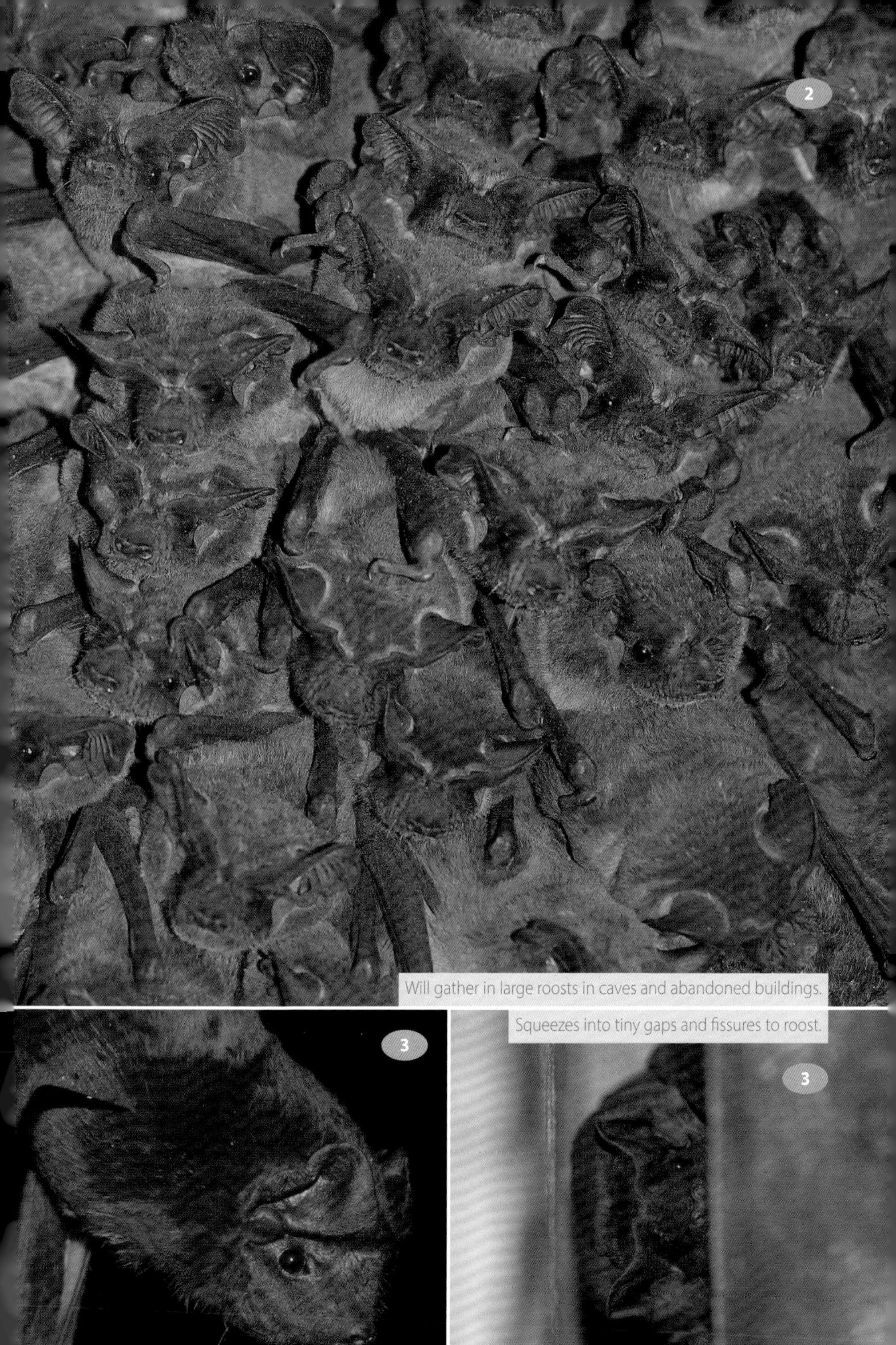

Will gather in large roosts in caves and abandoned buildings.

Squeezes into tiny gaps and fissures to roost.

Nectar- and pollen-eating bats

E 1 **Insular Single-leaf** (Long-tongued) **Bat** *Monophyllus plethodon*

WS 30 cm (12")

Endemic to the Lesser Antilles: widespread from **Anguilla to St Vincent**, including **Barbados**. Locally common within rainforests and over agricultural land; less often in dry forest. Forages for nectar, pollen and fruit, using its long tongue to reach deep inside flowers: an important pollinator of fruit and native trees. Roosts mainly in caves, mostly in small numbers.
ID: Small with brown fur; narrow, pointed snout; and small, heart-shaped nose-leaf. Ears are compact, triangular and set well apart. Broad, relatively short wings allow it to maneuver through vegetation and to hover and feed like a nocturnal hummingbird.

2 **Miller's** (Greater) **Long-tongued Bat**

Glossophaga longirostris WS 30 cm (12")

Restricted to **St Vincent, the Grenadines and Grenada**, where locally common in dry forests and cultivated areas, but less often in rainforests. Forages for nectar, pollen and fruit, hovering in front of flowers like a hummingbird: plays an important role in pollination and seed dispersal of native plants. Roosts in caves, man-made structures, rock crevices and trees.
ID: Fur brown to gray-brown; snout is narrow and elongated with a short, spear-like nose-leaf. Broad, slightly rounded wings.

Rare or highly restricted-range bat species

Trinidad Dog-like Bat *Peropteryx trinitatis*—Grenada

St Vincent Big-eared Bat *Micronycteris buriri* E DD—Endemic to St Vincent

Red Fig-eating Bat *Stenoderma rufum* E NT—Endemic to USVI, only on St Thomas and St John (also Puerto Rico)

Silvery Fruit-eating Bat *Dermanura glauca*—Grenada

Geoffroy's Tailless Bat *Anoura geoffroyi*—Grenada

3 **Angel's Yellow-shouldered Bat** *Sturnira angeli* E NT
Endemic to Montserrat, Guadeloupe, Dominica, Martinique

Paulson's Yellow-shouldered Bat *Sturnira paulsoni*
E NT—Endemic to St Lucia, St Vincent, Grenada

Flat-faced Fruit-eating Bat *Artibeus planirostris*—Grenada

4 **Great Fruit-eating Bat** *Artibeus lituratus*
St Vincent, the Grenadines, Grenada

Guadeloupean Big-eyed Bat *Chiroderma improvisum* EN
Endemic to St Kitts and Nevis, Montserrat, Guadeloupe

Allen's Mustached Bat *Pteronotus fuscus*—St Vincent

Davy's Naked-backed Bat *Pteronotus davyi*—Guadeloupe, including Marie-Galante, Dominica, Martinique, St Lucia, Grenada

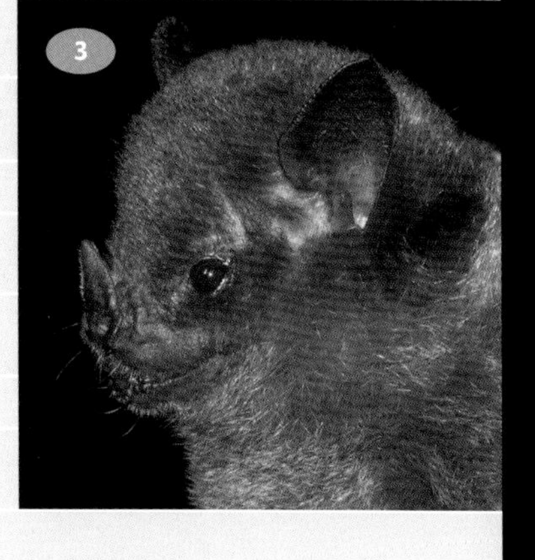

Common Black Myotis *Myotis nigricans*—Grenada

Barbadian Myotis *Myotis nyctor* E VU—Endemic to Barbados, possibly Grenada

Dominican Myotis *Myotis dominicensis* E VU—Endemic to Dominica, Basse-Terre (Guadeloupe)

Schwartz's (Martinique) **Myotis** *Myotis martiniquensis* E NT—Endemic to Dominica, Basse-Terre (Guadeloupe)

Guadeloupean Big Brown Bat *Eptesicus guadeloupensis* E NT—Endemic to Basse-Terre (Guadeloupe)

Amphibians

Frogs and toads are the only amphibians in the region. Most are small and nocturnal, and although they can be very vocal with distinct calls, they are difficult to track down, being hidden away along watercourses and deep within vegetation. There are 15 native species: most are either single-island or regional endemics. Whistling frogs are by far the most widespread group and, together with the introduced South American Cane Toad, are the species most likely to be seen. The only native toad, **Puerto Rican Toad** *Peltophryne lemur*, is presumed extirpated from the Virgin Islands but still occurs on Puerto Rico.

The region's amphibians are a vulnerable group; ten species are considered globally threatened, three of which are Critically Endangered. The main conservation threats are habitat loss, the impact of invasive species and the fungal disease *Chytridiomycosis.*

All amphibians are highly variable in both color and markings, and identification can be difficult. A growing challenge is to separate native from introduced species.

RARE ENDEMIC FROGS

E 1 Martinique Volcano Frog *Allobates chalcopis* L 20 mm (¾″)

CR **Endemic to Martinique:** rare and highly localized at high elevations in grassland, scrub and palm brakes. Active dusk and dawn but secretive, hiding under leaf litter and rocks. The only West Indian representative of the frog family Aromobatidae. Recent range contractions are possibly due to climate change, the species now thought to be restricted to the higher slopes of Mont Pelée.
ID: **Tiny; red-brown** with **black throat** and **orange lower belly**. Toes lack webbing.
VOICE: An insistent, almost bird-like, single squeaky whistle on an even pitch.

St Vincent Frog *Pristimantis shrevei* L 40 mm (1½″)

EN

Endemic to St Vincent: rare in rainforests and marginal grassland at higher elevations. Sites include the Vermont and Soufrière Trails. Nocturnal and mainly arboreal, foraging for invertebrates on vegetation. Larvae develop within the egg and hatch as tiny froglets.
ID: Color ranges from **dark brown to tan**; unmarked or with weak chevrons along back. A **dark line through the eye** extends to top of forelimb. Can show a **pale line from top of eye to snout** and **orange-red at inner base of hind leg.** Feet have long digits with toe pads but no webbing.
VOICE: Series of percussive clicks, often in short, quick bursts.

Grenada Frog *Pristimantis euphronides* L 39 mm (1½″)

Endemic to Grenada, where rare and localized in rainforests and marginal grassland at higher elevations. Sites include Grand Étang. Now Critically Endangered; threats include the fungal disease *Chytridiomycosis,* habitat loss and competition with the introduced Lesser Antillean Frog. Mainly nocturnal, foraging for ants and other small invertebrates both in low vegetation and on the ground. Larvae develop within the egg and hatch as tiny froglets.
ID: Ranges from very dark to pale brown; can show dark W or chevron markings along back and/or a broad pale line along body from the eye. A pale-bordered dark line runs from the snout to top of the eye, and a thin, curved dark line leads back from the eye; can show orange-red at inner base of hind leg. Feet have long digits with toe pads but no webbing.
VOICE: Intermittent short series of soft clicks.

DITCH FROGS

Large frogs found in a range of damp situations, mainly in forest habitats. After mating, the female lays eggs in a foam nest, created by beating glandular secretions into a froth; once hatched, larvae (tadpoles) develop in water.

E 1 Antillean White-lipped Frog *Leptodactylus albilabris* L 35 mm (1½")

Endemic to the Caribbean; only on the **Virgin Islands**, but occurs more widely in the Dominican Republic and Puerto Rico. Uncommon in muddy ditches, streams, ponds, marshy areas and drainage gutters among buildings. Forages for a wide range of invertebrates, including snails, beetles and spiders.
ID: Brown, variably marked with pale or reddish lines and blotches. Strong black line runs from snout through the eye above a **bold white line along upper lip**. Legs can appear banded; toes lack webbing.
VOICE: Repeated single note: "*kwit*".

E 2 Mountain Chicken (Giant Ditch Frog) *Leptodactylus fallax* L 167 mm (6½")

CR

Endemic to the Lesser Antilles, where restricted to **Montserrat and Dominica** following extirpation from St Kitts, Nevis, Guadeloupe and Martinique. Once common enough to be collected for food, it is now very rare and restricted to rainforests, often near ravines and streams. Nocturnal, foraging for a range of invertebrates, small frogs and lizards. Retreats to burrows or damp situations under rocks and leaf litter. Severely threatened by the fungal disease *Chytridiomycosis* and habitat loss. Monitoring suggests that fewer than 150 mature individuals remain in the wild. Local and international conservation actions include captive breeding programs.
ID: One of the largest frogs in the world. **Heavy-looking**, gray-brown with **dark blotches**, and a dark line through and behind eye. **Hind legs have heavy dark bands**; long toes lack obvious toe pads.
VOICE: Single soft "*chirrp*", repeated.

E 3 Windward Islands Ditch Frog *Leptodactylus validus* L 51 mm (2")

Endemic to the Caribbean, occurring only on **St Vincent, Grenada** and Trinidad and Tobago. Localized along forest margins in streams and ditches, in disturbed land and gardens, often at lower elevations.
ID: Broad-bodied with **short, rounded snout** and **obvious circular eardrum** behind eye. **Yellowish to brown** with **dark spots and blotches**; the **upper lip is often barred or marked with blotches**. Long toes lack webbing.
VOICE: A sharp, fast, two-note "*pip-pip*".

1

2

3
3

WHISTLING FROGS

The chiming calls of whistling frogs combine with the incessant chirping of cicadas and crickets to create a background chorus to evenings in the Caribbean. Males make these loud calls, inflating and deflating a throat sac, to both advertise territory and attract females. They can sometimes be heard in the daytime following rain, but are most vocal between dusk and dawn. Whistling frogs are in the genus *Eleutherodactylus*, which means 'free-toed' or '**unwebbed**'. These tiny frogs are difficult to locate, even when calling nearby. Most are 'sit-and-wait' predators, often jumping to catch small invertebrate prey. The female lays eggs among leaf litter and rocks; larvae develop within the egg and hatch as tiny froglets without an aquatic tadpole stage. Nine species occur in the region, but there is a remarkable diversity of *Eleutherodactylus* species across the West Indies, especially on the larger islands of the Greater Antilles.

Whistling frogs are highly variable in color and markings and are challenging to identify in the field. The three commonest species are most easily separated by their distinctive calls.

E 1 **Lesser Antillean** (Johnstone's Whistling) **Frog**

Eleutherodactylus johnstonei L 35 mm (1¼")

Endemic to the Lesser Antilles. Common **throughout** in all habitats from gardens to rainforests—the most widespread frog in the region. There is some uncertainty about which populations occur naturally, as the species has been widely introduced (including to the Virgin Islands) and is increasingly considered invasive on some islands. Fossil evidence suggests that it is native to several of the Leeward Islands, including Antigua and Barbuda.
ID: Small and compact. Gray-brown with **highly variable markings** that can include a **dark line through the eye**; pale side-stripes; a thin, pale dorsal line; and one or two **dark chevrons on the back**. Long toes with small but obvious toe pads.
VOICE: Persistent, rhythmic, short "*tree*", with a ringing quality.

E 2 **Martinique** (Robber) **Frog** *Eleutherodactylus martinicensis* L 47 mm (1¾")

NT **Endemic to Dominica and Martinique** and introduced to at least **St Martin/Sint Maarten, St Barthélemy, Antigua** and **Guadeloupe**. Locally common in damp areas within rainforests, agricultural land and gardens; less frequent in dry forests. Hides away in leaf axils and bromeliads and underneath stones and vegetation.
ID: Similar to Lesser Antillean Frog but larger with **longer rear legs** (although not easy to determine in the field). Brown but can be paler yellow-brown with paler underparts. **Broad head** with **dark line through the eye**. Can show orange-red at inner base of hind legs.
VOICE: A repeated, two-note, slurred, rising whistle: "*ooo-ee*".

E 3 **Puerto Rican Red-eyed Frog** (Antillean Coqui)

Eleutherodactylus antillensis L 43 mm (1¾")

Endemic to the Virgin Islands and Puerto Rico. Widespread and common in dry forest, grassland and urban areas, where found in bushes, grasses and bromeliads and underneath stones and vegetation.
ID: Gray-brown to red-brown, often with a pale dorsal line. A dark line runs from snout through the eye to top of front leg, with a **pale line** from the **snout over the** top of the **eye**, which can be faint. Distinctive **red eyes**.
VOICE: Call a short, liquid but sharp "*te-qui*": the first note is clipped and the second rises slightly.

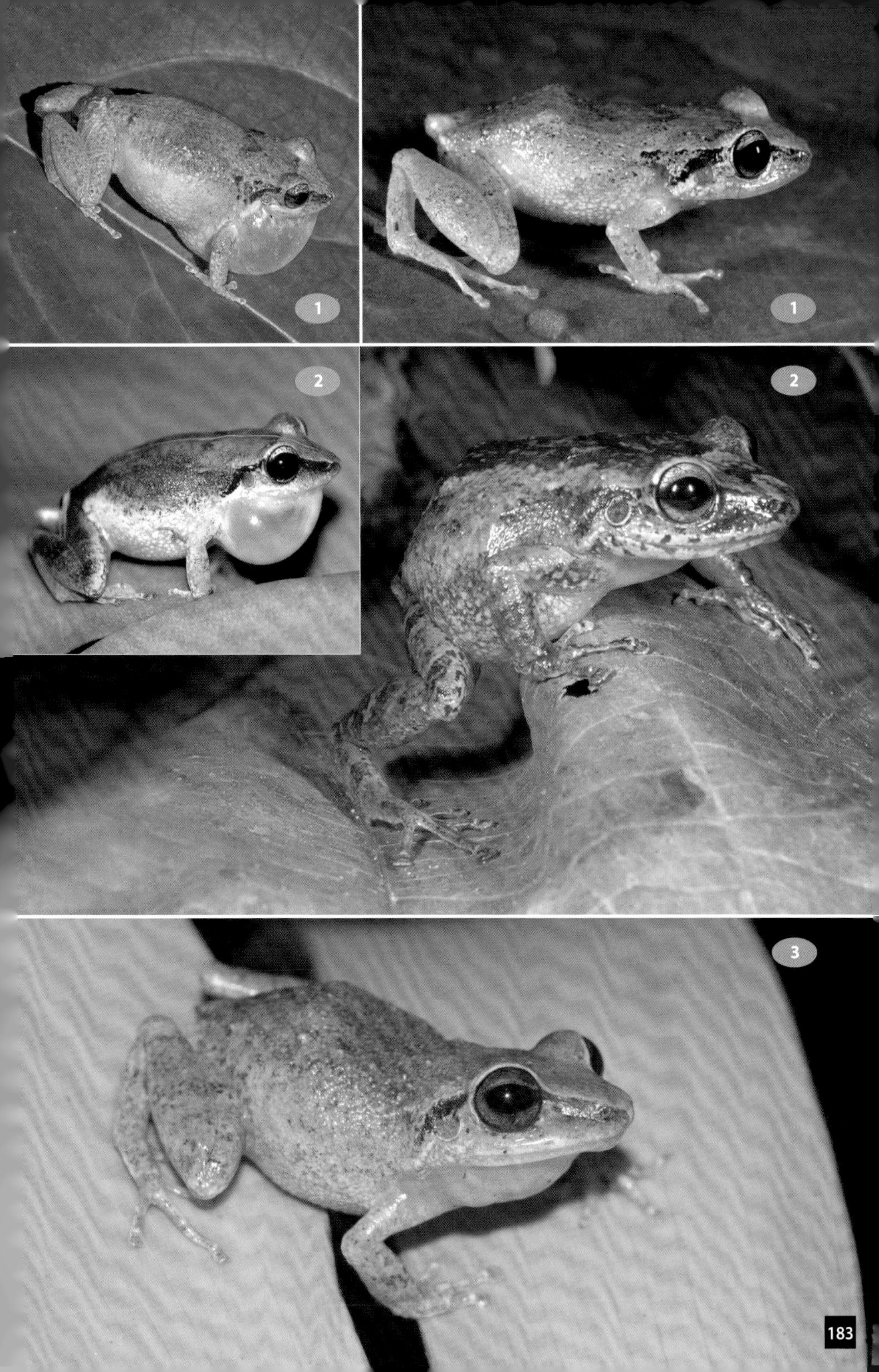
1
1
2
2
3

RARE OR LOCALIZED WHISTLING FROGS *Eleutherodactylus* species

Virgin Islands Khaki Frog *E. schwartzi* E EN—Endemic to the Virgin Islands, although may be extirpated from USVI

Puerto Rican Whistling Frog *E. cochranae* E—Endemic to St Thomas, St John (USVI), Tortola, Virgin Gorda (BVI), also Puerto Rico

Puerto Rican Coqui *E. coqui* E—Endemic to Puerto Rico, introduced to St Thomas, St Croix, St John (USVI)

Virgin Islands Yellow Frog *E. lentus* E EN—Endemic to the Virgin Islands

Guadeloupe Stream Frog *E. barlagnei* E EN—Endemic to Basse-Terre (Guadeloupe)

1 **Guadeloupe Forest** (Pinchon's Piping) **Frog** *E. pinchoni* E EN—Endemic to Basse-Terre (Guadeloupe)

2 **Dominica Frog** *E. amplinympha* E EN—Endemic to Dominica

INTRODUCED SPECIES

Several introduced species are now established. It is known that some arrived as adults or eggs in shipments of commodities or plants used in landscaping.

3 Common Snouted (Red-snouted) Treefrog *Scinax ruber* L 40 mm (1½")

A South American species introduced to **Martinique** and **St Lucia.** Uncommon, mainly at lower elevations. Appears flattened and long-bodied.

Venezuelan Snouted Treefrog *Scinax x-signatus* L 45 mm (1¾")

A South American species introduced to **Guadeloupe** and **Martinique**. Uncommon, mainly at lower elevations.

E 4 Cuban Treefrog *Osteopilus septentrionalis* L 110 mm (4¼")

Endemic to the Bahamas, Cayman Islands and Cuba. Now **widely introduced** and established on many islands in the Eastern Caribbean. Locally common in most habitats, including dry forest and gardens. Highly invasive, it outcompetes the smaller native whistling frogs for territories and appears to be increasing in distribution and number. A wide-ranging predator and capable climber, it feeds on invertebrates, froglets, young lizards and snakes and has even been seen in birds' nests! Female lays eggs in water, which hatch as aquatic tadpoles. Skin mucus is an irritant to humans.
ID: Much **larger, heavier and longer-bodied** than native whistling frogs. Ranges from olive-green to bronze-brown and has a **warty back**. Distinctive **long legs** can appear banded; toe pads are round; and **hind feet partially webbed**.
VOICE: Deep repeated croak, often in chorus.

5 South American Cane Toad *Rhinella marina (Bufo marinus)* L 180 mm (7")

A Central and South American species, widely introduced and established on at least the **Virgin Islands** and from **St Kitts and Nevis to Grenada**, including **Barbados**. The only toad in the region and the most commonly seen amphibian, often on roads or around exterior lighting at night. Female lays strings of eggs, which hatch into aquatic tadpoles. Cane Toads were deliberately introduced to control insect pests in sugar-cane plantations; it is a voracious predator, feeding on a wide range of invertebrates, lizards, frogs and small birds. It is included on the IUCN list of the 100 worst invasive alien species in the world. Secretes a toxic substance harmful to humans and domestic animals, and should be avoided.
ID: Stocky, yellowish to brown with **darker mottling** and **warty skin**. Short legs; feet have no obvious toe pads; hind feet are partially webbed. Immature can be paler with **dark markings** and **fine, pale dorsal line**.
VOICE: A deep, sustained, fast drumming.

1
2
3
4
5

Reptiles

There is an incredible diversity of reptiles in the Eastern Caribbean. They range in size from huge sea turtles, which can weigh over a ton, to tiny dwarf geckos—some of the smallest reptiles in the world, no bigger than your little finger. Ancestrally, terrestrial species would have reached the emerging volcanic islands through natural dispersal over water or when some islands were joined as island banks. Modern DNA-based studies are providing insights into the evolutionary history and relationships of the region's reptiles, recognizing an increasing number as single-island or restricted-range endemics.

The distribution of reptiles throughout the region has been complicated by human activity. Indigenous people arriving from South America are thought to have brought and dispersed tortoises and probably iguanas as food sources. More recently, reptiles have been part of a huge international pet trade, with inevitable escapes and releases. Other reptile species arrived incidentally, with both animals and eggs finding their way onto ships among commodities or within shipments of plants for landscaping. A combination of habitat loss, competition with introduced reptile species and the impacts of non-native invasive predators—especially Small Indian Mongooses, cats, rats and South American Cane Toads—has pushed many to the brink. Of the 145 reptiles in this guide, 106 are endemic to the region: of these, 78 are on the IUCN Red List of globally threatened species. Many are considered Endangered or Critically Endangered, with some possibly even extinct. There are now species action plans in place for many of the most vulnerable endemic reptiles: these include rodent eradication on smaller islands, captive breeding and translocation. Successful programs, combined with local support and education initiatives, are benefiting several species, including Anegada Rock Iguana, endemic groundlizards on Redonda (Antigua) and some of the Anguilla cays, Union Island Clawed Gecko and two snakes: Antiguan Racer and St Lucia Racer.

The Critically Endangered Redonda Anole.

IGUANAS

Iguanas are unmistakable: stout and seemingly ancient, with heavy scales and, in some species, a striking line of sharp spines along the back. Reaching over a meter in length, they are by far the largest lizards in the Eastern Caribbean. They are confiding on some islands, elusive on others, but are most easily seen in the early morning when basking on rocky outcrops and in mangroves, scrub and even gardens. They feed mostly on leaves, flowers and fruit, playing an important role in seed dispersal. If disturbed they will take evasive, often noisy, action: climbing higher in trees, running through vegetation or leaping into water, where they are capable swimmers.

Iguanas have elaborate territorial and courtship displays, communicating through head-bobbing, mouth-gaping, press-ups and extending the dewlap (a sagging flap of skin on the throat). Males also raise their body to appear bigger and more threatening to rivals. Disputes rarely develop, but they can lead to fierce fights involving biting and tail-whipping. After courtship and mating, the female excavates a burrow for egg-laying, often traveling some distance to use traditional beach sites. The young of all species tend to be a brighter green than adults.

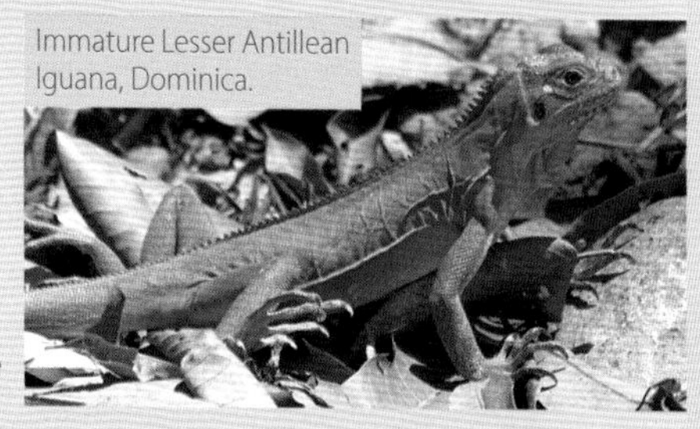
Immature Lesser Antillean Iguana, Dominica.

The status of iguanas throughout the region is complicated, particularly that of Common Green Iguana. This species was considered native to several of the Eastern Caribbean islands, further dispersed in recent decades through the pet trade or as a result of hurricanes. Although research is ongoing, in 2020 iguanas on the Virgin Islands, Saba, Montserrat, St Lucia and the Grenadines that were formerly considered Common Green Iguanas were ascribed to one of two newly recognized species for the Eastern Caribbean, either Caribbean Black Iguana or Southern Lesser Antilles Horned Iguana. This leaves the status of Common Green Iguana uncertain on some islands.

Anegada Rock Iguana and Lesser Antillean Iguana are both Critically Endangered, having suffered historic range contractions through habitat degradation, habitat loss and predation. Conservation efforts include translocation and habitat restoration. One of the main threats to endemic iguanas is hybridization and competition from introduced, invasive Common Green Iguanas.

1 **Anegada Rock** (Stout) **Iguana** *Cyclura pinguis*

HB 56 cm (22″); 105 cm (41″) including tail

Endemic to Anegada (BVI), where rare and difficult to see in sandy or rocky scrub. Mainly ground dwelling, this species is threatened by habitat loss and degradation and by predation from feral cats. There are probably fewer than 400 individuals remaining in the wild; an ongoing recovery plan has involved translocation, with the aim of establishing new populations on several smaller islands in the Virgin Islands archipelago.
ID: Large with **thick neck** and **heavy body with small spines**. **Gray to brown-black** overall but can have **blue** on spines, hind legs and base of tail. Immature is gray-green with dark-edged bands along body.

1

E 1 **Lesser Antillean Iguana** *Iguana delicatissima*

CR HB 43.5 cm (17"); 107 cm (42") including tail

Endemic to the Lesser Antilles, occurring only on **Anguilla, St Barthélemy, St Eustatius, La Désirade and Petit Terre (Guadeloupe), Dominica, Martinique** and some of their small offshore islands. Extirpated from St Martin/Sint Maarten, St Kitts and Nevis, Antigua and Barbuda and Guadeloupe (main island). Uncommon in dry forest and scrub, and along rocky and sandy coastlines. Mainly arboreal and easily overlooked when basking or foraging in trees. Vulnerable to hybridization with introduced Common Green Iguanas.
ID: Adult **body and tail unmarked slate-gray to olive-green**. Rows of **prominent white scales** above and below the mouth; **no obvious circular plate** at side of neck, unlike Common Green Iguana.

2 **Caribbean Black Iguana** *Iguana melanoderma*

HB 50 cm (19"); 182 cm (71") including tail

Occurs only on the **Virgin Islands, Saba and Montserrat**, also on Vieques (Puerto Rico) and in Venezuela. Locally common in forests and gardens; can be confiding.
ID: Gray-black with dark banding on body and tail, becoming darker with age. **Head** can be **boldly marked black and white**, with **bold black patch around eye** and black dewlap.

E 3 **Southern Lesser Antilles Horned Iguana** *Iguana insularis*

HB 50 cm (19"); 182 cm (71") including tail

Endemic to the Lesser Antilles, with two subspecies: *I. i. sanctaluciae* on **St Lucia**, where restricted to the northeast, and *I. i. insularis* on the **Grenadines**; with some uncertainty over populations on St Vincent and Grenada.
ID: Similar to Common Green Iguana but has **several small horns on center and sides of snout**. St Lucia subspecies has heavy black bands on body and a dark dewlap. The Grenadines subspecies has weaker or no bands on body and a paler dewlap and can turn pale pink-white with age (also known as 'Grenadine Pink Rhino Iguana').

4 **Common Green Iguana** *Iguana iguana* HB 50 cm (19"); 182 cm (71") including tail

Widespread, with historic and more recent introductions to most islands, but could occur throughout: now considered a non-native species (*p. 187*). Locally common in a range of habitats from coastal wetlands to scrub and dry forest; readily visits gardens to feed. Where it occurs alongside native iguana populations it poses a threat through competition and hybridization.
ID: Green-gray, typically with **dark banding** on body and tail and **obvious circular (sub-tympanic) plate at side of neck** (which Lesser Antillean Iguana lacks).

Adult, Montserrat.

Adult, the Grenadines. Adult, the Grenadines.

GROUNDLIZARDS AND AMEIVAS

A loud, sometimes startling, rustle in dry leaf litter is often the first sign of a foraging groundlizard. These stocky lizards can be common and confiding around buildings and gardens, and readily bask on rocks or low walls. They have a strong, pointed snout; thick neck; flattish, broad back; and very long hind toes. Males are larger than females, reaching a head-and-body length of 200 mm (8″), which is easily doubled by the thick, tapering tail. Groundlizards are members of the family Teiidae, which is restricted to the Americas and Caribbean. There are 11 species in the Eastern Caribbean: most are either single-island endemics or highly restricted in range. They are not present on every island, and no island has more than one species, making identification straightforward.

Groundlizards are diurnal, foraging in dry scrub, grassland and on beaches. Their diet is primarily insects and other invertebrates, but they scavenge carrion, fruit and food scraps and even take small reptiles and the eggs of ground-nesting birds. They excavate burrows in soft sand or use holes and crevices in rocks to provide shelter in the heat of the day and as cover from predators. In the breeding season there are occasional aggressive interactions between males, including lengthy chases and tail-whipping. The female typically lays up to three small clutches of eggs in a season, usually between May and October. Juveniles are often browner than adults, with obvious pale stripes running along the body.

Most species of groundlizard are threatened to some extent. Native predators include racer snakes and birds, but many populations have been devastated by introduced cats, rats and particularly Small Indian Mongoose, which has driven some species to extinction. Four endemic species are restricted to tiny islands or rocky cays and are especially vulnerable to predation by introduced rodents and extreme weather events. Conservation plans are in place for several species, with actions including rodent removal, translocation and habitat management.

E 1 **Common Puerto Rican Groundlizard** *Pholidoscelis exsul*

HB 200 mm (8″), plus tail

Endemic to the Virgin Islands and Puerto Rico.
ID: Large and robust. Brown to paler gray-brown with **heavy spotting**; can show **bold, dark, broken side-stripe**. Face, throat, belly and tail can be a pale blue-white.

E 2 **Anguilla Bank Groundlizard** *Pholidoscelis plei* HB 180 mm (7″), plus tail

Endemic to Anguilla, St Martin/Sint Maarten, St Barthélemy and some of their offshore islands.
ID: Gray to green-brown with **heavy pale spotting**, especially on lower back, hind legs and tail. Juvenile typically shows pale stripes along back and sides, darkening with age.

E NT 3 **St Christopher** (Red-faced) **Groundlizard** *Pholidoscelis erythrocephalus*

HB 140 mm (5½″), plus tail

Endemic to St Eustatius, St Kitts and Nevis.
ID: Dark green to brown with **fine dark markings**; can show pale side-stripes. Face and neck **bright red** with contrasting white throat.

Juvenile groundlizards are often more heavily striped.

E 1 **Antiguan Bank Groundlizard** *Pholidoscelis griswoldi* HB 120 mm (5"), plus tail

NT **Endemic to Antigua** (where uncommon), **Barbuda** and some offshore islands.
ID: Gray to brown with **widely spaced pale barring** across back and **fine, pale spots** on legs and tail (markings range from pale green to light blue).

E 2 **Montserrat Groundlizard** *Pholidoscelis pluvianotatus* HB 170 mm (6½"), plus tail

NT **Endemic to Montserrat**, where suitable habitat is much reduced following volcanic eruptions.
ID: Gray to brown with **fine but faint pale spotting**. Can show blue on face and sides.

E 3 **Dominica Groundlizard** *Pholidoscelis fuscatus* HB 200 mm (8"), plus tail

Endemic to Dominica, where uncommon at low elevations.
ID: Large and robust. **Blue-gray** with obvious **pale blue spots** on sides, legs and tail; face paler. Juvenile browner, more striped.

E 4 **Antillean** (Grenada Bank) **Ameiva** *Ameiva tobagana* HB 150 mm (6"), plus tail

Endemic to St Vincent, the Grenadines and **Grenada**. Highly localized or rare on main islands, more often around hotels and settlements where Small Indian Mongoose is less frequent. More widespread on some of the mongoose-free Grenadines.
ID: Green to brown; **face and throat** often **blue-gray. Extensively, but finely, marked** from head to tail with spots and barring. Juvenile more heavily marked with pale stripes and lines of dark markings on back and sides.

2
3i
3
4
4

Rare or restricted-range groundlizards

E St Croix Groundlizard *Pholidoscelis polops*

EN **Endemic to St Croix**, where extirpated from the main island and now found only on four small offshore islands and cays.

The following three species, largely black in coloration, are limited to tiny islands with dry conditions.

E 1 Sombrero Groundlizard

CR *Pholidoscelis corvinus*

Endemic to Sombrero, Anguilla.

E 2 Little Scrub Groundlizard

EN *Pholidoscelis corax*

Endemic to Little Scrub Island, Anguilla.

E 3 Redonda Groundlizard

CR *Pholidoscelis atratus*

Endemic to Redonda, Antigua.

At least three species (*Pholidoscelis cineraceus, P. major* and *P. turukaeraensis*) endemic to Guadeloupe and its archipelago, and possibly Martinique, are extinct and known only from fossils or early museum specimens.

WHIPTAILS

The region has two species of whiptail lizards, which are closely related to groundlizards.

E 4 Maria Islands (St Lucia) Whiptail *Cnemidophorus vanzoi*

CR **Endemic to St Lucia** but extirpated from the main island and now found only on three small offshore islands, including the Maria Islands.

5 Guyana Whiptail *Kentropyx borckiana*

Found only on **Barbados**, where it is largely restricted to the southern half of the island. Origins are uncertain: it also occurs widely in northeastern South America.

ANOLES (TREE LIZARDS)

Small, active and engaging, anoles are the most widespread and commonly encountered lizards, easily seen during the day along forest trails and in gardens and hotel grounds. They feed mainly on invertebrates, including ants, beetles and flies, but also take berries and ripe fruit. There are more than 150 species throughout the wider Caribbean, with 26 endemic to the Eastern Caribbean, mostly restricted to a single island or island bank. On each island, only one or two species occur, except for most of the larger Virgin Islands, where three are widespread.

Anole behavior has been particularly well studied, and where two species are present it is known that they exploit habitats differently. On many islands, both bush anoles and tree anoles occur, often differing in size. As a general rule, **bush anoles** are found in low shrubs and vegetation, where they typically face head-down, watching for prey before pouncing. **Tree anoles** forage higher in trees, working around trunks and branches to catch prey, although all species, especially immatures, can readily be seen on the ground, rocks, walls and buildings. Most adults have a head and body length of less than 100 mm (4"): this is easily doubled by the tail, which can regenerate if damaged or shed. All have distinct toes with toe pads and sharp claws, enabling them to climb vertical surfaces.

Anoles are territorial and can be aggressive, communicating through a range of behaviors, including push-ups and head-bobbing. Males have a large, colorful dewlap. When extended, this fold of skin underneath the chin acts as a warning to other males or as an attraction to females. After mating, the female lays several eggs, which are deposited singly in inconspicuous sites under rocks and bark or in leaf litter.

Natural predators of anoles include snakes and birds such as American Kestrel, Gray Kingbird and Carib Grackle. Most species have secure populations, but all are vulnerable to habitat loss and predation by introduced chickens and mammals, especially feral cats, rats and Small Indian Mongoose. An increasing threat is from introduced larger or more dominant anole species that out-compete native anoles for food and habitat.

Most anoles are highly variable in color and markings. In the species accounts, adult males are described: these are typically larger, brighter and more easily identified than females, although body color and markings within a species can vary dramatically between location and habitat. Females and immatures tend to be more cryptically marked, often with bold stripes along the back or sides; images of some species are included. All anoles shed their skin periodically and can look ragged.

Identification can be challenging, and is further complicated by the presence of introduced species. For the most part, however: know your island, know your anole!

Anguilla Bank Anole. Anoles display a range of easily observed behaviors, including push-ups.

Anoles: Virgin Islands

E 1 St Croix Anole *Anolis acutus*

HB 67 mm (2½"), plus tail

Endemic to St Croix (USVI): the island's only native anole. Common and widespread in dry forest but often seen on rocks and walls.

ID: Pale, ranging from light-green to pale gray-brown; appears plain but actually has **fine markings**. Dewlap pale yellow with white border.

1♀

1♂

Three species of anole are widespread across the larger Virgin Islands but absent from St Croix

2 Puerto Rican Crested Anole *Anolis cristatellus* HB 77 mm (3"), plus tail E

Endemic to BVI, USVI and Puerto Rico; absent from St Croix. Introduced to St Martin/Sint Maarten and Dominica. Common and widespread in all forest types. Mainly arboreal but does feed on the ground.
ID: Brown to greenish-gray with fine spots. Broad head and snout. **Adult male has a full crest (especially obvious on tail)**; dewlap red with greenish-yellow center.

3 Puerto Rican Bush Anole *Anolis pulchellus* HB 51 mm (2"), plus tail E

Endemic to **BVI**, **USVI** and Puerto Rico; absent from St Croix. Common and widespread in grassland and low, dry scrub.
ID: Olive-green with contrasting pale chin and throat; a **prominent pale side-stripe runs from face to rear leg**. Snout long and pointed; dewlap red.

4 Puerto Rican Spotted (Banded) **Anole** *Anolis stratulus* HB 61 mm (2½"), plus tail E

Endemic to **BVI**, **USVI** and Puerto Rico; absent from St Croix. Common and widespread in dry forest and scrub. Mainly arboreal.
ID: Brown with **dark spotting** on head and upper body that **can form bands**. Dewlap orange, edged yellow.

E CR Carrot Rock Anole *Anolis ernestwilliamsi*

Endemic to Carrot Rock (BVI), where rare and localized.

Antigua Bank Tree (Leach's) Anole *Anolis leachii*

Has been introduced to St Thomas (*p. 200*).

2
2
3
3
4
4

Anoles: Anguilla to Saba

E 1 Anguilla Bank Tree Anole *Anolis gingivinus* HB 70 mm (2¾"), plus tail

Endemic to Anguilla, St Martin/Sint Maarten, St Barthélemy and their small offshore islands; the only native anole on Anguilla and St Barthélemy. Locally common and widespread in scrub, dry forest and rocky areas (including walls and buildings).
ID: Pale gray-brown to olive-green, variably marked with small dark spots and dashes. **Broad, pale side-stripe** and pale line along upper jaw below eye are usually obvious. Dewlap bright orange-yellow. Female and immature have a broad pale line along back.

2 North American Green Anole *Anolis carolinensis*

Native to North America, introduced to Anguilla.

E 3 Anguilla Bank Bush (St Martin Bearded) Anole *Anolis pogus*

NT HB 58 mm (2"), plus tail

Endemic to St Martin/Sint Maarten; probably extirpated from Anguilla. Widespread in all habitats but more common in shady situations at higher elevations.
ID: Ranges from gray-brown to orange-tan, typically unmarked but can show faint bands across body. Bright blue eyering and eye-surround; dewlap white. Female duller with diffuse pale line along back; may show fine dark barring.

Puerto Rican Crested Anole *Anolis cristatellus*

Has been introduced to Sint Maarten (*p. 196*).

Cuban Brown Anole *Anolis sagrei*

Has been introduced to Sint Maarten and is now established but localized around Philipsburg; there are also records from Anguilla (*p. 204*).

E 4 Saba Anole *Anolis sabanus* HB 69 mm (2¾"), plus tail

NT **Endemic to Saba**, where it is the only native anole. Widespread in most habitats, including gardens and around buildings.
ID: Tan to pale gray, **boldly marked with large dark spots** that may join to form bands; dewlap green-yellow. Female duller, spots much reduced or absent.

Gray individual on rocks.

Anoles: St Kitts to Antigua

E 1 St Kitts (Statia) Bank Tree Anole *Anolis bimaculatus* HB 125 mm (5"), plus tail

Endemic to St Eustatius, and St Kitts and Nevis. Common and widespread in forests and rocky habitats; mainly arboreal but can be seen on walls and buildings.
ID: Large. Male has a **blue-gray head and neck**, merging to **bright green** on back and tail; an obvious pale side-stripe; and can show diffuse spotting. Dewlap pale orange-yellow; can show crest on neck. Female head and neck darker (brown to olive-green), with a bright green side-stripe. Both sexes have a bright green-yellow eye-surround and a pale line along upper jaw.

E 2 St Kitts (Statia) Bank Bush Anole *Anolis schwartzi* HB 52 mm (2"), plus tail

Endemic to St Eustatius, and **St Kitts and Nevis**. Common and widespread in forests and rocky habitats, including walls and buildings. Forages on the ground and in low vegetation, often in shaded situations.
ID: Small and slender. Mainly plain **gray-brown to orange-brown** but can show brighter orange legs and tail; lacks green coloration. Dewlap bright orange-yellow. Female can show light barring on back and a pale side-stripe. Both sexes have a pale eyering.

E 3 Antigua Bank Tree (Leach's) Anole *Anolis leachii* HB 123 mm (4¾"), plus tail

Endemic to Antigua and Barbuda; introduced to St Thomas (USVI). Common and widespread in drier forest habitats and rocky areas, including walls and buildings.
ID: Large. Head and neck grayish, merging to bright green on back, with pale throat and **yellow-green eye-surround**. Typically has **extensive, fine dark spotting** and a pale side-stripe. Male has pale orange-white dewlap and can show crest on neck.

E 4 Antigua Bank Bush (Watt's) Anole *Anolis wattsi* HB 58 mm (2¼")

Endemic to Antigua and Barbuda; introduced to St Lucia. Common and widespread in forests and rocky habitats, including walls and buildings.
ID: Small. Orange to olive-brown, although head and neck can be **blue-gray**, with a **pale line along upper jaw**. Dewlap bright orange-yellow. Female browner, can be boldly marked with pale side-stripe and dark markings along back. Both can show blue in the eyering.

E Redonda Anole *Anolis nubilis* HB 81 mm (3"), plus tail

CR **Endemic to Redonda** (Antigua). Numbers are increasing following successful rat eradication and the removal of goats, the latter enabling habitat recovery (*see* photo *p. 186*).

1♀
1♂
2♂
2
3♂
3♀
4♂
4♀

Anoles: Montserrat to Dominica

E 1 **Montserrat** (Plymouth) **Anole**

NT *Anolis lividus* HB 70 mm (2¾"), plus tail

Endemic to Montserrat, where the only native anole. Locally common in all forest types; range was reduced following volcanic activity in the 1990s.

ID: Bright green to gray-green; plain or with heavy spotting on head and back. **Eyering and eye-surround bright orange-red**; dewlap orange-yellow. Female duller and lacks bold spotting.

E 2 Guadeloupe Anole

Anolis marmoratus HB 85 mm (3½"), plus tail

Endemic to Guadeloupe, where the only native anole on the main island; it is also on Petite Terre and several smaller islets. Common in all forest types and around buildings. Males especially differ considerably in size and appearance across the island.

ID: Bright green to gray-green; often plain but can show spotting on body. **Head and neck** markings range from **plain green or blue to a striking mottled orange and black**. Dewlap bright orange-yellow. Female head and neck less marked; typically duller overall with pale line along back.

In the Guadeloupe archipelago there are three more endemic species on offshore islands, all of which are widespread and locally common.

E Les Saintes Anole *Anolis terraealtae*

E Marie-Galante Anole *Anolis ferreus*

E La Désirade Anole *Anolis desiradei*

E 3 **Dominica** (Eyed) **Anole** *Anolis oculatus* HB 96 mm (4"), plus tail

NT **Endemic to Dominica**, where the only native anole. Locally common and widespread in all forest habitats, agricultural areas and around buildings.

ID: Tan-brown to green-brown with **pale spotting** that ranges from heavy to fine, some spots with a **dark border**. **Pale eyering** and an orange-yellow dewlap (present but smaller on female). Male can develop bold black patches to sides and a spiky crest to tail.

Puerto Rican Crested Anole *Anolis cristatellus*

Has been introduced to **Dominica**, where it is spreading and considered invasive, posing a threat to the native anole (*p. 196*).

Colorful male, found in the southern part of Basse-Terre.

Anoles: Martinique to Barbados

E 1 **Martinique Anole** *Anolis roquet*

HB 86 mm (3¼"), plus tail

Endemic to Martinique, where the only native anole. Common and widespread in forests, agricultural areas, and around buildings and gardens. Differs in appearance with habitat and location across the island.
ID: Green with **prominent green eyering**. Male can have extensive areas of black or blue with bold white spots or dark chevrons, but markings may be faint or reduced. Dewlap pale orange-yellow. Female green to gray-brown, often with reduced markings.

E EN 2 **St Lucia Anole** *Anolis luciae*

HB 91 mm (3½"), plus tail

Endemic to St Lucia, where the only native anole. Locally common in forests, agricultural areas, and around buildings and gardens. Population is in decline where introduced anoles, especially Antigua Bank Bush Anole, have become established.
ID: Large. **Mainly plain brown**, but both sexes are highly variable in color, which ranges from greenish to pale gray-brown. Can show faint side-stripes and chevron markings along back and tail, eye-surround smoky gray. Male dewlap is pale yellow.

Antigua Bank Bush Anole *Anolis wattsi* (*p. 200*), **Barbados Anole** *Anolis extremus* (*below*) and possibly **Cuban Brown Anole** *Anolis sagrei* (*below*) have been introduced to **St Lucia**.

E 3 **Barbados Anole** *Anolis extremus*

HB 83 mm (3¼"), plus tail

Endemic to Barbados, where the only native anole. Widespread in all habitats and can be common in gardens. Introduced to St Lucia.
ID: Green with grayish to **blue-gray head** and dark spotting and mottling, especially to head and neck. Smoky blue **eye-surround**; male dewlap yellow-orange.

E 4 **Cuban Brown Anole** *Anolis sagrei*

HB 70 mm (2¾"), plus tail

An introduced species, native to the Bahamas and Cuba, now established at least on **St Martin/Sint Maarten, St Lucia, Barbados, St Vincent**, including **Canouan** and **Grenada**. Mainly found in localized populations in disturbed habitats and around buildings.
ID: Stocky. Brown to gray-brown; pale spots and thin dark lines can form **broken stripes** on back and sides. Can show **crest** to neck and back. Dewlap **deep orange-red** with pale border.

1♂

4♂

1♂
1♀
2♀
2♂
3♂
3♂
3♂

Anoles: St Vincent to Grenada

E 1 St Vincent Tree Anole *Anolis griseus* HB 136 mm (5½″), plus tail

Endemic to St Vincent, where widespread in all forest types.
ID: Large. Brown to dark green with **extensive but subtle dark markings**; spotting can form **bands or chevrons** across back and tail. Prominent **short pale bar** over front legs and pale side-stripe (not always obvious). Can show short crest of tiny spikes along neck, body and tail. Orange dewlap present in both sexes but larger in male.

E 2 St Vincent Bush Anole *Anolis trinitatis* HB 74 mm (3″), plus tail

Endemic to St Vincent, where widespread in all habitats. Mainly **arboreal**, perching on tree trunks, in low shrubs and on buildings.
ID: Small. Differs between location and habitat. Mainly unmarked **bright green, blue-gray** or **brown-green**, with an obvious eye-surround ranging from **bright blue to black**. Head and neck may be bright blue-gray to bright green, with a pale line along upper jaw. Male dewlap **pale yellow**. Female usually less bright, can show weak markings along sides and have a small, less obvious dewlap.

E 3 Grenada Tree Anole *Anolis richardii*

HB 140 mm (5½″), plus tail

Endemic to Grenada and the Grenadines (eight islands, including **Carriacou, Bequia and Mabouya**). Locally common and widespread in forests, agricultural areas and gardens.
ID: Large. Ranges from brown-green to gray-green with a pale side-stripe, and from almost plain to spotted. All have a **pale crescent under the eye** and a **pale bar over front legs** (not always obvious). Head pale blue to heavily mottled white; male can show crest on neck. Dewlap yellow-green.

E 4 Grenada Bush (Bronze) Anole

Anolis aeneus HB 80 mm (3″), plus tail

Endemic to Grenada and the Grenadines (most islands). Locally common and widespread in forests, scrub, agricultural land, and around buildings and gardens. Mostly uses low perches but readily catches prey on the ground.
ID: Small. Male mainly gray-brown to green with hints of bronze and **light, subtle speckling** that can show as bars on back and tail. **Eye-surround typically bluish**, dewlap gray-green-yellow. Female similar but generally a duller gray-brown with weaker markings, which can include a pale line along back.

Cuban Brown Anole *Anolis sagrei* *(p. 204)* has been introduced to St Vincent, Canouan and Grenada.

4♂

1
1♂
2♂
2♂
3
3♂
3

LEAF-TOED AND HOUSE GECKOS

A pale, almost translucent, lizard effortlessly scaling a smooth internal wall is likely to be a Tropical House Gecko, introduced from Africa over several centuries and now widely distributed throughout the Eastern Caribbean. It is most often seen in and around buildings at dusk, foraging for insects attracted to artificial lights. At least three other introduced species are present (*p. 210*).

The only native species of gecko are leaf-toed geckos, distinguished by their broad toe pads and thick tail. The most widespread is Northern Turnip-tailed Gecko. More arboreal than the non-native geckos, it is found mainly in forests and gardens. It was thought to be the only leaf-toed species present, but in 2011 Sint Maarten Thick-tailed Gecko was recognized as a full species and Barbados Leaf-toed Gecko rediscovered.

Geckos are mostly nocturnal: their large eyes have vertically slit pupils that expand in dim light and transparent protective membranes in place of eyelids. They are excellent climbers, having a combination of sharp claws and toes with highly modified scales that create adhesive toe pads. Their tails are easily damaged and readily shed to escape predators but quickly regenerate. Geckos are mostly silent but will make soft, chirping or clicking sounds, especially when threatened or during courtship. Females lay eggs in crevices, stone walls and tree hollows.

Native geckos

1 Northern Turnip-tailed Gecko

Thecadactylus rapicauda HB 125 mm (5"), plus tail

Occurs **throughout** but with some uncertainty about its origins; it may occur naturally on some islands. Locally common in dry forest, agricultural land, rocky areas and around buildings. Mainly nocturnal but can be found basking in early morning sun.
ID: Light gray to dark brown; cryptically marked with **spots, bands and chevrons**, often camouflaged against natural backgrounds. Stocky with a **broad head**; strong **thick legs and tail**; and distinctive **wide toe pads with partial webbing**. Tail shorter than combined head and body length.
VOICE: A sharp clicking or chattering.

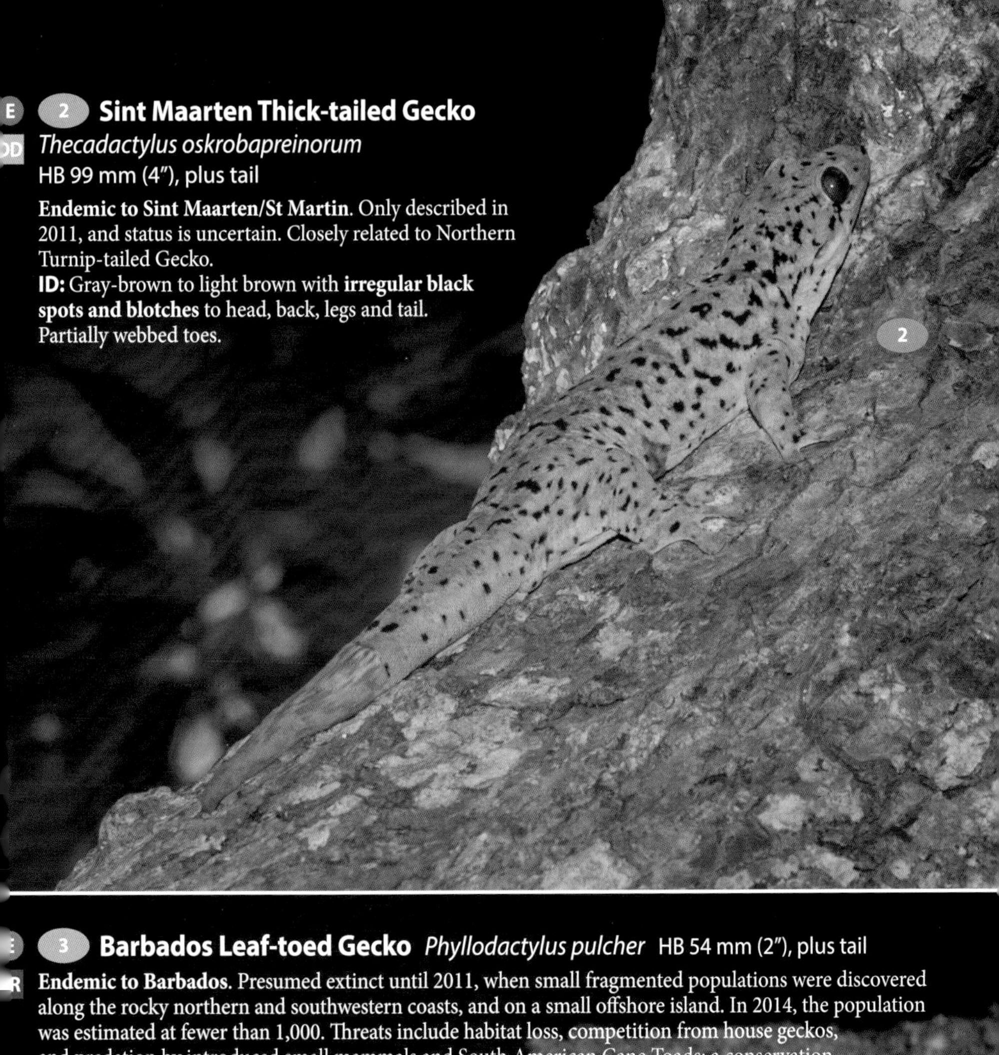

2 Sint Maarten Thick-tailed Gecko

Thecadactylus oskrobapreinorum

HB 99 mm (4"), plus tail

Endemic to Sint Maarten/St Martin. Only described in 2011, and status is uncertain. Closely related to Northern Turnip-tailed Gecko.

ID: Gray-brown to light brown with **irregular black spots and blotches** to head, back, legs and tail. Partially webbed toes.

3 Barbados Leaf-toed Gecko *Phyllodactylus pulcher* HB 54 mm (2"), plus tail

Endemic to Barbados. Presumed extinct until 2011, when small fragmented populations were discovered along the rocky northern and southwestern coasts, and on a small offshore island. In 2014, the population was estimated at fewer than 1,000. Threats include habitat loss, competition from house geckos, and predation by introduced small mammals and South American Cane Toads; a conservation recovery plan is in place.

ID: Small. Light brown with a pattern of dark markings and pale spots that can form loose bands across back. A pale stripe runs through the eye, with a line of dark spots below.

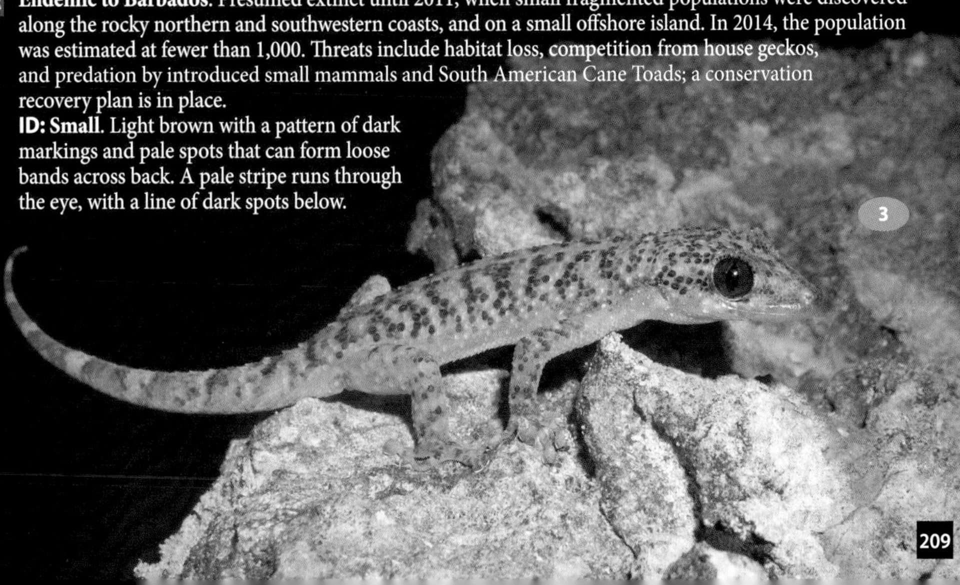

Introduced geckos

1 Spiny House Gecko

Hemidactylus palaichthus

HB 63 mm (2½"), plus tail

Small, strongly marked spiny gecko, introduced to **St Lucia** and its islets (including Maria Major) and distributed more widely on Trinidad and Tobago and in northern South America.

2 Tropical House Gecko *Hemidactylus mabouia* HB 68 mm (2¾"), plus tail

An African species, introduced and established **throughout**. Common on walls and ceilings inside buildings, less often externally. Stalks before pouncing quickly to catch insect prey.
ID: Gray-white to light brown: looks almost translucent. Ranges from pale and unmarked to dark and heavily marked with bands or chevrons on back and tail. **Broad head, flattened body**, and **small but visible narrow toe pads** with **no webbing**. Tail length similar to combined head and body length.
VOICE: A short series of chirps.

Pale individual on an internal wall.

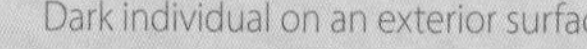

Dark individual on an exterior surface.

3 Common House Gecko *Hemidactylus frenatus*

A Southeast Asian species that is very similar to Tropical House Gecko. Widely introduced, it has been reported on **St Kitts, Dominica, St Lucia** and **Barbados**.

Mourning Gecko *Lepidodactylus lugubris*

Native to Southeast Asia and the Pacific region. Introduced and appears to be spreading, with records on at least **St Martin/Sint Maarten, Guadeloupe** and **Grenada**.

Tockay Gecko *Gekko gecko*

An Asian species, with small, isolated populations reported from **Guadeloupe** and **Martinique**.

DWARF GECKOS (GECKOLETS)

Tiny, unobtrusive and often exquisitely marked, dwarf geckos are rarely seen without active searching. They are among the smallest lizards in the world: most have a head-and-body length of less than 30 mm (1¼"), with the largest reaching only 40 mm (1½"). There are 14 species in the Eastern Caribbean, all either endemic to single islands or highly restricted in range. On most islands only one species is present; where two occur, identification can be difficult, as views tend to be fleeting and markings can vary. Further species may yet be separated and recognized, including a dwarf gecko on Redonda (Antigua).

Some species are diurnal, others more active between dusk and dawn. All are vulnerable to desiccation and avoid direct sunlight, remaining concealed in moist areas under leaf litter, logs, rocks and decaying vegetation. They are found in shady areas of coastal scrub, dry forest and rainforest, where they forage for small invertebrates, including ants, termites and spiders. Despite being difficult to see, population densities can be very high.

All are in the family Sphaerodactylidae, which translates as 'round finger', a reference to the small round pad at the end of each toe. Ranging from brown to gray, most are cryptically colored and finely patterned. Females typically deposit eggs singly among leaf litter, behind bark and in rock crevices. Natural predators include birds, snakes and larger lizards.

Population data are limited, but several species are threatened through habitat loss and predation, especially by rats and chickens.

Dwarf geckos of the Virgin Islands

1 **Puerto Rican Eyespotted** (Big-scaled) **Dwarf Gecko**
Sphaerodactylus macrolepis
HB 35 mm (1⅜") E

Endemic to USVI, BVI and Puerto Rico; recently reported as introduced to Prickly Pear East (Anguilla).
ID: Brown to gray; can be **boldly marked** with **heavy dark spots** along head, back and sides. Bold black mark with **two white spots at base of neck**.

Saint Croix (Beatty's) **Dwarf Gecko** *Sphaerodactylus beattyi* HB 30 mm (1¼") E EN

Endemic to St Croix (USVI)
ID: Gray to brown; **finely patterned** with dark markings. Spots can form stripes along tail. Pale iris.

Virgin Islands Dwarf Gecko *Sphaerodactylus parthenopion* HB 18 mm (¾") E EN

Endemic to Virgin Gorda (BVI)
ID: Tiny. Found in drier, rockier habitats than Puerto Rican Eyespotted Dwarf Gecko. **Dark brown**; finely patterned with darker markings. **Dark-bordered pale line behind eye.**

Dwarf geckos of the Lesser Antilles

1 **Anguilla Bank Dwarf Gecko** *Sphaerodactylus parvus* HB 24 mm (1")

Endemic to Anguilla, St Martin/Sint Maarten, St Barthélemy and offshore islands
Light to dark brown; **can be extensively marked** with **dark spotting. Dark stripe** through eye; **two white spots at base of neck.**

2 **Leeward Banded Dwarf Gecko** *Sphaerodactylus sputator* HB 39 mm (1½")

Endemic to Anguilla, St Martin/Sint Maarten, St Barthélemy, St Eustatius, St Kitts, Nevis and offshore islands
ID: Brown or gray, with bold, dark spots and **pale, often broken bands across neck, back and tail.** Head well marked.

3 **St Kitts Bank** (Saba) **Dwarf Gecko** *Sphaerodactylus sabanus* HB 29 mm (1⅛")

Endemic to Saba, St Eustatius, St Kitts and Nevis
ID: Brown with extensive **fine, dark and pale spots**, which can form lines. Can show faint dark stripe through eye.

4 **Antigua Bank Dwarf Gecko** *Sphaerodactylus elegantulus* HB 29 mm (1⅛")

Endemic to Antigua and Barbuda
ID: Brown and **finely spotted**, with a distinctive **pale iris.**

5 **Southern Leeward** (Fantastic) **Dwarf Gecko** *Sphaerodactylus fantasticus* HB 29 mm (1⅛")

Endemic to Montserrat, Guadeloupe and its offshore islands and **Dominica**
ID: Pale brown to green-brown; **patterns vary** between the islands. Body can show fine pale spots or bolder dark spots. Head ranges from blue to brown and can be boldly spotted and/or striped.

Les Saintes Dwarf Gecko *Sphaerodactylus phyzacinus* HB 25 mm (1") E EN

Endemic to Îles des Saintes (Guadeloupe)
ID: Yellow-brown to brown with bold dark bars or blotches.

Northern Martinique Dwarf Gecko *Sphaerodactylus festus* HB 40 mm (1½") E

Endemic to Dominica and northern Martinique
ID: Brown with bold dark spots or blotches and **two obvious, white-centered black spots** at base of neck.

6 **Southern Martinique** (Windward) **Dwarf Gecko** *Sphaerodactylus vincenti* HB 40 mm (1½") E

Endemic to southern Martinique, St Vincent and several islands in the Grenadines, where formerly considered *S. kirbyi*
ID: Brown to orange-brown; subtly and finely mottled. Some variation in markings between islands. Iris pale blue-green.

7 **St Lucia Dwarf Gecko** *Sphaerodactylus microlepis* HB 32 mm (1¼") E NT

Endemic to St Lucia, including Maria Major
ID: Dark brown to gray; markings range from **fine white spotting** to **darker bands along back**. May show yellow band, dark collar and/or two white spots at base of neck. Head can be gray or blue with dark chevrons.

8 **Union Island Clawed Gecko** *Gonatodes daudini* HB 30 mm (1¼") E CR

Endemic to Union Island (St Vincent)
ID: Beautifully marked: green-brown to gray with **pale cross-bands** and **several obvious red-bordered, white-centered black spots**.

SKINKS, TEGULETS, BACHIA AND WORM LIZARDS

This fascinating group of small, ground-dwelling reptiles spend most of their lives hidden among vegetation, leaf litter, rocks and walls, where they forage for invertebrates. They are diurnal but invariably elusive and difficult to see. All are viviparous, females giving birth to live young.

Until 2012 only a few species of skink in the family Mabuyidae had been identified in the Eastern Caribbean. A major systematic review (Hedges and Conn, 2012; *see* "Further reading", *p. 301*) has led to major changes, with 22 species now recognized in six genera. Most are considered Critically Endangered or Endangered; threats include habitat loss and predation by introduced mammals.

Sightings tend to be brief and can be inconclusive on islands where two or more species are present, so the characteristics of each family are a useful starting point for identification.

Family	**Skinks** (Mabuyidae)	**Tegulets, Tegus** (Gymnophthalmidae)	**Bachias** (Gymnophthalmidae)	**Worm Lizards** (Amphisbaenidae)
Genera (no. of species)	*Alinea* (2) *Capitellum* (3) *Copeoglossum* (2) *Mabuya* (8) *Marisora* (1) *Spondylurus* (7)	*Gymnophthalmus* (2)	*Bachia* (1)	*Amphisbaena* (2)
Typical HB	100 mm (4")	60 mm (2¼")	60 mm (2¼")	500 mm (20")
Habitat	Leaf litter or among rocks; can be found around buildings.	Leaf litter, grassy areas.	Mostly under rotting logs and damp vegetation.	Dry forest, grassland, disturbed or cultivated land, often in damp situations.
Behavior	Ground dwellers but climb low trees and walls.	Ground dwellers, scurrying through low vegetation.	Tend to remain hidden under leaf litter; will burrow.	Burrow in soil, creating tunnels, or remain under moist leaf litter.
ID	Appear very shiny. Lizard-like: sleek, with small limbs and a long, tapering tail. Most show a dark stripe through the eye and along the body.	Slightly flattened or angular, with very small limbs. Neck and body obviously broader than the long, tapering tail.	Thin, worm- or snake-like appearance, with tiny, well-separated limbs that can be difficult to see. No clear distinction between long body and long tail. Scales obvious in regular rings.	Snake-like, with cylindrical body, blunt head and tail. No limbs. Fine rings of scales.

1

Anguilla Bank Skink

Rare and highly localized skinks and worm lizards

All except Speckled Worm Lizard are endemic, most confined to a single island. Species are grouped in island banks.

Carrot Rock Skink *Spondylurus macleani* E CR—BVI

Virgin Islands Bronze Skink *Spondylurus sloanii* E CR—USVI, BVI

Lesser Virgin Islands Skink *Spondylurus semitaeniatus* E CR—USVI, BVI

Greater St Croix Skink *Spondylurus magnacruzae* E CR—St Croix (USVI)

Lesser St Croix Skink *Capitellum parvicruzae* E CR—St Croix (USVI)

Anegada Skink *Spondylurus anegadae* E CR—Anegada (BVI)

1 **Anguilla Bank Skink** *Spondylurus powelli* E EN—Anguilla, St Barthélemy, Tintamarre (St Martin)

St Martin Skink *Spondylurus martinae* E CR—St Martin, possibly extinct

Redonda Skink *Copeoglossum redondae* E EX—Redonda (Antigua), considered extinct

Montserrat Skink *Mabuya montserratae* E CR—Montserrat

Marie-Galante Skink *Capitellum mariagalantae* E CR—Marie-Galante (Guadeloupe)

Cochon's Skink *Mabuya cochonae* E CR—Îlet à Cochons (Guadeloupe)

Desirade Skink *Mabuya desiradae* E CR—La Désirade (Guadeloupe)

Grand-Terre Skink *Mabuya grandisterrae* E CR—Grande-Terre (Guadeloupe)

Guadeloupe Skink *Mabuya guadeloupae* E CR—Basse-Terre (Guadeloupe)

Petit Terre Skink *Mabuya parviterrae* E—Terre-de-Bas (Guadeloupe)

2 **Dominica Skink** *Mabuya dominicana* E—Dominica

Lesser Martinique Skink *Capitellum metallicum* E CR—Martinique, possibly extinct

Greater Martinique Skink *Mabuya mabouya* E CR—Martinique, possibly extinct

St Lucia Skink *Alinea luciae* E EX—St Lucia, now considered extinct

Barbados Skink *Alinea lanceolata* E CR—Barbados, possibly extinct

Lesser Windward Skink *Marisora aurulae* E VU—St Vincent, Grenadines, Grenada

Speckled (Black-and-white) **Worm Lizard** *Amphisbaena fuliginosa*—Grenada, possibly introduced from South America

Dominica Skink

E 1 **Greater Windward Skink** *Copeoglossum aurae* HB 105 mm (4″)

Endemic to the Caribbean, occurring only on **St Vincent, the Grenadines, Grenada**, Trinidad and Tobago.
ID: Shiny **gray-brown** with **scattered small dark spots** and a dark stripe extending from eye along body and tail.

2 **Smooth-scaled Tegulet** (Underwood's Spectacled Tegu) *Gymnophthalmus underwoodi* HB 48 mm (2″)

St Thomas (USVI) and from **St Martin/Sint Maarten to Grenada, including Barbados**, occurring more widely in South America. Thought to be an introduced species on the northern islands.
ID: Similar to Rough-scaled Tegulet but **lacks dark line along center of back**.

E NT 3 **Rough-scaled Tegulet** (Martinique Spectacled Tegu) *Gymnophthalmus pleii* HB 50 mm (2″)

Endemic to Dominica, Martinique and **St Lucia.**
ID: Shiny bronze-brown; can show **dark line along center of back**. Obvious pale line runs from above eye to top of forelimbs; broad, dark stripe extends from head along side of body.

E NT 4 **Antillean Bachia** (Earless Worm Lizard) *Bachia alleni* HB 57 mm (2¼″)

Endemic to the Grenadines and **Grenada**.
ID: Slender; brown to dark brown with **scales in obvious bands** around long body and tail. **Tiny limbs**.

E EN 5 **Virgin Islands** (Cope's) **Worm Lizard** *Amphisbaena fenestra* HB 242 mm (9½″)

Endemic to the Virgin Islands but absent from Anegada and St Croix.
ID: Brown; **worm-like** with **rounded head and no obvious distinction between head, body and tail**. Fine rings of **small, squarish scales**.

FOREST LIZARDS

Forest lizards (galliwasps) are found widely in the Greater Antilles, but only one species is present in the Lesser Antilles.

E CR **Montserrat Galliwasp** *Diploglossus montisserrati* HB 180 mm (7″)

This skink-like lizard is **endemic to Montserrat**, where it is very rare and highly localized in an area of rainforest in the Centre Hills.

1
2
3
4
4
TINY, WELL-SEPARATED LIMBS
5
WORM-LIKE, LACKS LIMBS

SNAKES

Pit vipers (fer-de-lance) and St Lucia Boa

There are two species of pit viper (or fer-de-lance) in the Eastern Caribbean: Martinique Lancehead and St Lucia Lancehead. Both are large, strong-bodied, highly venomous snakes, with a short, triangular (lance-shaped) head. Although mainly terrestrial, they do climb trees. Most active at night, they use heat-sensing pits between the eyes and nostrils to help detect prey, which is mainly small mammals and birds. Both species are Endangered, and their decreasing populations are threatened by habitat loss and incidental or deliberate human persecution.

Encounters with all snakes are rare, as are snakebites. Pit vipers are highly venomous, and any bites require immediate treatment.

Take necessary safety precautions and use experienced guides in areas where pit vipers are known to be present. Keep to trails and be aware of local health facilities and contacts.

E (1) **Martinique Lancehead**

Bothrops lanceolatus L 200 cm (78")

Endemic to Martinique. Uncommon in rainforests, marginal land, along river courses and less frequently in drier forest habitats. **Highly venomous; its bite is dangerous to humans**.

ID: Large and strong-bodied. Ranges from brown to gray, marked with often symmetrical patterns of dark patches bordered by pale cross-bands, although markings can be indistinct. **Head is broad and triangular with a short snout**; it is typically dark above, pale below. A **short, straight dark band runs behind the eye**.

1

1

2

Juvenile showing yellow tip to tail.
Note also the straight dark band behind eye.

E EN 2 St Lucia Lancehead

Bothrops caribbaeus L 200 cm (78")

Endemic to St Lucia. Uncommon in rainforests, marginal land, along river courses and less frequently in drier forest habitats. **Highly venomous; its bite is dangerous to humans.** The only other large snake on the island is the St Lucia Boa, which is found in similar habitats.
ID: Large and strong-bodied. Pale gray to brown, appears heavily scaled with subtle or indistinct markings. **Triangular head** with **short snout**: dark above, paler below. **Short, straight dark band runs behind eye**. Juvenile has bright yellow tip to tail.

E EN 3 St Lucia Boa *Boa orophias* L 300 cm (118")

Endemic to St Lucia. Uncommon in dry forests, rainforests and around cultivated land. Great care must be taken not to confuse it with the highly venomous St Lucia Lancehead (an unrelated but similar-looking species), which can be found in similar habitats.
ID: Large and heavy-bodied. Boldly marked with pale and dark patches highlighted with a yellowish border. Head broad, **snout long and obviously narrows**; can show a dark uneven line along center. **Bold black line behind eye widens to the rear**.

Bold dark line widens behind the eye.

Boas and treeboas

There are five endemic species of boa, which do not overlap in range. The largest are in the genus *Boa*. Closely related to the South American species, *Boa constrictor*, they are impressive, heavy-bodied snakes with striking, cryptic markings. They prey mainly on small mammals, including rats, mice, bats and also birds. The genera *Corallus* and *Chilabothrus* are smaller **treeboas** that feed primarily on anole lizards, rats, mice and small birds.

Boas are mainly nocturnal, resting by day concealed in trees or coiled in hollow logs or rock piles. They are primarily forest snakes but can be seen in marginal and agricultural land, especially where there is continuous canopy cover. They are viviparous, the female giving birth to a litter of young (typically fewer than 20).

Boas are uncommon, generally wary and evasive around people, and, although not always welcomed, their value in preying upon rodents is increasingly recognized. Most species appear to have relatively stable populations, but Virgin Islands Boa and St Lucia Boa are Endangered, with threats including habitat loss and persecution.

Boas are not venomous. They may bite if threatened, but instances are rare. Medical attention should be sought for any snakebite.

E 1 **Dominica** (Clouded) **Boa** *Boa nebulosa* L 260 cm (102″)

Endemic to Dominica; occurs in all forest types and along agricultural margins. Mostly nocturnal but occasionally seen basking in early morning sun.
ID: The **only large, heavy snake on Dominica**. Gray-brown to dark brown with **large irregular markings**. Head broad; dark patch behind the eye that widens to rear.

St Lucia Boa *Boa orophias*

The St Lucia Boa species account is located next to that for St Lucia Lancehead (*p. 219*), as the two species are broadly similar in appearance and share habitats.

E EN 2 **Virgin Islands** (Tree) **Boa** *Chilabothrus granti* L 120 cm (47″)

Endemic to the Virgin Islands and Puerto Rico, present on at least **St Thomas and Tortola**. Rare in dry forest and mangroves, mainly at lower elevations. Threatened by habitat loss and the impact of introduced predators; a recovery plan is in place.
ID: Relatively **small and slender**. Grayish; highly patterned with irregular blotches that can form bands.

E NT 3 **St Vincent** (Cook's) **Treeboa** *Corallus cookii* L 150 cm (60″)

Endemic to St Vincent; occurs in a range of habitats from rainforest to agricultural areas and disturbed ground.
ID: Wide range of color and markings from cream through orange to black. Most individuals are boldly marked with bands and blotches; some are dark overall with fine pale bands. Head is short and broad, with a narrow neck.

E 4 **Grenada** (Bank) **Treeboa** *Corallus grenadensis* L 165 cm (65″)

Endemic to Grenada and the Grenadines (at least ten islands); occurs in a range of habitats, including rainforest, agricultural areas and mangroves.
ID: Wide color variation (especially between islands): can be yellow, red, gray or dark brown. Can be unmarked or highly patterned with irregular markings.

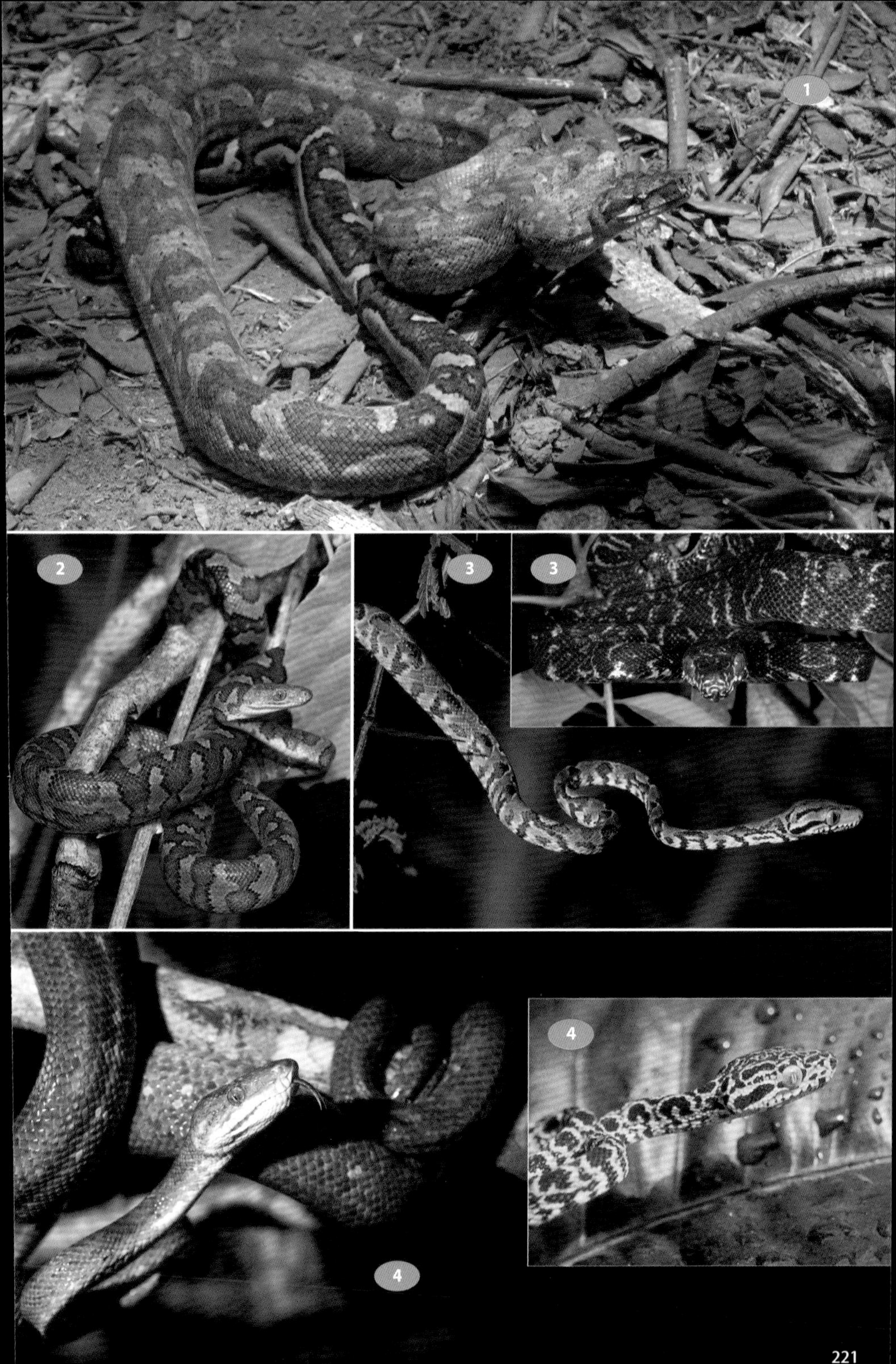
1
2
3
3
4
4

Racer snakes and ground snakes

Take an early morning hike on a forest trail or along a quiet road, and you may come across a racer or ground snake as it warms itself in the sun. These slim snakes, with a long tapering tail, are mainly terrestrial and active by day. They feed mostly on lizards and frogs but also take young snakes, mammals and invertebrates and even raid nests in small trees, where noisy mobbing birds can draw attention to their presence. They are oviparous; the female lays a clutch of eggs that typically takes two to three months to hatch.

There are 14 species in the region, all in the family Colubridae; most are endemic and restricted to a single island or island bank. They are vulnerable to habitat loss and predation; feral cats and especially Small Indian Mongoose have contributed to a reduction in numbers or even extirpation on some islands. Conservation actions are in place for some species to halt population declines or promote recovery.

The venom of racer snakes is reported as only mildly toxic to humans but may cause severe reactions in some people.

E 1 Puerto Rican Racer *Borikenophis portoricensis* L 92 cm (36")

Endemic to the Virgin Islands and Puerto Rico but extirpated from St John (USVI). Uncommon in all forest habitats but also hunts in open situations.
ID: Larger than Virgin Islands Miniracer. Gray to brown, with subdued markings that can form stripes. May show dark markings on snout and a **dark line in front of and behind the eye** that becomes a broken line running along the length of the body.

1

E **2** **Virgin Islands Miniracer** *Magliophis exiguus* L 32 cm (12½")

Endemic to the Virgin Islands and Puerto Rico: present on at least **St Thomas** (USVI), **Tortola** and **Virgin Gorda** (BVI). Uncommon in dry forest, scrub and agricultural land; often seen around rocks and walls.

ID: Very small and thin. Mainly brown to orange-brown, obviously paler, more cream below; can show subtle markings. An obvious **darker stripe** runs through the eye and continues as an unbroken line along length of body.

E N **3** **Anguilla Bank Racer** *Alsophis rijgersmaei* L 100 cm (39")

Endemic to Anguilla (including Scrub Island), **St Barthélemy** and its offshore islands; considered recently extirpated from St Martin/Sint Maarten. The only native snake in its range, found in dry forest and scrub, often around rocky areas.

ID: Ranges from gray to dark brown with subtle markings. Thin, **dark stripe behind eye**, typically continuing along length of body.

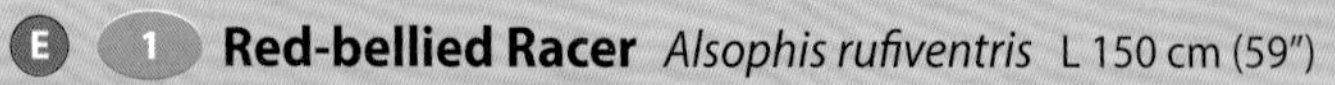

E 1 Red-bellied Racer *Alsophis rufiventris* L 150 cm (59″)

VU **Endemic to Saba and St Eustatius**, where the only native snake in its range; now extirpated from St Kitts and Nevis, where Small Indian Mongoose is present. Mostly terrestrial, found in all forest habitats.
ID: Gray-brown; well marked with **lines of broken spots**, which can appear as stripes. **Dark line behind eye** broadens to form a side-stripe. Any red on belly is difficult to see.

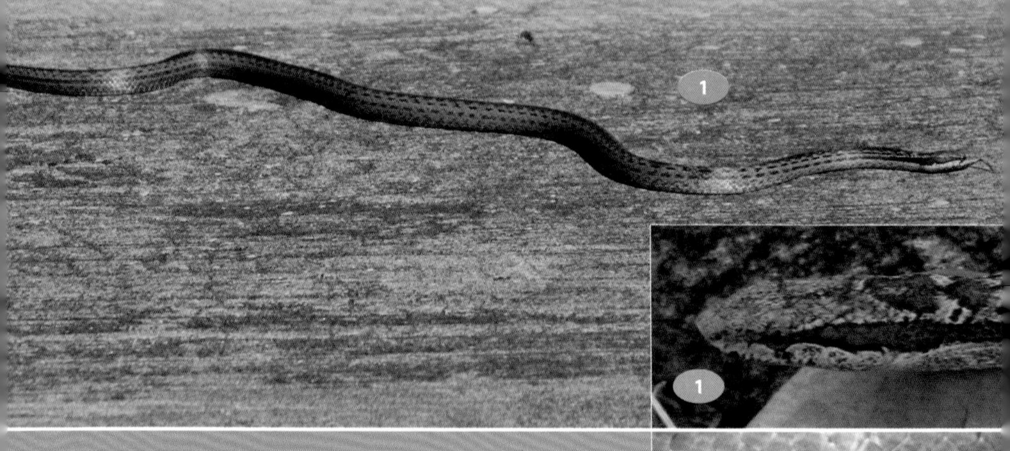

E 2 Antiguan Racer *Alsophis antiguae*

CR L 97 cm (38″)

Endemic to Antigua: extirpated from main island but persisted on Great Bird Island, where numbers were reduced to around 50 individuals in 1995. Following rat eradication, numbers increased, allowing reintroduction to another three small islands. A remarkable conservation story saw the total population grow to over 1,100 by 2015.
ID: Gray to brown with faint markings and side-stripes; can show darker cross-bands.

3 Montserrat Racer

E NT

Alsophis manselli L 94 cm (37")

Endemic to Montserrat, where the only native snake. Found in all scrub and forest habitats. **ID:** Dark **brown to black** with pale **yellowish markings** that can be striking.

4 Dominica Racer

Alsophis sibonius
L 94 cm (37")

Endemic to Dominica, where widespread, most often in dry forest. **ID: Very dark brown to black** with **pale markings** that can appear as bold spots or form loose bands. Much bigger and less boldly patterned than Leeward Ground Snake (*p. 226*), which also occurs on Dominica.

E 1 Leeward Ground Snake *Erythrolamprus juliae* L 46 cm (18″)

NT **Endemic to Dominica and Guadeloupe** but extirpated from Marie-Galante. Locally common on Dominica, now rare on Guadeloupe. Found mainly in dry forest at lower elevations.
ID: Small and slender. Dark with **distinctive diamond checkerboard pattern**, giving intricate black and white appearance. Some are all-dark.

E 2 Windward Tree Racer *Mastigodryas bruesi* L 83 cm (32″)

Endemic to St Vincent, the Grenadines and Grenada; introduced to **Barbados**. Uncommon in all forest types; readily climbs trees.
ID: Slender. Pale brown to gray, very finely marked, can show pale side-stripe. Paler throat and underside with a **short dark line from snout through eye**.

RARE OR HIGHLY RESTRICTED-RANGE SPECIES

Guadeloupe Racer *Alsophis antillensis* E CR

Endemic to Guadeloupe but considered extirpated from Marie-Galante.

3 **Les Saintes Racer** *Alsophis sanctonum* E EN

Endemic to Guadeloupe, found only on three islands in **Îles des Saintes**.

Martinique Ground Snake *Erythrolamprus cursor* E CR

Endemic to **Martinique** and **Rocher du Diamant** offshore: possibly now extinct.

4 **St Lucia Racer** *Erythrolamprus ornatus* E CR

Endemic to St Lucia: extirpated from main island, now only on **Maria Islands**.

5 **St Vincent Coachwhip** (Blacksnake) *Chironius vincenti* E CR

Endemic to St Vincent: rare and localized in one area of rainforest.

Common Mussurana (Windward Cribo) *Clelia clelia*

Only on Grenada, where status uncertain and possibly now extirpated. Occurs more widely in Central and South America.

3

4

5

Non-native snakes

Non-native snakes are occasionally reported. Most are single individuals that are likely to be escaped pets. The following, however, appear to have established breeding populations:

6 Red Cornsnake *Pantherophis guttatus* L 180 cm (72″)

Native to North America; introduced to the **Virgin Islands, Anguilla, St Barthélemy** and **Martinique**.

7 Black-headed Snake *Tantilla melanocephala* L 50 cm (20″)

Native to South America; introduced to **Mustique**, possibly **Union Island** and **Carriacou** (Grenadines) and **Grenada**.

6

7

Blindsnakes and threadsnakes

These small, worm-like burrowing snakes are found in forest habitats and on agricultural land. They hide away in soil or under leaf litter, logs and rocks and are rarely seen. Most are less than 300 mm (12″) in length and are some of the smallest snakes in the world. They forage for small insect prey, especially termites and ants, and their eggs and larvae. The female lays eggs that hatch as independent young; the introduced Brahminy Blindsnake is remarkable in that the female is able to reproduce without a male (a reproductive strategy known as 'obligate parthenogenesis').

Blindsnakes (also referred to as worm snakes) have a cylindrical body, rounded head and short, blunt tail. They are all gray to pink-brown with a paler underside. Threadsnakes are more marked, typically with yellowish side-stripes.

Virgin Gorda Blindsnake *Antillotyphlops naugus* E VU L 243 mm (9½″)—**Virgin Gorda (BVI)**

Anegada Blindsnake *Antillotyphlops catapontus* E DD L 265 mm (10½″)—**Anegada (BVI)**

Virgin Islands Blindsnake *Antillotyphlops richardii* E NT L 250 mm (10″)—**USVI and BVI**, and Puerto Rico

St Bart's Blindsnake *Antillotyphlops annae* E DD L 110 mm (4″)—**St Barthélemy**

1 **Leeward Blindsnake** *Antillotyphlops geotomus* E NT L 213 mm (8″)—**St Eustatius, St Kitts and Nevis, Antigua and Barbuda**

Montserrat Blindsnake *Antillotyphlops monastus* E NT L 258 mm (10″)—**Montserrat**

Guadeloupe Blindsnake *Antillotyphlops guadeloupensis* E L 162 mm (6″)—**Guadeloupe**

2 **Dominica Blindsnake** *Antillotyphlops dominicanus* E L 385 mm (15″)—**Dominica**

3 **Grenada Bank Blindsnake** *Amerotyphlops tasymicris* E EN L 263 mm (10″)—**Grenada and Union Island**; may occur elsewhere on the Grenada Bank.

Martinique (Two-lined) **Threadsnake** *Tetracheilostoma bilineatum* E L 110 mm (4″)—**Martinque**

4 **St Lucia Threadsnake** *Tetracheilostoma breuili* E EN L 110 mm (4″)—**St Lucia and Maria Major**

Barbados Threadsnake *Tetracheilostoma carlae* E CR L 104 mm (4″)—**Barbados**

5 **Brahminy Blindsnake** *Indotyphlops braminus* L 203 mm (8″)

This Asian species, also known as 'flowerpot snake', was an accidental introduction, probably among the roots of ornamental plants shipped into the region. Found on at least **Anguilla, St Martin/Sint Maarten, St Eustatius, St Kitts, Guadeloupe** including **Les Désirade, Montserrat, Martinique, the Grenadines, Grenada** and **Barbados**. **ID:** Thin, worm-like appearance. Typically very **dark brown-black**, much darker than native blindsnakes, although some individuals may be paler. Contrasting paler grayish (not white) underside. Tail has tiny **spike at tip**.

TORTOISES, TERRAPINS AND SEA TURTLES

Tortoises A hike through scrub or dry forest can provide a surprising encounter with a Red-footed Tortoise. Native to Central and South America, this species' route to the Eastern Caribbean is uncertain, but they are thought to have been introduced by indigenous people from South America as a food source several centuries ago. Tortoises are diurnal but most active in the early morning and late afternoon. They feed on leaves, flowers, fallen fruit and cacti, and also scavenge for carrion. Following courtship and mating, the female makes a shallow excavation to lay a small clutch of eggs, typically fewer than ten.

1 Red-footed Tortoise

Chelonoidis carbonarius L 300 mm (12")

Widespread but uncommon: present on at least **Anguilla, St Barths, Saba, St Kitts, Nevis, Guadeloupe** and several of the **Grenadines**.
ID: Dark **high-domed shell**, gray-black with **paler spots** in center of large plates (scutes). **Orange-red to yellow scales on head and front of forelimbs**.

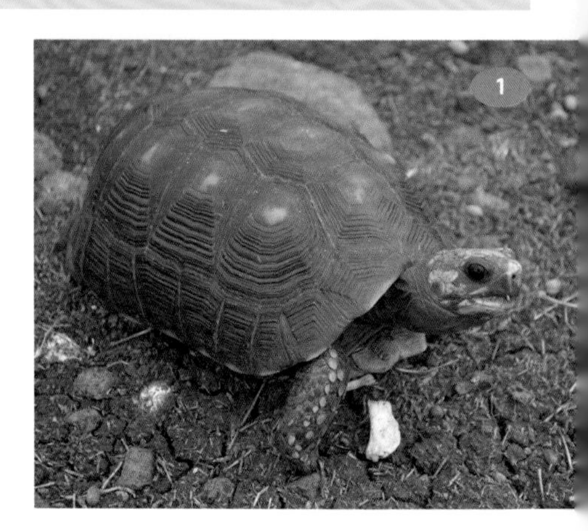

Yellow-footed (Brazilian Giant) Tortoise *Chelonoidis denticulata*

This popular pet species, native to South America, has been reported from **St John** (USVI) and **Guadeloupe**, but its status is unclear.

Freshwater terrapins

Pond terrapins have been widely introduced through the release of unwanted pets into ponds, rivers and reservoirs, where they can be seen basking on banks and stones. Their full ecological impact in the region is unclear, but they feed on a range of native aquatic plants and invertebrates. Red-eared Slider is recognized as one of the 100 worst invasive alien species in the world.

2 Red-eared Slider

Trachemys scripta elegans L 280 mm (11")

Introduced from USA and Mexico, now present on at least the **Virgin Islands, St Martin/Sint Maarten, St Eustatius, Guadeloupe** (including **Marie-Galante**) **and Martinique**.
ID: Low, streamlined carapace is dark brown or olive, often with light yellow lines and markings; has a **wide red band behind** the **eye**. If disturbed while basking, slides into water.

Puerto Rican (Central Antillean) Slider *Trachemys stejnegeri*

Endemic to Hispaniola, Bahamas and Puerto Rico: introduced to **Guadeloupe**, including **Marie-Galante** and **Les-Saintes**, and to **Dominica**.

West African Mud Turtle *Pelusios castaneus*

An African freshwater turtle, introduced to **Guadeloupe**.

Sea turtles

The sandy beaches and secluded bays that are so characteristic of the Caribbean have long been visited by sea turtles, and many are ancient nesting sites. Five of the world's seven species have been recorded: Green, Hawksbill and Leatherback Turtles all have important breeding populations. Sightings are typically of either Green Turtles surfacing for air while foraging for seagrass in shallow bays, or Hawksbill Turtles feeding around coral reefs, where they are often seen by divers and snorkelers.

Sea turtles are present year-round in the Eastern Caribbean, but individuals of some species migrate long distances to forage in the temperate waters of the Northwest Atlantic, returning to mate and breed in the area where they hatched. After mating at sea, the female hauls herself out onto the nesting beach, where she excavates a large nest-hole for egg-laying. Most will lay a small number of clutches in a breeding season, which runs broadly from April to September. Eggs typically take two months to hatch; the hatchlings head straight out to sea and spend their early years among floating vegetation such as sargassum. It can take a sea turtle 20–30 years to reach maturity.

All sea turtles are threatened to some degree by habitat loss, pollution, disease, beachside development (including light pollution and disturbance on nesting beaches), and rising sea-levels and temperatures associated with climate change. Sea turtles are also known to become entangled in fishing nets, and there is a global history of exploitation for shells, meat and eggs. Population declines in the region have resulted in legal protection and stimulated many local conservation initiatives from governments, conservation organizations and volunteers. Energetic conservation groups are active in beach and nest protection, nest monitoring and education programs. Many have phone hotlines to report nesting females and may offer local opportunities to become involved. Contacts can be found locally or through WIDECAST (widecast.org).

Hawksbill Turtle

1 **Loggerhead Turtle** *Caretta caretta* L typically 100 cm (39″) but can reach 120 cm (47″)

Uncommon to rare **throughout**; mainly a non-breeding visitor to inshore waters with occasional reports of nesting, mainly in the southern islands. Powerful jaws enable this turtle to feed on hard-shelled mollusks as well as jellyfish and squid.
ID: Head **large and broad**; dark scales less distinct than Green Turtle. Carapace **red to orange-brown**, very **deep at front**, tapering down towards rear; looks less patterned overall. Flippers relatively short compared to other species.

2 **Green Turtle** *Chelonia mydas* L typically 100 cm (39″) but can reach 120 cm (47″)

Uncommon breeding species **throughout**, most often seen foraging in shallow bays with seagrass beds, where views tend to be a brief glimpse of a head. Both immatures and adults can be seen year-round, but some adults migrate long distances to foraging areas. Overall numbers are declining globally, but with protection, some local populations are stable or increasing.
ID: Head **well marked** with **dark-centered scales** and **blunt rounded beak**. Carapace smooth, **brown** and subtly streaked. Flippers heavily spotted with dark scales on upper surface.

3 **Hawksbill Turtle** *Eretmochelys imbricata* L 90 cm (35″)

Uncommon breeding species **throughout**; some individuals are likely to be migratory. Most often seen foraging for sponges and mollusks in coral reefs and lagoons. Nests high on the beach, often among vegetation such as Sea Grape, where vulnerable to disturbance. Formerly exploited for its colorful shell ('tortoiseshell'), as well as for meat and eggs; despite now being protected, global populations are still in decline.
ID: Head **well marked** with dark-centered scales, **sharp pointed beak** (hence common name). Its colorful shell is **mottled brown, orange and gold** and has an obvious **serrated rear edge**. Flippers heavily spotted with dark scales on upper surface.

1

2

EN 1 **Leatherback Turtle** *Dermochelys coriacea* L 140 cm (55″) but can reach 180 cm (71″)

An uncommon breeding species **throughout**, turtles here are part of the Northwest Atlantic subpopulation. Primarily an open-ocean (pelagic) species; ranges long distances to feeding areas in the northern Atlantic to forage for jellyfish and sea-squirts, only returning to inshore waters and undisturbed sandy beaches for mating and egg-laying. This is the largest of the sea turtles, typically weighing 250–500 kg (550–1,100 lb) but can reach as much as 900 kg (2,000 lb). The unique carapace lacks the horny plates of other species, being covered in a **thick layer of leathery skin** (hence the common name).
ID: Large and dramatic, with a heavy body and dark, blunt head. Carapace **dark blue-black**, finely spotted and **tapering strongly to the rear**, with **distinct ridges** running along the back. Front flippers long, dark and spotted.

VU **Olive Ridley Turtle** *Lepidochelys olivacea* L 72 cm (28″)

A rare migrant to the region with occasional records from at least **Antigua and Barbuda, Guadeloupe** and **Martinique**. Able to dive deep to feed on crustaceans, mollusks and algae. Olive Ridley and Kemp's Ridley are the smallest sea turtles in the region. Carapace is **heart-shaped**, a dark **olive-green**.

CR **Kemp's Ridley Turtle** *Lepidochelys kempii* L 72 cm (28″)

A possible vagrant to the region; breeding populations lie along the Caribbean coast of Mexico, Bahamas and southern USA. Similar to Olive Ridley Turtle, but carapace is slightly wider and looks more circular.

Shoreline and land crabs

Encounters with shoreline and land crabs can be surprising and unexpected, from a colony of brilliant Blue Land Crabs on the floor of a mangrove swamp to a solitary Hermit Crab crossing a forest trail. Found from sandy and rocky shorelines to rainforest streams, they are easily overlooked and certainly under-recorded. Over 20 species are present and can be seen year-round. With the exception of Yellow Land Crab, which is endemic to the Lesser Antilles, all are distributed more widely beyond the Eastern Caribbean.

Crabs are crustaceans, belonging to the order Decapoda, meaning 'ten legs' (jointed in five pairs), the front pair modified as claws for feeding. One or both claws are enlarged in the male of some species, used for courtship display and in disputes with other males. Their eyes are at the end of stalks that retract into sockets on the carapace (the hard protective shell). Eye color, and stalk length and position on the carapace, can help in identification.

Crabs extract oxygen from water through gills in a chamber near the base of the legs. Land crabs need to keep their gills moist and are able to find sufficient water by excavating burrows into damp sediment or seeking damp areas under rocks and logs. Freshwater crabs are further adapted, having a lung-like lining to the gill chamber, enabling oxygen to be absorbed from air.

Most species are nocturnal but may be active during the day, especially in the early morning and late afternoon. They typically move with a scuttling sideways motion along the ground, although some are nimble and agile, able to climb rocks, walls and trees; all can be surprisingly fast, especially if disturbed. Crabs feed on fish, shellfish, shrimps, carrion, plant material and detritus, using their claws to hold or break up food and move it to their mouthparts. Many of the coastal species, especially fiddler crabs, are preyed upon by gulls, shorebirds and herons. Some land crabs are harvested for culinary use.

Most land crabs retain a link to the sea through their reproductive cycle. After mating, the female retains fertilized eggs in an 'apron' underneath the abdomen; females produce a remarkable number of eggs, sometimes many thousands. When the eggs are mature, she returns to the sea to release them, where they hatch as free-swimming larvae. For some species this is a synchronized event involving large migrations of females, often during a full or new moon. Larvae grow through four or five planktonic stages and a bottom-dwelling stage before leaving the sea as small, fully formed crabs. The freshwater Yellow Land Crab has a different reproductive cycle that is covered in its species account.

More information about the distribution of crabs can be found on the CRUSTA website (crustiesfroverseas.free.fr), which includes extensive surveys for the French Antilles along with information on distribution in the wider Eastern and Southern Caribbean.

Colony of fiddler crabs.

FIDDLER CRABS

Tiny and often occurring in vast numbers, fiddler crabs are found in shallow intertidal waters around mangroves, coastal lagoons, salt-ponds and river mouths, where they feed on algae and detritus brought in by sea or freshwater flows. They are active by day, excavating and aggressively defending individual burrows. Males have an enlarged claw that is waved to attract the attention of females or deter other males. The origin of the name 'fiddler crab' is uncertain, but one version is that the obvious enlarged claw of the male is held like a violin and 'played' by the regular movements of the smaller claw, which is used for feeding! Fiddler crabs are preyed upon by waterbirds, especially herons, egrets and Whimbrels. Identification to species level is not easy; they are so small that fine details are hard to observe in the field. Distribution is unclear on some islands, but two species—Burger's Fiddler Crab and Mudflat Fiddler Crab—are common and occur **throughout**.

	① **Burger's** (Salt Pond) **Fiddler Crab** *Minuca burgersi*	② **Mudflat Fiddler Crab** *Minuca rapax*
Size	CL 12 mm (½") | CW 16 mm (⅝")	CL 20 mm (¾") | CW 30 mm (1¼")
Carapace	**Very small.** Dark red-brown to paler gray, with subtle mottling; only **slightly tapered** to rear from mid-carapace. Appears squarer than Mudflat.	**Small.** Pale, mottled gray; tapers **sharply to rear** from mid-carapace. Overall appearance is more angled than Burger's.
Male enlarged claw	**Orange to red; deep at base,** which is densely covered in small nodules (tubercles). Whiter fingers are **broader and shorter** than those of Mudflat.	**Pale orange-yellow; narrower at base,** which is more sparsely covered in small nodules (turbercles) than Burger's. **Fingers** are whiter towards tip, and **longer and thinner**—giving an elongated appearance. Top finger typically curves beyond lower finger.
Walking legs	Base segments (merus) of rear of legs narrow; upper edge flatter.	Base segments (merus) of all legs obviously deep; upper edge more rounded.
Eyestalks	Stalks pale; eyes gray-brown.	Stalks pale; eyes gray-brown.
Habitat	Coastal lagoons, salt-ponds, mudflats and mangrove fringes; often in open situations.	Mudflats and mangrove swamps.

Atlantic Hairback Fiddler Crab *Minuca vocator* CL 22 mm (1") | CW 40 mm (1½")

Widespread, occurring on at least the **Virgin Islands, St Martin/Sint Maarten, Guadeloupe** and **Dominica**. Uncommon on mudflats, around mangroves and mouths of streams and rivers; typically in more shaded situations.

ID: Carapace gray with short hairs forming **distinct markings**. Less angular overall: sides are **smoothly rounded**, tapering less sharply to rear. Male enlarged claw orange to yellow with narrow base and long fingers. Legs a darker yellow-gray; **all segments narrow** and **obviously hairy**. Eyestalks possibly darker than Burger's or Mudflat Fiddlers, and more widely separated.

Uncommon to rare fiddler crabs

Species	Recorded on at least...
Thin-fingered Fiddler Crab *Leptuca leptodactyla*	USVI, Guadeloupe, Martinique
Atlantic Mangrove Fiddler Crab *Leptuca thayeri*	St John (USVI), Guadeloupe, Martinique
Greater Fiddler Crab *Uca major*	St Croix (USVI), Guadeloupe, Martinique
Brazilian Fiddler Crab *Uca maracoani*	Martinique; may occur farther south

1
Carapace broader at rear, more square-shaped.
1
1
Base segments of rear pair of legs narrow; upper edge flatter.
2
2
2
Base segments of rear pair of legs deeper; upper edge rounded.
Carapace narrower at rear, more angular.

MANGROVE AND MARSH CRABS

1 Mangrove Root Crab *Goniopsis cruentata* CL 63 mm (2½")

Widespread but uncommon; may be under-recorded and possibly occurs throughout. Found among mangrove roots and on muddy banks and margins, this species is quick, agile and a capable climber, able to cling to mangrove roots above flowing water. Forages for plant material, detritus and carrion.
ID: Bright, chunky, with a squarish, straight-edged carapace that is dark with **white spotting**. Legs deep at base, dark orange-red with bright spots or stripes. Claws are **similar in size, deep** with **serrated edges** and strikingly **pale orange and white**. Short orange eyestalks with dark eyes are set near corners of carapace.

2 Mangrove Tree Crab *Aratus pisonii* CL 22 mm (1")

Widespread, on at least the **Virgin Islands, St Martin/Sint Maarten, Antigua, Guadeloupe** and **Martinique**. Locally common in mangrove swamps, mostly on Red Mangrove, but can be difficult to find among the tangle of roots and branches. An agile and able climber, scuttles quickly through trees; when threatened, retreats behind branches or drops into water. Feeds on leaves, algae and invertebrates.
ID: Small and **cryptically marked**. Carapace is square, slightly tapered to the rear, dark brown and **finely patterned**, but markings can be obscured by mud. Leg segments deep, **flattened at base** with obvious sharp tips; claws are short and deep, similar in size. **Short eyestalks** are **set at corners** of carapace.

3 Atlantic Mangrove Ghost Crab *Ucides cordatus* CL 70 mm (2¾")

Widespread but uncommon, occurring on at least the **Virgin Islands, Antigua, Guadeloupe, Dominica, Martinique** and **Grenada**. Found in mangroves and on mudflats, often alongside other species. Typically seen at the entrance to its burrow, quickly retreating if disturbed.
ID: Carapace pale and distinctively domed with **deep, rounded** sides tapering to rear, and **surface grooves and ridges** that form an **obvious H**. **Large claws** are similar in size and purple with white tips. Walking legs typically purple-red, covered in fine silky hairs. Eyestalks short and pale, set towards center of carapace.

4 River Crab *Armases roberti* CL 27 mm (1")

Widespread, occurring on at least **USVI, Guadeloupe, Dominica, Martinique, St Lucia, Barbados** and **St Vincent**. Locally common in mangroves and along shady margins of freshwater streams and rivers, where it excavates a burrow in soft soil. Mainly coastal but will venture farther inland. Forages for algae, searching among rocks, mangrove roots and debris.
ID: Small. Carapace brown with paler markings, **square-shaped** and slightly ridged at front. **Legs long** and **flattened**; carapace and legs have **rough surfaces**. Claws small, similar in size, and dark **purple-red with orange fingers**. Distinctive **green eyes** on short eyestalks set towards corners of carapace.

Uncommon to rare mangrove and marsh crabs

Species	Recorded on at least...
Humic Marsh Crab *Armases ricordi*	Virgin Islands, St Martin/Sint Maarten, Guadeloupe, Martinique
Armases rubripes	Guadeloupe

1
1
2
2
3
3
4
4

HERMIT CRABS

Caribbean Land Hermit Crab (Soldier Crab) *Coenobita clypeatus*

CL 50 mm (2″), although rarely seen outside of a seashell

Locally common **throughout** in mangroves and coastal dry forests but will venture farther inland. Hermit crabs lack a hard carapace, so inhabit empty mollusk shells to protect their soft and vulnerable abdomen, moving through a series of increasingly larger shells as they grow. West Indian Top Shell *Cittarium pica* is commonly used, but there are increasing reports of hermit crabs using discarded plastic containers. This species is mostly seen on the ground, foraging for a range of plant and animal matter using the two pairs of long antennae for taste, smell and as 'feelers'. An able climber, it can be easily overlooked in trees and shrubs.
ID: Typical view is of **orange-red legs** and long, **fine antennae**, which are all visible outside a moving seashell. One claw is enlarged and **purple-red**: most easily seen when the crab is fully retracted inside its shell.

SHORELINE CRABS

Atlantic Ghost Crab *Ocypode quadrata* CL 50 mm (2″)

Widespread and locally common from the **Virgin Islands to Barbados**. Mostly restricted to secluded, less-developed beaches, where it excavates a burrow near the tide-line; piles of sand and radiating tracks can be obvious. Among the fastest of land crabs, moving quickly to catch prey, then retreating back into the burrow: the genus name *Ocypode* translates as 'swift-footed'. Omnivorous, feeding mainly at night on plant material, detritus, insects and shellfish.
ID: Carapace is squarish, typically **very pale** gray to straw colored, but can be darker on volcanic beaches. One claw is larger; the **walking legs are long, thin and hairy**. Eyestalks are set near center of carapace with **obvious bold black eye**.

3 Sally Lightfoot Crab *Grapsus grapsus* CL 75 mm (3″)

Widespread, probably found throughout, and locally common along rocky shores, jetties and seawalls. Can be obvious in the splash zone, clinging to rocks and walls with sharp-tipped legs as waves wash over. Grazes on algae, catches small prey and clears up detritus. Nimble and agile, running out of sight if disturbed; the name may have originated from a famous light-footed Caribbean dancer!
ID: Flattened carapace and legs; color varies from **dark brown**, maturing to **bright orange-red**, with **striking patterns** and paler markings. May show bright blue on head and legs. Large claws of similar size are red-purple with pale tips. Eyes gray but can be a brighter blue; eyestalks short.

Uncommon to rare shoreline crabs

Species	Recorded on at least...
Variegate Shore Crab *Geograpsus lividus*	Virgin Islands to St Lucia and Barbados
Globose Shore Crab *Cyclograpsus integer*	Virgin Islands to Dominica
Mottled Shore Crab *Pachygrapsus transversus*	USVI, St Martin/Sint Maarten, Antigua, Guadeloupe, Martinique, Barbados

1
1
2
2
3
3

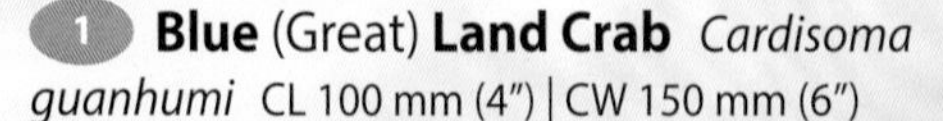

LAND CRABS

1 **Blue** (Great) **Land Crab** *Cardisoma guanhumi* CL 100 mm (4″) | CW 150 mm (6″)

Locally common **throughout** in mangrove swamps, coastal woodlands, and even gardens and hotel grounds. Excavates a burrow down to damp sediment, leaving an untidy pile of dug-out material near the entrance hole. A colonial species; **hundreds of crabs** may be present at a site. Forages for leaves, fruit, carrion and invertebrates.

ID: Largest land crab in the region, with deep carapace and large, heavy claws. Immature crabs are mainly tan to orange; when fully mature, male can become a **striking violet-blue**, while female is typically a paler gray-brown. Long eyestalks tend to reflect carapace color and retract into large, deep sockets.

2 **Black** (Purple) **Land Crab** *Gecarcinus ruricola* CL 75 mm (3″) | CW 100 mm (4″)

Widespread from the **Virgin Islands to at least Martinique**, occurring along coasts and riverbanks and in forests; reaches altitudes of more than 300 m (980 ft) on Dominica and Saba. Mostly nocturnal: when foraging, can be seen crossing roads at night.

ID: Compact, **rounded carapace**. Mostly seen in a **dark purple-black** or **brighter orange** form; can show vein-like lines on sides of carapace. Large claws are similar in size. Legs range from **purple-black** to bright **orange-red**; outer segments are edged with small spines. **Dark eyes** on **short stalks** may contrast with small, very pale eye sockets near center of carapace.

3 Blackback Land Crab

Gecarcinus lateralis

CL 45 mm (1¾") | CW 60 mm (2½")

Locally common **throughout** in mangroves and coastal forests, where it scavenges and forages for plant material. Excavates a burrow above the tideline. In parts of its range, is also known as Red Crab, Moon Crab or Bermuda Crab.

ID: Carapace wide and rounded: **two-tone**, bright **orange-red** with distinctive **black center**. Legs and large, similar-sized claws are **bright orange-red**. **Dark eyes** are on **short stalks**, with small eye sockets near center of carapace.

4 Yellow Land Crab (Cyrique) *Guinotia dentata* CL 60 mm (2¼") | CW 100 mm (4")

Endemic to the Lesser Antilles, occurring only on **Guadeloupe, Dominica, Martinique, St Lucia** and **St Vincent**. Locally common along mountain streams, lakes and rivers, especially in forested areas; recorded to 850 m (2,800 ft) at Lake Boeri on Dominica. An entirely freshwater species, it excavates a burrow along a stream-bank or retreats to damp areas among tree roots or rocks. Forages mainly for carrion, small fish, invertebrates and some plant material. Breeds year-round: female carries fertilized eggs that hatch as young crabs rather than initially developing as external larvae. On St Vincent, this is one of the main prey items of Common Black Hawk.

ID: Carapace **broad**, mostly **yellow**, but can be dark brown or even largely black. Carapace and large yellow claws have **distinctive, finely serrated edges** (the Latin specific name *dentata* translates as 'toothed'). Walking legs are slightly flattened, often browner. **Short** yellow eyestalks with dark eye retract into **rounded eye sockets** set close to center of carapace.

Dragonflies and damselflies

Spend any time visiting wetlands and you will come across dragonflies. These attractive insects are mainly associated with freshwater habitats and, less often, with brackish wetlands. Some species breed high on rainforest streams and are found only on the larger volcanic islands; others readily disperse in search of new or temporary pools and are found more widely. Females and immatures of several dragonfly species 'hawk' insects away from water and can be seen over coastal scrub, grassland and along forest margins, often gathered in large, mixed groups. Some of the larger dragonflies are twilight feeders that can be seen foraging at dusk and dawn, while migratory species may occur sporadically on any suitable wetland. Fascinating to watch, dragonflies are dazzling fliers, often flashing vibrant blues, reds or greens, and are highly effective aerial predators feeding on a range of flying insects.

The term 'dragonfly' is commonly used to describe damselflies as well as dragonflies. Both groups are in the order Odonata—damselflies in the suborder Zygoptera (meaning 'yoked wings' or 'paired wings'), dragonflies in Anisoptera (meaning 'unequal wings': hindwings are typically broader than their forewings). Over 50 species have been recorded in the Eastern Caribbean: five are endemic to the region, with the rest found more widely in the Caribbean and/or the Americas. The most widespread species are described; rare or restricted-range species are listed, but data are patchy for all species, so your records can add significantly to local knowledge (submitted locally or through iNaturalist).

Dragonflies are active by day. As their body temperature is regulated by ambient temperature, in the tropics they are on the wing year-round. Mature males are typically brighter colored than females and immatures. They can be conspicuous when defending a territory or searching for females, either from a perch or by patrolling a section of water suitable for egg-laying and larval development. Courtship varies and can take place either in flight or within marginal vegetation, where mating pairs can be seen connected 'in tandem' (*p. 249*) or in a 'wheel' (*p. 248*). The female lays eggs singly or in clusters, sometimes when connected to the male; a female dipping its abdomen regularly into water or aquatic vegetation will be egg-laying ('ovipositing').

The life cycle of a dragonfly is in three stages:

- **Egg:** typically laid underwater, often on or in aquatic plants.
- **Nymph** (larva): underwater larval stage. Nymph undergoes several molts before finally climbing onto vegetation above water level.
- **Adult:** nymph sheds larval skin (exuvia), emerging as an adult; the exuvia can often be seen on waterside vegetation. Newly emerged dragonflies (tenerals) are paler than adults: full coloration develops over several days. With maturity, some species develop a blue or white powdery bloom (pruinosity) on the thorax and abdomen. Life expectancy ranges from a few weeks for damselflies to a few months for larger dragonflies: in reality, weather events and predation mean this may be shorter.

Distribution information is taken from Meurgey *et al.* (2012) and Catling *et al.* (2015) and personal observations, complemented by advice from Dennis Paulson. *See* "Further reading", *p. 301*.

DAMSELFLY OR DRAGONFLY?

1 Damselfly

Small, dainty, with very thin body. Most species are similar in shape.

When perched, wings are held closed along body, except spreadwings, which hold wings slightly opened and angled backwards.

Front and rear wings are broadly similar in shape: usually fine and narrow.

Eyes small and separated.

Flight weak and typically low; less often over open water.

Feed by catching invertebrate prey in flight or by searching slowly through fringing vegetation (gleaning) close to water. Perch on low vegetation, often vertically but can be horizontally.

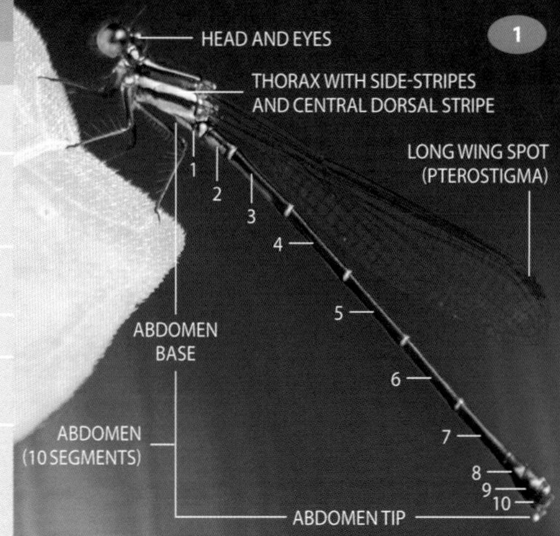

2 Dragonfly

Species differ in size and shape; generally more robust with heavier body.

When perched, wings are held at right angles to body or slightly forward.

Front and rear wings differ in shape: rear wings are usually broader, but this is not always obvious.

Eyes large and very close to one another, almost touching.

Flight strong and fast and can include hovering and rapid changes of direction; often over open water.

Broadly separated into two main types based on foraging and perching behavior: **Larger, long-winged species** that spend long periods on the wing catching insects in flight. May forage away from water, often at height. Tend to hang vertically when perched on vegetation (*e.g.*, darners and gliders).
Compact, shorter-bodied species that fly low, often skimming the water surface. Frequently return to favored perches, darting up to catch passing insects. Perch horizontally or with abdomen slightly raised, often on low exposed stems or stones, less often away from water (*e.g.*, dragonlets and saddlebags).

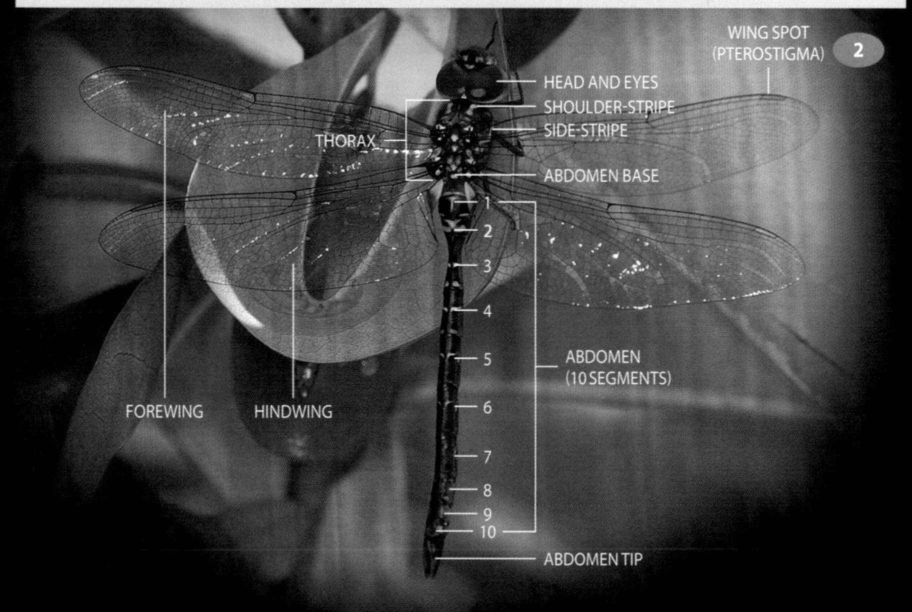

DAMSELFLIES

Spreadwings Large damselflies found on shallow, marshy ponds and lakes, especially those with emergent vegetation. Flight is slow, often low over water; settles with wings partially spread.

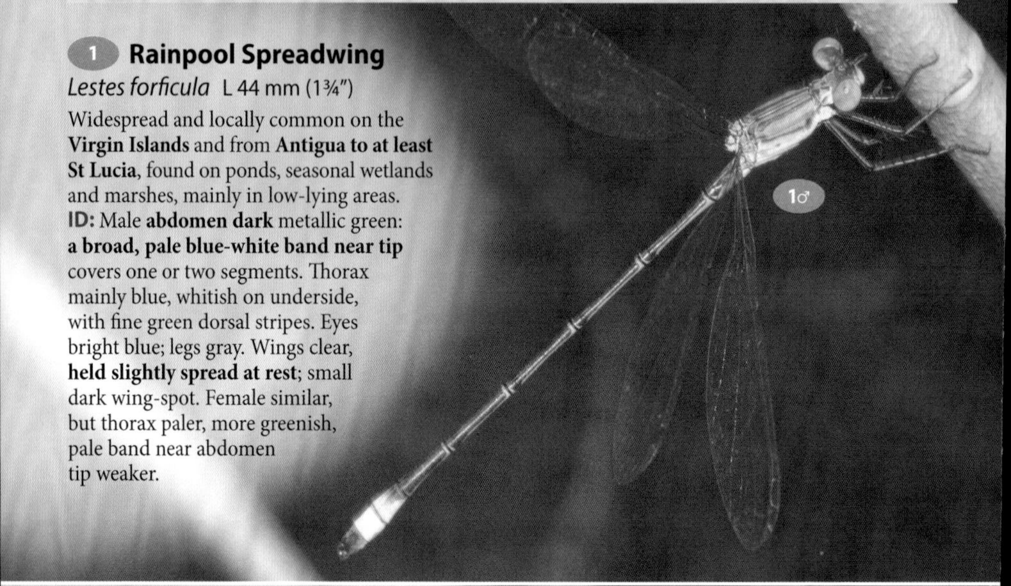

1 Rainpool Spreadwing

Lestes forficula L 44 mm (1¾")

Widespread and locally common on the **Virgin Islands** and from **Antigua to at least St Lucia**, found on ponds, seasonal wetlands and marshes, mainly in low-lying areas. **ID:** Male **abdomen dark** metallic green: **a broad, pale blue-white band near tip** covers one or two segments. Thorax mainly blue, whitish on underside, with fine green dorsal stripes. Eyes bright blue; legs gray. Wings clear, **held slightly spread at rest**; small dark wing-spot. Female similar, but thorax paler, more greenish, pale band near abdomen tip weaker.

1♂

2 Blue-striped Spreadwing

Lestes tenuatus L 44 mm (1¾")

Uncommon, occurring on at least **Guadeloupe, Dominica, Martinique, St Lucia** and **Grenada**; localized on shady ponds in dry forests. **ID:** Male similar to Rainpool Spreadwing, but **pale band to abdomen tip is smaller** (restricted to one segment or even just a spot). Thorax has an **obvious blue shoulder-stripe** and darker side-stripe. Female duller; **lacks pale band or spot** near tip of abdomen.

2♂

Antillean Spreadwing *Lestes spumarius* not shown

Recorded once: from a flooded river valley on **St Lucia** in 2011.

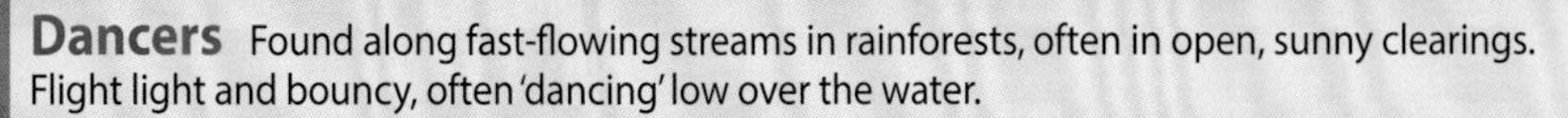

Dancers Found along fast-flowing streams in rainforests, often in open, sunny clearings. Flight light and bouncy, often 'dancing' low over the water.

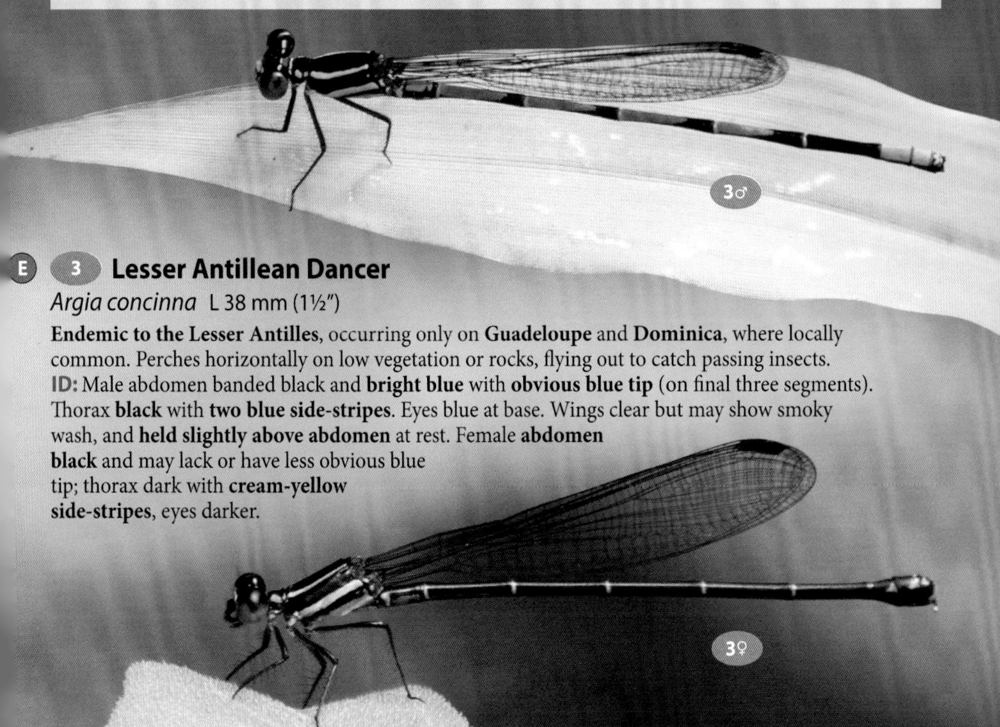

E 3 Lesser Antillean Dancer

Argia concinna L 38 mm (1½")

Endemic to the Lesser Antilles, occurring only on **Guadeloupe** and **Dominica**, where locally common. Perches horizontally on low vegetation or rocks, flying out to catch passing insects. **ID:** Male abdomen banded black and **bright blue** with **obvious blue tip** (on final three segments). Thorax **black** with **two blue side-stripes**. Eyes blue at base. Wings clear but may show smoky wash, and **held slightly above abdomen** at rest. Female **abdomen black** and may lack or have less obvious blue tip; thorax dark with **cream-yellow side-stripes**, eyes darker.

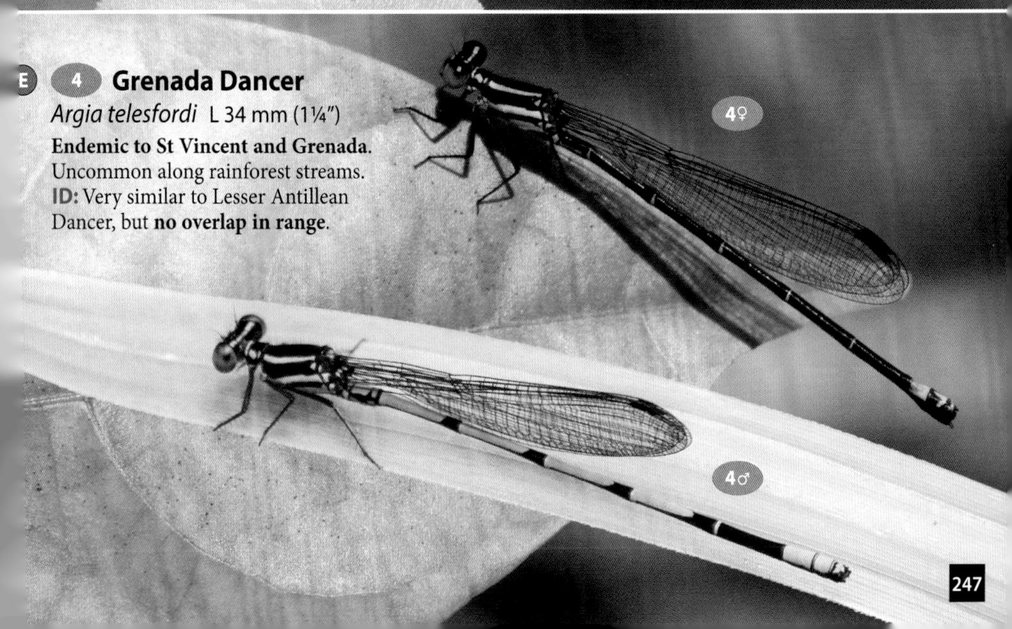

E 4 Grenada Dancer

Argia telesfordi L 34 mm (1¼")

Endemic to St Vincent and Grenada. Uncommon along rainforest streams. **ID:** Very similar to Lesser Antillean Dancer, but **no overlap in range**.

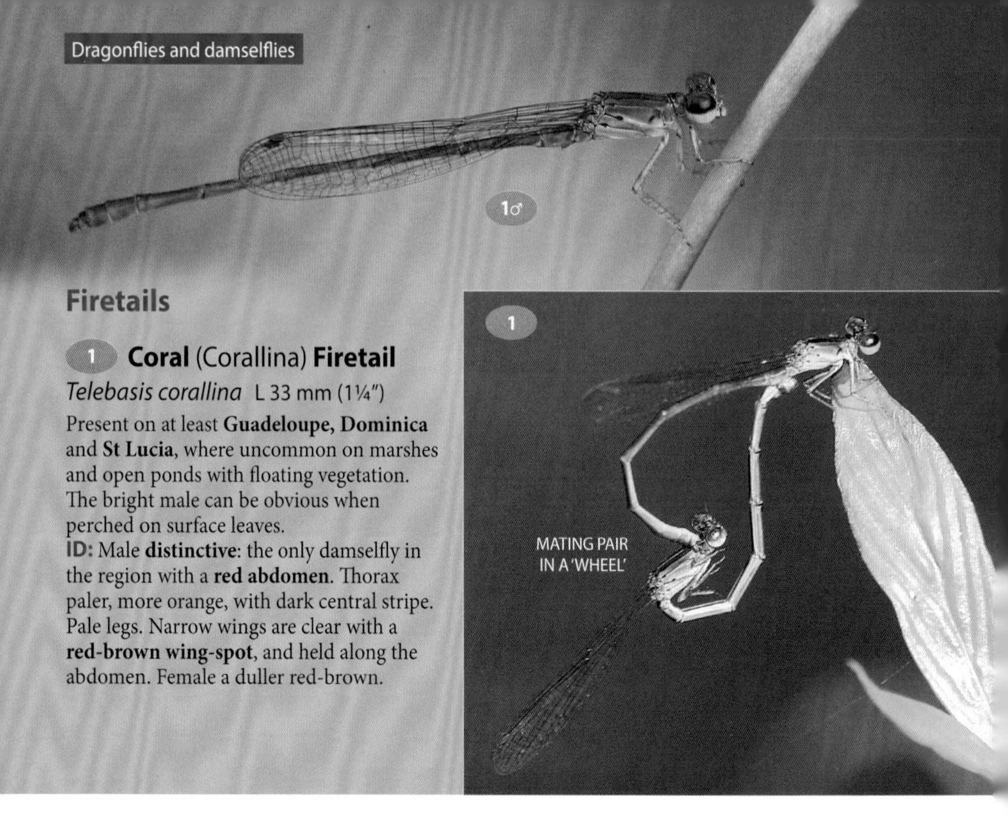

Firetails

1 **Coral** (Corallina) **Firetail**

Telebasis corallina L 33 mm (1¼")

Present on at least **Guadeloupe, Dominica** and **St Lucia**, where uncommon on marshes and open ponds with floating vegetation. The bright male can be obvious when perched on surface leaves.
ID: Male **distinctive**: the only damselfly in the region with a **red abdomen**. Thorax paler, more orange, with dark central stripe. Pale legs. Narrow wings are clear with a **red-brown wing-spot**, and held along the abdomen. Female a duller red-brown.

Threadtails

Distinctive, with a long, very thin abdomen (broadening slightly at tip). Unhurried and delicate in flight: almost seems to fly in slow motion. The three species in the region do not overlap in range.

E 2 Emerald Threadtail *Protoneura viridis* L 37 mm (1½")

Only on the **Virgin Islands**, where uncommon and localized along streams and on ponds.
ID: Male abdomen dark with pale band near tip (segment 7); thorax metallic green with yellow underside. Legs and eyes yellow-green. Female similar, but pale band is at tip of abdomen (segment 9) and thorax and eyes are bright metallic blue-green.

E 3 Guadeloupe Threadtail *Protoneura romanae* L 36 mm (1½")

NT **Endemic to Guadeloupe**, where uncommon and localized, mainly along rainforest streams on Basse Terre and less frequently in marshy forests on Grande Terre.
ID: Very similar to Lesser Antillean Threadtail, but no overlap in range.

E 4 Lesser Antillean Threadtail *Protoneura ailsa* L 36 mm (1½")

NT **Endemic to Dominica, Martinique** and **St Lucia**, where uncommon along shaded rainforest streams and rivers; also occurs in dry forests at lower elevations in southwestern Martinique. Flight is low over water, under banks and among tree roots; settles in fringing vegetation.
ID: Male abdomen distinctive: **very long and slim, black** with narrow pale bands. Thorax **red** with an orange base. Eyes **bright red**; legs pale yellowish. **Wings are short and clear** with a dark wing-spot. Female abdomen slightly shorter and thicker; thorax has green stripes on top.

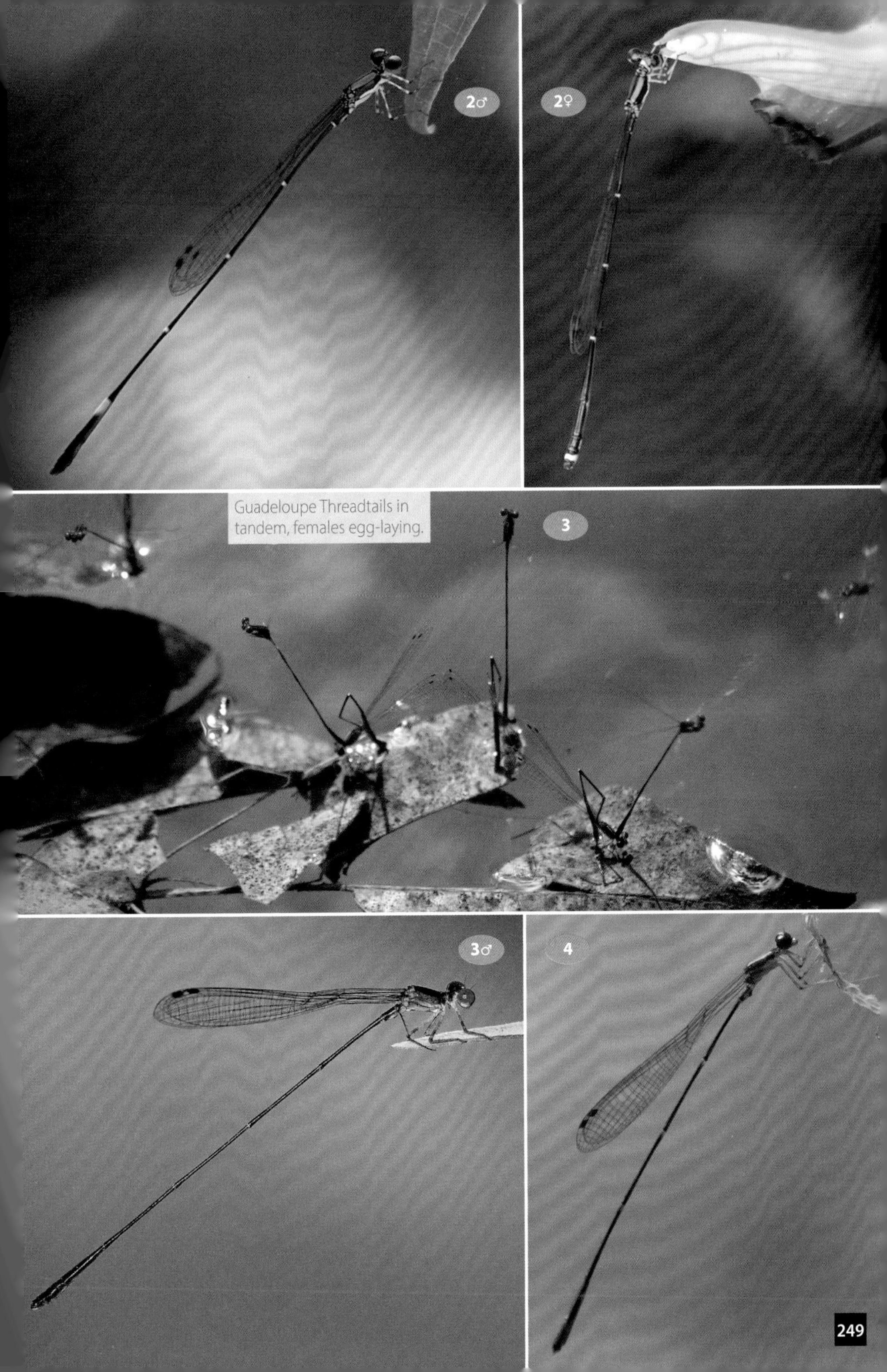

Guadeloupe Threadtails in tandem, females egg-laying.

Bluets

Antillean Bluet *Enallagma coecum* L 39 mm (1½″)

Endemic to the Caribbean: widespread on the **Virgin Islands** and from **Nevis to at least St Lucia**, possibly St Vincent. Uncommon and localized along slow-flowing rivers and streams and around ponds. Flight is smooth: often hovers low over water.
ID: Male abdomen **black, blue at base**, with black U shape on second segment, and a **striking pale blue tip**. Thorax striped black and blue, with obvious blue shoulder-stripes. Eyes black. Narrow clear wings with long wing-spot are **held along abdomen at rest**. Female similar, but abdomen less blue at base and narrower blue band near tip.

Forktails

Very small damselflies found on a range of ponds and shallow wetlands. Forage through vegetation for insects. Less often seen over water than Antillean Bluet.

2 Rambur's Forktail *Ischnura ramburii* L 36 mm (1½″)

Found **throughout**. The commonest damselfly: can occur in large numbers on open and seasonal ponds. Often widely dispersed: readily finds and colonizes new wetlands.
ID: Male abdomen **dark green-black** with **obvious blue band** near tip (complete on segment 8 and base of segment 9 at least). Thorax is green or blue at base and black above, with pale shoulder-stripe. Eyes black above, green below; legs dark. Clear wings with small dark wing-spot are **held along abdomen** at rest. Female occurs in at least two color morphs: can be similar to male, or can have an **orange** thorax with a black central stripe and an orangey base and underside to dark abdomen.

3 Tiny Forktail *Ischnura capreolus* L 25 mm (1″)

Present but uncommon on at least the **Virgin Islands, Montserrat, Guadeloupe, Martinique** and **St Lucia**. Typically flies low among vegetation on sunny ponds and marshes, including grazed areas, and can be hard to spot.
ID: Tiny. Male similar to Rambur's Forktail but distinctly smaller and **dark legs are pale on inner edge**. Blue band near tip of abdomen differs (partial on segment 8, complete on segment 9). Female can be similar to male, or thorax can be greenish with black shoulder-stripe, but is often **bright yellow** with a **thin dark central stripe**.

4 Citrine Forktail *Ischnura hastata* L 27 mm (1″)

Present on at least the **Virgin Islands, Guadeloupe, Dominica** and **Martinique**. Uncommon on marshes, swampy wetlands and ditches with emergent vegetation. A dispersive species, known to be carried long distances on the wind.
ID: Tiny. Male **abdomen yellow** with dark markings, **plain yellow towards tip**. Thorax black but pale at base with fine, pale-green shoulder-stripe. Eyes are black above, paler green-yellow below; obvious **pale legs**. Female **abdomen orange**, becoming dark towards tip; **thorax mostly orange with dark central stripe**. With age both male and female can become darker, more blue-gray overall (pruinosity).

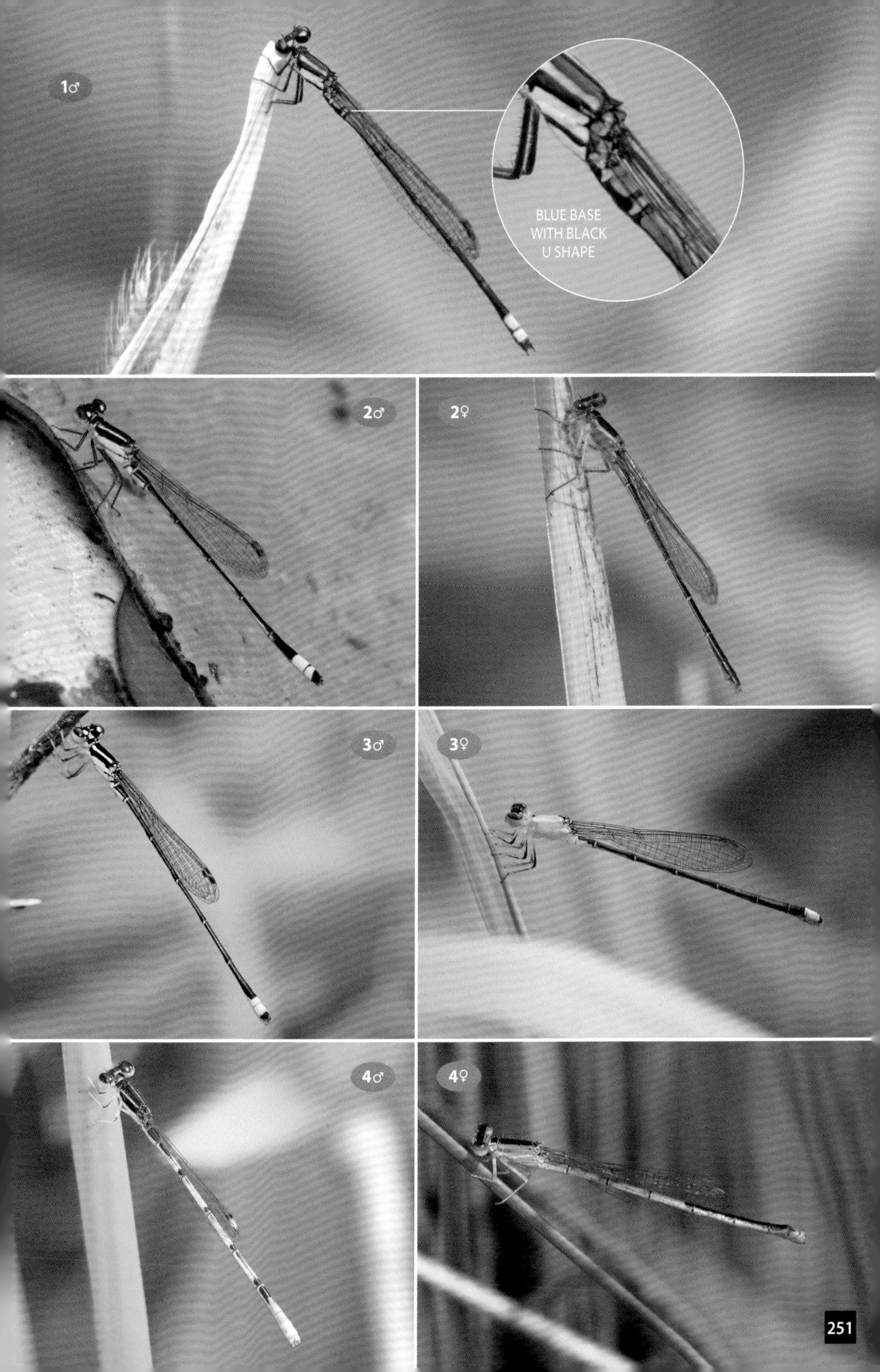
1♂
BLUE BASE
WITH BLACK
U SHAPE
2♂
2♀
3♂
3♀
4♂
4♀

DRAGONFLIES

Darners (hawkers)

The largest dragonflies in the region; **all are uncommon** with fragmented distributions on lowland ponds and marshes or shaded forest pools. Their flight is strong and fast, often at height, with long periods spent on the wing foraging for insects, typically settling vertically at rest. Several similar species occur, but they can be elusive and may be under-recorded.

1 Common Green Darner *Anax junius* L 78 mm (3″)

Recorded on at least the **Virgin Islands, Barbuda, Guadeloupe** and **Martinique**. A highly migratory species; some Caribbean records may be of migrants from North America.
ID: Male abdomen **blue** with **dark central line** widening to an all-dark **tip**; thorax **unmarked green**. Obvious dark, round 'target' spot on forehead. Wings clear with long, pale wing-spots. Female abdomen more brown-green; wings may show amber wash.

2 Pale-green Darner *Triacanthagyna septima* L 66 mm (2½″)

Found on at least **Guadeloupe** (including **Marie-Galante**) and **Martinique**. A **twilight feeder**, it may be under-recorded.
ID: Abdomen long and slender; brown with very fine greenish bars and central line at base. Thorax **unmarked green**; eyes green-blue when mature, green-brown on female and immature; **legs pale yellow**. Wing-spots brown.

3 Caribbean Darner *Triacanthagyna caribbea* L 67 mm (2½″)

Found on at least **Guadeloupe, Martinique** and **St Lucia**, possibly also Dominica. A **twilight feeder**.
ID: Male Similar to Pale-green Darner, but abdomen **narrows at base** and thorax is **strongly banded green and brown**. Eyes blue in mature male, browner in female. Female is similar to male, but abdomen does not narrow at base.

4 Turquoise-tipped Darner *Rhionaeschna psilus* L 69 mm (2¾″)

Only on **Guadeloupe** and **Dominica**.
ID: Male abdomen brown with small, pale, broken bands; **irregular, blue 'anvil' mark** at **narrow** base; and blue beneath the tip. Thorax dark brown with green shoulder-stripe and **two obvious, greenish, angled side-stripes**. Female similar but duller.

RARE OR RESTRICTED-RANGE EMPERORS AND DARNERS	
Species	Recorded on at least…
Vagrant Emperor *Anax ephippiger*	Virgin Islands, St Barthélemy, Guadeloupe, Dominica: a rare transatlantic migrant
Amazon Darner *Anax amazili*	Guadeloupe, St Vincent
Blue-spotted Comet Darner *Anax concolor*	Guadeloupe, Dominica
Blue-faced Darner *Coryphaeschna adnexa*	Guadeloupe
Twilight Darner *Gynacantha nervosa*	Martinique, St Lucia

1♂
1♀
2♂
3♂
4♂
LOOK FOR BLUE
'ANVIL' SHAPE
NEAR BASE OF
ABDOMEN

Clubskimmers and sylphs

e 1 Slender Clubskimmer

Brechmorhoga praecox grenadensis
L 47 mm (1¾″)

Only on **Guadeloupe, Dominica, Martinique, St Lucia** and **Grenada**. A rainforest species, uncommon and localized along mountain streams, especially shallow stretches with gravel or rocky beds. **Perches vertically**. Immatures forage in groups away from water, along forest trails and in forest clearings.
ID: Abdomen slender and **flattened**, widening to form **clubbed tip; dark brown** with two obvious, **elongated pale spots**. Thorax dark with **two pale, angled side-stripes** and pale shoulder-stripes forming **U shape**. Face and **eyes blue**, legs dark. Clear wings with dark wing-spots.

E 2 Antillean Sylph *Macrothemis celeno* L 43 mm (1¾″)

Endemic to the Caribbean, present on at least the **Virgin Islands, Nevis** and **Guadeloupe**; uncommon along forest streams.
ID: Abdomen **slender, black** and can show pale spots at base. Thorax has obvious pale **bluish spots on top and sides**. Striking **pale blue eyes**. Wings are clear with small dark wing-spots, but female may show amber wash.

Pennants

Fly low over water, regularly returning to a favored perch on a twig or stem, settling with abdomen horizontal or raised.

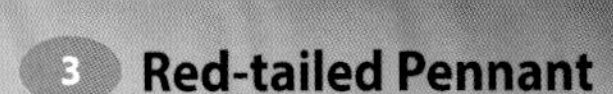

3 Red-tailed Pennant

Brachymesia furcata L 46 mm (1¾")

Widespread, occurring on at least the **Virgin Islands, Nevis, Montserrat** and **from Guadeloupe to Grenada and Barbados**. Locally common, mainly in coastal areas on large, open ponds and marshes. **ID:** Male abdomen **flattened** and swollen at base; **bright red** with **two obvious black spots** near tip. Thorax unmarked red-brown; eyes and face dark red. Wings (often held slightly forward when perched) are clear with long, pale red-brown wing-spots and can show brown wash at base of hindwing. Female similar but duller, more red-brown.

4 Tawny Pennant

Brachymesia herbida

L 46 mm (1¾")

Widespread, occurring on at least the **Virgin Islands** and **from Nevis to Grenada**. Locally common on low-lying open wetlands, including newly created ponds. Perches on vegetation low above water. **ID:** Abdomen flattened, swollen at base; **yellow** with **strong black central line** but becoming **all-dark at tip**. Thorax **brown** and **distinctively hairy**; eyes and legs dark. Wings have obvious **amber wash** and pale brown wing-spots.

Dragonlets and skimmers

1 Band-winged Dragonlet *Erythrodiplax umbrata* L 45 mm (1¾")

Found **throughout**: one of the most widely distributed species. Common on ponds, marshes and temporary pools, even small puddles. The male is the most obvious and easily recognized dragonfly in the region. Typically perches horizontally with wings held slightly forward.
ID: Male **abdomen and thorax dark**; can develop blue-gray pruinose bloom. Wings clear with **distinctive bold, black central bands**. Female abdomen **yellow** with **brown central stripe** and broken side-stripes leading to an **all-dark tip**. Thorax brown with **obvious pale central stripe**. Wings clear, can show amber tips.

2 Seaside Dragonlet *Erythrodiplax berenice* L 35 mm (1½")

Locally common on the **Virgin Islands** and **Guadeloupe**; uncommon to rare elsewhere. Found in mangroves and brackish lagoons: the only dragonfly breeding in these saline habitats.
ID: Male small and slender. **Abdomen and thorax black**, becoming pruinose blue with age. **Eyes dark purple-black**; wings **clear** with long, dark wing-spots. Female **abdomen yellow** with darker sides and tip; can become black or blue with age. Thorax **finely striped yellow and black**.

3 Red-faced Dragonlet *Erythrodiplax fusca* L 28 mm (1")

Only on **St Vincent, the Grenadines** and **Grenada**. Uncommon on shallow ponds and streams.
ID: Male abdomen a **striking pale blue, dark red at base and tip**. Head, face and thorax **dark red-brown**. Wings clear with long dark wing-spots; can show obvious **red patch** at base of hindwing. Female similar to female Band-winged Dragonlet but is smaller, and abdomen has an unbroken side-stripe.

Red-mantled Dragonlet *Erythrodiplax fervida*

Rare and restricted to **St Vincent and Grenada**.

E 4 Lesser Antillean (Antillean Purple) Skimmer
Orthemis macrostigma L 56 mm (2¼")

Endemic to the Lesser Antilles, widespread from **St Martin/Sint Maarten to St Vincent and Barbados**. Common on ponds, marshes, ditches and man-made wetlands: one of the region's most obvious and easily seen species. *Orthemis* skimmers are also found on the Virgin Islands, St Vincent and Grenada but need confirming to species level.
ID: Male abdomen **bright red**, broad and slightly flattened. Thorax **pink-red** becoming pruinose purple-red with age. Eyes purple-red. Wings are clear with **long, dark wing-spots, held slightly forward at rest**. Female paler and browner; thorax has three thin, pale side-stripes and **pale central stripe extending onto base of abdomen**.

1♂
1♀
2♂
2♀
3♂
3♀
4♂
4♀

Dashers, setwings and pondhawks

1 Spot-tailed Dasher *Micrathyria aequalis* L 33 mm (1¼")

Widespread on **Nevis** and from **Guadeloupe to Grenada**; absent from Barbados, with occasional records elsewhere. Locally common on lowland ponds and marshes, perches with **wings held well forward** and abdomen often raised.
ID: Small. Male abdomen slender, **pale blue to black** with **two obvious white triangles** near slightly **enlarged black tip**. Thorax gray-blue: can develop gray-blue pruinose bloom. Face white, **eyes bright green-blue**. Slender, clear wings with dark wing-spots. Female abdomen broader and black with pairs of yellowish, elongated triangular spots; thorax dark with **irregular, fine, yellowish stripes**; eyes a duller green blue.

2 Three-striped Dasher *Micrathyria didyma* L 41mm (1½")

Found from **Guadeloupe to Grenada**; absent from Barbados. Uncommon on coastal marshes and shaded forest ponds. Typically perches with wings held forward and slightly spread.
ID: Male abdomen black with pale, elongated side-spots and **two pale, squarish spots** near the slightly enlarged black tip. **Thorax striped black and yellow**. Eyes red on top. Wings slender with dark wing-spots. Female similar, but with stronger yellow markings along abdomen.

3 Brown Setwing *Dythemis sterilis* L 44 mm (1¾")

Widespread from Nevis to Grenada; absent from Barbados. Locally common in open situations along forest streams. Perches at the ends of twigs and vegetation, with **wings typically held well forward** of head.
ID: Abdomen **strikingly thin**; black with **elongated yellow spots** before all-dark tip. Thorax brown with pale central stripe and **yellow side-stripes**. Eyes bright red-brown; legs dark. Wings clear with black wing-spots; female **can show faint brown wash.**

4 Great Pondhawk *Erythemis vesiculosa* L 60 mm (2¾")

Widespread, probably occurs **throughout**. Locally common on ponds and coastal marshes and along forest margins. Typically occurs in small numbers at any site but usually conspicuous and easy to see. An aggressive predator: perches low on rocks and twigs, flying up to catch insects, including dragonflies of its own size. Long spines on legs are used to catch and hold prey.
ID: Abdomen long, **slender and flattened; bright green** with **dark bands** that widen to form all-dark tip. Thorax **unmarked green**; head and eyes green. Wings are slender and clear with long, green-gray wing-spots; typically held slightly forward.

1♂
1♀
2♂
2♀
3♂
3
Subspecies only on St Vincent, *D. s. multipunctate.*
4
Great Pondhawk with
Rambur's Forktail prey.

Amberwings

1 **Slough Amberwing** *Perithemis domitia* L 23 mm (1″)

Restricted to the **Virgin Islands**, where uncommon on marshes and ponds. A small skimmer that perches on twigs and vegetation, often with wings slightly raised and spread.
ID: Tiny. Male abdomen **broad, brown with yellow central stripe**; thorax brown with angled yellow shoulder- and side-stripes. **Wings** distinctively **bright amber** with prominent red wing-spots. Female browner, **wings more marked**, with **amber base, dark border and spots**.

Gliders

Long-winged with broad hindwings, gliders are able to spend long periods in flight; most hang vertically when perched.

2 **Hyacinth Glider** *Miathyria marcella* L 40 mm (1½″)

Widespread but uncommon from **St Kitts and Nevis to St Lucia** on lowland ponds and marshes with floating vegetation, particularly invasive Water Hyacinth *Eichhornia crassipes* and Water Lettuce *Pistia stratiotes*. Often seen foraging away from water.
ID: Perches vertically or slightly angled. Male abdomen broad and **flattened**, narrowing at base and tip; **yellow-orange** with **dark central line** and dark tip. Thorax red-brown with two whitish side-stripes. Can develop purple pruinose bloom. Eyes red-brown; legs dark. Wings have small dark wing-spots and may show amber wash and veins. **Hindwing** has obvious **dark base**, resembling saddlebags (*p. 262*). Female similar but duller.

3 **Wandering Glider** *Pantala flavescens* L 50 mm (2″)

Widespread from the **Virgin Islands to Grenada**; absent from Barbados. Locally common on ponds, lagoons and seasonal wetlands; egg-laying has even been recorded in puddles and swimming pools! Spends much time on the wing; flight strong, includes lengthy glides. Often seen foraging away from water in open habitats. A migratory species, this is one of the great insect travelers, capable of wandering long distances, even over oceans.
ID: Male abdomen broader at base, **orange-yellow** with a **reddish central line** that broadens at tip. Thorax yellow-brown, **looks yellow overall in flight**. Face yellow; eyes red. Wings have small red wing-spots and can show **amber wash at tip**; **hindwing** obviously **broad at base**. Female similar, but abdomen lacks orange tones.

RARE OR RESTRICTED-RANGE GLIDERS	
Species	Recorded on at least ...
Garnet Glider *Tauriphilia australis*	Guadeloupe, Martinique, St Lucia
Spot-winged Glider *Pantala hymenaea*	Virgin Islands, St Barthélemy, Guadeloupe, Martinique, Grenada; an occasional migrant

4 **Evening Skimmer** *Tholymis citrina* L 53 mm (2″)

Found on at least **Guadeloupe, Martinique and St Lucia**, where uncommon and localized on shaded coastal and forest ponds and in swamps and mangroves. A **twilight species** that can be seen foraging at dusk and dawn along trails, in open areas and around external artificial lights. Immatures forage together in groups.
ID: Abdomen and thorax **unmarked pale gray-brown** to darker brown. Eyes darker gray-brown to green; legs pale. Wings clear with dark wing-spots and an irregular **amber patch in central hindwing**. **Perches vertically**, often hanging from a twig.

1♂
2♂
1♀
3♂
4

Saddlebags

Spend long periods on the wing, often foraging for insects low over water, then settling horizontally on a low perch. These species typically have an obvious dark base to the hindwing ('saddlebag').

1 Vermilion Saddlebags

Tramea abdominalis L 50 mm (2")

Widespread from the **Virgin Islands to Grenada and Barbados**. The most commonly seen saddlebags on ponds and seasonal wetlands; a pioneer species at new sites.

ID: Male abdomen **bright red with two black spots near tip**; thorax duller. **Face** and eyes **red**; legs dark. Wings clear with small **red wing-spots** and obvious **dark red base** to **hindwing**. Female similar to male, but face and thorax browner.

2 Antillean Saddlebags

Tramea insularis L 49 mm (2")

Only on **Nevis** and from **Guadeloupe to Grenada**; absent from St Vincent and Barbados. A migratory species. Very similar to Vermilion Saddlebags and difficult to separate in the field. **Face and eyes** much **darker**; forehead a dark metallic purple.

3 Sooty Saddlebags

Tramea binotata L 51 cm (2")

Only on **Guadeloupe, St Lucia** and possibly **Barbados**. Uncommon on ponds and open wetlands.

ID: Male abdomen and thorax **black**; can develop blue-gray pruinose bloom. Wings clear with small dark wing-spots and **narrow black base to hindwing**. Female abdomen red-brown with thin black bands and **strong black tip**.

RARE OR RESTRICTED-RANGE SADDLEBAGS

Species	Recorded on at least ...
Striped Saddlebags *Tramea calverti*	St Barthélemy, Guadeloupe, Martinique; a migratory species
Red Saddlebags *Tramea onusta*	Virgin Islands
Keyhole Glider *Tramea basilaris*	Guadeloupe, Martinque; a rare vagrant from Africa

Butterflies

From the tiny Hanno Blue flitting over short coastal grassland to the long-winged Julia Heliconian flashing vibrant orange along a shaded forest trail, butterflies are on the wing year-round in the Eastern Caribbean. There are over 60 resident species, many of which are found more widely in the Caribbean and the Americas. At least 11 are endemic to the region, while others occur as distinct subspecies on individual or groups of islands. You can see them in gardens and along forest trails, but often the easiest way of finding a range of butterflies is to stop at any small patch of grassland or scrub that is rich in flowering plants.

Butterflies are active and dynamic insects. Many are restless when feeding, visiting a succession of flowers for nectar; others readily settle to feed on rotting fruit. Some white and sulphur butterflies gather to 'mud-puddle', taking in salts and minerals from areas of damp mud or fresh animal dung. In some species the male patrols or defends a territory, chasing away rivals and searching for females. After pairing and mating, the female lays eggs on particular plant species that provide a larval food source. This marks the start of a life cycle from egg via larva (caterpillar) and pupa to adult. Many species breed throughout the year, while others are linked to dry or wet seasons. One of the main threats to butterflies and many other invertebrates is the reduction of native larval food plants through habitat loss, together with the impact of invasive plant species.

All common or widespread butterflies are described; for completeness, rare or highly localized species are listed. Some of these occur in a number of subspecies, several endemic to the region, with subtle variations in appearance that are not easily distinguished in the field. Knowledge of status, distribution and population trends varies between islands and can be limited, so sharing your sightings will add valuable data (submitted locally or through iNaturalist). Ongoing research is leading to revisions in classification, with changes being made to both scientific and common names; it is likely that some subspecies will be recognized as full species in the future.

Many butterflies are distinctive, so identification can be straightforward, but views in the field are often brief and inconclusive. Where possible, similar species are grouped together on a page, which means that they are not always in strict systematic order. If distinctly different, males and females are each described.

SKIPPERS

Brown or orange butterflies, named after their erratic, skipping flight. Typically lacking bold markings and coloration, they are tricky to identify, requiring careful attention to fine details—and can be easily overlooked.

Large skippers with short tail, or no tail, to hindwing

Mainly found in open areas, scrub and dry forest margins.

e 1 Mercurial Skipper *Proteides mercurius* FW 36 mm (1⅜″)

Present in three subspecies on at least **Guadeloupe, Dominica, Martinique, St Lucia, St Vincent** and **Grenada**. Flight is strong and rapid, the male chasing intruders from its territory. Settles on the underside of leaves and twigs with wings closed but also basks or nectars with wings partially open.
ID: Large with **long forewings** that extend well beyond hindwings when closed. Upperwings dark brown, with contrasting **golden-yellow** at base. A row of four pale spots across center of forewing and two tiny spots near forewing tip can also be visible on underwing. Underside of hindwing is **darker at base** with **obvious large pale patch** in center. Head and thorax **golden-yellow**; abdomen heavy and banded.

2 Zestos Skipper *Epargyreus zestos zestos* FW 27 mm (1″)

Widespread but uncommon from the **Virgin Islands to Grenada**, typically found close to the ground in low scrub and forest margins, often near the coast. Flight is fast and low, tending to settle with wings closed, rarely showing upperwings.
ID: Long forewings; very short tail on hindwing. Upperwings brown, slightly paler at base, with band of **large golden spots** across center of forewing and three tiny dots near wing-tip. Underside of hindwings broadly banded, paler **purple-brown and darker brown**, often stronger in female.

e 3 Hammock Skipper *Polygonus leo* FW 23 mm (1″)

Widespread and locally common from the **Virgin Islands to at least St Lucia**. Flies quickly and erratically in and out of vegetation, typically in low- to mid-canopy forest. Individuals or small groups **rest on underside of leaves** with wings closed but nectar with open wings.
ID: Upperwings dark brown, can show **violet-blue at base**. Forewing has **three large, broadly rectangular white spots** near center and **three tiny squarish spots** in a line near tip, all visible on underwing. Under hindwings are **banded** with an **obvious dark spot** near base of leading margin and can show purplish hue. Very short tail.

4 Manuel's Skipper *Polygonus savigny (manueli) punctus* FW 25 mm (1″)

Widespread but uncommon from **St Martin/Sint Maarten to Grenada**, found in scrub and dry forest at lower elevations, often around coasts. Settles on or underneath leaves, often high in bushes.
ID: Similar to Hammock Skipper with some overlap in range and not easy to separate. The **three tiny white spots** near upper forewing-tip are slightly more rounded, less square. Underside of hindwing paler brown; lacks purple hue with smaller or **no obvious dark spot** near base of leading margin.

1
1
2
2
3
3
OBVIOUS
DARK SPOT
4
4
SMALL OR NO SPOT

1 Yellow-tipped Flasher (Roy's Skipper)

Astraptes anaphus anausis (Telegonus anausis) FW 26 mm (1")

Uncommon, occurring on at least the **Virgin Islands** and from **Montserrat to Grenada**. Typically found at lower to mid-elevations along forest margins, trails and adjoining areas rich in flowering plants. Often rests on the upper surface of large leaves.
ID: Upperwings brown with two **darker brown bands** across both wings, which are **visible on the underwings; very short tail**. Settles with **wings angled backwards**. The subspecies *A. a. anausis* found in the Eastern Caribbean lacks the obvious yellow-edged hind margins and tail that account for its common name.

e 2 Lesser Sicklewing *Eantis minor (Achlyodes thraso)* FW 26 mm (1")

Occurs on at least the **Virgin Islands** and from **Montserrat to Dominica**. Uncommon in both dry forest and rainforest. Flight is low and swift, typically along forest margins, but readily stops to bask or nectar with wings spread. Taxonomy has been subject to change and may still be unsettled.
ID: Distinctive forewing shape with **slightly hooked tip**. Male upperwings dark with **purplish hues** and subtle markings, including a **paler band around outer margins**. Female similar but paler.

Two very similar **duskywing skippers** in the genus *Ephyriades* occur. Both settle with wings open and are difficult to separate in the field, especially females. There is continuing uncertainty over distribution and status of *Ephyriades* species in the region, including *E. zephodes*, which occurs on Hispaniola and was formerly considered to occur in the Virgin Islands.

3 Caribbean (Hairy) Duskywing *Ephyriades arcas arcas* FW 21 mm (⅞")

Widespread from the **Virgin Islands to Guadeloupe**, where locally common in scrub and dry forest. Flight is swift and erratic, in and out of shrubs, but this butterfly can be conspicuous when settled or nectaring on low flowers.
ID: Male upperwings are striking **dark purple-black**, with a 'fold' near the leading margin of forewing. A tiny white spot near tip of underside of forewing is difficult to see (but is absent entirely in Florida Duskywing). Female upperwings brown and obviously banded. Upper forewings have an **uneven line of large white spots** across center and smaller white spots near tip, which together form a **loose circle**.

e 4 Florida (Jamaican) Duskywing *Ephyriades brunnea dominicensis* FW 18 mm (¾")

Endemic subspecies occurs on at least **Nevis, Dominica** and **Guadeloupe** (and may be considered a full species in the future). Uncommon in forest clearings, margins and disturbed land at lower elevations. Flight is low and erratic; readily settles on low flowering shrubs and flowers to nectar with wings spread.
ID: Forewings slightly narrower and more pointed at tip than Caribbean Duskywing. Male **upperwings brown**, slightly darker at base (this subspecies, unlike others, has no spots on upper forewing). Underwings plain with no white spot on forewing-tip. Female similar to Caribbean Duskywing, including forewing spots forming loose circle, but wings more obviously **banded dark brown and purplish** (especially when fresh).

4♀ *E. b. brunnea*, photographed on Cuba (but no discernible differences in the field between females of these two subspecies).

1
1
2
3♂
3♀
4♂
4♀

Large skippers with obvious tail to hindwing

These skippers are found in grassy areas and along forest margins.

1 **Long-tailed Skipper** *Urbanus proteus domingo* FW 25 mm (1″)

Common **throughout**: the most widespread of the long-tailed skippers. Flight is erratic, often looping in and out of vegetation, then settling with wings fully or partially open.
ID: One of the largest skippers. Distinctive with **long tail** and **blue-green** on **head, body** and **base of upperwings**. A loose circle **of bold white translucent spots on forewing** is visible on underwing. Bold dark barring and spotting on underside of hindwing **does not reach leading margin**.

E **St Vincent Longtail** *Chioides vintra* FW 23 mm (¾″)

Only on **St Vincent, the Grenadines** and **Grenada**. May be endemic, as there is some uncertainty about the distribution of *Chioides* in the wider region.
ID: Uniform brown, **lacks any blue-green**. Upperwing has three small spots near tip in an **even row** and a **dark triangular spot** near tip of underwing. Under hindwing markings include two large dark spots at edge of leading margin.

E 2 **Dark Longtail** (Stub-tailed Skipper) *Thorybes (Urbanus) obscurus* FW 23 mm (¾″)

Endemic to the Lesser Antilles: widespread from **St Martin/Sint Maarten to St Vincent** including **Barbados**. One of the few skippers reaching higher elevations in rainforests. There is some uncertainty about the respective distribution and status of this species and the very similar Dorantes Longtail, but there may actually be no overlap in range.
ID: Similar to Long-tailed Skipper but **lacks blue-green** and **tail** is **noticeably shorter**. Upperwings darker brown, forewings have **fewer and smaller spots**. Three small spots near tip of forewing **not in an even row**. Dark bands on underside of hindwing are less distinct.

3 **Dorantes Longtail** (Skipper) *Thorybes (Urbanus) dorantes* FW 23 mm (¾″)

Present only on the **Virgin Islands**, more widely in the Greater Antilles and southern USA. Similar to Dark Longtail, but no overlap in range.
ID: Similar to Long-tailed Skipper (which overlaps in range) but browner, **lacks blue-green**, and has fewer and less distinct spots on upper forewing.

1
1
2
2
3
3

Small golden-orange skippers

These species occur in open areas with low vegetation. Distinctive when settled, as the hindwings are half closed and the forewings are raised above the body.

1 **Fiery Skipper** *Hylephila phyleus phyleus* FW 17 mm (¾")

Found **throughout**: the most common small orange skipper. Often conspicuous in rough grassland and along open forest margins from low to mid-elevations. Flight is rapid and mostly low. Territorial males patrol over vegetation, regularly settling on leaves or other vantage points.
ID: Male upperwings **rich orange** with **jagged dark wedges on outer margins**. Underwings **pale orange** with **indistinct circle of small dark spots**. Female upperwings dark brown with uneven lines of **large, squarish orange spots** showing as **paler areas** on underwings.

E 2 **Dictynna Skipper** (Lesser Whirlabout) *Polites (Hedone) dictynna* FW 14 mm (½")

Endemic to the Lesser Antilles, present on at least **St Kitts, Dominica, St Lucia, St Vincent, the Grenadines** and **Grenada**. Uncommon in rough grassland and gardens and along tracks and trails. Flies slowly through ground cover.
ID: Upperwings mostly **golden-orange** with **solid, less jagged dark outer margins**. Male has a **dark bar in center of forewing**, absent in female. Underside of forewing has a dark brown patch at base, not always visible; underside of hindwing is a **plain orange-brown**.

E 3 **Fiery Broken-dash** *Polites (Wallengrenia) ophites* FW 15 mm (½")

Endemic to the Lesser Antilles and Trinidad: present on at least **St Kitts, Guadeloupe, Dominica** and **Martinique**. Uncommon in open grassland and along forest margins from low to mid-elevations. Flies low amid vegetation; can be unobtrusive. Upperwings of both male and female are much more strongly marked dark brown than on the similar Dictynna Skipper.
ID: Male upper forewing orange, with **broad dark brown outer and inner margins** and **bold dark 'broken dash'** at center. Hindwings orange with **dark leading margin**. Underwings **unmarked** pale orange-brown. Female upperwings much **browner** with **orange patches** on upper forewing.

E 4 **V-mark Skipper** *Choranthus vitellius* FW 14 mm (½")

Endemic to the Caribbean, present on at least the **Virgin Islands and St Martin/Sint Maarten**. Uncommon in grassy clearings in scrub and dry forest. Flight is slow, mostly low over vegetation.
ID: Similar to Fiery Broken-dash, but no overlap in range. Upper forewings bright orange with **dark brown wing-tips and outer margins**, and **dark V mark** near center. Upper hindwings have dark leading and outer margins; under hindwings are pale **unmarked** orange.

1♂
1♀
1♂
1♀
2♂
2
2
3♂
3♀
3
4
4

Small to medium-sized brown skippers

Five similar species that settle with their wings closed, held vertically along abdomen, or partially open (*see p. 270*). Male and female of each species are similar.

1 **Brazilian** (Canna) **Skipper** *Calpodes ethlius* FW 26 mm (1″)

Can occur **throughout** wherever canna plants *Canna* spp. have been introduced, often in formal gardens and cultivated areas. Most active early morning and evening. Flight is strong and powerful. Larvae may be dispersed through shipments of ornamental canna.
ID: Long forewing **extends beyond hindwing** at rest. Upperwings dark brown at outer margins, paler brown at base. **Four large pale spots** in center of forewing and **three very small spots towards tip**, visible on under forewing. Underwings brown, with **three or four small white spots forming a line** on hindwing.

2 **Purple-washed** (Sugar Cane) **Skipper** *Panoquina lucas lucas (sylvicola)* FW 18 mm (¾″)

Can occur **throughout**, more often on islands with sugar cane; larval plants include sugar cane and a range of grasses. Uncommon in scrub and on rough grassland, mainly at lower elevations.
ID: Similar to Brazilian Skipper but smaller. At rest, long forewing **extends beyond hindwing**. Largest white spot in center of upper forewing is **arrow-shaped**, and there are three **tiny spots** near tip. Under hindwing **purplish** or brown with **six to seven pale spots** (*i.e.*, more than Brazilian) near center, forming a **vertical line** on closed wing.

e 3 **Violet-banded** (Nyctelius) **Skipper** *Nyctelius nyctelius agari* FW 19 mm (¾″)

Present from at least **Antigua to St Vincent**. Uncommon in rough grassland, dry scrub and along forest margins. Flight is swift and darting.
ID: Upperwings mid-brown, with **pale spots** in center of forewing. Of these, **one is obviously larger and squarer**, while **three very small spots** form a line **set back from wing-tip**; all are visible on underwings. Under hindwing banded dark and pale violet (when fresh), with **obvious dark spot** near leading margin.

e 4 **Obscure** (Beach) **Skipper** *Panoquina panoquinoides* FW 13 mm (½″)

Widespread but may be present **throughout**. Localized in dunes, beachside scrub and mangrove fringes. Flight is low and fast over coastal grasses.
ID: Dull brown overall. Upper forewing has four yellowish or white spots (rarely visible as wings held closed at rest). Underwings show obvious **pale veins** and **two very small** white spots near tip. A broken **line of three pale spots** on hindwing can be faint and difficult to see.

5 **Three-spotted Skipper** *Cymaenes tripunctus tripunctus* FW 15 mm (½″)

Only recorded on the **Virgin Islands**, where locally common in grassland and along forest margins and scrub at lower elevations. Bouncy flight; readily settles on low vegetation with closed wings.
ID: Brown overall with obvious **paler wing-veins**. Upper forewing has two pale central spots and a **line of three tiny spots near tip** that are **visible on underwing** at rest (hence name). Underwings paler, with uneven **line of faint spots in center of hindwing**.

1
1
2
2
3
3
4
5

Checkered skippers

Small, highly patterned butterflies of grassland, scrub and forest margins.

1 Tropical Checkered-Skipper *Burnsius (Pyrgus) oileus* FW 14 mm (½")

Found from the **Virgin Islands to Dominica**. A distinctive species over most of its range. Common along roadsides and trails and in rough grassland. Flight low with rapid changes of direction; readily settles with wings open.
ID: Male upperwings **finely checkered very dark brown and white**; appears **blue and hairy** at **base of upperwings and body**. Underwings paler: hindwing lightly patterned, with a distinctive small **dark rectangular spot** in center of leading margin. Female similar, but **upperwings browner**, less boldly checkered.

2 Orcus Checkered-Skipper *Burnsius (Pyrgus) orcus* FW 14 mm (½")

Found from **Martinique to Grenada, including Barbados**. Formerly a subspecies of Tropical Checkered-Skipper but is now considered a separate species with no overlap in range. Similar to Tropical Checkered-Skipper but **lacks small rectangular spot** at center of leading margin of under hindwing.

e 3 White-patterned (St Vincent Grizzled) Skipper
Chiomara asychis FW 17 mm (¾")

Restricted to **St Lucia, St Vincent, the Grenadines** and **Grenada**; occurs more widely in Central and South America. Uncommon in clearings and along shady trails in dry forests. Flight weak and fluttery; often settles with wings open.
ID: Upperwings **brown**, strongly marked with **white bands and squares** and an **obvious large white patch** on hindwing. Underwings much paler with reduced dark markings.

Grassland margins with low flowering plants attract a range of butterflies.

1♂
1♀
1
2
SMALL RECTANGULAR SPOT
IN CENTER OF LEADING
MARGIN OF HINDWING
2♂
2♀
3
3

Mid-sized white butterflies

Two species of white butterfly are present in the region; both are widespread and similar in appearance. They can be seen over grasslands, low scrub and along sunny margins and readily congregate at muddy puddles (mud-puddling) and on fresh animal dung, often with sulphur butterflies (below). Both are known for sporadic large-scale migrations, but the Eastern Caribbean populations are more sedentary. They are most often seen settled with wings closed or slightly spread.

	1 **Great Southern White** *Ascia monuste* e	2 **Florida White** *Glutophrissa (Appias) drusilla* e
Distribution	The most numerous white butterfly; occurs **throughout** in two subspecies. Large numbers can be seen low over open habitats.	Found **throughout** in three subspecies; more common on the northern islands. Usually seen in smaller numbers.
Size	FW 31 mm (1¼")	FW 28 mm (1⅛")
Male upperwing	**Chalky white**. Forewing has fine **black wing-tip** and **outer margin** with distinctive **jagged black wedges** that extend along veins.	Brilliant **clean white** with very **fine black leading margin** to forewing (can be visible at rest).
Male underwing	Forewing white, wing-tip pale yellow to pale brown. Hindwing ranges from plain yellow to white, with darker or more pronounced veins.	Creamy-white with **small yellow patch** at base (not always easy to see).
Female upperwing	Bold dark wing-tip and outer margin with **jagged wedges along veins**.	White with fine **black border to outer margin of forewing**, visible on underwing. **No wedges along veins**.
Female underwing	More **heavily marked**, especially hindwing, with **pale brown along and between veins**.	Unmarked creamy-white with **small yellow patch** at base, not always easy to see.
Antennae	**Obvious blue-white tip** to antenna club.	**Small white tip** to antenna club.

Large sulphur butterflies

Mostly seen in flight, settling only briefly with wings closed, making identification difficult. Sexes differ slightly: females are usually paler and can appear white at distance. Males in particular gather for prolonged periods on wet mud, often with other species. Most commonly seen along forest margins and in gardens, often flying at height.

3 Cloudless Sulphur *Phoebis sennae sennae* FW 33 mm (1¼")

Occurs **throughout**; the most common and widespread large sulphur. Fast-flying and wide-ranging, this is a sun-loving species, hence its common name.

ID: Male upperwings **pure yellow, margins slightly paler**. Underwings yellow, **lightly but variably marked** with pink-brown lines and spots. Two small **dark-bordered white spots in center** of both wings are more obvious on hindwing. Female upperwings paler, yellow-cream. Underwings more marked, can show fine pinkish border to outer margin.

1♂
DISTINCTIVE
BLACK WEDGES ON
OUTER MARGINS
1♂
1♀
2♂
2♀
PHOTOGRAPHED
ON CUBA
3♂
3♀

Photographed on Cuba.

e 1 Large Orange Sulphur *Phoebis agarithe* FW 37 mm (1½")

Widespread but uncommon in two subspecies from **St Kitts to Grenada**, including **Barbados**; may be absent from some islands. Often difficult to see, as it normally flies high in the canopy but will descend to nectar on low flowers.

ID: Mostly settles with wings closed. Underwings **deep yellow**, lightly spotted and speckled, with a short, **unbroken vertical red-brown line** on forewing and two dark-edged **white spots** in center of hindwing. Upperwings, typically only seen in flight, are an **unmarked rich orange** in male, paler in female, with **dark reddish spots on outer margin** and **single spot in center** of forewing.

2 Apricot Sulphur *Phoebis argante argante* FW 35 mm (1⅜")

Present on at least **St Lucia, St Vincent** and **Grenada**, where uncommon along forest margins.

ID: Similar to Large Orange Sulphur, but male has small **black dots at outer margin** of upperwings and short, **broken** (interrupted) vertical red-brown line on under forewing. Female upperwing has larger dots at outer margin of both wings and a dark spot in center of forewing; underwing markings similar to male but stronger.

3 Straight-lined Sulphur *Rhabdodryas (Phoebis) trite watsoni* FW 33 mm (1¼")

Widespread but uncommon, occurring from at least **St Kitts to St Vincent**. Tends to fly high in the forest canopy, making it very difficult to see and identify. Males descend and congregate at wet mud.

ID: Similar to Cloudless Sulphur, but underwings are an unmarked **pale green-yellow** (slightly paler and more cream in female) with obvious **vertical green-brown line** across both wings, which gives its common name.

4 Statira (Migrant) Sulphur *Aphrissa statira statira* FW 31 mm (1¼")

Uncommon migrant, recorded at least on **Tortola** (BVI), **Guadeloupe, Dominica, Martinique, St Lucia** and **St Vincent**.

ID: Male upperwings two-toned: **basal half lemon-yellow, outer half** obviously paler. Underwings **unmarked** pale yellow with a distinctive **whiter patch** towards base of upperwing (not always visible). Female more marked; upper forewing has a **dark central spot, dark wing-tip** and a **dark outer margin** (all visible on underwing). An irregular line of reddish spots runs across underwings, with two uneven pale spots in center of hindwing.

Straight-lined and Statira Sulphurs mud-puddling.

Small yellow butterflies

These butterflies are found in scrubby herb-rich grassland and margins. Their flight is low and erratic. All settle with wings closed, rarely showing upperwings.

1 Little Yellow (Little Sulphur) *Eurema lisa euterpe* FW 17 mm (⅝")

Common **throughout**: the most numerous and widespread small yellow. Flight is low and weak; males congregate to mud-puddle.
ID: Male upperwings **sulphur-yellow** with **bold black wing-tips and outer margins**, jagged on inner edge. Female upperwings paler; black outer margin is incomplete on forewing, fragmented on hindwing. In both sexes, **underwings** are yellow to cream with small dark dots along outer margins, and hindwing has **two very small black spots at base**, black spot near center and large **reddish spot near wing-tip** (overall **more marked than other small yellows**).

2 Leuce Yellow *Pyrisitia leuce antillarum* (formerly Hall's Sulphur *Eurema leuce*) FW 19 mm (¾")

Locally common, at least on **St Martin/Sint Maarten, St Kitts and Nevis, Guadeloupe, Dominica** and **St Lucia**. Often in forest clearings and margins; tends to fly higher than other small yellow species.
ID: Wings broad and rounded. Upperwings **lemon-yellow**, slightly paler in female, with narrow **black tip** to forewing and **no black border to hindwing**. Male underwings largely **unmarked yellow**; female is similar but has an **obvious reddish spot** near tip of each wing and two very small black spots in center of hindwing.

e 3 Pale Yellow *Pyrisitia venusta emanona* (formerly Little Yellow *Eurema venusta*) FW 17 mm (⅝")

Widespread from **Montserrat to Grenada**, where locally common along dry forest margins and clearings.
ID: Upper forewing **bright lemon-yellow** with fine dark line along leading margin, **dark wing-tip and outer margin**. Hindwing is **contrastingly pale yellow to white**. Underwings **pale yellow** and largely unmarked but can show a faint dark spot in center of hindwing. Female similar to male, but upper forewing paler and under hindwing can show subtle dark markings.

Barred Yellow and Banded Yellow

Two very similar species that occur **throughout** with subtle seasonal variations in their underwing markings. Male upperwing bar is the most reliable identification feature but is difficult to see, making identification challenging.

4 Barred Yellow *Eurema daira palmira* FW 17 mm (⅝")

ID: Male upper **forewing yellow** with bold dark wing-tip and outer margin. Inner margin has a **slightly down-curved gray-brown bar** above a **narrow and complete yellow-orange line**. Hindwing white with broad dark outer margin. Female similar, but upperwing lacks dark bar. Under forewings of both sexes are pale yellow; hindwings are whiter, unmarked or with dusty spotting. Female can show two very small dark spots in center of hindwing and dark spots along outer margin.

5 Banded Yellow *Eurema elathea elathea* FW 17 mm (⅝")

ID: Male upperwings similar to Barred Yellow, but inner margin has a **straight, very dark bar that broadens towards base** above a **narrow but incomplete yellow line**. Female similar but lacks dark bar. Underwings of both sexes are similar to Barred Yellow, so difficult to separate.

1
2♀
3
♂ caught in spider's web, showing pattern on upperside of forewing: complete yellow-orange line on inner margin with a slightly down-curved gray-brown bar above.
4♂
4♀
4♂
♂ showing pattern on upperside of forewing: incomplete yellow-orange line on inner margin with a straight gray-brown bar above.
5♂
5

Hairstreaks

Small inconspicuous butterflies of low vegetation and scrub. Males of some species flash blue or purple upperwings in flight, which is rapid and low. All typically settle with closed wings, showing fine patterning on underwings; most species have one or two delicate tails on the hindwing.

1 **Amethyst** (Antillean) **Hairstreak** *Chlorostrymon maesites* FW 10 mm (⅜″)

Widespread but uncommon from the **Virgin Islands to Grenada**; may be absent from some islands.
ID: Upperwings brilliant purple-blue in male, paler in female. Underwings **bright yellow-green** with **broken vertical black** line on both wings, **partially edged white** on hindwing only. A **broad** gray and rust-colored **partial band** runs along the hindwing's outer margin. **Two obvious tails** of unequal length on hindwing.

2 **Silver-banded** (St Christopher's) **Hairstreak**

Chlorostrymon simaethis simaethis FW 13 mm (½″)

Widespread but uncommon from **St Kitts to Grenada**, including **Barbados**.
ID: Upperwings purple in male, browner in female. Underwings **bright green** with **unbroken dark-bordered vertical white** line on hindwing that continues on forewing. An untidy pale gray band runs along the **full outer margin** of hindwing; obvious **single tail**.

3 **Cramer's Scrub-Hairstreak** (Bubastus Hairstreak)

Strymon bubastus ponce FW 14 mm (½″)

Found **throughout** in scrub and dry forest at lower elevations; the most common hairstreak.
ID: Upperwings brown; male has a single dark spot in center of forewing, and both sexes have **two or three dark spots** on outer margin of hindwing (all spots are difficult to see). Underwings gray-brown; hindwing well marked, including **two bold dark spots** on leading margin and **obvious, orange-bordered dark spot** on outer margin (similar to Hanno Blue, *p. 284*). **No tail.**

E 4 **Columella Scrub-Hairstreak** (Hewitson's Hairstreak) *Strymon columella*

FW 13 mm (½″)

Endemic to the Virgin Islands, Puerto Rico and **the Lesser Antilles**: present on at least **St Martin/Sint Maarten, St Barthélemy, St Kitts, Antigua** and **Dominica** where rare and localized.
ID: Upperwings dark brown, with two or three **black spots** on outer margin of hindwing. Underwings gray-brown and well marked: **dark spots form loose lines** on both wings; hindwing has **two obvious spots** near base, **large orange patch** at outer margin and a **single tail**.

5 **Caribbean Scrub-Hairstreak** (Drury's Hairstreak)

Strymon acis acis FW 14 mm (½″)

Widespread but uncommon from the **Virgin Islands** (subspecies *S. a. mars*) **to** at least **Martinique**.
ID: Upperwings dark brown with **red spot** near outer margin of hindwing. Underwings smooth-looking and pale gray-brown, with incomplete, dark-edged white line on forewing. Hindwing is **strikingly marked** with two **small white spots** near base, a **strongly angled**, dark-edged white line, and a **large orange patch** with a black spot near **two tails** of unequal length.

E 6 **Angerona** (Bronze) **Hairstreak** *Electrostrymon angerona* FW 13 mm (½″)

Endemic to the Lesser Antilles; widespread and locally common from **St Kitts to Grenada**.
ID: Upperwings dark brown, male often with coppery sheen. Underwings paler with a white-edged **black line**. Forewing has fine **orange line** on leading margin. Hindwing **unmarked at base** with **strong orange patch**, bold dark spots and white line along outer margin. **Two obvious tails** of unequal length.

1
2
3
4
5
6

E 1 **Godman's Hairstreak** *Allosmaitia piplea* FW 16 mm (¾")

Endemic to the Lesser Antilles. Widespread, on at least **Nevis, Montserrat, Guadeloupe, Dominica, Martinique, St Vincent** and **Grenada**. Found from coastal scrub to rainforest but appears little studied.
ID: Slightly larger than other hairstreaks. Upperwings **dark brown-black** with **blue at base**, female more gray-blue. Underwings brown with **vertical, white-edged dark line** across hindwing (**weaker on forewing**). Large, **bright orange-red spot** near outer margin of hindwing is similar to, but smaller than, that on Angerona Hairstreak. **Single long tail**.

E 2 **St Vincent** (Giant) **Hairstreak** *Pseudolycaena cybele* FW 30 mm (1¼")

Endemic to St Vincent. Rare and localized along forest margins; sites include La Soufrière Trail. Flight is strong and swift; readily perches on low plants.
ID: Large and unmistakable. Upperwings are a brilliant blue; underwings are **pale mauve** and **strongly spotted**. Two tails of unequal length.

Blue butterflies

Tiny blue butterflies of open sunny areas, especially short grassland. They mostly settle with wings closed, showing finely patterned underwings. Male upperwings are usually bright blue, but underwings are similar in both sexes.

3 **Hanno Blue** *Hemiargus hanno watsoni* FW 10 mm (⅜")

Common **throughout**. The region's most numerous and widespread blue butterfly, often occurring in large colonies. Flight is fast and erratic; readily settles to nectar on low-growing flowers.
ID: Upperwings **vivid blue** with thin dark border in male. Female **browner** but can show some blue at base of wings and on body. Underwings **pale silvery-gray**, subtly marked with small spots and a **single obvious bold, dark spot** with pale orange border on outer margin of hindwing.

4 **Miami** (Thomas's) **Blue** *Cyclargus thomasi woodruffi* FW 11 mm (⅜")

Widespread but uncommon from the **Virgin Islands to St Kitts**. (Taxonomy may be unsettled.) Easily overlooked among other small butterflies along flower-rich margins.
ID: Upperwings **bright blue** with fine dark margins and **two dark spots** on outer margin of hindwing; female similar but duller. Underwings gray-brown, strongly marked with broken **white bands** across both wings. Underside of hindwing very similar to Hanno Blue but with **two obvious black spots** on outer margin (the upper one edged orange and blue) and two to three **bold spots near base**.

5 **Cassius Blue** *Leptotes cassius cassiodes* FW 13 mm (½")

Probably occurs **throughout**; may be under-recorded. The subspecies *L. c. catilina* occurs on the **Virgin Islands**. Locally common in scrub and rough grassland margins. Typically flies higher than other blues in shrubs and small trees. Flight quick and fluttery; can be hard to follow.
ID: Male upperwings unmarked **violet-blue**; female paler blue with **dark leading and outer margins on both wings**. Underwings pale gray-brown with heavy, irregular **stripes across both wings**. **Two obvious blue-black spots** with pale yellow-orange surround on outer margin of hindwing.

1

2

OBVIOUS SINGLE LARGE, ORANGE-BORDERED, DARK SPOT AT OUTER MARGIN OF HINDWING
3

3♂

3♀

TWO OBVIOUS DARK SPOTS AT OUTER MARGIN OF HINDWING AND FOUR BOLD SPOTS NEAR BASE
4

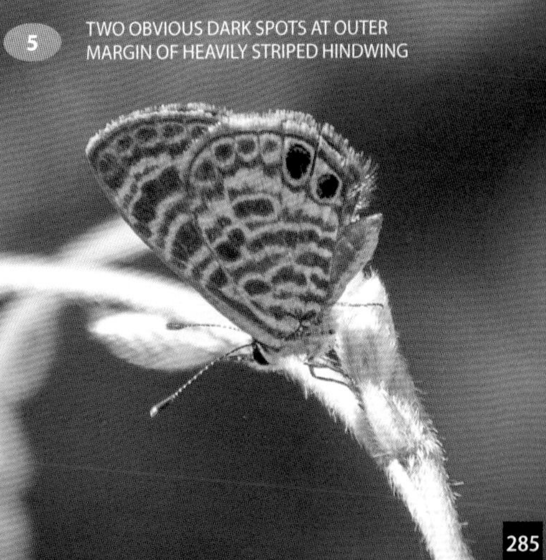
5
TWO OBVIOUS DARK SPOTS AT OUTER MARGIN OF HEAVILY STRIPED HINDWING

Distinctive large butterflies

These large, conspicuous butterflies are found in gardens, open areas and forest margins.

1 **Monarch** *Danaus plexippus* FW 48 mm (1¾″)

Locally common **throughout**. Monarchs in the Eastern Caribbean are mostly a sedentary subspecies, *D. p. megalippe*, that is present year-round in small numbers. Flight is strong but often **slower with glides** when nectaring. Larva feeds on leaves of poisonous milkweed plants *Asclepias* spp., retaining their toxins as an adult, making both stages unpalatable to predators.
ID: Large. Upperwings **bright orange-brown** with **black veins** and **bold black margins with two rows of white spots**. Male has small dark spot (sex brand) on a vein at center of hindwing. Underwing reflects upperwing pattern, but the hindwing is often paler.

2 **Gulf Fritillary** *Agraulis (Dione) vanillae* FW 32 mm (1¼″)

Found **throughout** in open sunny situations, the most common and widespread large orange butterfly. Flight is strong and low; often settles to bask with wings open.
ID: Long forewings. Upperwings **bright orange**, slightly browner in female. Forewing has **black spots** and **blackened veins**, hindwing a **band of small black circles** on the outer margin. Underwings boldly marked with **silver-white spots and patches** extending onto thorax and abdomen.

3 **The Mimic** (Danaid Eggfly) *Hypolimnas misippus* FW 40 mm (1½″)

Widespread from **Antigua to at least St Lucia**, including **Barbados**. Native to Africa and Southeast Asia, now established in the region and appears to be spreading. Uncommon or rare in open scrubby grasslands and gardens. Females are known to mimic other species that are distasteful to predators; in the Eastern Caribbean they are broadly similar to Monarch but more closely resemble Plain Tiger *Danaus chrysippus*, an African species.
ID: Male striking and unmistakable, with obvious **large white spots** on **black upperwings**. Underwings brown, with **bold white central band**. Female is very different: upperwings typically orange with **bold black and white wing-tips, and 'lacey' black and white outer margins**. Underwing pattern is similar to upperwings but paler.

2
2
3♂
3♂
3♀
3♀

e 1 **Julia Heliconian** (Flambeau) *Dryas iulia* FW 39 mm (1½″)

Locally common **throughout** in six recognized subspecies; may be absent from some low-lying islands. Flight can be fast, but butterfly is fluttery and restless when weaving low among vegetation.
ID: Long forewings. Upperwings vibrant **golden-orange**, less bright in female. **Limited dark markings** on forewings vary between subspecies and can vary between male and female. Underwings paler with subtle markings, but all have a **characteristic white streak** on leading margin of hindwing.

Virgin Islands *D. i. iulia*

Guadeloupe *D. i. dominicana*

Dominica *D. i. dominicana*

St Lucia *D. i. lucia*

Martinique *D. i. martinica*

Grenada *D. i. framptoni*

♂ and ♀, Virgin Islands

2 **Zebra Longwing** *Heliconius charithonia charithonia* FW 46 mm (1¾")

Present on at least **the Virgin Islands, Saba, St Kitts, St Eustatius, Antigua** and **Montserrat**, possibly Dominica. Locally common in all forest types. Striking and unmistakable. Flight slow and deliberate; readily settles with wings open. Known to roost communally in trees. **ID: Long, slender forewings**. Upper and underwings distinctively **black with lemon-yellow bands**.

3 **Red Rim** *Biblis hyperia hyperia*

FW 32 mm (1¼")

Present on at least **the Virgin Islands, St Eustatius, St Kitts and Nevis, Montserrat, Guadeloupe, Dominica** and **St Lucia**; appears to be absent from low-lying islands. Uncommon in clearings and along trails in all forest types. Readily settles with wings open. **ID:** Unmistakable. Upperwings **dark velvety-brown** with paler outer margin on forewing and striking **red band** along outer margin of hindwing. Underwings similar but paler.

1 Ruddy Daggerwing (Southern Dagger Tail) *Marpesia petreus damicorum*

FW 39 mm (1½″)

Uncommon on at least **Saba, St Kitts, Guadeloupe, Dominica** and **St Lucia**, mainly in rainforests. Most easily seen in flight, which is slow with glides. Settles with wings closed both above and underneath leaves and can be difficult to find; basks with wings open.

ID: Forewings slightly hooked. Upperwings bright orange-brown, with **three fine black lines** running from leading margin across both wings and **two obvious tails** with prominent spots in front. Underwings paler with subtle bands and **single dark vertical line**. Underside of head, body and legs **strikingly white**.

e 2 Orion Cecropian *Historis odius caloucaera* FW 64 mm (2½″)

Uncommon on at least **Guadeloupe, Dominica, Martinique, St Lucia** and **Grenada**. Mostly solitary, but groups gather to feed on rotting fruit. Flight strong and rapid; typically settles **underneath branches** with wings closed, resembling a dead leaf. Larva feeds on *Cecropia peltata* saplings, which can be common in regenerating forests.

ID: Large and broad-winged; **forewing** has **rounded hook-tip**. Upperwings **dark brown** with **extensive orange at base**. A **single white spot** near forewing-tip is obvious on underwings, which are cryptically marked with **broad brown and gray bands**.

E 3 Dominican Leafwing (Godman's Leaf Butterfly) *Memphis dominicana*

FW 31 mm (1¼″)

Endemic to Dominica (subspecies *M. d. dominica*), **Martinique** and **St Lucia** (*M. d. luciana*). Uncommon and difficult to find along shady trails. Settles **underneath leaves and branches**, often above head height. Flight is strong and direct.

ID: Upperwings largely orange with two obvious pale squares on dark forewing-tip. Underwings gray, **finely striped** in cryptic pattern resembling a dead leaf. Hindwings have scalloped edges, a line of greenish spots and an **obvious tail**.

2
2
3
3
Museum specimen.

Large, boldly patterned butterflies

Found in gardens and along forest margins, where they may settle with their wings open.

e 1 **Polydamas Swallowtail** *Battus polydamas* FW 47 mm (1⅞")

Found **throughout** but uncommon and may be absent from low-lying islands. Present in nine subspecies, each with subtle differences in appearance, suggesting sedentary populations. Flies effortlessly at speed, quickly disappearing out of sight along a road or trail. Readily settles but is restless when feeding. **ID:** Upperwings **black** with **obvious cream-yellow band** near outer margin of both wings; an old name is 'Gold Rim'. **Underwings dark** with a pale band of spots on forewing (not always visible) and line of **red spots** on hindwing. Outer margin of hindwing **scalloped**; despite its name, **no obvious tail**.

2 **Malachite** *Siproeta stelenes stelenes* FW 50 mm (2")

Present on at least **St Croix** and **Nevis**, possibly elsewhere. Uncommon to rare in all forest types; can be difficult to find. Flight slow and gentle; settles in trees with wings partly open, often at height. **ID:** Strikingly marked. Upperwings black with obvious **bright green bands and spots**, which are broadly repeated on **red-brown underwings**. **Outer margin** of hindwing is scalloped and has a small tail.

3 **Lime Swallowtail** *Papilio demoleus* FW 48 mm (1⅞")

Native to Asia and Australia; first recorded in the Caribbean in 2004, since when it has spread and is now present on at least **St Croix** (USVI), **Anguilla, St Martin/Sint Maarten** and **St Eustatius**. Uncommon along forest margins and in clearings. Larva feeds on the leaves of lime and other citrus trees, with potential impacts on agricultural production. Flight strong, often low; readily settles with open wings. **ID:** Upperwings black, **heavily marked with irregular pale spots** and obvious **orange-red spot** on inner margin of hindwing. Underwings strikingly marked **black and white**, with orange-red band (sometimes weak). Black and white stripes extend from base of hindwing onto thorax and abdomen. No obvious tail.

2
2
3
3

Medium-sized butterflies

Butterflies of sunny, open grassland and forest clearings, usually settling close to the ground with open wings.

BUCKEYES

Two very similar species that overlap in range. Their taxonomy has been unsettled, with recent changes in both common and scientific names. They are difficult to distinguish in the field, with some variability in color and markings: the underside of the hindwing may offer the most useful identification features.

1 **Tropical** (Caribbean) **Buckeye** *Junonia zonalis (genoveva)* FW 29 mm (1⅛")

Found **throughout**; common and familiar in sunny open habitats. Flight fast and low to the ground; readily settles with wings open.
ID: Upperwings strongly marked with eye-spots and **cream-white band** near tip of forewing (visible on underwing). Orange band near outer margin of hindwing is typically narrow. Underside of hindwings are **well marked**, with a **pale line** down the center; **eye-spots tend to be visible**. Antenna stem paler than Mangrove Buckeye; club mainly white with small dark spot near tip.

2 **Mangrove Buckeye** *Junonia neildi (evarete)* FW 29 mm (1⅛")

Present from at least **the Virgin Islands to Guadeloupe**. Uncommon and localized in mangroves; the main larval food plant is Black Mangrove *Avicennia germinans*. Often flies high around shrubs; settles on mangrove leaves.
ID: Upperwings typically darker than Tropical Buckeye, strongly marked with eye-spots and duller pale band near tip of forewing, and the **orange band** near outer margin of hindwing is typically **wider**. Under hindwings tend to be **plainer** brown, with **eye-spots not clearly visible**. Antenna stem darker; club mainly brown, with small pale spot near tip.

PEACOCKS (ANARTIAS)

3 **White Peacock** *Anartia jatrophae jatrophae* FW 24 mm (¾")

Locally common **throughout** in scrub and grassland and along forest margins. A distinctive species that is easily seen, as it readily settles with wings open on stones or low plants. Males aggressively chase one other when defending territories. Flight is slow and fluttery with glides.
ID: Upperwings **pale silvery gray-brown**, finely marked with **dark spots** and orange-buff outer margins. Underwings similar but paler; very small tail on hindwing.

4 **Red Peacock** (Red Anartia) *Anartia amathea* FW 27 mm (1")

Recorded on at least **Antigua, Barbados** and **Grenada**, with sporadic influxes from South America, especially to the southern islands. Uncommon and localized in small colonies. Habitats include open grassy forest margins. Flight is quick and erratic; restless when feeding. Wings are typically held open at rest, slightly pushed forward and lower than body.
ID: Upperwings strikingly **red and black** with **rows of white spots** on both wings. Underwings similar but paler. Female paler, more **orange-brown**.

1
1
2
2
3
3
4♂
4♀

Mestra

 **South American** (St Lucia) **Mestra** *Mestra hersilia hersilia (M. cana)*

FW 23 mm (7/8″)

Found from at least **St Lucia to Grenada**, possibly Barbados. Uncommon and localized in dry forest and scrub, especially in clearings with low flowering plants. Flight is low, weak and fluttery.
ID: Upperwings mainly **pale orange**, subtly patterned with **gray and whitish bands and spots**. Orange underwings have similar markings that on the hindwing appear as **two obvious vertical white bands**.

Rare or highly localized butterflies

Species	Distribution
Green Flasher *Astraptes talus*	Marie-Galante (Guadeloupe), Martinique
Anegada Skipperling *Copaeodes eoa* E	Endemic to Anegada
Anegada Ringlet *Calisto anegadensis* E	Endemic to Anegada
Drury's Broken-dash *Wallengria drury* E	Virgin Islands
2 **Yellow Angled-Sulphur** *Anteos maerula*	Guadeloupe
Dominican Snout *Libytheana fulvescens* E	Endemic to Dominica
3 **Gray Ministreak** *Ministrymon azia*	On at least St Martin/Sint Maarten, St Kitts and Guadeloupe
4 **Fulvous Hairstreak** *Electrostrymon angelia*	Virgin Islands, Guadeloupe
Dominican Hairstreak *Electrostrymon dominicana* E	Endemic to Dominica
Juno Silverspot (Longwing) *Dione juno*	Grenada to Dominica; appears to be spreading north.
Dingy Purplewing *Eunica monima*	Migratory species; recorded on at least Tortola (BVI) and St Barthélemy
Antillean Crescent (Pygmy Fritillary) *Antillea pelops* E	St Kitts
5 **Pale** (Caribbean) **Cracker** *Hamadryas amphichloe*	Guadeloupe
6 **Painted Lady** *Vanessa cardui*	Migratory species; recorded on at least Martinique, Dominica, Guadeloupe
Troglodyte *Anaea troglodyta minor*	St Barthélemy, St Eustatius, St Kitts and Nevis, Antigua, Montserrat, Guadeloupe; rare with scattered records, some historic.

1
1
2
3
4
5
6

Other common invertebrates

In addition to the groups already covered (dragonflies, damselflies and butterflies), there is a bewildering array of other invertebrates in the region, many of which are little studied. These include molluscs (snails, slugs and chitons), annelids (earthworms and leeches) and the largest class, arthropods. The latter are animals with a rigid or protective external skeleton, a segmented body and pairs of jointed appendages, such as legs. There are four main types of arthropod: insects; myriapods (such as millipedes and centipedes); arachnids (including spiders and mites); and crustaceans (including slaters or woodlice, shrimps and crabs). Among the more familiar insects found in terrestrial habitats are dragonflies, earwigs, grasshoppers and crickets, thrips, beetles, bees, wasps, ants, flies, midges, moths and butterflies. Many species are nocturnal; moths and other insects can be seen around external lights, and the constant chirping of cicadas and crickets is part of a night-time chorus, most intense in forested areas.

The number of invertebrate species in the region is considerable, with far too many to even list in this publication. Some are obvious and easy to see, others difficult to find or identify; recent surveys suggest there are still new species to discover! A biodiversity assessment on Montserrat in 2005–08, for example, increased the number of invertebrates known from the island from 318 to more than 1,240, with at least 100 of these being endemic. Surveys on St Vincent and the Grenadines have recorded over 2,000 species of insects and 220 species of arachnids. Forest habitats such as mangroves, dry forest and rainforest are especially rich in invertebrates.

Invertebrates have an invaluable role within ecosystems; some species are pollinators, including for commercially grown plants, while others are active in the decomposition process, helping to recycle nutrients from plants and dead animals back into the soil. They are part of often complex food webs, feeding on plants, fruits and other invertebrates, and in turn being preyed upon by birds, bats, amphibians and reptiles.

Data on the distribution and population of invertebrates are limited on some islands but steadily increasing. Individuals, local and international organizations, governments, and academic and research institutions are helping to develop a clearer picture of the region's invertebrates. An increasing number of non-native species are being recorded. Some of these are invasive and cause harm to people, agriculture and native wildlife. Sending your observations to local nature conservation organizations, relevant government departments and online databases such as iNaturalist will help increase knowledge of the region's invertebrates.

This section cannot be comprehensive but aims to illustrate just a few of the more widespread, common and obvious species.

LAND SNAILS

Mostly small and widely distributed throughout the region. Several endemic species.

***Pleurodonte* spp.** There are several species of these small (typically L 20 mm or ¾") land snails in the region, including Lesser Antillean endemics. Some are threatened; at least one from Martinique, *P. desidens*, is considered extinct.

Giant African Land Snail *Lissachatina fulica*
An introduced invasive species that grows to L 20 cm (8") and consumes a range of plants. It is widely distributed in the region.

TERMITES

Found throughout in all forest types, the dark nests of three *Nasutitermes* termites are most commonly seen. These nests can be large and obvious. They are usually on tree trunks, constructed using a mixture of chewed wood and mud, and held together with saliva and fecal matter. Termites avoid sunlight and predators by building enclosed tunnels that run from the nest to nearby sources of the decaying wood on which they feed (*see* 3).

MOTHS

There are thought to be in excess of 500 species of moth in the region, although data are patchy on most islands, and undoubtedly there are additions to island lists and discoveries to be made!

3 Termite nest.

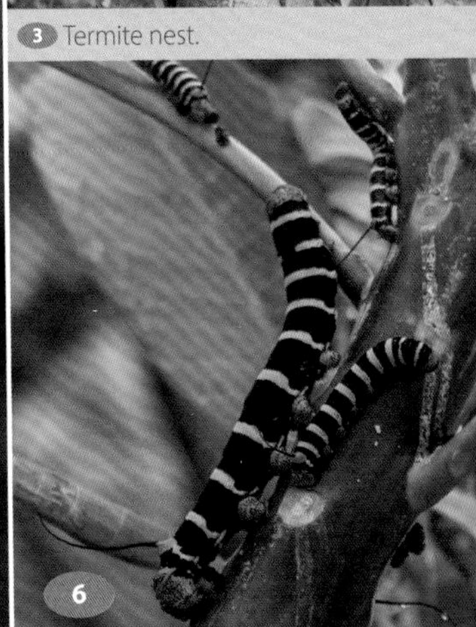

4 **Black Witch Moth** *Ascalapha odorata*. Found throughout, mostly seen on shady trails and tracks in rainforests. Often active during the day; when disturbed it flutters away, typically landing out of sight where it is difficult to find. Its large size (WS up to 17 cm or 6½"), dark color and fluttery flight give it a bat-like appearance, making it one of the region's most distinctive species.

5 **Ornate Bella Moth** *Utetheisa ornatrix*. Found throughout and locally common in dry, sunny grasslands; one of the more obvious day-flying moths (WS 46 mm or 1¾"). Both the caterpillar (larva) and adult moth sequester toxins from the host plant, *Crotalaria* sp., making them unpalatable to predators.

6 **Tetrio Sphinx Moth** *Pseudosphinx tetrio*. Larva: L can exceed 15 cm (6"); adult: WS 14 cm (5") Found throughout. Caterpillars often occur in large numbers wherever there is frangipani *Plumeria* sp. or allamanda *Allamanda* sp., which they can quickly defoliate. One of the most noticeable of all moth and butterfly larvae in the region, but the adult is less often seen.

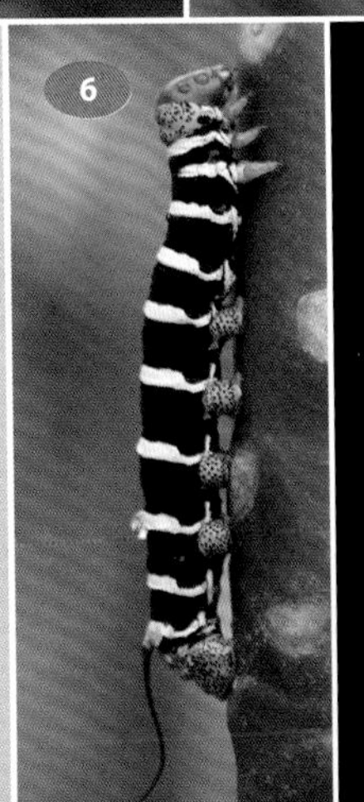

BEETLES

Where invertebrate surveys have taken place, beetles are by far the most numerous insect recorded in the region. Their front pair of wings are hardened, forming wing-cases (elytra). Beetles exhibit a huge array of color, shape and size (*see* 7).

GRASSHOPPERS, CRICKETS AND KATYDIDS

Members of this group are easily recognized by their very long hind legs (adapted for making long jumps) and heavy cylindrical body. Most species produce sounds through stridulation, by scraping ridges on legs or wings against one another, like a card on a comb. Most species feed on plants.

MILLIPEDES AND CENTIPEDES

Centipedes prey on a wide range of small invertebrates and are found mainly in leaf litter; millipedes, which can be large and conspicuous in forests, eat decaying plant and animal matter, playing an important role in decomposition.

7 **Dixon's Striped Firefly** *Aspisoma ignitum* Remarkable, tiny firefly beetles use bioluminescence, which is thought to either attract a mate or deter predators. They are always a delight to see in a Caribbean evening!

8 **Katydids** (or **bush-crickets**), like this superbly camouflaged *Microcentrum* sp., are most active at night and are recognizable by their distinctive loud "*kay-ti-did*" song.

9 **Bumblebee** (Yellow-banded) **Millipede** *Anadenobolus monilicornis*. Native to the wider Caribbean and can be common, especially in damp forests, where it readily climbs trees. L can reach 10 cm (4").

SPIDERS

10 One of the most widespread and commonly seen spiders is the distinctive **Silver Garden Orbweaver** *Argiope argentata*. Females are larger than males, with BL up to 35 m (1½"). Both sexes spin a large, intricate web, often between the low stems of shrubs, weaving in conspicuous zigzag structures known as 'stabilimenta', the purpose of which is uncertain.

FURTHER READING

BOOKS

Landforms, history and ecology

Allan, C.D. (ed.) 2017. ***Landscapes of the Lesser Antilles***. Springer Nature.
Beard, J.S. 1949. ***The Natural Vegetation of the Windward and Leeward Islands***. Clarendon Press.
Flannery, T. & Schouten, P. 2001. ***A Gap in Nature: Discovering the World's Extinct Animals***. Text Publishing.
Higman, B.W. 2021. ***A Concise History of the Caribbean***. 2nd edition. Cambridge University Press.
Kricher, J.C. 2017. ***The New Neotropical Companion***. Princeton University Press.

Birds

Bond, J. 1985. ***Birds of the West Indies***. Harper Collins Publishers.
Bradley, P.E. & Norton, R.L. 2009. ***An Inventory of Breeding Seabirds of the Caribbean***. University Press of Florida.
Chenery, R. 2022. ***Birds of the Lesser Antilles***. Christopher Helm.
Keith, A., Raffaele, H.A., Wiley, J.W., Raffaele, J.I. & Garrido, O.H. 2020. ***Birds of the West Indies***. 2nd edition. Christopher Helm.
Kirwan, G.M., Levesque, A., Oberle, M. & Sharp, J. 2019. ***Birds of the West Indies.*** Lynx Edicions.
Lowrie, K., Lowrie, D. & Collier, N. 2012. ***Seabird Breeding Atlas of the Lesser Antilles***. Environmental Protection in the Caribbean.
Wege, D.C. & Anadon-Irizarry, V. 2008. ***Important Bird Areas in the Caribbean: Key Sites for Conservation***. Birdlife International.

Mammals

Gannon, M.R., Kurta, A., Rodríguez-Durán, A. & Willig, M.R. 2005. ***Bats of Puerto Rico: An Island Focus and a Caribbean Perspective***. University of West Indies Press.
Gomes, G.A. & Reid, F.A. 2015. ***Bats of Trinidad and Tobago***. Trinibats.
Shirihai, H. & Jarrett, B. 2019. ***Whales, Dolphins and Seals: A Field Guide to Marine Mammals of the World***. Bloomsbury.
Kurta, A. & Rodríguez-Durán, A. (eds.) 2023. ***Bats of the West Indies***. Comstock Publishing Associates.

Amphibians and reptiles

Hedges, S.B. & Conn, C.E. 2012. A New Skink Fauna from Caribbean Islands (Squamata, Mabuyidae, Mabuyinae). *Zootaxa* 3288: 1–244.
Henderson, R.W. & Powell, R. 2009. ***Natural History of West Indian Reptiles and Amphibians***. University Press of Florida.
Thorpe, R.S. 2022. ***Reptiles of the Lesser Antilles***. Edition Chimaira.

Land and coastal crabs

Chace, F.A. Jr. & Hobbs, H.H. Jr. 1969. ***The Freshwater and Terrestrial Decapod Crustaceans of the West Indies with Special Reference to Dominica***. Smithsonian Institution Press.
Masunari, S., Martins, S.B. & Anacleto, A.F.M. 2020. An illustrated key to the fiddler crabs (Crustacea, Decapoda, Ocypodidae) from the Atlantic coast of Brazil. *Zookeys* 943: 1–20.
Poupin, J. 2018. ***Les Crustacés Décapodes des Petites Antilles***. Musée National d'Histoire Naturelle.

Dragonflies

Catling, P. M. & Kostiuk, B. 2015. A dry season survey of the dragonflies of St Kitts and Nevis, northeastern Leeward Islands. *Argia* 27: 20–24.
Meurgey, F. & Picard, L. 2011. ***Les Libellules des Antilles Françaises***. Biotope/Musée National d'Histoire Naturelle.
Meurgey, F. & Poiron, C. 2012. ***An Updated Checklist of Lesser Antillean Odonata***. Musée d'Histoire Naturelle.
Paulson, D.R. 2011. ***Dragonflies and Damselflies of the East***. Princeton University Press.

Butterflies

Riley, N.D. 1975. ***A Field Guide to the Butterflies of the West Indies***. Collins.
Smith, D.S., Miller, L.D. & Miller, J.Y. 1994. ***The Butterflies of the West Indies and South Florida***. Oxford University Press.
Turner, T. & Turland, V. 2017. ***Discovering Jamaican Butterflies and Their Relationships around the Caribbean***. Caribbean Wildlife Publications.

Books about individual islands or island groups

Anguilla

Hodge, K.V.D., Censky, E.J. & Powell, R. 2003. ***The Reptiles and Amphibians of Anguilla, British West Indies***. Anguilla National Trust.
Holliday, S.H., Hodge, K.V.D. & Hughes, D.E. 2007. ***A Guide to the Birds of Anguilla***. Royal Society for the Protection of Birds.

Barbados

Buckley, P.A., Massiah, E.B., Hutt, M.B., Buckley, F.G. & Hutt, H.F. 2009. ***The Birds of Barbados***. British Ornithologists' Union/British Ornithologists' Club.

Dominica

Evans, P.G.H. & James, A. 1997. ***Dominica: Nature Island of the Caribbean***. Faygate Printing.

Guadeloupe and Martinique

Breuil, M. 2002. ***Histoire Naturelle des Amphibiens et Reptiles Terrestres de l'Archipel Guadeloupéen***. Musée National d'Histoire Naturelle.
Brévignon, L. & Brévignon, C. 2003. ***Papillons de Jour des Antilles Françaises***. P.L.B. Editions.
Dewynter, M. (ed.) 2018. ***Atlas des Amphibiens et Reptiles de Martinique***. Biotope/Musée National d'Histoire Naturelle.
Meurgey, F. & Picard, L. 2011. ***Les Libellules des Antilles Françaises***. Biotope/Musée National d'Histoire Naturelle.
Meurgay, F., Guezennec, P. & Guezennec, C. 2017. ***Insectes des Antilles Françaises***. P.L.B. Editions.

Montserrat

Holliday, S.H. (ed.) 2009. ***A Guide to the Centre Hills of Montserrat***. West Indies Publishing Ltd.
Pienkowski, M., Pienkokski, A., Wensink, C., Francis, S. & Daley, J. 2015. ***Birding in Paradise: The Caribbean Emerald Isle of Montserrat***. UK Overseas Territories Conservation Forum.

Saba, St Eustatius and St Maarten

Powell, R., Henderson, R.W. & Parmalee, J.S. Jr. 2015. ***The Reptiles and Amphibians of the Dutch Caribbean: Saba, St. Eustatius, and St. Maarten***. 2nd edition. Dutch Caribbean Nature Alliance.

St Martin
Yokoyama, M. 2013. ***The Incomplete Guide to the Wildlife of Saint Martin.*** 2nd edition. Les Fruits de Mer.

St Kitts and Nevis
Catling, P.M. & Kostiuk, B. 2015. ***A Field Guide to the Butterflies of St Kitts and Nevis, and the northeastern Leeward islands, West Indies.*** Privately published.

St Lucia
Keith, A.R. 1997. ***The Birds of St Lucia, West Indies.*** British Ornithologists' Union.

St Vincent, the Grenadines and Grenada
Coffey, J. & Ollivierre, A. 2019. ***Birds of the Transboundary Grenadines.*** Birds of the Grenadines.
Henderson, R.W. & Powell, R. 2018. ***Amphibians and Reptiles of the St Vincent and Grenada Banks, West Indies.*** Edition Chimaira.
Wiley, J.W. 2021. ***The Birds of St. Vincent, The Grenadines and Grenada.*** British Ornithologist's Club.

Virgin Islands
Raffaele, H.A., Petrovic, C., Colón López, S.A., Yntema, L.D. & Salguero Faria, J.A. 2021. ***Birds of Puerto Rico and the Virgin Islands.*** 3rd edition. Princeton University Press.

WEBSITES

birdscaribbean.org—a vibrant international network committed to conserving Caribbean birds and their habitats
butterfliesofcuba.com—a comprehensive guide to the butterflies of Cuba (includes several species also in the Eastern Caribbean)
caribherp.org—amphibians and reptiles of Caribbean islands
ccs-ngo.com—Caribbean Cetacean Society
crustiesfroverseas.free.fr—a database of Crustacea (Decapoda and Stomatopoda), with special interest for those collected in French overseas territories
durrell.org—conservation work includes species recovery projects in the region
ebird.org—database for recording observations and checklists; freely shared to power data-driven approaches to science, conservation and education
fauna-flora.org—works on species and habitat recovery in the region
inaturalist.org—an identification tool for all plants and animals that generates data for science and conservation
iucnredlist.org—IUCN Red List, with global conservation status of species
rarespecies.org—conservation and research organization active in the region
rewild.org—works with local communities and partners to protect and rewild habitats
rspb.org.uk—works with local partners on conservation of birds and habitats
widecast.org—Wider Caribbean Sea Turtle Conservation Network

ACKNOWLEDGMENTS

We are grateful for all the help and support we have received in the course of researching and writing this book. This is the guide we wanted when we first visited the region (Anguilla in 2000), when most species were unfamiliar to us. It has proved a much bigger task than we ever imagined, and our thanks go to the many people who have helped along the way. We have tried to ensure it is as up-to-date and accurate as possible; any errors that may remain are entirely ours!

We are indebted to the team at Princeton University Press. In particular we must thank Andy Swash of Princeton WILDGuides for his early encouragement, incredible support and advice throughout; Robert Kirk for recognizing our vision and steering the guide through to publication; and Jacqui Sayers and Rob Still for their enthusiasm and expertise throughout the editing and design stages, especially as the guide neared completion. James Lowen did a fantastic job of copy-editing, as did Shane O'Dwyer, and David and Namrita Price-Goodfellow of D & N Publishing, with the design.

We want to thank everyone who has joined us out in the field through the last 20 years, sharing the passion and knowledge they each have for their own islands. From north to south, with apologies for anyone we have missed, we are particularly grateful to: Susan Zaluski (BVI); Farah Mukhida and the team at the Anguilla National Trust, together with Karim Hodge, Oliver Hodge, Gina Brooks and the late Ijahnya Christian (Anguilla); Hannah Madden (St Eustatius); Percival Hanley (St Kitts); Stephen Mendes and James Scriber Daly (Montserrat); Anthony Levesque (Guadeloupe); Bertrand "Dr Birdy" Baptiste (Dominica); Adams Toussaint (St Lucia); Glenroy Gaymes (St Vincent); Anthony Jeremiah and Sonia Cheetham (Grenada); and Eddie Massiah (Barbados).

So many incredible specialists have been enthusiastic and generous with their time, knowledge and contacts, and we are especially grateful to the following individuals and their organizations. **Birds**: Lisa Sorenson, Anthony Levesque, Mark Yokoyama, Jeff Gerbracht (Birds Caribbean); Natalia Collier, Adam Brown (EPIC); David Wege (BirdLife International); Charlie Butt, Lyndon John (RSPB); Juliana Coffey (Transboundary Grenadines); Chris Batty and Andy Swash. **Bats**: Geoffrey Gomes and the team at Trinibats, Allan Kurta, Melissa Donnelly. **Marine mammals**: Jeffrey Bernus, Valentin Teillard and Raven Hoflund at the Caribbean Cetacean Society. **Amphibians and reptiles**: Jenny Daltry (FFI and Re:wild); Karen Eckert and the team at WIDECAST; Robert Henderson. **Land crabs**: Joseph Poupin, Broughton Taylor. **Dragonflies**: Dennis Paulson, François Meurgay. **Butterflies**: James Hogan (Oxford University Museum of Natural History), Jeffrey Glassburg, Tim Norriss, Brenda Kostiuk and Paul Catling.

This book would not have been possible without the generous support of the many photographers who kindly provided images; every single individual is credited and very much appreciated. We particularly want to thank the following, who opened their image libraries for us: Jenny Daltry, Frantz Delcroix, Melissa Donnelly, Pierre and Claudine Guezennec, Robert Henderson, Jeremy Holden, Anthony Levesque, Tim Norriss, Dennis Paulson and Netta Smith, Mike Pollard, Robert Powell, Toby Ross, Rich Sajdak, Andy and Gill Swash, Mark Yokoyama, the Caribbean Cetacean Society, Trinibats and WIDECAST.

Our thanks also go to the many people we met on our visits to the islands who made our research trips all the more special, enjoyable and valuable. Closer to home we would like to thank Ruth Holmes for providing enthusiastic feedback on our early text.

And finally to our family, for their input and unwavering support and encouragement: Charlotte, Lucy, Phil and Ed. We dedicate this book to them and our grandchildren.

PHOTOGRAPHIC CREDITS

The authors have endeavored to source images that were taken in the region, especially for local subspecies. In the few instances where this was not possible, the nearest and/or most similar subspecies has been substituted.

The following organizations have been particularly helpful in providing images and expertise:

The contribution of every photographer is gratefully acknowledged and **each image not taken by the authors** is listed by page number, together with the photographer's initials. Full details of their images are in the section-by-section credits that follow:

Adam Riley [AR]: 63. **Allan Hopkins** [AH]: 242. **Andy and Gill Swash** (WorldWildlifeImages.com) [AGS]: 52, 54, 55, 59, 64, 65, 67, 68, 72, 77, 80, 83, 98, 99, 101, 113, 114, 115, 120, 122, 123, 131, 132, 133, 149, 154, 155, 157. **Anthony Levesque** [AL]: 68, 70, 71, 75, 78, 79, 83, 85, 87, 88, 91, 93, 106, 108, 111, 115, 124, 125, 139, 147, 149, 151, 155, 157, 158, 169, 203, 251, 267, 271, 273, 277, 278, 279, 281, 283, 287, 289, 295, 297. **Apurv Jadhav** / Alamy [AJ]: 229. **Arya Satya** / Alamy/NPL [ASa]: 287. **Brian E. Small** / Agami [BES]: 57, 59, 72, 91, 96, 99, 115, 120, 123, 125. **Caribbean Cetacean Society** [CCS]: 16, 159, 160, 161, 163, 164. **Caroline S. Rogers** (Sea Turtle Conservation Bonaire) [CSR]: 16, 233. **Chris van Rijswijk** / Agami [CVR]: 59. **Daniel Hargreaves** (Trinibats) [DHa]: 171, 173. **Daniele Occhiato** / Agami [DO]: 97. **David Hollie** [DHo]: 106, 111, 119, 121, 127, 133, 134, 137, 140, 143, 147, 151, 153. **David Kjaer** (courtesy of the estate of David Kjaer) [DK]: 169. **David Monticelli** / Agami [DaMo]: 53. **Denis Simon** [DSi]: 267. **Dennis Paulson** [DP]: 246, 251, 253, 255, 262. **Denzil Morgan** [DeMo]: 54, 63. **Doug Wechsler** / Alamy/NPL [DW]: 227. **Dubi Shapiro** / Agami [DuSh]: 73. **Dustin Smith** [DS]: 221. **Frantz Delcroix** [FD]: 54, 61, 67, 70, 71, 74, 75, 77, 79, 81, 96, 111, 117, 119, 121, 124, 129, 131, 134, 135, 137, 139, 140, 143, 147, 149, 157, 158. **Gabriel Kombluh** [GK]: 119. **Geoffrey Gomes** (Trinibats) [GG]: 177. **Glenn Bartley** / Agami [GB]: 70. **Greg and Yvonne Dean** (WorldWildlifeImages.com) [GYD]: 117. **Greg Lavaty** [GL]: 68. **Ian Davies** / Agami [ID]: 54. **James Lowen** [JL]: 94. **Jason Ondreicka** / Alamy [JO]: 227. **Jay McGowan** [JMG]: 60, 61, 75, 91. **Jeffrey Glassberg** [JG]: 269. **Jenny Daltry** (F&F/Re:wild) [JD]: 12, 29, 186, 189, 192, 193, 194, 198, 199, 201, 203, 204, 205, 208, 210, 212, 214, 217, 218, 219, 223, 224, 225, 226, 229. **Jeremy Holden** [JH]: 27, 210, 213, 219, 227, 229. **Jim T. Johnson** [JTJ]: 253. **John Kuenzli** [JK]: 113 **Judd Patterson** [JP]: 139, 142, 151, 267. **Juliana Coffey** [JC]: 230. **Keith Clarkson** [KC]: 121, 123, 129, 157. **Laurens Steijn** / Agami [LS]: 63. **Laurent Malglaive** [LM]: 267. **Lee Gregory** [LG]: 149. **Mael Dewynter** [MDW]: 178. **Mark Gash** [MG]: 99. **Marc Guyt** / Agami [MGu]: 113, 115. **Mark Hulme** [MH]: 181, 202, 225. **Mark Yokoyama** [MY]: 16, 18, 35, 40, 53, 57, 67, 93, 169, 170, 171, 173, 185, 188, 199, 201, 208, 210, 211, 212, 217, 228, 237, 265, 271, 283. **Markku Rantala** / Agami [MR]: 55. **Martijn Verdoes** / Agami [MV]: 63. **Melissa Donnelly** [MD]: 173, 174, 175, 176, 177,

203, 215. **Melvin Grey** (Trinibats) [MGr]: 176. **Menno van Duijn** / Agami [MVD]: 55. **Mike Pollard** [MP]: 50, 51, 53, 62, 72, 78. **Mike Rutherford** [MR]: 165, 166, 185, 208, 298, 299. **Mike Watson** [MW]: 63. **Milos Andera** / NaturePhoto [MA]: 169. **Natalia Rivera-Viscal** [NRV]: 117. **Netta Smith** [NS]: 246, 261. **Nils Servientis** (Bivouac Naturaliste) [NSe]: 218. **Oxford Museum of Natural History** [OMNH]: 291. **Paul Reillo PhD** (Rare Species Conservatory Foundation) [PR]: 127. **Pete Morris** / Agami [PMA]: 54, 113, 149. **Pete Morris** [PM]: 99, 104, 105, 111, 113, 119, 127, 129, 134, 136, 143, 151, 154, 169. **Pierre and Claudine Guezennec** [PCG]: 183, 185, 213, 227, 239, 243, 245, 248, 249, 251, 253, 254, 257, 259, 261, 287, 290, 291, 292, 297. **Probreviceps** / iNaturalist [PRO]: 194. **Ralph Martin** / Agami [RM]: 52. **Rich Sajdak** [RS]: 12, 179, 181, 183, 221, 226. **Robert Powell** [RP]: 179, 181, 183, 185, 187, 221, 222, 223, 229. **Roberto Pillon** / iNaturalist [RPi]: 232. **Rob Riemer** / Alamy [RR]: 232. **Roger and Liz Charlwood** (WorldWildlifeImages.com) [RLC]: 125. **Scott Eckert** / WIDECAST [SE]: 234. **Sea Turtle Conservation Bonaire** [STCB]: 231. **Terence Zahner** [TZ]: 117, 135, 136, 141, 153. **Tim Norriss** [TN]: 259, 261, 265, 271, 273, 275, 277, 278, 279, 281, 283, 293. **Toby Ross** [TR]: 194, 201, 205, 208, 212, 217, 227. **Tom McFarland** / WIDECAST [TMF]: 232. **Tom Preney** [TP]: 180, 183. **Trevor Codlin** [TC]: 83. **Valery Rebizant** [VR]: 265. **Vaughan Turland** [VT]: 249, 293. **Will Leurs** / Agami [WL]: 61, 157.

Front cover image: Jenny Daltry

INTRODUCTORY SECTIONS

p12: Grenada Treeboa [RS], Union Island Clawed Gecko [JD].
p16: St Martin [MY], Fraser's Dolphins [CCS], Hawksbill Turtle [CSR].
p18: Mangrove swamp [MY].
p27: St Lucia Dwarf Gecko [JH].
p29: Redonda Anole [JD].
p35: Central Hills [MY].
p40: Shekerley Mountains [MY].

BIRDS

p50: [MP].

Seabirds

p51: [MP].
p52: Sooty Tern [AGS], Bridled Tern [RM]. p53: Brown Noddy [MY], Sooty Tern [DaMo], Bridled Tern [MP].
p54/55: Brown Noddy, Sooty Tern [both DeMo], Bridled Tern [FD], Least Tern bottom [PM], Roseate Tern bottom [ID], Common, Sandwich, Gull-billed, Royal (all), Caspian Terns, Laughing Gull bottom [all AGS], Laughing Gull juv [MR] Lesser Black-backed Gull [MVD].
p57: Least Tern 1b [BES], 1j [MY], Sandwich Tern 3b [BES].
p59: Royal Tern 1b [BES], Laughing Gull 1stW [AGS], Lesser Black-backed Gull 3n [CVR], 3j [AGS].
p60/61: Red-billed Tropicbird [WL], White-tailed Tropicbird [FD], Sargasso Shearwater (both) [JMG].
p62: Brown Boody 1ad [MP]. p63: Brown Booby [LS], Red-footed Booby 2 dark [AR], 2 light [MV], Masked Booby 3ad [MW], 3i [DeMo].
p64: Magnificent Frigatebird ♂ [AGS].
p65: Brown Pelican 2b [AGS].

Waterbirds

p67: White-cheeked Pintail (flight) [MY], Blue-winged Teal ♂ [AGS], (flight) [FD].
p68/69: Black-bellied Whistling-Duck (flight) [AL], Fulvous Whistling-Duck [AGS], (flight) [GL].
p70: Ring-necked Duck ♂ [AL], ♀[AL], Lesser Scaup ♂ [FD], ♀[GB]. p71: Masked Duck ♂ [FD], ♀[AL].
p73: Least Grebe 1n [AGS], Pied-billed Grebe 2b [DuSh], 2n [BES], American Coot 3 main [MP].
p74: Purple Gallinule [FD]. p75: Clapper Rail [FD], Sora 4ad [AL], 4j [JMG].
p77: American Oystercatcher (both) [FD], Whimbrel (flight) [AGS].
p78: Black-bellied Plover (flight), 1b [both AL], 1n [MP], Southern Lapwing [AL]. p79: American Golden Plover 3 (b-to-nb) [FD], 3j [AL].
p80: Collared Plover [AGS]. p81: Wilson's Plover 2b [FD].

p83: Ruddy Turnstone 1b [AL], Sanderling (flight) [AGS], 2n [AL], Red Knot (flight) [AL], 1st W [TC].
p85: Least Sandpiper (both), White-rumped Sandpiper (flight), Western Sandpiper 4j [all AL].
p87: Pectoral Sandpiper 1j [AL].
p88/89: Greater Yellowlegs 2b, 2n, 2j, Lesser Yellowlegs 3b [all AL].
p91: Willet 1n [AL], 1b [BES], Short-billed Dowitcher 2j [AL], 2n [JMG], Wilson's Snipe (both) [AL].
p93: Great Blue Heron 2j [AL], Tri-colored Heron 3ad [MY], 3j [AL].
p94: Western Cattle Egret 4n [JL].
p96: Least Bittern 4♂ [BES], 4♀ [FD]. p97: Black-crowned Night Heron 3j [DO].
p98: Scarlet Ibis [AGS]. p99: Belted Kingfisher 3♂ [BES], 3♀ [MG], Ringed Kingfisher 4♂ [PM], 4♀ [AGS].

Landbirds

p101: White-winged Dove [AGS].
p104/105: Ruddy Quail-Dove, Grenada Dove [both PM].
p107: Scaly-naped Pigeon (main) [DHo], White-crowned Pigeon (main) [AL].
p108: Yellow-billed Cuckoo (both) [AL].
p111: Antillean Nighthawk [AL], flight [FD], Rufous Nightjar [DHo], White-tailed Nightjar 3♂ [PM], 3♀ [FD], American Barn Owl (both) [PM].
p113: Black Swift, Lesser Antillean Swift, Gray-rumped Swift (under) [all PM], White-collared Swift [MGu], Short-tailed Swift [AGS], Gray-rumped Swift (upper) [JK].
p114/115: Caribbean Martin 1♂, 1♀ (flight) [both AL], Barn Swallow 2♂ (perched and flight) [AGS], 2j [MGu], Cliff Swallow 3 (upper) [AGS], 3 (under) [BES], Bank Swallow (both) [AGS].
p117: Antillean Crested Hummingbird 1♂ [TZ], 1♂ (flight) [FD], Puerto Rican Mango [NRV], Purple-throated Carib 4 (left) [GYD].
p119: Blue-headed Hummingbird 1♂ [GK], Rufous-breasted Hermit 2 (left) [PM], Guadeloupe Woodpecker 3 (left) [DHo], 3 (right) [FD].
p120: Red-tailed Hawk (flight) (both) [BES]. p121: Broad-winged Hawk (flight) 2 under [KC], 2 upper [DHo], 2 (perched) [FD].
p122/123: Hook-billed Kite 2j, 2♂, 2 (flight) [all AGS], Common Black Hawk 1 (perched) [BES], 1 (flight) [KC].
p124/125: American Kestrel 1 (flight) [FD], Merlin 2 (flight) [AL], 2j [RLC], Peregrine Falcon 3 (flight) 3 left [AL], 3 right [BES].
p127: Red-necked Parrot 1 (perched) [PM], (flight) 1 upper [DHo], Imperial Parrot all [PR].
p129: St Lucia Parrot 1 (perched) [PM], 1 (flight) [FD], St Vincent Parrot 2 (flight) [KC].
p131: Yellow-bellied Elaenia 3 left [AGS], 3 right [FD], Puerto Rican Flycatcher [FD].
p132/133: Lesser Antillean Pewee (Dominica) [DHo], Fork-tailed Flycatcher all [AGS].
p134: St Lucia Wren [PM], St Vincent Wren [DHo], Grenada Wren [FD]. P135: Rufous-throated Solitaire [FD], Black-whiskered Vireo (main) [TZ].
p136: Spectacled Thrush [TZ], Cocoa Thrush [PM]. P137: Red-legged Thrush [FD], Forest Thrush (Dominica) [DHo].
p139: Scaly-breasted Thrasher 2 left [JP], 2 right [AL], Martinique Thrasher [FD].
p140: Northern Mockingbird [DHo], Tropical Mockingbird [FD]. p141 Gray Trembler [TZ].
p142: St Lucia Oriole [JP]. p143: Montserrat Oriole (both) [PM], Martinique Oriole [FD], St Lucia Oriole [DHo].
p147: Barbuda Warbler [DHo], Plumbeous Warbler [AL], St Lucia Warbler, Whistling Warbler [both FD].
p149: Adelaide's Warbler [PM], Black-and-white Warbler [AGS], American Redstart 4♂ad [AGS], 1stW [FD], Northern Parula [LG], Blackpoll Warbler [AL].
p151: Lesser Antillean Tanager 1♂ (Grenada) [PM], 1♂ (St Vincent) [JP], Lesser Antillean Euphonia 2♂ [DHo], 2♀ [AL], Bananaquit 3 (Grenada) [AL].
p153: St Lucia Black Finch 2♂, 3♀ [both DHo], Lesser Antillean Saltator [TZ].
p154: Blue-black Grassquit 2♂ [PM], 2♀ [AGS]. p155: Yellow-bellied Seedeater 3♂, 3♀ [both AGS], Grassland Yellow-Finch (both) [AL].
p157: Rufous-vented Chacalaca [WL], Helmeted Guineafowl, Red Junglefowl [both AGS], Channel-billed Toucan [KC], Village Weaver 6♂ [FD], Northern Red Bishop 7♀ [AL].
p158: Orange-cheeked Waxbill, Red Avadavat [both AL], Scaly-breasted Munia, Chestnut Munia [both FD].

MARINE MAMMALS
p159: Pantropical Spotted Dolphin [CCS].
p160/161: Short-finned Pilot Whale (both) [CCS], Sperm Whale upper [CCS], Humpback Whale (tail flukes) [CCS].
p163: Dolphins all [CCS].
p164: Spinner Dolphin (both) [CCS].

LAND MAMMALS
p165: Robinson's Mouse Opossum [MR].
p166: Opossums all [MR].
p169: Common Red-rumped Agouti [PM], Black Rat [MA], Brown Rat [DK], House Mouse [MY], Northern Raccoon [AL].

BATS
p170: Cave roost [MY]. p171: Greater Bulldog Bat upper [MY], lower [DHa].
p173: Jamaican Fruit Bat left [MY], right [DH], Antillean Fruit-eating Bat (both) [MD], Lesser Antillean Tree Bat upper [MY], lower [MD].
p174/175: Insect-eating bats all [MD].
P176: Insular Single-leaf Bat [MD], Miller's Long-tongued Bat [MGr]. p177: Angel's Yellow-shouldered Bat [MD], Great Fruit-eating Bat [GG].

AMPHIBIANS
p178: Martinique Volcano Frog [MDW]. p179: St Vincent Frog [RP], Grenada Frog [RS].
p180: Antillean White-lipped Frog [TP]. p181: Mountain Chicken [MH], Windward Islands Ditch Frog left [RS], right [RP].
p183: Lesser Antillean Frog left [RS], right [RP], Martinique Frog left [PCG], right [RP], Puerto-Rican Red-eyed Frog [TP].
p185: Guadeloupe Forest Frog [PCG], Dominica Frog [RP], Common Snouted Treefrog [MR], Cuban Treefrog [MY].

REPTILES
p186: Redonda Anole [JD]. p187: Anegada Rock Iguana [RP].
p188: Common Green Iguana [MY]. p189: Southern Lesser Antilles Horned Iguana (both) [JD].
p192/193: Antigua Bank Groundlizard, Dominica Groundlizard 3i [both JD].
p194: Sombrero Groundlizard [TR], Little Scrub Groundlizard [JD], Redonda Groundlizard [JD], Maria Islands Whiptail [TR], Guyana Whiptail [PRO].
p198/199: Anguilla Bank Tree Anole 1♂, 1♀, North American Green Anole [all JD], Anguilla Bank Bush Anole 3♂, Sab Anole 4♂ [both MY].
p201: St Kitts Bank Tree Anole 1♀, St Kitts Bank Bush Anole 2, Antigua Bank Tree Anole 3♂ [all JD], St Kitts Bank Bush Anole 2♂ [MY], Antigua Bank Bush Anole [4♀] [TR].
p202/203: Montserrat Anole [MH], Guadeloupe Anole 2♂ [AL], Dominica Anole upper [JD], lower [MD].
p204/205: St Lucia Anole (both) [TR], Barbados Anole 3♂ left, Cuban Brown Anole [both JD].
p208: Northern Turnip-tailed Gecko upper [TR], lower [MR]. p209: Sint Maarten Thick-tailed Gecko [MY], Barbados Leaf-tailed Gecko [JD].
p210: Spiny House Gecko [JH], Tropical House Gecko lower [MY], Common House Gecko [JD]. p211: Puerto Rican Eyespotted Dwarf Gecko [MY].
p212/213: Anguilla Bank Dwarf Gecko [JD], Leeward Banded Dwarf Gecko, St Kitts Bank Dwarf Gecko [both MY], Antigua Bank Dwarf Gecko [TR], Southern Leeward Dwarf Gecko [PCG], St Lucia Dwarf Gecko, Union Island Clawed Gecko [both JH].
p214: Anguilla Bank Skink [JD]. P215: Dominica Skink [MD].
p217: Greater Windward Skink, Smooth-scaled Tegulet, Antillean Bachia (both) [all JD], Rough-scaled Tegulet [TR], Virgin Islands Worm Lizard [MY].
p218: Martinique Lancehead (both) [NSe], St Lucia Lancehead 2 (both) [JD], 2j [JH], St Lucia Boa right [JD].

p221: Dominica Boa [RP], Virgin Islands Boa [DS], St Vincent Treeboa left [RS], right [RP], Grenada Treeboa (both) [RS].
p222/223: Puerto Rican Racer, Virgin Islands Miniracer [both RP], Anguilla Bank Racer left [JD].
p224/225: Antiguan Racer, Dominica Racer [both JD], Montserrat Racer [MH].
p226/227: Leeward Ground Snake [JD], Windward Tree Racer [RS], Les Saintes Racer [PCG], St Lucia Racer [JH], St Vincent Coachwhip [TR], Red Cornsnake [JO], Black-headed Snake [DW].
p228/229: Leeward Blindsnake [MY], Dominica Blindsnake [RP], Grenada Bank Blindsnake [JD], St Lucia Threadsnake [JH], Brahminy Blindsnake [AJ].
p230: Red-footed Tortoise [JC]. p231: Hawksbill Turtle [STCB].
p232/233: illustrations all [TMF], Hawksbill Turtle [RR], Loggerhead Turtle [RP], Green Turtle [CSR].
p234: Leatherback Turtle (both) [SE].

SHORELINE AND LAND CRABS

p237: Burger's Fiddler Crab 1 top, 1 right [both MY].
p239: Atlantic Mangrove Ghost Crab left [PCG].
p242/243: Black Land Crab (both) [AH], Blackback Land Crab [PCG].

DRAGONFLIES AND DAMSELFLIES

p245: lower [PCG].
p246: Rainpool Spreadwing [DP], Blue-striped Spreadwing [NS].
p248: Coral Firetail (both) [PCG]. p249: Emerald Threadtail 2♂ [VT], Guadeloupe Threadtail 3♂ [PCG].
p251: Antillean Bluet [AL], Tiny Forktail (both) [PCG], Citrine Forktail 4♀ [DP].
p253: Common Green Darner 1♂ [JTJ] 1♀ [DP], Pale Green Darner, Caribbean Darner [both DP], Turquoise-tipped Darner [PCG].
p254: Slender Clubskimmer, Antillean Sylph [both PCG], Red-tailed Pennant [DP].
p257: Red-faced Dragonlet (both) [PCG].
p259: Three-striped Dasher 2♀ [PCG], Brown Setwing 3♂ [TN].
p261: Hyacinth Glider [PCG], Wandering Glider [TN], Evening Skimmer [NS].
p262: Antillean Saddlebags [DP].

BUTTERFLIES

p264: Zestos Skipper left [VR], right [TN], Hammock Skipper left [MY].
p267: Lesser Sicklewing [AL], Caribbean Duskywing 3♂ [JP], Florida Duskywing 4♂ [DSi], 4♀ [LM].
p269: Dorantes Longtail (both) [JG].
p271: Fiery Skipper 1♂ upper [AL], 1♀ (both) [TN], V-mark Skipper 4 left [MY].
p273: Brazilian Skipper (both) [AL], Purple-washed Skipper left [TN].
p275: Tropical Checkered-Skipper 1 [TN].
p277: Great Southern White 1♂ (both) [TN], Florida White 2♂ [AL], 2♀ [TN], Cloudless Sulphur 3♂ [AL], 3♀ [TN].
p278: Large Orange Sulphur [AL], Apricot Sulphur [TN]. p279: Statira Sulphur 4♂ upper [TN], 4♂, 4♀ centre [both AL].
p281: Leuce Yellow, Pale Yellow, Barred Yellow 4♂ [all AL], Banded Yellow bot [TN].
p293: Amethyst Hairstreak [TN], Silver-banded Hairstreak, Caribbean Scrub-Hairstreak [both AL], Columella Scrub-Hairstreak [MY].
p287: Mimic 3♂ upper [PCG], 3♀ left [ASa], 3♀ right [AL].
p289: Red Rim [AL].
p290/291: Ruddy Daggerwing 1 left, Orion Cecropian [both PCG], Dominican Leafwing right [OMNH].
p292: Polydamas Swallowtail upper [PCG]. p293: Malachite 2 upper [VT] 2 lower [TN].
p295: Red Peacock 4♂ [AL].
p297: Yellow-angled Sulphur, Painted Lady [both PCG], Gray Ministreak, Fulvous Hairstreak, Pale Cracker [all AL].

OTHER COMMON INVERTEBRATES

p298/299: Pleurodonte spp., Tetrio Sphinx Moth [both MR].

INDEX

E

F

N

O

P

Q

R

S